THE LIGHT REAPERS

End of the World

GARY HICKMAN

Black Rose Writing | Texas

First printing

This is a work of fiction. Names, characters, businesses, places, events, and incidents are either the products of the author's imagination or used in a fictitious manner. Any resemblance to actual persons, living or dead, or actual events is purely coincidental.

ISBN: 978-1-68433-734-7
PUBLISHED BY BLACK ROSE WRITING
www.blackrosewriting.com

Printed in the United States of America
Suggested Retail Price (SRP) $20.95

The Light Reapers is printed in Book Antiqua

*As a planet-friendly publisher, Black Rose Writing does its best to eliminate unnecessary waste to reduce paper usage and energy costs, while never compromising the reading experience. As a result, the final word count vs. page count may not meet common expectations.

DEDICATION

To my wife, Wendy:

Throughout our thirty years together, we have been through everything the world could throw at us and we are still standing. You have been there by my side even when I didn't necessarily deserve it. Thank you for being an inspiration and I love you very much.

To my kids, Carly and Noah:

Carly, thank you for showing me strength and perseverance. Seeing you fight through severe Lyme disease inspires me to move forward regardless of the odds.

Noah, thank you for reminding me how to walk to the beat of your own drum. You are truly your own man and I am proud of who you are.

To Jennifer Rowell:

Thank you for being supportive through this entire process. I appreciate your excitement and willingness to help work on this book to make it the best it can be.

THE LIGHT REAPERS

End of the World

Igitur qui desiderat pacem, praeparet bellum
"Therefore, let him who desires peace, prepare for war."

~ Publius Flavius Vegetius Renatus ~

PROLOGUE

Near Kandahar, Afghanistan, weeks prior

The walls rattle as an RPG explodes against the side of the building. The insurgents had the Light Reapers Team trapped in this hovel for the last ten minutes. "Jesus Christ!" yelled Neville. Not one for a loss of words, Sargent Neville dove to the floor and rolled against the opposite wall.

The building they were using for cover was a blown-out hovel in the Dahle region. It was reinforced with clay brick, but that didn't offer much protection.

Some family had abandoned it long ago because of the fighting in the region. It was tight quarters with all eight members of the team. "Nuts to butts" so to speak.

The building was approximately 12x12, but the addition of the broken furniture made it a tighter space for the team members and their gear. A table sat to the east side, probably used for dinner. There was a piece of furniture on the west wall that looked to have been a couch. The rugs that littered the floor were packed with sand and dirt.

This mission had been a cluster-fuck since day one. Intel was spotty, and there were "kids" trying to run the operation. Team leader, Captain Webb, didn't even want to know the ages of those in S2 running this mission. It caused him acid reflux to even think about it.

"Cap'n, we gotta move!" Priest yelled. Master Sargent Priest commanded most of the moments of jocularity on the team, but this was not one of those moments. He was laying down suppressive fire towards the location of that last RPG.

"I'm working on it," yelled Webb. Rounds ricocheted all over the room. Acrid, cordite smoke, dirt, and sand filled the already dusty room. Priest's throat was dry and pasty. He tried to peer through the smoke, searching for a way out of the building that would allow him to flank these insurgents.

"Frag out!" screamed Staff Sargent Abarra as he threw a grenade through the front window. It bounced down the backside of the ridge just a few yards in front of the building.

Just before Abarra yelled, Priest locked eyes on a side door on the eastern wall. When he heard "frag out," Priest sprinted the two or three strides and slammed his shoulder through the weak door.

He came out on the other side and rolled up on his feet like a cat. "Don't let the fat fool ya," he mumbled to himself. He used this line many times as a valuable, but painful, lesson in how not to underestimate your opponent. He was a martial arts instructor, and when sparring with a young, cocky black belt, he would ham it up by stretching, moaning, and groaning before the sparring match. The young black belt would soon incur a minor hit to their pride, along with a few bumps and bruises.

Priest dove for cover behind a small retaining wall two yards outside the broken door. He immediately heard rounds hitting all around him and felt their impact in the dirt. He had attracted some insurgent's attention. Priest worked his way down the retaining wall where it opened up at the mouth of a ravine which the insurgents were using for cover. Priest clicked on his comms, "I'm headed across the ravine from east to west. Cover me, and we'll push the off button on these fuckheads."

Abarra barked, "Copy. Shaw, get your big ass to that window and lay down some shit!"

"Copy that," Staff Sargent Shaw said and brought his M48 to rest on the window frame. He started dropping .50 cal rounds downrange, clipping off the top ridge of the ravine.

The insurgents tried to duck down deeper into the gorge to escape the rapid weapon fire coming their way. Some were successful, some weren't. "Get some, goat fuckers," Shaw bellowed, tobacco juice dribbling down his chin. Shaw had the tobacco wad nice, warm and juicy. He had a nasty habit of spitting a glob of tobacco spit in the face of every insurgent taken prisoner. Right between the eyes. Outlaw Josie Wales was one of his favorite movies. Shaw seemed to value insurgent POW's about as much as Josie Wales did the stray dog in the film.

Webb shouted to his men, "Check your fire; Priest is getting close. We don't want to take his fucking head off."

Just as he hoped, they preoccupied the insurgents with Shaw and his barrage of rounds, so Priest could traverse most of the ravine basically untouched. He rounded another curve in the terrain with his M4 locked into his shoulder, where he finally spied the chaos of the insurgents. Two of them had their heads down, running right at him, looking for cover.

"Hello ladies," Priest said before he opened up a three-round burst on each.

The insurgent on the right took two rounds center mass. The third round trailed up the man's jaw, taking most of the right side of his face with it. Teeth shot out the side of his face while his tongue lolled out of the cavern that had been the lower half of his jaw. Blood spewed from his face, and he dropped face-first to the ground.

The insurgent on the left had a split second more to react and ducked to his left for a half measure. One round blew through his forearm, while the other two embedding themselves in the side of his torso. The exit wounds exploded with blood and pieces of his ribs. He screamed as the rounds ripped through his body, only to be silenced by a follow burst that Priest laid into him. Those he expertly placed in the side of his head, obliterating it like an M-80 inside a ripe watermelon. Blood, brain matter, and shards of a skull painted the ground as the insurgent went limp and collapsed with his ass in the air. Priest shook his head and moved on. "Way too many jokes for this situation, which I don't have time for," he thought.

Shaw kept up his suppressive fire on the ridge of the ravine but trailed his firing to the left, staying 20 yards ahead of Priest.

Webb yelled out, "Myles, go back up Priest, and cover his six."

"Copy," Myles yelled back. Corporal Myles ran out the door, down the retaining wall and into the ravine.

Webb keyed Priest, "Priest, you copy?"

A second or two of silence, "Busy here, Captain," Priest blurted, showing only a slight bit of sarcasm.

"Myles is coming up on your six, don't shoot him."

Priest retorted, "No guarantees, but good copy."

Webb looked over his shoulder to see something unusual to most, but normal for this team. Sargent Shin was meditating, and Neville was now playing cards with Doc. "Are you shit heads aware of what is going on out here?" Shin never opened his eyes from his meditative state.

"Yes, Shaw is providing suppressive fire along with Abarra. You are providing oversight to Priest in the ravine."

"Okay," Webb said. "What about you two?" referring to Neville and Doc.

"Damn Cap'n., I'm sure nobody needs sniping," Neville objected.

"I didn't hear anybody calling for a medic," Doc exclaimed. "Besides, nobody else can fit next to Shaw and use the rest of the window as a firing position with his big ass in the way," Doc quipped.

Shaw spit some tobacco juice. "Yep, that's about right. This window only accommodates one man… or the two of ya'll!" he chuckled.

"Keep firing, or I'll come over there and slap the shit out of that big, corn fed, redneck head of yours," Doc bitched.

"Yep, that will be about the time you cease to exist, son," Shaw muttered.

"Pipe down, you assholes, Priest is coming close to finishing things off,", Webb barked.

It didn't take long for Priest and Myles to reach the rest of the insurgents. Priest fired into the group. Myles threw a grenade on the far side of the group. "Frag out!" he yelled.

The two dropped to the ground for cover. BOOM! Dirt, blood, and scraps of flesh rained down, followed by screams. The two Reapers trudged through the destruction and systematically ended the screams for good.

CHAPTER 1

Present: 101st Airborne Division, Ft Campbell, KY

The Light Reapers are a special operations group within the 101st Airborne Division, ran by Captain Marcus Webb, call sign "Spider". Marcus Webb was a tall, thirty-eight-year-old black officer from the streets of Philly, who commanded a lot of attention when entering a room.

Webb's second in command was Master Sargent Alec Priest, call sign "Father". Built like a brick wall with a bald head and sizable grey beard, Priest intimidated most people with just a look. He had extensive combat experience, but often told jokes in the middle of combat which brought his sanity into question.

The next in line was SFC Gabriel Abarra, call sign "Bacardi". Abarra, from Puerto Rico, was an expert troop manager and former drill Sargent who liked to jack around with the rest of the team. A short man in stature, but large in character. The lines in Abarra's face represented his twenty-plus years of military life.

Next, Staff Sargent Jeremiah Shaw, call sign "Cotton". Hailing from Alabama, he was an enormous man standing 6'4", weighing 280lbs and with a baby face that was a tremendous hit with the ladies. As the team's entry breach expert, his size came in handy.

Then there was Sargent Renaldo Neville, call sign "Voodoo". An expert sniper and recon soldier, Neville had a sarcastic attitude but performed his missions flawlessly. He was from a mixed-raced family and grew up in bayous of Louisiana.

The spiritual member of the group was Sargent Sung Shin, call sign "Gandhi". He was from South Korea and a Buddhist. Shin was an expert with numbers and calculations, so his spotting skills were important for Neville as a sniper. When he was spotting for Neville, they both shared the call sign, "Overlord".

Their medic was Sargent Joseph Mancini, call sign "Doc". The team called him Doc as units in the military tended to do. Being from the Bronx, he had a heavy NY accent and a WTF attitude. He had a habit of providing graphic narration during combat.

Their newest recruit was Corporal Dominic Myles, call sign "Motown". From the streets of Detroit, he was an excellent fighter and loyal soldier. After a heartfelt plea from his mother, he gave up the thug life and joined the military.

The Light Reapers are a quick deployment unit, which maintained constant deployment readiness. Their equipment, standards, and tactics differed from the regular military. They played by their own rules and stayed out of the political theater and dog and pony shows. They executed Black Ops flawlessly and were not on the radar of any Congressional chamber.

The team was cleaning and checking their gear when Webb ran into the load-out room. "Priest, Abarra, you're with me. Major briefing, now!"

"Up to the principal's office again?" Priest lamented.

Abarra hit him jokingly on the shoulder, "Come on, you probably have detention again."

The three made their way to the 101st Airborne Division HQ building. HQ was a magnificent building designed with the building's atrium doubling as a museum, with bronze statutes of eagles and soldiers lining the walls, and the front of the building is the highlight as you walk into the round room. Hanging high above the statues were oversized battle streamers and photos of every Medal of Honor winner. A revolving display in the back highlighted important battles and times for the division. Overhead, hung a life-sized paratrooper, his parachute dangling from the windows above.

Arriving at the top floor, Priest and Abarra followed Webb into the division office suite. Standing in the doorway of the War Room was Colonel Madison, the commander and handler for the Black Ops branch of the 101st Airborne. All three reported with a respectful salute.

"Sit down, gentlemen," Colonel Madison motioned to a large conference table in the middle of the War Room.

The War Room was impressive – a wall of monitors on one wall and a single massive screen on the opposite wall. Old school maps were hanging on any wall space available that wasn't being taken up by some form of technology. The maps weren't used so much anymore, but Madison was nostalgic and liked the reminders of the old school. Seated was a team of communications and mission controllers in front of various computers on tables were against one wall.

Colonel Madison was an avid runner with a lean body along with close-cropped, graying hair and blue eyes, standing about six feet with digicam ACU's. Madison reminded Priest of Cal Ripken Jr. He was drinking coffee out of an enormous mug, even though it was 15:00 hours in the afternoon. Madison was an all-day coffee drinker. Priest thought, "All that running will not help him if his kidneys give out from all the java."

"Gentlemen, we have a potential problem that may require your expertise." Madison continued without waiting for a response. "We have intel that some bad operators are working together to bring about an objective that could affect the rest of the world."

Webb furrowed his brow and gave a long glance to Priest, who returned the concerned look. Madison continued, "With the intel we have received, the players in this arena are Pakistan, Palestine, and Iran. There has been some secondary intel that countries like Russia and China are in the mix as supporters, but we have not confirmed that. What makes this highly unusual is that these three countries have agreed to join. The desired outcome for the three is the same, but the intended target is different for each. The targets identified for each country are: Pakistan's target is India. It's no secret there has been a feud here for decades. Palestine's target is easiest to figure out."

"Israel," Abarra offered.

"Correct. They have wanted Israel removed off the face of the earth for decades. Finally, we have Iran. Who is their target, you may ask? All of us infidels, plus their Muslim neighbors. They want to target the different sects of Islam who they think are not in the will of Allah. Their primary targets right now are Afghanistan, Iraq, and Saudi Arabia."

Webb spoke up, "I assume we are not talking about military power? There is no way these countries have enough troops or firepower to take over these adversarial countries. So, I guess they are looking at other ways?"

"Maybe chemical or biological," Priest added.

Madison continued, "They are conducting experiments in a "neutral country" hoping to throw us off. We are tracking them and found a working compound in Hakkari, Turkey, next to the Iran/Iraq border."

"So, I assume we want to destroy the facility and everything associated? Are we to gain any intel there?" Webb said.

"The intel we have alludes to them working on a virus that has various effects on people. We intercepted communications implying they may not want the complete destruction of the people in the areas."

Priest piped up, "They don't want to obliterate all the people, so they want to take prisoners?"

Madison continued, "Correct. So, this virus, chemical weapon, medical cocktail, whatever you want to call it, apparently can make people subservient. How it achieves this, we don't know. We tried to get an asset inside, but they have made this operation tight and exclusive. They aren't letting many people in the clubhouse on this one. We have heard rumors that they have test subjects, but we have no visual evidence of this. Oh, the other bit of wonderful news. As of 19:38 hours last night, the whole sight went dark. No activity, no lights or communications, period."

"So, we are to go into the target area with almost no intel, contemporaneous communications, and no layout of the interior of any building?" Webb inquired

"Justo en la boca del infierno?" Abarra sarcastically uttered.

"Pretty much," Madison replied. All three men sitting at the conference table looked at one another with that "should have seen this coming," look. Madison caught the glances but said nothing. "All the mission requirements will be briefed on the flight to your objective. As far as the mission criteria, it's simple, make it to the lab area, assess the situation, infiltrate the facility, secure the formula and any other intel, then exfil. You will encounter enemy combatants all over the compound and should engage appropriately. Questions?"

CHAPTER 2

Hakkari, Turkey:

The night was devoid of light and the cloud cover blocked any limited moonlight that peeked through. The landscape of Hakkari was mountainous terrain with lots of rocks and desolate vegetation. The choice of putting the furtive research facility here was one of deception and pretext. That the perceived outcome of the research was not to benefit any of the governments of the players involved alluded to a volatile situation. To base their research in a "neutral" country separate from any of the target countries was a calculated decision. If any of the home countries of the terrorists involved found out about their plan, they would surely stop them and there is no telling what would happen to them.

The special ops Blackhawk with the stealth rotors silently navigated the hilly terrain end route to the infill point, 3 klicks SW of the Hakkâri facility.

Webb keyed his comms to the team. "Ok, we're 10 minutes out. Let's go over it one more time. Neville and Shin, you will take up Overwatch position on the designated high ground, directly east of the facility. Give us some initial surveillance on personnel and validation of the facility layout. The rest of us will infiltrate in a three-prong approach. Three, six, and nine o'clock. Watch your crossfire and check your targets. Doc and I will take three o'clock and provide cover and suppressive fire if needed. Priest and Shaw, you two will enter from nine o'clock and will be the breech team. Abarra and Myles, you guys will be at the six o'clock position and will stay in cover to provide support and any silent elimination of enemies who show up late for the party. Questions?"

The Blackhawk came in silent and smooth. It hovered about 50 feet from the ground, just low enough that it was hidden by a couple of hill peaks. The crew chief dropped the rope outside the left door. Webb and Myles, fast roped out first, touched down on the ground, pivoted to a prone position, and started providing support while the others exited the Blackhawk. Priest and Shaw were out last. Priest laid his comms, "We're down. All personnel on site." Upon the notification, the Blackhawk crew took off to await exfil notification.

The facility was like most others in this region. Plain bunker-looking buildings scattered about the compound. The primary research facility was toward the rear of the compound, almost backed up against a hill. Other various buildings were also on the compound to include a barracks to the east of the research facility. This is where Webb and Doc posted in case enemy soldiers came pouring out. So far, it's been quiet. To the left of the research facility was a maintenance building and facility support storage. "Ok, maintain radio silence until we get a sit rep from Overlord," Webb whispered.

Moments later, "Overlord to team, do you copy?"

"Copy, Overlord," Webb replied.

"Things look quiet; unnervingly so. I see no personnel, no activity, no utilities in operation. Nothing," Neville advised.

Priest keyed, "Are we sure our intel is fresh?"

"I confirmed before our last operational briefing that we had the latest intel." Webb answered.

"Well, we will not be confirming squat unless we get moving. Breech team is heading in. Watch our ass, Overlord." Priest continued.

"We're on it. Proceed."

Priest and Shaw made their way to the research facility front. Peering through the dark glass, Priest saw nothing. He dropped his NVG's to the front of his helmet. As the green light activated, he tried to make out the inside layout of the facility. The front was a typical lobby with a front desk, either reception or security. There were two armchairs with a sofa in between them, all surrounding a large coffee table. There was a bank of elevators on the far wall to the right of the front desk.

Priest keyed his comms, "The front lobby is dark; no personnel. The power appears to be out. I don't see any standby lights on, nothing on the computers at the front desk, or the call buttons on the elevators. I don't even see any emergency lights on. Overlord, do you see any signs of life or power at all?"

"Negative. No ground lights, street lights, nothing. The entire facility looks dead."

"Copy that," Webb added. "Priest, proceed cautiously. Could be an ambush, but no power is calling too much attention to the scene if they want to spring something."

"Copy that." Priest tried the front door, and it was open. Shaw and Priest exchanged quizzical looks and proceeded on.

Inside, the lobby was eerily quiet. Even as experts of stealth, it still seemed like their footfalls sounded like they were stomping through like a full-size marching band. Several long moments passed when Priest's voice came over the comms. "First floor is clear. No personnel so far, and it looks like most of the equipment was left."

"Copy that," Webb acknowledged.

Abarra silently whispered to Myles, "This isn't right. Something is off. A full functioning lab, and now there is nothing?"

"Heading down to the next level," came Priest's voice.

After a monotonous process of clearing rooms and levels, Priest and Shaw ended up at the main research facility lab. They came to two enormous steel doors with 12"X12" windows in each, about five feet high.

Shaw looked through the left window into the lab. "The lab space looks empty, still no power visible feeding any of the equipment."

"Let's take a look," Priest replied.

Shaw entered first and took up cover to the left, and Priest covered to the right. The lab was a large room with various working counters laid out in a row in the middle of the room. Along each wall were glass-door cabinets containing various beakers, bottles, and other research materials. The left and right sides of the room were desks situated with computers and servers, which all were powered off.

Shaw and Priest separated from each other to inspect the computers and servers on opposite sides of the lab. Priest updated the Team, "We are in the main lab facility and all the hard drives from the computers and servers are missing. We have also cleared the drawers and filing cabinets. There is absolutely nothing here. They have cleaned everything out. This place is completely sanitized. The intel is shit."

Webb shouted, "Ok, get the hell out of there, I don't like it. This mission is fucked!"

"Copy that!" Priest and Shaw made it to the second-floor landing, and as they were silently making their way to exit the building, they stopped in their tracks.

"Wait…you hear that?" Shaw called. "It sounds like shuffling."

"Shit, it does. Stand by; we may have someone in the facility. Maintain silence until further notice," Priest said.

Shaw and Priest made their way out of the stairwell into the second-level hallway. The dark hallway was long with multiple doors on each side. They inched their way down the hall. Priest shouldered his M4 at the ready with Shaw checking his M48. They strained to hear the sound they heard in the stairwell. At first, nothing. Then they heard the shuffling again. Then they heard a noise… an unfamiliar noise.

"What the hell is that?" whispered Shaw.

"I don't know. I can't place it. It almost sounds like a clicking."

"Yeah, it's creepy."

Priest and Shaw were on their way down the hallway towards the sound. "Click, click… click, click" Shaw motioned toward the fourth door on the left. They set up on each side of the door. "Click, click… click, click"? The sound was louder now, and the cadence that reminded them of the Tick-Tock sound of a clock.

Priest give the signal to breech quietly. Shaw tried the door, and it is unlocked. "Click, click… click, click. "He slowly opened the door to a medium-size conference room. The NVG's washed the room in an eerie green tint as they search for the source of the sound.

They spotted a figure sitting in a chair with its back to them at the end of the conference table. Priest noticed that the figure's head was tilting from side to side in unison with the click-click sound……click-click.

Shaw moved silently up to the figure, slowly swung the chair around, and backed away. In the chair sat a man. His blood-covered face wearing an oversized smile. He tilted his head to one side, then the other side while continuing to make the clicking sound. He was missing his left eye, which is just a bloody socket.

He met eyes with Shaw and then lunged out of his chair with an ear-piercing scream. The movement startled Shaw at first, but Shaw, being trained in hand-to-hand combat, threw a palm strike to the man's face. The strike caused the man to stumble back.

Shaw then raised his M48 and fired a three-round burst right in the man's face. The rounds exploded out the back of the man's head, taking off the right side of his skull. Brain matter slid out of his skull and splattered on the ground. The rest of the man's body hit the floor a split second later. "Holy shit," Shaw barked. "Never seen nothing like that."

"Who has?" Priest searched the body for identification and found a door access key with the man's picture… Dr. Ahmadi. "He is one of the missing biologists from Pakistan."

"What the hell is he doing all the way over here in Turkey?" Shaw asked

"Spider, we have a situation. This op is FUBAR! We need to beat feet," Priest barked into his squad comms.

"Copy that, Father. Make your way out and we'll cover your six. Bacardi, get us an Uber, ASAP. Time to blow this popsicle stand. Everyone on me."

Priest and Shaw exited the facility after a few moments and posted up on Webb.

He looked at both men, "Sit rep."

Priest chimed in first, "The facility is clean… sanitized. No documentation, no hard drives, no USB's, nothing."

Abarra spoke next, "Exfil in 20. We will just need to pop smoke."

"Got it. What is the deal with the doctor in the..."? Webb trailed off. He heard faint clicking noises. Not just one, but many. By the look on the faces of the rest of the team, they heard it too.

Just then, the comms activated, "Spider, this is Overlord."

"Go ahead."

"It looks like there are a dozen civilians coming your way."

"Which direction?"

"Rock Around the Clock Spider, every direction. They don't seem to move with a purpose. Instead, they seem to be listening. Almost seems like they aren't all there. Like they are on something."

Priest gave Webb a serious look, "If these civilians are anything like the doctor we encountered, this is going to hit like a shit storm."

"I'm not one to shoot civilians without cause." Abarra exclaimed.

Priest looked at Abarra with concern, "Yeah, me neither, but the thing we encountered was not a mild-mannered doctor. That thing was a raging beast without thought, remorse, or a trace of humanity. Overlord, zoom in on one civilian and give me a behavior read."

"Copy. Ok, female civilian approaching to your 11 o'clock. 200 yards. She is covered in blood, head to toe. Eyes seem unfocused at the moment. She is moving her head from side to side. She seems to make some sound with her tongue, but obviously I am too far away to hear."

"That is the fucking clicking noise we heard the doctor making. Along with the abnormal head movements," Priest whispered.

Webb keyed, "Does it look like she is in shock?"

"Negative. I've seen shock and battle rattle. Doesn't look the same here."

Webb looked at Priest under furrowed brows, "What caused the doctor to snap and go ape shit?"

"When he saw Shaw. Before that his back was to us, and we were operating in stealth."

"Ok, I guess we will test a theory. Team, circle the wagons."

The team set up in a circle with their backs to the center. "Watch your fire lanes. We have 360-degree contact, and I will bait the fox to the henhouse. Apparently, these people have some serious problems, so take a second to assess. But if you need to push the off button, then so be it."

As Webb finished, the clicking was getting increasingly louder. "Overlord, we are getting ready to poke the bear here. Assess and provide support."

"Copy."

Webb looked to his left and fist bumped with Doc to acknowledge he was ready. This continued around the entire team in the circle until it reached back to Webb, who received a fist bump from Shaw to his right. Webb then let out a loud whooping yell and waited. He didn't need to wait long. Blood-curdling screams answered the yell from all directions.

"Ah, Spider, that did the trick. There is recognition in the girl's face. She is going nuts and coming your way at a high rate of speed. Engage?"

"No, hold off until you hear one of us fire. We're still trying to assess."

"Copy that."

Abarra was the first to acknowledge, "Contact 11 o'clock." The girl who was under Overlord's surveillance was the first to come into view of the team. The rest of the team, highly disciplined, kept their focus on their firing lanes.

Webb, who was on the opposite side of the circle from Abarra, "Sit rep!"

"She is definitely not in her right mind. We have guns trained on her, and she is still coming, screaming like a banshee."

"Ok, engage first. If no compliance, then take her down."

Abarra yelled, "Ma'am, stop where you are and put your hands up!" She didn't comply and was closing the gap.

150 yards? Ma'am, stop where you are and put your hands up." Nothing.

100 yards? "I will be forced to shoot if you do not comply." No recognition.

50 yards? It is when all other civilians came into view running and screaming toward the team. The screams made your blood run cold.

It was nothing like Corporal Myles had ever heard before. He was from Detroit, had seen people die, had heard people die. He witnessed drug deals go bad, people betrayed, people seek revenge for several things. Nothing he had seen was even close to this. Myles jumped as Abarra let loose with a three-round burst toward the approaching girl. All three landed center mass, and she went down.

"Target down!" Abarra said. He rotated his sight picture to another target when he noticed movement from the girl he just shot. "Oh, diosmio que demonios," Abarra said under his breath. "Three-center mass and the target got up and is still coming."

"Body armor?" Priest spoke.

"Negative, I can see her bra under her shirt."

"Shit, we aren't dealing with normal combatants. Put one in her head. See if she gets up then," Priest yelled.

Abarra confirmed his sight picture and sent a round down range. The girl's head snapped back, and she crumpled to the ground. Abarra watched her for a couple seconds. "Yep, that did it. She's down for the count."

"Everybody hear that? Head shots to put these ," Priest barked.

Webb then keyed for Overlord. "Overlord, take out all hostiles. Repeat, eliminate all hostiles."

"Copy." By this time the entire team was engaged with the civilians running at them like wild beasts. They were charging out, screaming with no regard to their safety or survival. They were laser focused on getting to the team.

Based on what Shaw had witnessed in the conference room, he knew it would not be good if the people reached them. He opened up with the M48, sending round after round of .50 cal ammunition, which cut the approaching group down by the score. Legs were being surgically removed, along with arms, chunks of torsos and sections of skull. Even with one person having their lower half blown off, their desire to make it to the team never wavered. He kept crawling, dragging what was left of his lower torso and legs. Shaw put a couple in the guy's head.

Doc was freaking out. As a medic he had seen a lot of gore in combat, but nothing like he was seeing right now. "Holy fucking shit. Look at that guy over there. I blew half his fucking hip off and he is still coming. His guts are all over the ground, and he is still moving. His eyes are gone too. How can he see where the fuck he is going?"

Webb barked, "Shut up and kill the son of a bitch already."

"Ok, but shit, there is hardly anything left to shoot on this motherfucker!"

"Shoot him in the head, in the fucking head," Priest shouted.

Doc fired into the crawling man's face. "Holy Mary and Joseph. Did you see his head explode? I blew his head apart, and it looked like cauliflower."

"Doc, shut the fuck up!" Webb bellowed.

Myles could hear the screaming and see the faces of the civilians charging at them. He could feel the concussion of the guns sending rounds down range. But he was in a fog. He felt like he was wearing a concrete suit. All his limbs felt weighted down. His head ached, his eyes burned, and something muted his hearing. The scene was blurry in front of him, and he couldn't make out where he was or what was going on. Abarra was shaking his shoulders, finally snapping him out of his funk. He found himself slumped forward, and his weapon hanging down, not pointed toward the oncoming civilians.

"Are you all right? Hey Myles, what the hell is going on with you? Are you with us?" Abarra shouted.

Abarra's voice started somewhat muffled but quickly cleared, and Myles could make out what was being said. "Yeah, yeah… I'm good," Myles grunted out. "I'm good to go."

Myles sighted on two people running at him about 100 yards away. Immediately the closest one went down after the side of his head exploded. A split second later, the woman followed, nosediving into the ground with such force it snapped her neck and left her head laying at a weird angle.

"Two down. Motown, you better wake up and engage your targets!" Overlord said, sounding annoyed. Myles just stared at the two bodies lying dead in front of him.

"What's wrong?" Abarra asked quizzically.

"Never been this close to targets before. Never been this close. It's different. I saw their faces, heard their screams," Myles trailed off. Luckily for Myles, all targets were finally down.

Webb keyed, "Anymore targets in the area? Overlord, sit rep."

"Negative, Spider. Area is all clear."

"Ok, stay and provide support while we take click of what the actual fuck just happened."

"Copy Spider, we are T-minus, 2 minutes for exfil."

"Thanks, Overlord. Give out our coordinates here for the birds. This area is all clear, and I don't feel like humping to the previous exfil point."

"Copy that."

Webb turned back to the rest of the team, "Ok, we got 2 minutes, so what the fuck just happened?"

"Well, it's obvious these weren't regular people," Priest answered "They look like local support personnel, but something happened to them to make them almost indestructible to everything except a headshot. My guess is they were somehow exposed to what was being researched here."

"Yeah, I would agree," Webb acknowledged.

Abarra nodded his head in agreement.

"Man, the one guy kept crawling with his guts trailing behind. All that dirt was sticking to them almost made them look like octopus tentacles."

"Jesus, Doc. What the fuck is wrong with you?" Abarra asked. "You are a medic. You've seen this shit before."

"No, not like that. When was the last time you saw a guy with no lower half crawling around with his guts behind him? I've never seen that shit. Any of you seen shit like that before? I mean holy shit, that was some fucked up shit..."

"Ok, we get it. Pipe down," barked Priest.

"Doc, get some blood and tissue samples from two corpses. We'll take them back for HQ to analyze. I don't know if they'll stay viable, but it's all we got," Webb ordered.

Doc did as Webb instructed and finished just as the chopper came in to exfil.

The stealth Blackhawk hovered in silently, but the rotor wash stirred up dust and debris. The Blackhawk sat down smoothly and waited for the team to load up.

Neville and Shin came running up and gave Webb and Priest a nod and everyone mounted up. Priest plugged into the bird's comms, "Get us the hell out of this shit hole!"

CHAPTER 3

101st Airborne Division, Ft Campbell, KY

The Reapers exited the Blackhawk, still shellshocked somewhat by the previous events. Myles had been quiet the entire way back from Turkey; a helicopter back to their forward base, a military hop from Turkey to the UK, another hop from the UK to the US and then a helicopter ride back to Ft. Campbell. Silence the whole way.

Abarra sidled up to Myles, "You feeling alright? You've been quiet the entire trip back. Come on, talk to me."

Myles stopped walking and dropped his eyes to the ground.

"We were shooting civilians, regular people. It was a massacre, and we acted like it was business as usual." He grew silent again.

"I know it was tough, but those weren't regular people. Multiple rounds didn't drop those people for good which was a telltale sign. They should have passed out from the pain. None of that happened. Hell, they should have at least ran the other way when we started firing. To put then in the same category as normal civilians is dangerous."

Abarra put his arm around Myles and gave him a shake. The two continued to walk into the flight hangar.

As the rest of the team entered the hangar, Webb called the Reapers to form up on him.

"Okay Reapers, let me hear it. We all know that mission was fucked all the way around. It wasn't the first time we have had to engage civilians, but this was unlike before. I didn't like it either, so talk freely."

"What the fuck are we dealing with Cap?" Neville spoke up. "Except for head shots, those people were indestructible."

Okay,"Yeah, and what about that damn screeching?" Doc jumped in.

"Not to mention that creepy ass head movement and the clicking," Shaw finished.

Webb listened intently and shared a look or two with Priest.

"Okay, okay, I hear all of you. Believe me, I have all the same thoughts as you. Priest and I discussed this, but of course, we have no intel to tell us what the hell just happened. We can, however, relay our assumptions."

Webb looked at Priest, and he nodded. Webb cleared his throat.

"Here is what we believe; the formula that this gaggle of scientists either created or altered has turned into some kind of virus that doesn't kill its victim, but changes them into the mindless machines. We believe they exposed the civilians we engaged to this virus, and we got a front-row seat to opening night. If they unleash this stuff on the population, I am not sure what we will come across. If that is how they intend to use it."

"Hopefully we have someone on staff here who can tell us what is going on with this virus and what we are dealing with. We are running blind and I don't want to jump headfirst into a hornet's nest," Priest added.

Myles continued to seem disengaged, and it caught Priest's eye.

"Myles, what is it? You're part of this team, so out with it, son."

Myles slowly raised his head.

"I froze. I didn't even get a shot off. I just sat there and watched the whole thing go down. Watched people running toward us, screaming and screeching. I just sat there and did nothing. They could have over-run us."

Priest walked over to him and put his hand on his shoulder.

"You covered my ass a couple weeks ago in Afghanistan. You didn't hesitate at all. What makes this so different?" Priest asked with concern, causing the lines on his face to deepen.

"I don't know. I guess you can put a face on your enemies that looks the same most of the time. I can look at them with the same clothes, same weapons and the same purpose. Which is to destroy us. B-b-but these were regular women and men. No AK-47's to recognize, no matching uniforms or head coverings. They all had different clothes and I could see their faces were different. With that blood all over their face, the normal picture of the enemy was not what I was seeing out there. It just wasn't the same." Myles said with a far-off look in his eyes. Like he was replaying the scene in his head.

Shaw shook his head, "We don't know where this shit is going to lead. We know the virus and all the other personnel were gone. If this isn't over, and my gut tells me it ain't, then we are going to be dealing with a lot more people just like those."

Myles looked around at the rest of the team, and a look of resolve flashed across his face.

He nodded his head, "I got it. Understood. I'm good to go." Myles said confidently.

Priest slapped him on the shoulder, and they started walking again.

"Believe me, Myles. We are all confused as fuck and we are just as worried as you are. We would be stupid if we weren't. However, we'll get through this together. Reapers always do. HUA!"

"HUA, Sarge!" Myles repeated.

"Out-fucking-standing." Priest joked.

It was 09:30 when Priest completed his debrief to command. Four hours of recollection, combat analysis, various questions, and repeats of the same information had him exhausted. They hadn't let him eat, sleep, shit or shower since they had returned to base. It was old news to him; he had been here a hundred times before. With as many missions as he'd been on, this was just part of doing business.

Webb jogged up to him, "You finished?"

"Yeah, feel like something the cat dragged in and then threw underneath the refrigerator."

Webb laughed. He always like Priest's humor. He looked at him and could tell Priest was almost dead on his feet.

Priest was shorter than Marcus Webb, only about 5'10" or so. Priest was normally clean shaven, bald most of the time, unless out on a mission for an extended period. Priest kept a gray beard, about 3 to 4 inches below his chin. His call sign being "Father" suited him well. They gave him that call sign as a play of words with his last name, "Priest." Priest had blue eyes that seemed kind and evil at the same time. It just mattered on which Priest you came across.

Webb had met Priest on another mission, about three or four years ago. The Special Operations were re-orging and were merging into several teams and different MOS's. Webb had completed various tours in Iraq and Afghanistan.

Priest was older and had spent time all over the world. Even places the regular public did not realize conflicts were even happening. He had served in the Philippines, South America, Somalia, Yemen, and the list went on and on. They had pulled Webb into the SPO with basically no direction. Command knew they needed people, and Webb's resume was impressive. He was young for a captain, so most of the teams didn't want to work with him.

SPO worked differently than the rest of the military, and their enlisted teams had the stroke and set their own rules. All teams had to have an officer or officers as part of the team for command continuity issues.

They had given Priest, Webb's DD214, and many of his evaluations. Priest was impressed with Webb's credentials and could decipher an ass kisser from a hard charger. The first time they met, Priest introduced himself, and they went to have a beer. The rest they say is history, and Webb had been in command of the Light Reapers Team since that day.

Priest admired Webb. He like that Webb didn't play the race card, didn't use his childhood or upbringing as an excuse for anything. He just busted his ass and worked hard, gaining Priest's respect and loyalty. Hell, he had respect from the entire team.

Priest knew Webb had it hard growing up in inner city Philadelphia. Webb had talked a lot about his family and upbringing whenever he and Priest had some downtime and talked over a few beers. He never talked about it to get sympathy, just more than a matter of fact. Priest could relate to that as his own childhood was full of turmoil and strife. Having a violent drunk of a father, Priest understood Webb's situation of home never being a sanctuary.

Webb and Priest made their way to the barracks where they were temporarily assigned. Since they were SPO and rapid deployment, the Army never really gave them a home on Fort Campbell. The barracks they stayed in were open bay style, like they had in boot camp.

They looked at each other and rolled their eyes as they approached the building. The rest of the team had already set up in the barracks, and Myles, Neville and Doc were already asleep. Shin was meditating, and Shaw was cleaning his M48.

Abarra met Webb and Priest halfway down the bay. "You guys finally finished?"

"Yeah, they raked us over the coals," Webb said tiredly.

"You two look like shit."

"Thanks," Priest chuckled.

"We grabbed some chow for you guys before the chow hall closed. Get something to eat and put your ass in the shower. You guys reek."

"Yes, mother. Really, we appreciate it."

"No problem, Priest, anytime."

The two ate, grabbed a shower and were asleep before their head hit the pillow.

After a few hours of sleep, Priest woke up to arguing in the barracks.

"I don't understand why my call sign is Gandhi," Shin said.

"Because you do that meditation stuff, and you're about peace and shit," Doc explained.

"Gandhi was Hindu, I am Buddhist. It's not even close."

"Well, it's kind of the same."

"No, he was Indian, and I am Korean," Shin said with an annoyed look on his face.

"Your countries are on the same continent, right?"

"You are an idiot," Shin said in Korean. "Ok, you are from NY, correct?"

"The Bronx, born and raised."

"So, it would be the same as if I called you a country redhead."

"That's redneck." Shaw spoke up, "And don't compare greaser over there to us fine, well-mannered, Alabama country folk."

"Doc, you are dumb as a bag of hammers, you know that?" said Priest, putting in his two cents.

"Sorry, Sarge, I didn't think I was that loud. I didn't mean to wake you up."

"Doc, you are loud when you are just thinking, much less when you open your mouth." Doc looked bewildered, which made Priest chuckle to himself.

"Shin, you are with Neville most of the time during missions where a sniper team is needed. Together, your call sign is Overlord. We hardly ever use Gandhi."

"I know, but I am just confused about when I got the name."

"Well, I can't remember either, but it stays. I'm too old to learn new shit."

Shin just threw up his hands and walked away. Shin's parents had come over during the Korean War to escape the communist occupation of North Korea. He explained to Priest some time ago that his parents loved the U.S. and were grateful for the opportunities they had. Shin figured a way to give back and make his parents proud at the same time was to serve his country. He had planned to get out after his initial enlistment was up, but by that time, he was in the Light Reapers and decided to re-up. Shin was Neville's spotter; and could calculate distances, speed, trajectory, and many other valuable statistics. He and Doc seemed to bicker like two brothers.

Speaking of Doc, he had joined the military honoring a request from his father. Actually, the request was more like Pops would kick the shit out of him unless he got himself together. His Pops dragged his ass to the recruiter. Doc had always cared about people and thought about becoming a nurse. Thinking along the nurse track, he became a combat medic and had joined the Light Reapers about two years ago.

The team went home with Doc twice, and his momma about killed everyone. She kept making so much food even Shaw almost fell into a coma with the amount she was shoving at them. Momma Mancini was a kind woman and made it a point to hug every one of the team before they left her house. She also graced everyone before they left by placing her hands on both sides of their face and reciting a prayer for them.

Priest looked around, and Shaw notice he was searching for someone, "Looking for Webb?" Priest nodded. "They called him up to the TOC at HQ to get our next briefing. We were going to wake you up, but they said brass only."

"Well, I appreciate the sleep."

"You have a second, Sarge?" Shaw asked reservedly.

"Sure, Shaw, what's up?" "You know me, and I'm not one to complain. That job we did in Turkey was completely fucked up. That didn't feel right at any level."

"Yeah, I feel the same way. During my debrief, I couldn't help thinking there was something Command knew, but weren't telling us."

"I just hope it doesn't come back to bite us in the ass."

"You and me both."

After an hour, Webb appeared back in the barracks. His face was pensive, and he looked like he had been arguing. The veins in his temples and neck hadn't completely gone down to normal.

Abarra addressed him, "Marcus, everything all right?"

"Fuck no, everything ain't all right. It appears the shitty intel we received on our last mission wasn't the last pile of shit we will receive. It seems we were a day late and a dollar short on infiltrating the research facility."

"Yeah, no shit," Neville said with his Cajun accent.

Webb continued, "It turns out that ISIS hit the facility just a day before we had arrived and stole the virus. From the wonderful intel we have, it appears ISIS has taken the virus to their cell in Dearborn, Michigan."

"What? In the good old USA? Fucking bastards. Don't bring that shit over here!" Doc was livid.

"Man, this shit just got real-real," Priest muttered.

"Exactly. So, they could deploy us to Dearborn to find the cell, eliminate it and confiscate the virus." Webb was looking more and more worried as he spoke.

Abarra squinted, "So this means we are to engage US citizens? Posse Comitatus?"

Webb shook his head, "I hope not, and we need to avoid that as much as possible. The ISIS personnel involved are here on college Visa's studying engineering."

"So, when do we roll out," Miles asked.

"Ok, slow your roll. Coordination is being conducted with local authorities and the FBI. They are handling the situation. We are on standby, just in case. The only reason they are even considering us is that we have already engaged people who were affected. So, we are in an advisory capacity at this moment. So, get some chow, sleep, shower, etc. while you have the chance. Just be available if they need us, Hua?"

"Hua."

CHAPTER 4

23:10 Fort Campbell, KY

The young corporal assigned to Fort Campbell drove through the mostly empty streets with trepidation but with purpose. They gave him orders and the look on his lieutenant's face gave him a foreboding feeling. He knew this wasn't just a dog and pony show and was something severe. He had never seen it that busy in the HQ building before.

The corporal rolled up to the barracks the team was staying in and slammed on the brakes. He jumped out of the SUV and busted through the barrack doors. Halfway through the door, they met the corporal with clicks, clacks, and eight barrels pointed straight at him.

"Oh, shit!" The corporal uttered as a little dribble of piss ran down his leg. It was painfully clear that the corporal had never dealt with a special ops unit before.

Shaw was the closest to him. "Holy dog shit, son. You almost got turned into a piece of swiss cheese as many rounds as you could have gotten nailed with.... WHOO-hoo."

"Uh-uh," The corporal stammered.

"Out with it, son," Shaw poked.

"Uh, Captain Webb... Colonel Madison, has requested your presence, along with MSG Priest and SSG Abarra immediately. Things seem to have unraveled quickly."

The three of them looked at one another with trepidation. "Ok, let's go then." Webb, Priest, and Abarra followed the corporal out the door.

Shaw hollered, "Who the hell will wipe this piss up off the floor?" They met his question with silence. "Myles, you're up, son," Shaw said as he laid back down.

"Shit," Myles murmured under his breath. "Being the lowest rank sucks."

"Yep, I get it. It sucks. Goodnight, John Boy." Shaw responded as he laid down to fall back to sleep.

The three Light Reapers made it to the War Room within minutes. Colonel Madison was sitting at the head of the conference table, rubbing his temples. He looked haggard with dark circles under his eyes, like he had been up for days. Colonel Madison's XO, Major Harrell, motioned them in and left to get the coffee for the meeting. Madison looked up and motioned for the three to have a seat. He took a couple of deep breaths and then sighed.

"Boys, we are in a world of shit, if you haven't figured that out by now. Command always seems to be a step behind, and we are getting ready to take a bite of a big ass, shit sandwich. So here it is in a nutshell. ISIS made it to Dearborn, Michigan, with the virus. Yes, they made it through security and customs with the virus. Loyalists, radicals or paid off workers who probably gained some financial independence with some 1.5 billion in cash Obama sent to Iran, take your pick. Here is the raw deal on that. While relieving those terrorists of the virus, they damaged the container. Because they were transporting the virus in a damaged container, it caused the virus to spread among the people they came in contact with during their travel. Yes, it is exactly what you are thinking, that shit has now spread halfway across the fucking planet. With the virus being as extremely contagious as it is, who knows how many people were exposed to it. We got a fucking pandemic here."

"How bad is it, sir?" Webb inquired.

"Bring up the news on the primary screen, Harrell." Harrell typed a few characters on his keyboard. The images came up on the screen but seemed like something from a bad movie, instead.

The two news anchors, who probably looked perfect and plastic on a normal day, were far from that now. The man and woman looked visibly rattled and read their prompts with a robot-like mechanical demeanor. They were in shock from the scenes playing in a loop on the screen behind them. Because of the obvious gore, they blurred most of the scenes out. Although by the look of the anchors, it was apparent they had seen the full and unhindered video.

The scenes were of various cities and the complete chaos that was ensuing. People were running after other people; their clothes and faces covered with blood. Those who were displaying the signs of being infected were ripping into others who were not. The EMT's that were looking to help the injured were being attacked along with the police who were trying to maintain order. The police were getting off some shots into the people who were attacking, but without the headshots, they weren't staying down. The cameras showing the carnage had lost their operators long ago and were lying on the ground showing this bizarre dance from a skewed angle. The ending scene of the camera in Detroit was a young girl walking toward the camera, tilting her head from side to side, click-clicking. The screen then switched to nothing but static. The female anchor burst into tears and left the news desk.

Madison waved his hand, and Harrell ended the feed. Webb, Priest, and Abarra just sat there in silence. All three had seen plenty of combat, probably more than their fair share. They had killed and witnessed killing. They had seen death, destruction, mutilation, and the like. The usual "killing field" was some far-off land, and it didn't compare to seeing the same thing happening in your city. It gave it an entirely new perspective, seeing the carnage in your own country, in your own city, in your own backyard.

Madison spoke solemnly, "This is what we are up against, and there are many issues in addressing this situation. We are trying to determine just how many cities the virus has affected. Not to mention, how are we to eliminate the infected without taking an equal amount of collateral damage? We could end up with zero value out of these cities. Infected and non-infected, all dead because we may not discern between the two in time. Command is contemplating deploying troops, National Guard, Reserves, and even Active Duty, to get a handle back on the major cities. Chicago, DC, Atlanta, and LA are just some of those mentioned. General Steward from Central Command is asking that your team deploy to ground zero in Dearborn to see if you can assess the spread, speed, and completeness of the virus take over."

"And you said what?" Priest pried.

"I said no, but Stewart, who outranks me, said yes. Not only did he say your team will deploy, but you are also taking a CDC Ph.D. with you."

"Ah, hell no," Abarra laughed.

"Ah, hell, yes," Madison retorted. "Last time I checked, none of you had any experience in bio-genetics, viruses, microbiology, or any other sciences that require an intellectual brain."

"Well, that was uncalled for. That hurt my feelings." Priest feigned being hurt at the statement.

"Maybe one of your men could rub something on your raw asshole," Madison continued. "This is what will happen. You will fly over, assess the situation, and get Dr. Costa on the ground for samples, a live specimen, whatever the doctor needs."

"Damn, babysitting duty," Abarra chimed in. "This will be dangerous enough without having to lug around a civilian."

Madison looked at the team. "Are there any questions?"

"It sucks, but it's pretty cut and dry," Priest said.

Madison nodded. "Go get some sleep; your team rolls out at 0500. Dismissed."

There wasn't much to discuss after that. All three walked back to the barracks without saying a word. Webb and Priest briefed the rest of the team on the mission. After the grumbles, bitching, and whining, the team consented to the task and finally settled down to sleep.

CHAPTER 5

0500 Fort Campbell, KY

The team walked out on the flight line to a waiting Blackhawk already spinning up. The morning was brisk, and the sun had not completely come up over the horizon yet. The sky was a splash of purples and pinks, and Neville stopped to admire the scene. "This is the same picture I see when I look out from my porch, back home on the bayou."

"Ah, Buddha smiles upon us," Shin reflected.

"The dawn is nice, but make sure Buddha will cover our ass," joked Shaw.

Abarra looked over at Myles, "You sure you're up for this?"

"Don't have many choices now, do I?"

"Yeah, I guess not."

"I'm good to go, Sarge." Abarra nodded and left it at that.

The team loaded in the chopper and lifted off the tarmac. For Op Sec purposes, Webb briefed the rest of the team on the Blackhawk. They would fly to Indianapolis to refuel, pick up the doctor, and then on to Dearborn/Detroit area. The CDC building is in the northwest region of Dearborn. There had been prior communications with the research team there. The team was to take Dr. Costa there to coordinate with the scientists who had obtained blood samples and were in the process of analyzing the infected blood's properties.

To the southeast of the CDC is the Nationwide Insurance building, which has a clear view of most of the city. We will drop Neville and

Shin off on the top of this building to provide support for the rest of the team who will deliver Dr. Costa to the CDC facility. Exfil will be the top of a parking garage three blocks Northeast of the CDC building.

After the Team received their briefing on the mission details, they settled back for the flight to Indianapolis International Airport.

Sitting next to Priest, Shaw turned his head toward him. "Sarge, none of this gives me a warm and fuzzy."

"You know something I don't know?"

"No, just a gut feeling that the shit is getting ready to hit the fan."

"Well, to be honest with you, I have a bad feeling about the whole thing. Just keep your head on a swivel and let your training guide your steps."

"Copy that."

Captain Webb was checking his gear when the copilot came over his comm. "We are 15 mics out of Indy Airport. We are trying to hail the airport for clearance but have not raised them yet."

"Is that normal?" Webb asked.

"No, sir."

"Can you raise Fort Campbell's command? Colonel Madison?"

"Negative. We tried that, and still nothing."

Webb switched to squad comms, "Ok, ladies, we have an issue. The bird cannot establish comms with the airport or with HQ, and that means we are not sure what is going on at the airport or what conditions we are jumping in the middle of. We are prepared no matter what the situation!" The team all leaned forward and bumped fists.

Minutes later, "Sir, we are coming into the airport, but still no communication."

"Copy that." Webb eyed the team, "Drop your cocks and grab your socks. Here we go."

CHAPTER 6

As the airport came into sight, it looked like a war-torn area of Syria or Libya instead of the Indianapolis Airport. Multiple planes were sitting, wrecked into each other, and on fire. Bodies were lying all over the ground, and blood was everywhere. "Jesus Christ," the crew chief mumbled, looking out on the destruction.

"What the fuck happened?" Doc asked. He was leaning out of the side door, wide-eyed and in disbelief.

"Sum bitch. Looks like Turkey all over again," Shaw chimed in.

Priest looked at Webb, "Could the virus have spread this quickly?"

"Dunno. Maybe this is why we can't raise anyone on the comms?" Webb broke off as they heard a screeching yell. It was loud enough to be heard over the rotors.

"There," Shin pointed at a woman on top of one of the maintenance buildings running toward the landing chopper. The woman continued to run towards them, her clothes and mouth smeared with blood. She jumped with her arms outstretched toward them, still screaming. Her jump came up short of the chopper, and she plummeted three stories to the concrete below. Hitting face first, her head exploded upon impact with the concrete. The momentum drove her body over the back of her head and snapping her neck. The woman lay there in an awkward position with her body folded in half until her spine broke in two.

"Holeee, Mother Mary, and Joseph. Do you see that shit? Her neck folded in half like a taco. Her body just flipped over her head like some Exorcist bullshit."

"Dude, we saw it happen. We're sitting right here," Myles said, trying to keep his breakfast down.

While Webb communicated with the pilot about contacting HQ, Priest barked out orders to the team. "Everyone out, pull security, and we will regroup on the ground." The bird set down, and the team poured out, setting up at tactical intervals to provide 360-degree support. The chopper took off, and the team struggled to hear after the whine of the rotors faded away. It didn't take but a second or two for the team to hear screaming again. They called contact acknowledgments out.

"Contact at 9 o'clock."

"Contact on our 6."

"Contact at 2 o'clock."

"Contact at 4 o'clock."

Myles shouted, "Do we engage these civilians?"

"Do they look like regular civilians?" Webb growled. "Engage the fucks."

There was an immediate cacophony of small arms fire as the team fired in several directions. The smell of cordite, sweat, and body odor took on a life of its own. The entire team felt the sounds and concussion of the minor battle. Shaw was relentless on his M48 as he was mowing down legs, torsos, and faces.

Three men wearing maintenance overalls came charging at the team from around a full baggage cart. There was hate on their faces, and rage reddened their eyes. The inhumane scream coming out of their mouth made the hair on the back of their necks stand up.

Shaw let loose with a couple of three-round bursts; the first took out the pelvis of the black guy in front. It cut him in half and separated his torso from his legs. The momentum kept the upper half of his body moving forward. Intestines were flapping after his torso like flags whipping in the wind. His body rolled head over torso across the concrete. The man's intestines were wrapping around as he flipped. When he finally stopped, they wrapped him up like a present.

Priest chuckled, "Don't open until Christmas!" Shaw cackled at that.

Priest's weapon took out the worker on the right. One round ripped through his throat, taking out most of it. Without enough to hold the head up, the infected looked like a bobblehead as it flapped around on just the spine. His second-round entered through the infected left cheek and removed most of the back of his skull when exiting.

Shaw made quick work of the third infected as he raked the burst across the infected face at eye level. He cut the top of the infected head clean off, and it hit the deck like a bag of wet cement. Brain matter and blood shot out of his mutilated head and across the tarmac when he hit.

Abarra and Myles were directly opposite in the circle. They had two infected coming in their direction. One was a runner, and the other was missing part of its right leg from the ankle, and its right foot was missing. The runner was 50 yards away when Abarra sent three rounds vertically, starting at his sternum and ending at his forehead. That dropped the infected, which slid on the asphalt for a few feet.

Myles launched a 40mm grenade from his M203. Foomp! The grenade hit a couple of yards behind the infected, which shredded its torso, and the concussion took it off its feet. It did not get back up. "WHOO, suck on that!" Myles yelled.

"Our nuts will dangle in the stewpot unless we get some help over here," Neville shouted.

"We do not put our testicles in our pots, or our bowls for that matter. Does everyone in the US do that?" Shin inquired.

"It means we will be in a world a shit if we don't get help." A horde of about fifteen was running toward Neville and Shin's position.

"Rotate over and collapse the gaps," Webb barked. Webb, Doc, and Abarra moved closer to Neville's position, squeezing the gap in the circle to help with preventing the position from being overrun. All others spanned out to cover more of the circle's circumference.

"Jesus, Mother Mary, and Joseph. We've got a shitload of these things over here," Doc remarked.

"Shut up and take these things out," Abarra snapped. They all kept sending rounds downrange.

"Reloading," yelled Webb. He backed off the line to reload. A scream from his right startled him, and he looked up just in time to see a teenage girl missing half her left shoulder jumping at him. Webb didn't have time before she launched herself on top of him. He hit the ground with her on top of him, knocking all the air out of his lungs. "Shit!" he howled. "Get this bitch off me!"

Her left arm was virtually useless, but she was incredibly strong and renewed her effort to rip and bite his face off. She kept fighting, but Webb could hold her off with one hand while grabbing her left wrist and the other around her throat. As she struggled against his defenses, Webb dropped his hand off her wrist and reached to his thigh to pull his Glock. Just as he reached the butt of his pistol, the screaming and struggling stopped. She slumped over and rolled off to the left. Webb looked over at her and watched as Shin pulled his combat knife out of her temple.

"You ok, sir?"

"Yeah, thanks, Shin. That was a wild ride." Shin reached his hand out and helped Webb up to his feet. "How many more infected are…." Webb trailed off. All the rest of the horde were lying across the tarmac, dead.

Webb snapped out of his reverie, "Ok, we are completely exposed out here. We need to find Dr. Costa, if she was still alive. Thoughts?"

"We need to split the team in half and conduct two searches for her. Comms are out, but our squad comms are still operational," Priest spoke.

"Sounds good. Doc, Abarra, Miles, and I will search in the terminal. Priest, you take Shaw, Neville, and Shin. You guys search the flight line and maintenance buildings. Once we locate her, we rally back here, and we will call in our exfil. We still have comms to the bird," Webb added.

"How long do we look for her?" Shaw asked.

"As long as it takes. She is our only mission right now. Unless this whole airport becomes completely overrun, we stay until we locate her," Webb answered.

"Copy, Sir."

Webb looked at all of his Team, "Ok, move out."

CHAPTER 7

Team Priest–Tarmac and Maintenance Buildings

The team moved behind one of the maintenance buildings for cover.

Priest turned to Shin, "Give me the landscape."

Shin pulled out his range scope and moved to the edge of the building to get a lay of the land. "There are three mid-size hangers to the right. One contains a plane. The other two are empty. I see no movement in any of the three. To the left, there are two small maintenance sheds, which seem to be closed. About 50 yards from these are four utility garages for the support vehicles. There seems to be no movement.... wait a minute. There is movement near one building. I see 1, 2, 3... 5 men and 1 woman. They look to be click clicks. The woman is not one of them."

"Shit, this can't be good," Priest said under his breath. "Are they raping her?"

"Yes, they just ripped her clothes off and now," Shin stopped. His mouth slightly open and closed. Priest noticed his jaw tightening. "They did not rape her."

"Whew, that's a relief," Shaw said.

"No, it's worse. They tore her belly apart, and she is still alive."

"Fuck!" Neville whispered. It would have been a yell.

"They removed her intestines and draped them over themselves, dancing with them. They are pulling other organs out and tossing them in the air like catching a ball. They are covered in her blood."

Shin dropped his scope and faced Priest, "She is still alive. Neville needs to kill her. Put her out of her misery." Neville moved forward but Priest stopped him.

"We can't."

"Why not?" Neville's eyes were full of rage.

"You pop one off at this distance and they will hear it and come after us. It will give away our position. Plus, we don't know how many more of those things are out there we just can't see or haven't seen yet."

"But she is being tortured!" Neville whispered with more rage and venom than before.

"Son of a bitch, Neville. You think I like this any more than you do? Fuck no, but we got to be smart about this. We're not playing with the normal scumbags."

Neville knew he was right. Hell, they all knew he was right, but it didn't stop their guts from wrenching. Didn't stop the hopeless and sinking feeling of guilt. This is part of what they do, they save people. Unfortunately, not this time and it felt like shit.

Priest was just glad they couldn't hear her screams from the distance, or this might have been a different conversation.

Shin spoke, "Finally she has died. Not before they pulled her eyes out and ate them. I have seen nothing like this before."

"Hell, none of us has," Priest lamented.

"Three have returned into the garage. The other two remained outside. Buddha bless us," Shin said in Korean.

"What now?" Shaw asked.

"Uh-uh, one of them is rolling around in her blood. The other.... The other one is playing with the body or what's left of it."

"Jesus Christ," Neville breathed.

"Yeah, we are not dealing with our run-of-the-mill warlords, terrorists or dictators. These fucking things have no remorse, no fear, no instinct for self-preservation. Just killing... in fucked up ways. We can't scare them, reason with them, and they outnumber us. They don't care about any of that. We have to avoid them or kill them until we can regroup back at HQ and figure out how to eliminate these things off the damn planet." Priest finished. "Shin sit rep."

"The other two have gone back in the building, and I don't see any other movement outside."

"Ok, we need to access that building and eliminate all hostile, so we can continue our search for the doctor. Neville, Shin, can you make your way to the left, behind one of those hangars? Cover our ass while we take that building."

"Can do." Neville nodded.

"Let me know when you're in place."

"Copy, give us five."

Priest and Shaw waited for confirmation that Neville and Shin were in place. Five minutes went by. Six, Seven, Eight. Priest wanted to contact them, but if they were in a compromising position, he would give their location away. About ten seconds later, Priest heard from Shin.

"Father, this is Gandhi. We're in position. Sorry about the extra time, but we found a maintenance ladder, and we are now on top of the hangar. Much better vantage point."

"Ok, sounds good. Just don't scare me like that."

"Copy that. So, we can see into the building, and the five infected are still there. They are all congregating around a table in the far west corner. Completely opposite of your present location."

"Copy that. Do you see any other entry points into the maintenance building?"

"Hold one.... yes, at the back of the building in the east corner. If you enter there, you will have approximately 20-30 yards of space between that entry point and the infected at the table. We can provide support from here, but if they all charge as one, it will be difficult to take them all out before they reach you. Be advised."

"Understood." Priest looked over at Shaw, "What do you think? Pop the door, roll a grenade and see how many are left?"

"Sounds good, but we better be ready to boogie if noise brings any more runnin."

"Concur. Overlord, we are going to make our way to the back of the building, toss a grenade and then mop up what's left. If you have a shot take it, then direct your support outward and keep any infected off our back from elsewhere on the grounds," Priest instructed.

"Good copy. Be careful."

Priest and Shaw made their way to the back of the maintenance shed that they were using for cover. With Priest on point and Shaw covering their six, they slowly made their way to the back of the maintenance garage. "Ok, Overlord. Getting ready to deliver our present."

"Copy, Father. We're ready."

Priest and Shaw both pulled a frag grenade and pulled the pins. They held on to the spoons. Priest counted down. "Three, Two, One." Priest kicked open the door and he and Shaw threw their grenades toward the group of infected. Priest quickly shut it among the screams and screeches of the infected. BOOM! BOOM! Two explosions, one right behind the other.

"Father, I see two down, and Voodoo just took out a third. You have two left, but not in the best shape. They are crawling toward you now. Switching support field of view. You are blind."

"Copy Overlord." Priest and Shaw entered back through the door and pulled their knives. They easily dispatched the two-remaining infected. "No sense in wasting ammo," Shaw said.

"Amen." Priest barely got amen out of his mouth when they started hearing shots. Priest and Shaw ran out. "Overlord, sit rep."

"There were a few latecomers to the party. We punched their dance card."

"Holy shit, Shin. Was that a joke?"

"Not mine, Neville's. I just repeated it."

Priest giggled, "Thought we finally got him to loosen up."

"No dice," Shaw answered.

"Father, it looks like there is a black SUV about 300 yards due west from your location on the flight line. It is surrounded by infected, so I assume that there may be regular civilians inside. Advise."

"Copy that. Keep eyes on them, and we will play the boogie man and assault them from behind. If you see any others running to join the party, take them out."

"Copy that."

Priest and Shaw took off toward the direction of the SUV; Shin spotted. Bang! The reports of Neville's sniper rifle. Bang! Another.

Then another shot as Priest came in view of the SUV. It was still about 150 yards, but he could make out the SUV and the infected surrounding it.

"Father, I made a test shot on the quarter panel and the SUV is bulletproof."

"You heard him, Shaw. Make them dance."

"Fucking A." Shaw let loose with his M48. It was amazing how accurate he was with it while running. The big son of a bitch had a firm hold on his M48, and it probably didn't buck much in his massive grip.

The infected hanging off the SUV finally realized there were uninfected easier to get to and started for the team. "Here comes company," Shaw roared.

"And without an invitation, must be the in-laws," Priest added.

The nearest infected, a man in a tattered business suit, was about 150 yards as Priest aimed through his reflect sight. As his finger squeezed on the trigger, businessman's head exploded like a watermelon. His headless body fell, and the momentum slid his body a couple feet. "Thank you, Neville," Priest thought to himself.

Neville and Shin were sighting in the horde, making its way toward the rest of the team. "Ah, business man down. He slid same like in baseball," Shin quipped.

"Safe," Neville chided in.

"Ok, 25 yards behind, target large woman in big dress."

"Just say fat bitch in the moo moo."

"What does cow sound have to do with this woman?"

"Never mind."

The rifle report, "Cow down. Ok, nine to go. Make that eight. Ah, 7."

Shin called the next target, "Target from the stewardess back. We will work from the rear."

"She's called a flight attendant, Shin. You're so sexist."

"I don't think of myself as sexy. Do you think woman do?"

"Dude, never mind. I can't even bust on you because you don't understand most of the references."

"I am very intelligent. I graduated at the top of…"

"No life stories, just sight for me."

Shaw was mopping up the last two infected while Priest made his way to the SUV. He peered inside to see a frightened woman and two men in business suits with Glocks in their hands. She looked up at Priest with a total shell-shocked look. "Dr. Costa?" Priest asked.

The woman just looked at him for a long moment. She looked as if she was waiting for her mind to re-engage with reality. She finally nodded yes slowly. "Ma'am, we need to get you out of here and to the CDC lab in Dearborn. Could you please unlock the door?" She looked at him with sheer terror and violently shook her head no.

"Doctor, I know things are a little crazy right now, but I'm going to need to you to trust me. We have men here to protect you, but we need to get you out of here and in the air to Dearborn quickly." She still shook her head, but much slower this time. One of the men in the suits hit the unlock button and climbed out. He nodded to Priest.

"David Kennedy, Agent with the Secret Service, this is my partner Thomas Bolin and yes, Dr. Isabelle Costa. They assigned us to the doctor and tasked with making sure she met up with your team and with providing security for her as she traveled to the CDC in Dearborn. We had two others with us who entered the terminal to get coffee. They never returned. And before you ask, yes, one of them had the keys or we would have driven off. Those crazy people swarmed us so quickly, jumping in and locking the door was all we had time to do."

Priest was going to ask how his team got there, but they needed to get the doctor out of there. "Doctor, are you ok?"

"Yes... Yes, I am fine. I have never seen such aggression. I have seen what this virus does. I have treated people with similar symptoms but never seen a level of aggression such as this."

"Do you believe that the original virus was tampered with or changed in some way?" Priest added.

"It had to have been. This behavior is nothing like I have seen in early test cases."

Priest cocked his head, "I'm confused. I thought an alliance with rogue players from terrorist countries created this. We just stormed their lab facility about a week ago. No one has seen any of the test results. ISIS snatched the research and fled to Dearborn."

"If ISIS stole the virus and transported it to Dearborn, I am unaware of that, however, you were wrong about where the virus originated from."

Priest and the team exchanged looks with each other. Priest's demeanor changed slightly, which Dr. Costa noticed. He didn't enjoy being on the outside of the bubble when it came to intel. So far, this entire mission had been a lesson in shitty intel, and Priest was not happy about it. "Ok, we need to move back to the hangar we just cleared of infected. Tell us the rest on the way."

Dr. Costa continued, "The virus originated as a joint effort between German and Dutch scientists. They coordinated together to develop a medicine to combat ALS and Alzheimer's. They created the original formula to reach people whom scientists thought could still be reachable. They created the medicine to open communication pathways with patients, who, up to this point, couldn't be communicated with. It was realized later that it could be modified to condition the mind or serve as a proxy to allow suggestion or commands. All the moons had aligned for this to happen."

"How so?"

"Well, the patient's mind must be intact, they may be low on the proteins which help build the body's immunity which could otherwise fight against the virus along with some other factors."

"So, I assume that the crackpots in Turkey, changed the original recipe to artificially bridge that gap and bring about the factors needed, which now allows the infected person to respond to suggestion," Priest inquired.

"Yes, that is correct. From what I just witnessed; whatever changes they made to the formula have somehow affected the regulation of basic human emotion. It seemed to significantly ramp up violence, anger and confrontational consciousness, while subduing compassion, empathy and kindness. It also seemed to have removed other core human traits like self-preservation and their ability to feel pain. It also has affected their body's ability to continue to function after receiving considerable damage."

"Yeah, you don't have to tell us about it. Only head shots will take these things down," Shaw expressed.

The doctor nodded, "Yes, this information needs to be communicated."

"Also, how contagious it is and the speed in which it infects the body," Priest added.

"That too," the doctor agreed.

"Ok, let me hail the Cap, and we will get the hell out of here."

CHAPTER 8

Team Webb–Airport Terminal

Webb moved to look around a kiosk near a departure gate. His team was in one of the departure gates, sections off the main terminal. This part of the airport was filled with more narrow hallways and a lot of ambush-prime real estate, like various kiosks, alcoves and shop fronts. The floor at their location was carpeted, but the main walkway was tiled or poured epoxy. The hard floor, couple with the echoes in the high-ceiling terminal, provided an early warning alarm.

Webb turned to the team, "Ok, we need to search this airport for the doctor and do it quickly. I am open to options for the most efficient way to make this happen." The team brainstormed the best way to achieve this.

"The phone," someone said.

Webb responded, "What?"

"The phone." Everyone turned to Myles.

"The phone?" Abarra said.

"Yeah, you know Mr. Smith, please pick up the white courtesy phone."

"You idiot," Doc stared at him. Myles looked down.

"Whoa, wait a minute. Maybe he is on to something. We could use the intercom on the phone, ask for anyone to call our phone if they hear us. It won't immediately give our position away, and it may stir up these infected and give their position away. Myles, you're a genius. Doc, apologize." Webb stared at Doc.

"What?"

"Apologize to Myles, now. That's an order."

"Sheesh, ok. Sorry, bro."

Webb snickered as he snuck over to the gate counter. He looked at the counter and luckily there was a phone list taped to the inside. He picked up the handset and pushed the numbers for the intercom. The terminal speakers squealed loudly and made everybody jump.

"If there is anyone trapped in the terminal, call number 92053. We are the US Army, and we are trying to escort civilians out of here safely. We are looking for Dr. Costa. Dr. Costa, we are here to secure you and transport you to Dearborn CDC. Please contact us and give me your location. Time is of the essence."

As soon as Webb started speaking, the screams and wails reached their ears.

"Damn, that stirred them up," Myles whispered.

"Yeah, but they have no idea where we are," Abarra replied. They heard footsteps coming at them quickly. People were running toward them.

Webb was thinking, how do they know where we are? The small crowd of infected came running down the walkway and stopped near the team's location. The team heard an assortment of growling, heavy breathing and clicks.

Abarra looked around the half wall he was hiding behind to see what was going on. The horde was standing there looking around, their heads twitching left to right, and they made that clicking sound with their tongues. Abarra moved back behind the wall and looked at Doc. "God damn tick tocks. Which means they are still highly functioning."

Doc nodded with clear fear in his eyes. One of the infected looked around and hissed.

"There is prey here.... click, click. We need to find them and infect them, or maybe kill them. Infect or kill, infect or kill, infect or kill, click, click. Wait for the phone to ring. Infect or kill, click, click, infect or kill."

The rest of the group recited, "Infect or kill, infect or kill. Click, click… click, click."

"I can't stand that clicking," Doc whispered through clenched teeth

Abarra grabbed his shoulder, "We'll make it through this. Just keep it together." Doc nodded.

Webb thought about what the infected had said, "Oh shit!" He reached up and turned the ringer off just as the phone starting lighting up. "Holy shit, that was close," he thought to himself. Webb picked up and whispered, "Hello, Dr. Costa?"

"Uh-no, this is Allison Reeves. I am a TV news reporter. We were here to get our news chopper ready to take off for the day, when some crazy people started attacking my producer and cameraman. They just started biting them and ripping them apart." Webb could tell she was crying. "Oh God, can you help us? Please help us!"

Doc saw Webb was on the phone, and he turned to Myles and Abarra and gave them the hand sign for cover. Abarra and Myles nodded in understanding. As they watched the horde, Webb continued to whisper on the phone. The horde was making so much noise with the clicking and hissing, they couldn't hear Webb's voice. They continued to rustle around, looking for the uninfected in all the shops.

"Ok, calm down. Did you say, us?"

"Yes, I am in here with Doug, our helicopter pilot."

"Do you know where you are?"

"We are at Ruth Chris's Steakhouse. They chased us through the airport terminal, and we were able to get away and hide in the walk-in fridge. We heard you come over the intercom, but had to wait until there were no sounds of those crazy people, before I risked coming out to call you."

"Ok, go back in there, and we will come get you out." Webb said in a calm tone.

"Ok, please hurry."

As Webb hung up the phone, he suddenly had an idea. He looked at the phone list. He saw the number for the information desk. Hoping that the desk was a good way away from them, he called the number.

A distant phone started ringing, and the horde went ape shit. They started whooping and screaming and ran off toward the sound of the phone.

Webb watched the horde take off, and then he stalked out of his hiding spot. The rest of the team joined him. "Ok, on me," Webb whispered.

They made their way down the terminal, listening for the infected. They came to the directory on a billboard in the middle of the walkway. "Hmm, Ruth Chris's is here," Webb said, pointing to the restaurant which was in the main terminal just east of their present location. "We need to make it here."

"Is that where the doctor is?" Abarra asked.

"Negative. This is a reporter plus one at this location needing extraction."

"That's not the mission," Abarra added.

"Yeah, I know, but they are people in trouble, and they contacted us. You just want to leave them here?" Webb asked with a minor annoyance in his voice.

"No, of course not. I am just stating the facts." Abarra said stoically.

"Duly noted. Let's move out."

CHAPTER 9

Webb's team made its way to the first juncture with other corridors off the main terminal. Webb gave the hand sign for stop, and the team knelt down. He then motioned for Doc to check out the left corridor and Myles the right corridor. The two made their way stealthily to observation points at each corridor.

Doc got to within 10 yards, dropped and low crawled behind a trash can. He peeked around and observed for a couple minutes. Giving the hand sign for ok, Doc slid back and made his way back to the team.

Myles executed the same maneuvers, looked around the corner and watched for a few minutes. He pulled back quickly and motioned over his shoulder, indicating twelve contacts down the corridor at an estimated distance of about 60 yards.

"Shit," Webb breathed. He eased over to Abarra. "Of course, they have to be down the corridor we need to take to get to the reporter woman."

Abarra thought for a second, "We could go back outside and come in from the outside of the terminal. Maybe get the rest of the team."

"Yeah, I like that plan. Let's move."

Myles looked back and Webb motioned for him to fall back and post up with the team. Myles slid back away from the corner and turned to get up. As he pivoted around his rifle hit a metal freestanding sign for free ear piercing at Claire's. The sign scraped the ground and then fell against the wall with a loud clang. Myles stopped and looked back at the team with terror in his eyes. The infected let out a scream and start running toward the sound.

"Aww fuck," Doc spit out, as he makes his way back to the team.

"Run, Myles! Fucking run!" Abarra screamed. Myles ran but tripped over the metal stand that he had just knocked over.

Webb ordered, "Cover fire, cover fire!" Myles struggled to get to his feet as the infected came in view, turning the corner. The team started sending rounds down range into the charging group of infected. Myles regained his feet and began running. Unfortunately, this cut the fire lane for half the team. With their angle of fire, they couldn't fire into most of the infected without hitting Myles.

Various "travelers", dressed in an array of destination attire, came running around the corner. The tropical couple wearing Hawaiian shirts, Bermuda shorts and sandals, the businessman with the tailored suit and expensive Stacy Adams shoes, the college kids in sweats bearing their respective schools, fraternities or sororities.

All of their clothes were soiled and stained with blood and gore from past victims. Many were showing signs of being victims themselves. Some had portions of their throats missing, while others were missing limbs, trying to run on stumps which were missing a foot or lower leg. Regardless of their state, they were all in a frenzy, trying to reach Myles to infect him. Since first coming in contact with the infected, this seemed to be their driving force, their reason to exist, the only thing occupying whatever mind remained.

The team spread out as best they could to alter their lanes of fire and put rounds into the infected horde. Abarra moved to his right, firing his M4 on full auto. The crowd was dense enough that all rounds were hitting home. Head shots weren't the priority at the moment. They were just trying to keep the infected off of Myles and buy some time.

"Dammit," Doc spat. They are too close to Myles to use the 203, or I would have that fucking crowd decimated by now."

"Yeah, I know, but just keep firing," Webb yelled.

The infected were directly behind Myles and they were gaining ground. Unfortunately, Myles had 60 pounds' worth of gear on and the infected had nothing slowing them down. Doc could take out a few legs in the horde, making some infected go down, tripping up those behind them. Webb and Abarra were mowing down as many as they could without hitting Myles. Their M4's were in accord with each other as they sent tens of rounds into the quickly approaching infected. Myles was screaming as he ran, but even with his conditioning, he was quickly slowing down.

Suddenly, a woman came running out of nowhere, bypassing the horde. She was infected, but was running like a cheetah on the Serengeti. The woman was easily passing the rest of the infected like a thoroughbred coming from the outside at the Kentucky Derby. She was the fastest of the infected anyone had seen.

"Holy shit, she is almost on top of him, but I can't sight her in. Myles is in the way!" Webb exclaimed. "Anyone else have a shot?"

"I might in a couple seconds," Doc replied.

"Well, take it as soon as you can." Webb barked

"Come on, come on, just a few more yards, and then I got your bitchass," Doc pleaded. Just as the knuckles on his finger were whitening on the trigger, the woman dove for Myles. Doc's shot went wild over her head and embedded in the wall next to the pizza place. "Shit," he yelled. By the time he adjusted his aim for another shot, she was on top of Myles riding him to the ground.

Myles was yelling at the top of his lungs, "Get her off me. Get her the fuck off me!" He was face down trying to fight her off.

For the next couple of seconds, time stood still. Doc fired a round from his M4 that struck the infected woman in the shoulder, spinning her off of Myles. He struggled to get up and as he regained his feet; the woman was up again and jumped on his back. Doc sighted on her again and pulled the trigger. The bullet struck her in the left temple that snapped her head back and she slumped off.

Myles ran, still yelling as the rest of the team continued to send rounds in the throng. The M4's sang in unison as they sent 5.56mm projectiles into the infected, producing clouds of blood and gore along with scattering bits of skull and bone all over the floor and walls.

"We need to back out of here and find another way through on the outside of the terminal. This little party is going to bring every infected throughout this whole fucking building." While Webb barked out orders, Myles continued to yell. Abarra grabbed Myles' shoulders and shook him, "Calm the fuck down, you're safe."

It was then that Abarra noticed Myles was holding the back of his neck and saw the blood seeping out from between his fingers. Abarra's face turned ghostly white as the blood drained from it.

Webb noticed his face, "What's wrong?"

"Nothing, let's get the fuck out of here." Abarra yelled as the team continued firing.

Doc roared, "You guys make your way out. I'll cover your six."

Abarra escorted Myles toward the outside doors, while Webb and Doc laid down suppressive fire.

Doc loaded a 40mm grenade in his M203, "Here comes the pain, bitches." Foomp! The grenade landed in the middle of the infected mass and exploded in an enormous wall of flame and smoke. An eruption of gore, blood and body parts rained down like a hailstorm as Webb and Doc turned and sprinted toward the terminal doors to outside.

As Webb ran, a voice came over his comms. "Spider, this is Father. Do you copy?"

"Go ahead, Father."

"We have the asset, repeat, we have the asset. Get the fuck out of there."

"Copy that, we are already making our way out. We have some company, so be advised."

"Copy that. We will wait for them. When able, get that exfil in here ASAP."

"Copy, I'm on it." Webb and Doc were almost to the terminal exit. "Eagle one, eagle one, this is Spider. Do you copy?"

After a few seconds, "Copy Spider, this is Eagle one."

"We need exfil ASAP. Asset is in custody, and we need exfil. Location is hot, I repeat location is hot. Do you copy?"

"Copy that. Immediate exfil requested and location is hot. We will provide support during exfil. ETA five mics."

"Copy that Eagle One, Spider out."

20 seconds later, Webb and Doc made it out of the terminal. The rest of the team moved to form up on Webb.

Priest spoke, "Maintain a defensive perimeter. Shaw and I will take 12 and 6 o'clock."

"Doc..." Abarra spoke up with his voice shaking, "Myles is injured, and I need you to take a look. I'll take 3 o'clock." Webb looked over toward Myles.

Doc moved over to Myles, "Let me take a look, dude." Myles reluctantly removed his hand, and Doc saw what looked like a bite with a good size piece of flesh and tissue missing. Doc looked over at Webb and shook his head.

Webb muttered under his breath, "Shit." He now is burdened with a decision to make and knows that this is the primary method of how the virus is spread. What he doesn't know is how long it takes the virus to spread and take over one's thoughts, actions and reasoning. He dropped his face into his palm in sorrow and frustration.

"How bad is it, Doc? I'm alright, right?" Myles pleaded. "How bad is it? I'm good to go, right?" Doc said nothing.

Priest looked over his shoulder at Webb. They locked eyes, and Priest shook his head. Webb saw the empathy in Priest's eyes, nodded, and turned his head to provide security.

Priest let out a long-troubled sigh. "Doc, please restrain Corporal Myles.

"Wait, what?" Myles looked at Priest and then to Doc. "No, I'm good to go Sarge. I'm good to go." Tears began streaming down Myles' face. "I... I... I'm good to go Sarge." He could barely get the words out.

Doc pulled Myles' hands behind his back, slowly, respectfully. "I'm sorry brother, I really am." Myles dropped to his knees and began sobbing.

One by one the team walked over to Myles and gave hugs, some kissed him on the top of his head. Myles' sobbing continued for a few minutes or so.

In the distance, the faint sound of Blackhawk's rotors reached the team's ears. Suddenly, the team heard a clicking noise.... click, click,

click, click, which caused Doc to jump back and Priest to pull his Walther PPQ. Priest spun around and aimed the pistol at Myles' head, which was moving from left to right.

"You need the poison. Do I see prey or brothers, which ones are you? The poison makes you invincible. The poison brings freedom... click, click, click, click. Do you want the poison?" Myles said. His voice sent chills down the spines of the team.

"Fuck that", Shaw yelled.

Myles growled and then lunged at Priest, who quickly put a 45-caliber round right in his forehead. Myles stopped short and slumped to the ground...dead.

"Son of a bitch," Abarra cried.

"What the fuck, Myles? What the fuck?" Doc yelled through tears.

"Overlord to Father. What the hell was that shot? Do you have contact? I don't see any infected."

"Negative. Myles was bitten, and he turned... so we sent him home."

"I shall say blessings for him," Shin said.

Priest took a knee and recited the Lord's Prayer over Myles as the rotors got louder, and Shin spied the bird.

"Bird is inbound."

"Copy that," Webb said. "You two make your way down so we can load up. Priest, before we roll out of here, we have a couple of civilian survivors on the other side of the terminal who are trapped. We need to get them out."

Priest looked at him, "We don't want to compromise our mission getting Dr. Costa to Dearborn. We cannot delay getting her there."

"I have contacted those civilians and told them we were coming for them." Webb explained.

Priest lowered his head in thought and after a long moment, he sighed, "We can't leave people out here. I'll take Shaw and Doc, and we'll get the civilians out. You take Abarra, Neville and Shin with you to Dearborn. You'll also have Kennedy and Bolin. Gear them up, which gives you two more troops."

"I don't like the idea of splitting the team." Webb replied.

"I don't either, but if you have something better, I'm all ears."

Webb didn't. He knew Priest was right. "Ok, so be it. We'll give you a lift to the other side of the terminal and then proceed to the CDC in Dearborn."

"Ok, drop us on the roof so we can assess the best way to get these people out."

The Blackhawk landed, and the team loaded Dr. Costa on board. They grabbed Myles' gear and weapon for the Secret Service guy, loaded up with Priest, Shaw, and Doc being last.

The Blackhawk took off and rose above the terminal. The area was all clear until they crested over the opposite side of the terminal building and saw a crowd of infected milling about. Some were trying to get in the building, while some were looking around for the noise. The crew chief started laying down fire with his mounted M134 Minigun.

"Good God almighty," Shaw howled. "That bad boy is chewing the shit out of them."

The mass of infected looked up as the rounds rained down. They all howled and screamed at the helicopter, reaching for those inside. The infected were climbing over top of each other to get to those that they needed to infect. They were met with a deluge of 5.56mm rounds which removed eyes, ears, jaws and sections of upturned heads. The rounds cut through the upturned faces and plowed through the torsos and legs of those standing behind them.

Usually people will run away from danger or certain death, but the infected didn't even seem to care about the fact that they were dying by the tens and hundreds. It didn't even register on any of their faces, but the team didn't have time to contemplate the philosophy behind it all and focused on dismounting the chopper.

Priest keyed his comms. "Hover over the roof and we'll unload there." The pilot acknowledged and brought the Blackhawk to hover about 3-4 feet from the roof. The crew chief continued to spit rounds into the mass of infected, while all three jumped out and waved to the crew chief. With the acknowledgement, the crew chief spoke into his helmet's mic and the bird ascended, rotated to the right, and took off on its way to Dearborn, Michigan.

In his gut, Doc felt a sinking feeling as he watched the Blackhawk fade from sight.

CHAPTER 10

The scene was something completely out of a horror movie as the blood flowed in little streams down the pavement. Pieces of flesh and indistinguishable body parts lay scattered the ground for hundreds of feet. The team could hear blood dripping and squishing sounds as the gore settled, sliding and sinking off of piles of destroyed bodies.

"Jesus Christ," Shaw breathed. "I used to slaughter cows and pigs back on the farm, but I have seen nothing like this."

Doc quipped, "I've seen my share of blood, guts and wounds as a medic. I'm with you as far as never seeing this much carnage before." Priest said nothing. He just stood there staring at the unbelievable scene. Doc continued, "Damn, look at that. There's a head over there that flew 20 feet. Look at all the guts laying over there. It's like up to your calf. That's some deep guts."

The amount of body parts stacked up in front of the maintenance door was unbelievable, and it would take a while to remove all that meat. Not to mention, they would have to wade through all that blood, all the intestines and other bodily fluids to even get to the door.

"Damn Doc, shut up already," Priest bellowed. "Ok, boys. Let's get to it. See if there is a way, we could gain access to those people without having to go through that door."

The team spread out and went in search of any alternate entry point. After a time, Shaw speaks up and calls over, "I think I might have found something." Priest and Doc run over to Shaw who is standing at a roof access door.

"Well, that is a way in and it definitely looks viable. Let's check it out." Priest nodded.

Shaw checked the door which was locked. Shaw pulled a pry bar from his breach kit, wedged it between the door and the jam, and gave it a good shove with his massive bulk. The door creaked open and Shaw peered in with his mag light. The stairway was clear, so they made their way down with Shaw on point, Priest as clean up and Doc covering their six. They stopped twice when they heard something, but determined it was on the other side of the walls.

As they reached the bottom, they found themselves in a maintenance area. It was a fairly long corridor with pipes running down each side. Cable trays were hanging from the ceiling, which contained power and fiber optic cable. They could also see several doors along the hallway on their right with the store numbers on them. Shaw made a comment about the doors showing numbers only and not the business names.

Priest whispered, "Ok, we know which business they are in. We just need to find the actual location and suite number. We need to search this maintenance space for maps, a directory, anything that gives us a layout of this terminal." They went a little further, and the space opened slightly to a desk and a workshop. As they made it to the desk, they heard screams and pounding, followed by another's screams.

"Shit, they must still find non-infected," Shaw said. Priest nodded concurrence. After a quick search, they found some building drawings and schematics. Since Ruth Chris's was one of the cornerstone businesses meant for this terminal in the planning stages, it was listed by name on the drawings.

"Ok, it looks like Ruth Chris's is 120A-G. Doc, where are we now?"

Doc walked down to the closest door and came back. "Continuing forward will take us to increasing suite numbers. The closest door is Suite 88."

"Shit, well I guess it could be worse and we could be standing at number one. Ok, let's move out swift but silent." The walk down to

Suite 120 was uneventful except for the occasional scream, growl, or sounds of groups running back and forth. They finally reached the door for Suite 120A. "Ok, let's do a little recon and see what we are dealing with."

Shaw reached for the door and turned the handle, discovering it was unlocked. He pulled the handle, cracked the door open enough to peer through. His eyes go wide as he took in the dramatic scene. He was in the steakhouse's rear, looking toward the dining room, and from his vantage point the carnage was clear. A multitude of bodies in various states of butchery lay strewn along the restaurant floor. Chairs were on their backs, tables laid toppled over, and they had smeared blood all over countless table cloths.

Uneaten food scattered the floor of the restaurant, pools of blood and various bloody drag marks. The restaurant appeared empty, so Shaw motioned the Team forward. They made their way through the restaurant to the wall separating it from the terminal corridor. Shaw peered around the wall to scout out possible next movement and viewed body parts strew across the entire field of view. Legs, arms, heads, and pieces that were not recognizable were lying in pools of blood. Tangled intestines were stretched down the passageway and wrapped around benches and poles, definitely done on purpose.

Shaw pulled his head back. "Man, these are some sick fuckers. It looks like they were playing with the innards, like it's a game or something."

Out of nowhere, there were various screams, laughs, yells, and shrieking. The team jumped at the noise.

"Shit," Doc said under his breath. They then heard running coming their way down the adjacent corridor. They looked out to see a group of people running with a pack of the infected right on their heels. There was a man in the back who looked to be a traveling businessman. His apparent constant snaking, restaurant eating and lack of exercise had eventually caught up with him as he was much slower than the rest of the people running and had fallen behind. He was breathing heavily and finally his legs gave out as the pack jumped on him. The man let out a blood-curdling scream as several of the infected took bites out of his body. The infected bit chunks of flesh and meat from his face, neck, arms, legs and blood was everywhere.

They quickly jumped off him and were running for the rest of the group. We left the businessman where he lay while blood continued to pump out of his massive wounds and pool around him. His breathing became shallow, challenging, and was coming at a quick pace. He moaned one last time and finally stopped breathing.

"Holy shit," whispered Priest. "This is some fucked up shit."

Doc was about to respond with something, but heard something that stopped him. Breathing, moaning, and the squeak of shoes on a wet floor. They looked back to the businessman and watched him get up, staring around like he wasn't sure where he was. He heard the screaming coming from down the hallway and took off after the sounds. "What the fuck," Doc whispered. "We now have confirmation as we did with Myles on how quickly this virus takes over."

"Yeah, too fucking quick," Priest replied. "Ok, let's find these two civilians and get the hell out of here. They should be in the restaurant's walk-in fridge, in the kitchen, I am assuming. We find the kitchen, then we find the walk-in fridge." Priest whispered.

They made their way toward the rear of the restaurant and right in front of Shaw were the double doors leading to the kitchen. Priest and Doc posted up on each side of the opening, then Shaw slowly opened the door. Without warning, a figure busted its way through the door, knocking Shaw back on his ass. The figure landed on top of him and began trying to bite his face. Shaw recovered quickly enough to fend off the infected. Just as Shaw got his hand around the man's neck, the figure stopped fighting and slumped over to his right. He saw Priest standing there with his combat knife dripping with blood and what seemed to look like brain matter.

Doc offered his hand and helped Shaw back up.

"Damn," Shaw whispered. "If that had been a female, she would have reminded me of my old girlfriend back in Alabama."

Priest motioned for them to be quiet by putting his index finger to his lips, "Hopefully, they didn't hear that," he whispered. They all stopped to listen to see if the infected were coming back and heard nothing. Priest motioned them into the kitchen. It was an enormous kitchen with a prep area to the right and order pick up counter directly ahead. Behind the counter was a grill that still had steaks on it that were on fire and looking like charcoal. All three looked at the ruined steaks and shook their heads. Damn shame, all that beef wasted was the look they gave each other. Doc pointed to a hallway to the left of the grill, which they all followed with Priest on point. The hall led back to another room, and against the back wall was the door for the walk-in.

Priest continued on and found a light switch next to the door. There was also a 12 x 12 window in the walk-in fridge's door. Priest flicked on the light and peered in. He immediately saw a young woman who met his eyes, began screaming and backing away from the door. Luckily for them, she couldn't be heard through the door. Doc shoved his head in the window to see what was going on and smiled at her, which elevated her hysteria.

Priest thought she would pass out. "Breathe, lady, breathe." He knew he had to get her calmed down before he opened that door, or every infected in the whole terminal would hear her screaming. An older man came next to her and tried to calm her down, while Priest attempted to make hand motions to let her know things were ok. He then put his finger to his lips for her to be quiet. When she had calmed down some, and he opened the door. He put his arm in first with his palm down and moved it up and down, motioning that it was ok, calm down. He finally got his face in the door and spoke to both of them.

"It's ok, we are here to get you out. Shhh, everything is all right, but we need to move and move now to get out of this place safely. Are you both ok to move? Can you walk?" Both nodded. Priest kneels and looks at the woman. "I'm MSGT Alec Priest and I believe you were talking to our Commander, Captain Webb?"

"Yes, I was. I am Allison Reeves. I am a reporter for a local news station, and this is Doug Harris. He is the pilot of our Channel 4 news helicopter." Priest shakes both of their hands.

"This is SGT Joseph Mancini or Doc as we call him, and that big son of a bitch over there," Priest throws his thumb over his shoulder, "is SSGT Jeremiah Shaw."

"Ma'am," Shaw dipped his head toward Allison

"So, Doug, is your helicopter somewhere here on the airport?"

"Yes, it is," Doug replies.

"Is it functional?"

"It is, or it was when I left it last."

"Ok, how many does it seat?"

Doug looked down at the floor, and somberly said, "four."

"It seats four, but is it powerful enough to take the weight of five?" Priest asks.

"Well, yes, it can easily handle that much weight. You know, it has some equipment we could dump to lighten the load if we had the time."

"Hmm, ok." "Where is it located?"

"It is on the flight line at the east end of this terminal."

Priest said, "Ok boys, we are bailing out the same way we came in. Doc, you take point and lead the two civilians down the hall and up the stairs to the roof where we will regroup. Shaw and I will cover your six and follow. Everyone clear?" They all nodded. "Ok, let's roll."

With Doc in the lead, next Allison, Priest, Doug, and finally Shaw guarding their rear, they stop at the kitchen door to listen for movement. They heard nothing, so Doc slowly opened the door, stepped out into the restaurant and headed for the maintenance door. He then motioned for the rest to follow his lead.

They made it halfway to the maintenance door when Priest catches movement out of his peripheral vision. He turns to see the businessman is standing there. His head was tilting from left to right and making a clicking noise. Click, click, click-click. "I see some who need the poison. The wonderful poison to be like me, like us... Click click, click." He then breaks into a run for the group.

"Move! Doc, get them to the door," Priest bellows. Doc makes a run for the maintenance door, with Allison and Doug right behind him. Priest squares up to fight businessman as to not draw attention to their location by using his rifle.

Businessman is about 15 feet away when Shaw shoots out toward him. Shaw connects and delivers the most devastating clothesline Priest has ever seen. All 275 pounds of Shaw lunges with his arm like a hook, connects with Businessman's neck and hits with such force; it breaks Businessman's neck and flips him head over heels to leave him in a quivering mass of flesh and broken bones.

"Fuck me!" Priest utters in amazement as Shaw runs back to him. "Remind me to never piss you off." They chuckle as they sprint to the maintenance door. As they make it through, Priest yells at Shaw, "Make that door in-op?"

"Copy." Shaw grabs a large screwdriver and a hammer off the workbench near the door. He wedges the screwdriver in the metal frame behind the door and hit it with the hammer which lodges the screwdriver in the frame. As he turns to run, he hears banging and screaming on the other side of the door. He yells, "They are at the door. Move!" The rest of the group had already reached the roof as Shaw bursts out of the door meets up with the group.

They kneel there for a few minutes to catch their breath. Priest looks around to everyone there, "Everybody all right? Anyone hurt?" All of them shake their heads. Except for being scared to death and a little winded, they seemed to be okay. He looks around the roof, thinking of their next steps.

Priest explains, "Ok, we run across the roof to the easternmost point, where Shaw and myself will escort Doug to his chopper. We will pull security while he gets it running, while Doc and Allison stay up on the roof until we are ready to take off. Everyone clear?" They all nod. "Ok, let's move!"

CHAPTER 11

The hum of the engine, along with the rocking motion of the rotors, lulled a few of the team to sleep. Webb was awake because he had too much responsibility on his hands, too much going on in his head. He conducted a quick scan around to see Dr. Costa dozing, along with Bolin, but Kennedy was awake. He gave Webb a nod.

Abarra was nodding off. "Thank God," Webb thought. They hadn't had time to process the loss of Myles, except Abarra. He was close to Myles and took him under his wing to educate and train him as best he could. Myles was making progress and was turning into a damn fine soldier. Abarra had taken Myles's death hard and took responsibility for his death, even though it was not his to take.

It had been Webb who gave the order to perform surveillance, not Abarra. Webb felt guilty but didn't feel the brunt of the blame as Abarra did. Myles had gotten himself killed. He was sloppy, although this is something Webb would never articulate out loud. He figured Doc was probably feeling some of that guilt, so there was enough to go around.

Gratefully, Abarra had calmed his mind enough to get some rest. Abarra was a powerful man, an excellent soldier, and an excellent friend. He was one who could be hard on you but always cared for his team and didn't have a problem shedding a tear for a fallen brother.

Scanning the cabin, Webb noticed the crew chief cock his head and then lean in between the pilot and copilot. They were discussing something and then the crew chief sat back down. Webb tapped him on the arm, "Hey, what's going on?"

"They have a detected an approaching aircraft which isn't answering communications. Nothing to worry about, though." Webb leaned back in this jump seat. As they flew farther, the crew chief cocked his head and looked like he was listening to something and Webb thought he heard him say, "copy." The crew chief seemed to intensify his search out the gunner's port.

After a few moments, the crew chief pointed and spoke into his helmet's mouthpiece. Webb looked to where he was pointing and could faintly make out an aircraft approaching in the distance. Webb connected into the Blackhawk's comm. "Do you think this is civilians trying to escape?"

"Most likely. We hope that is what it is, but they won't answer our calls. We can't go firing on civilian aircraft just because we aren't sure who they are," the copilot replied.

"Yeah, but we are not in normal circumstances here and there could be anything piloting that aircraft," Webb continued to watch the aircraft approach. The copilot just seemed to wave him off.

The crew chief came over the comms again, "Sir, the aircraft seems to have an intercept path to us."

"Yeah, it sure looks like it, the co-pilot responded

"Should I engage?"

"Negative, we need to verify before we shoot citizens out of the sky."

"Copy that." By this time, they could make out it was a single winged plane, most likely a crop duster. The plane was moving about sporadically, like the pilot was drunk. The crew chief was getting antsy. "Sir, that plane is making a B-Line for us, coming right at our three o'clock."

"I see them, but we are still trying to hail them. Following protocol," the copilot added. The crew chief looked at Webb over his shoulder and shook his head. Webb continues to watch the drama unfold. The pilot adjusted their course, but plane also adjusted its course as well to continue its perceived intercept of their Blackhawk.

Neville gave Webb a worried look, "Sir, I am getting really nervous about this."

"Understood, Sargent." Webb unplugged from the Blackhawk's comms. He tapped the crew chief's shoulder, "The pilot and copilot, what are their ranks?"

As if he knew where Webb was going, he smiled, "Both are Warrant Officers, Sir."

"That's what I thought. They know flying. I know combat. You take direction from me from this point on. Understood?"

"Yes, sir," the crew chief said as he saluted with an enormous grin on his face.

"Charge that weapon, Specialist, and fire on my command." Webb instructed. The crew chief did so.

Webb plugged back into the Blackhawk's comms. "Is that aircraft still making a B-Line for us?"

"Affirmative sir," said the Specialist.

"We don't know that for sure," said the copilot with a condescending tone.

"What? We wait until they are on top of us before we prepare?"

"Captain Webb, we cannot blow civilians out of the sky because of paranoia."

"Paranoia? You haven't seen what the fuck is going on down there. It's a mother fucking blood bath. Paranoia is one thing, but being stupid is another."

"Sir, the aircraft is about 200 yards and closing. Straight for us, I might add," the Specialist remarked.

"Sight on that aircraft, Specialist, and wait for my signal. If that plane doesn't change course, then we will remove it from the sky."

"Captain, I don't think this is wise..."

Webb cuts him off, "Last time I checked, I outrank everyone on this fucking aircraft, Goddamnit. With that being the case, I don't give a shit what you think. You will take direction from me. Are there any questions?" They didn't respond. "Out fucking standing! Specialist report."

"150 yards and closing."

"Any acknowledgment from them?"

"Negative," the copilot responded.

"Ok, Specialist, send a couple warning shots across the bow. Let them know to back off and change course." The Specialist raked a burst of rounds over the top of the aircraft, but the plane stayed on course. "Ok, this is getting too close for comfort and I am not willing to get Dr. Costa killed. Specialist, take it out."

"Copy that." The Specialist pulled the butterfly trigger and the six mini-gun barrels whirled. It started sending 5.56mm rounds toward the plane. The first group of rounds went too low and missed the target. "Sorry, Sir. I have never fired on an aircraft before, much less one while in the air myself."

"Understood son, do your best. You have the most experience on that weapon." Webb looked forward and could see the worry on Dr. Costa's face and he gave her a confident nod. The Minigun spit out more rounds towards the plane and a few hit the left-wing. The plane shuddered a bit but regained control. "Specialist, take that fucking plane down now!" Webb barked.

"I'm trying, sir."

Abarra slid the side door open and fired his M4 at the plane, "It's getting friendly close!"

"Pilot, change course, but keep the mini-gun side toward the plane. It's the only firepower we have."

"Copy." The pilot pulled the cyclic stick up, and the Blackhawk ascended two hundred feet. The plane tracked the movement and kept its collision course.

"Fuck gentlemen, let's splash that bastard already!" Webb roared. The plane was approaching quickly. Seventy-five yards, fifty-yards. As the Minigun sprayed the plane across both wings, and a few rounds hit the propeller and engine. The plane faltered, but not enough to prevent a collision, so the pilots shifted the helicopter sideways, but it was too late.

"Shiiiit!" the Specialist yelled. He and Abarra continued to fire at the plane. The Minigun chattering and the barrels were getting red.

Twenty-five yards and then boom! Rounds hit the engine, and the plane exploded.

All at once, multiple things happened. The explosion sent shrapnel into the side of the Blackhawk and through the open door, while everyone did their best to protect themselves. Kennedy and Bolin both covered Dr. Costa to protect her. Abarra tried to sliding the door shut, and Webb turned his back, hoping his plate carrier would take the damage. The explosion also sent a shock wave that ravaged the side of the Blackhawk and sent it rocking.

Alarms wailed from the cockpit, and the helicopter went into a spin. The pilots fought to gain control of the aircraft. The doctor was screaming; the team was yelling, and the pilots were cussing. As the helicopter continued to spin, the pilots struggled to fight the cyclic stick while it jumped around in their grip like a crazy rooster.

Webb grabbed the handhold straps to steady himself and saw Bolin slump over. He reached to right the man up and noticed the blood on his back. He looked harder and noticed Bolin had a piece of shrapnel sticking a few inches out of his back. Webb put his fingers on his neck and did not feel a pulse.

The alarms continue to beep incessantly, making it hard to hear anyone. Everyone was holding on for dear life while the pilots cursed the helicopter. The bird tipped to one side, and then the spin slowed. They were gradually losing altitude, but it seemed like the Blackhawk was straightening out.

Approximately 60 seconds later, they were at a hover, and the alarms had silenced. All onboard looked at each other with no one saying a word. Eyes were as big as manhole covers, and Abarra was whispering a prayer in Spanish. Webb snapped out of his stupor to assess the situation.

"Is everyone ok?" It was when Dr. Costa realized Bolin was dead. Kennedy did as well and stared at the floor as Dr. Costa cried.

Webb put a hand on Kennedy's shoulder, "Sorry, Kennedy. He was an honorable man."

"Yeah, he was. This job was all he knew, all he wanted. No wife, no kids, just this."

"Sorry, man," Abarra added.

"Thanks."

The pilots took a breath and regained their composure, then continued their flight to Dearborn. Everyone was silent, mostly.

After a while, Webb spoke through the bird's comms. "Any contact with CDC yet?"

The copilot shook his head, "Negative."

"What about Command? Any of our friends answering there?"

"Negative on that, Sir. The radio has been dead silent since we rolled out on this mission. Except for your squad comms, we haven't heard a peep out of anyone: Command, the airport, not even other aircraft. It's as if the entire world has gone quiet."

Webb turned to Abarra and pointed toward the pilots, "No comms, as if the world has gone. No people, no radios, nothing."

"That can't be good."

"Yeah, well, regardless, we have a mission to complete." Webb turns to the doctor. "We haven't had communications with anyone, including the CDC in Dearborn. Have you had contact with them at all recently?"

She looked around, worried. "Our last communication with them was two days ago. With what has gone on recently, that might as well be two months, much less two days."

"Copy that." Webb sat back against the Blackhawk's cabin panel. He shut his eyes for a second to run through scenarios in his head. He tried to plan for everything, thinking about what is happening next and how to handle it.

"Captain?" The copilot came over Webb's comms. "We are about ten miles out."

"Copy that." Webb pushed his squad comms, "Ok, boys. We are about ten miles out. Neville and Shin, we will drop you off on the roof of the insurance building. A quick assessment of the surrounding area, then concentrate on covering our asset into the CDC building." Both acknowledged. "We go in, get whatever the doctor needs, and roll out. Kennedy and Abarra will escort Dr. Costa to our exfil point two blocks away. I will stay back and help cover Overlord's six while we make our way to the exfil point. Questions?"

The doctor spoke up, "I might need some time in that CDC lab, since I can't take everything I need from there. Some things might have to be completed there."

"Doctor, if everything is intact then you may have all the time you want. Though, we do not understand what the situation on the ground is. If it is anything like what we've seen already that CDC facility could be completely compromised."

"Captain, I need those samples, and any other information or the world may not stop this."

"We will do what we can, Dr. Costa, you have my word."

"Captain, approaching objective. We have a visual...." The copilot broke off in mid-sentence.

"Say again. I didn't copy it." The team opens the side doors and looks out. Webb articulates what everyone else is thinking. "Dear God, what the hell?"

The chopper hovered over the remains of the CDC building. The entire block looked like something out of a war-torn France during WWII. Smoke was rolling out of storefronts, broken windows, burned-out cars, and dead bodies littered the streets.

Neville turned to Webb, "Do you think there is anything left in that lab worth saving, Sir? Just say the word, and we will deploy."

Webb grabbed Dr. Costa's arm, "Doctor, do you believe there is anything left in there you can use, anything that isn't compromised?" Dr. Costa was staring down at the destruction. "Doctor, doctor!"

Dr. Costa shook her head and looked back at Webb, "Yes, sorry. We need to see what we can salvage out of there. Anything could help us identify this virus and possibly help to find an antidote."

"Ok, you heard the lady, we need to see what we can pull out of there. Neville and Shin deploy and take your position."

Neville and Shin fast roped onto the insurance building's roof, then the chopper rose higher and moved off the building roof. With Neville using his rifle scope and Shin his range scope, they surveyed the area for movement, especially near the facility the breach team was getting ready to deploy to.

Neville scoped the situation out, "What you got, Shin?" "I do not see any movement in several surrounding blocks."

"I do not as well."

"Spider, this is Voodoo, do you copy?"

"Voodoo, this is Spider, go ahead."

"We do not see any movement in the surrounding blocks. All is quiet. No infected, but no civilians either."

"Copy that Voodoo. Watch our six. We are getting ready to deploy."

"Copy, we are on point." The rest of the team, including the doctor and Kennedy, exited the bird on the CDC roof. The bird took off as to not draw any unwanted attention as they found the roof access door and entered the building.

CHAPTER 12

Shaw and Priest low crawled, along with Doug, to the edge of the terminal building. They were all in the prone position and looked out across the flight line where planes were towed in for maintenance. They also used the area as a hub for some private jet charters helicopters, including the state police or Life Flight, and a few network news choppers. There were two private jets parked there with a Boeing 727 that looked like they towed it in for repair. They parked the 727 to the left and parallel to the terminal building. The two private jets were each parked in front of a maintenance hangar.

Doug's news chopper was two hundred yards away to the right of the terminal building. It was sitting by itself out in the open, which presented the team with a Catch 22 scenario. On one side, it was in the open, allowing the team to see anything coming, which presented no change for an ambush. On the other side, it was in the open, so anything remotely within view of the helicopter would see them making a run for it. Not an ambush situation, but stealth was out the window, and they risked being overrun.

Priest moved back from the edge and turned on his back to look at the sky. "Damn, that will be risky no matter what. Doug, how long does it take to get that bird prepped enough to take off?"

"Well, forgoing all the pre-flight checks, about 5-6 minutes to start the engines, 1-2 minutes to achieve lift RPM. So anywhere from 7 to 10 minutes."

"Shit! That's too much time. We will need a distraction to draw the infected away so they don't hear the chopper spinning up or see anyone running to it."

"I could go to one side of the building and start shooting and bring them over." Shaw said.

"Yeah, I am just worried that once they hear the engines fire up, it will drown out all other sounds, and they'll swarm the chopper."

"That's if there are any of those things out there." Doug chimed in

"Oh, they're out there. Bet your ass on that." Priest flipped over and crawled back to look over the ledge. He was thinking about what he could use as a distraction as he scanned the area. He stopped on an item sitting about 200 yards from their location. In a small ditch to the east of the terminal building sat a Dodge Challenger. Priest pointed it out to Doug and Shaw. "Dude, how about the car?" Priest said in a subdued tone as he thought about it.

Shaw piped up, "Well, if we assume the keys are in it and it's not stuck, yeah, you could use it to draw the horde away."

Priest chuckled, "Wonder if it's a Hell Cat, that sure would be nice. Never could afford one of those. I think it's worth the risk to find out if it is operational."

"Well, knowing how stubborn you are, I guess there is no chance of talking you out of it. I guess I will just have to cover your crazy ass."

"Ok, Mr. Shaw, let's make it happen."

They found an awning for one of the businesses that Priest could jump down onto. The issue was that it was too high to grab from the ground, so once you were down, you were down. Priest jumped to the awning and stopped to listen for any infected. He didn't hear any but it didn't make him feel any better, because he knew they were out there somewhere. He was sure he would probably find out soon enough.

Priest took a deep breath, jumped to the ground with a grunt and took off as fast as his legs would carry him. He was older than anyone else on the team, but he was pretty fast for an old fart.

As soon as he cleared the corner of the terminal building, he heard multiple screams and shouts. The hair on his arm stood on end with a chill running through him. Was that adrenaline, or was that fear? As he glanced back, he saw more infected coming at him from some buildings to his left-front. "Get there, please let me get there, he swore to himself." The screams from behind were getting louder, as they were gaining on him.

"Shit, shit, shit," he yelled. Just then he heard... chunk.... chunk... chunk... chunk! The sound of Shaw's M48 cutting through the infected was recognizable.

The infected from the front were still closing in. Priest could raise his rifle and take some of these fuckers out, but that would slow him down, and then the infected might catch up. He just had to keep chugging and make it to the car. The infected were closing the gap and were now only 100 yards from him.

"Go old man, move your fucking ass!" Priest yelled at himself. Giving him one last burst of courage or maybe fear, but whichever it was it allowed him to reach the car. He jumped in, shut and locked the doors, and took a breath. Priest reached down with eyes closed and holy shit, the keys were in it. He turned the key, and the car started and idled with a harmonious rumble.

The infected had reached him and were banging on the glass as he slapped the vehicle in reverse and punched it. The car shot out of the ditch and sped backward. He hit the brakes, slapped it in drive, and stomped on the gas. The tires smoked as they spun on the pavement, then the car launched itself forward, hitting three infected with the front of the vehicle. He continued to keep his foot on the gas, and the vehicle fishtailed, taking two infected out on the right side.

Priest looked down at the steering wheel and saw the Demon emblem. "Holy Shit. Get some," he yelled. He sped down the flight line while blowing the horn, which captured the infected attention, and they took off after the car.

Shaw and Doug made it to the news chopper and Doug immediately went to his storage panel on the side. He started rifling through it as Shaw looked around the nose of the chopper.

"What are you doing?"

"Looking for a wrench or my socket set to remove that equipment on the right side. It's just broadcast transmission equipment." Doug answered.

Shaw looked at him, annoyed. "We don't have time for that." Shaw slung his M48 on his back, opened the right-side door and shoved his arms inside. His massive hands grabbed ahold of the first piece of equipment and with a heave, ripped it out and threw it on the ground.

Doug looked over at him in amazement. He held the wrench he just pulled out in front of his face, stared at it for a second and then tossed it back where he had gotten it from. He ran to the pilot's seat and started the engine. Shaw had all the equipment removed in minutes. A scene of broken screws, bent brackets and mangled metal remained in place of the equipment, but he had all the equipment cleared out.

As Shaw was standing right at the pilot door, he looked at Doug, then looked at Priest running around in the car, "You think he is having too much fun out there?"

Doug glanced up, "Yep, sure looks like it," and shakes his head. "He ain't all there, is he?"

"Nope, he sure ain't."

By now, Priest had close to two or three dozen infected chasing him, trying to get to him, trying to infect him and join their ranks. Priest had the crowd of contaminated about 500 yards away from Shaw and Doug.

As Shaw patrolled around the news chopper, a pack of infected came running out of a nook in the terminal building approximately some distance away. Shaw's M48 barked out .50 caliber rounds that shredded the pack of infected in mere seconds. The figures of humans, once running toward them, were now piles of blood, viscera, and unrecognizable fragments of bone, skin and hair. "Damn, looks like chunky soup," Shaw remarked.

He turned around and walked back to Doug, who was shouting over the whine of the engine and beating of the rotors. "We're ready to go, bring your boy in."

Shaw nodded. "Cotton to Father, do you copy?"

"Go ahead, Shaw.... WHOO hoo!"

"Time to put your toy away and get the fuck out of here."

"Shit, copy that, on my way." Priest spun the car around one last time and sped toward the news chopper. With that 700 hp, he reached 140mph, then dialed back before executing a power slide to a stop. He jumped out with a grin on his face five miles wide and ran to join Shaw and Doug.

Shaw just shook his head, "Get your dumb ass in here." Priest got in the copilot seat and belted in.

They jumped in, Doug took off and flew over to where Doc and Allison were on the roof. Shaw helped Allison in and Doc right after.

"Get us the hell out of here!" Priest shouted.

"Don't have to tell me twice," Doug ascended and then directed the chopper northeast toward Dearborn.

CHAPTER 13

The Dearborn CDC facility was not in the condition the Team expected it to be. They immediately entered the stairwell and halted to gage their bearings.

Webb turned to Dr. Costa. "Do you know the building layout?" She shook her head. "Ok, we have zero intel on the layout so we're going in blind. Do you have a guess on where we should look first?"

"Well, if it is like most labs, most of the elements we use like nitrogen and oxygen are usually in tanks on the ground floor. I would think reception and offices are on the first floor, so starting on the floor below that would be our best bet."

"Sounds solid to me." Webb looks to Abarra & Kennedy, "Any objections?" They both shook their heads. "Ok, we are on the fourth floor, so we have to traverse four floors. I will take point, Kennedy will follow, Dr Costa behind him and Abarra will cover our ass. Questions?"

With Webb in the lead, the team made their way down three floors, encountering no infected. As they approached the first-floor landing, Webb gave the visual for stop and he cocked his head to listen to the varied sounds.

The fires on the first floor were loud and sounds of building debris falling everywhere made it even harder to make out anything. This made listening for the infected almost impossible, but Webb shook his head and continued down the stairs toward the first underground level. There was a strange sound coming from below them, sounding like a wet thunk, thunk, thunk in the stairwell.

Webb signs stop to the Team as he slowly continues down the stairs. As he turns the corner of the landing, a graphic scene unfolds in front of him. A shirtless man with his back to Webb had a weapon in his hand, chopping into a body at lying at his feet. His weapon looked like a chair leg, which had a chunk of metal sticking out from the end that resembled of a hatchet. Long open wounds trailed down the man's back and blood was dripping to a pool on the floor.

The body at his feet, which looked like a woman, had no head, and the man was working on removing one of her legs. On the left stairwell railing were the woman's bowels and other entrails, spread out like on display at a posh art gallery. As the man brought the object down again and again, his head was tilting left and right like Webb had seen many times before, along with a clicking noise he made between giggles.

The man stopped chopping on the body to turn and admire the display of insides on the railing. He was moving his hand along the intestines slowly like they mesmerized him and had a look of reverence on this face. His daze cleared as he turned a little more to the left and noticed Webb standing there. The man's face was completely covered in blood so thick; it was difficult to make out his facial features. All Webb noticed was the man's wide eyes projecting out from the mask of red. He tilted his head to regard Webb for a few seconds, then pointed his "hatchet" toward the woman's body and spoke with a hiss.

"She didn't want the poison. The sweet, sweet poison. She paid the price. She has lovely pieces though," he said as he strokes the innards hanging on the railing. He points his hand made hatchet at Webb, "You want the poison, yes?" It was more of a statement than a question as far as his tone.

Webb thought quickly and answered, "Yes, I want the poison."

The man smiled and hissed. "Yes, yes, you do. You see, don't you? You see, the joy it brings?"

"Yes, I do. I want to join my brothers."

The man smiles even wider, opened his mouth and hissed as he approached Webb slowly. Webb hadn't seen this behavior before and really never had a conversation with one of the infected.

Kennedy looked at the Dr. Costa and then Abarra. "Is he talking to that fucking thing?"

Abarra shrugged, "Sounds like it."

Dr. Costa whispered, "They seem to keep their mind and skills for time, albeit, a very distorted mind."

"That's even more creepy," Kennedy added as they continued to listen to what was going on below them.

The man approached Webb with his arms open wide, "The poison will embrace you. You can join us and truly know." As the man got within arm's reach, Webb moved like lightning, pulled his combat knife and shoved the blade right under the man's chin, up through the roof of his mouth and into his skull cavity. The infected man's eyes rolled back in his head and his body went limp, with his arms still opened wide. Webb removed the knife, wiped it on the man's pants, then sheathed it. "All clear," Webb said, and the rest came down the stairs.

Dr. Costa recoiled at the entrails draped over the railing and almost screamed at the sight of the mutilated body of the woman.

"Sorry Doc, but we got to keep moving."

"That poor woman.... he-he mutilated her." Dr Costa muttered.

Kennedy grasped her arm and helped her over the body and around the pool of blood. They all continued out of the stairwell on the lower floor.

They surveyed the dark corridor. Sparse light glowed from the emergency lights, which were spread quite a distance away from each other. There were papers and other debris littered up and down the hallway. There were four doors along each side and one at the end of the hallway which were all open.

Webb shook his head, knowing how dangerous this was, because they had to cover both doorways at the same time or risk being surprised from the rear. He was going on his own to clear the rooms, because Kennedy needed to stay with Dr. Costa and Abarra was to cover their rear. Webb was contemplating the situation when his comms activated and Shin's voice came over the comms. This caused Webb and all the others to jump out of their skin. Kennedy accidentally fired a round into the ceiling when he jumped.

"Mother fucker," Webb reeled on him. "What the hell is your finger doing on the fucking trigger? It stays on the guard until you are ready to fire. Didn't they teach you that shit in the Secret Service?"

"Sorry, sorry. I am nervous. I've never dealt with shit like this before."

Abarra stared at Kennedy, "You better unfuck yourself right here and now. Do you understand?"

Kennedy listened but didn't look at Webb or Abarra.

"Ok, go ahead Gandhi."

"Sir, Father checked in and they are on their way to provide support."

"Did they get the two civilians out?"

"Affirmative."

"Well, there is no sense in them coming here. Hold one. Tell them to stand by." Webb said.

"Copy. Sir, there is another piece of news. We have multiple hordes of infected coming this way from all directions. They may have heard the chopper when we infiltrated. With the numbers we are estimating, we may require support to repel them. Have you found what you need, yet?"

"Negative, we need more time."

"What are your orders, then Sir?" Webb paused for a few seconds. "How long until we have contact with the horde?"

"Hard to say, sir. They don't seem to be in a hurry to get here. I do not think they know our exact location, because they seem to be still searching. If I was to guess, we're looking at approximately 15 mics."

"Copy that. Ok Doctor, we have 10 minutes to look for samples, evidence, whatever the hell you can find, then we need to be out of here."

Dr. Costa nodded in agreement.

"Gandhi, tell Father to find a staging area close by in case we need an RFQ. You guys monitor their progress, let us know if things change. We'll be out in 10 mics."

"Copy that."

The team cleared all the hallway doors and posted up at the last door on the end of the hallway. This was the only door they had come across that was closed. Webb took the left, Abarra the right. Kennedy escorted Dr. Costa into one of the other rooms in that hallway and waited. Webb tried the door, and it was unlocked. He nodded to Abarra and counted using his fingers, one, two, three.

They breeched the room and Webb quickly surveyed. It was a destroyed lab environment with equipment scattered all over the floor. Microscopes, specimen slides, analyzing equipment, papers, etc. were underfoot as they entered. A good amount of blood was indiscriminate around the lab as pools, smears, and splatters.

"Ok, Doc. Abarra and myself will pull security while you and Kennedy look for whatever you can find. You got 10 minutes and then we have to bail."

Dr. Costa began frantically looking through documents and test equipment while Kennedy searched the room for a computer. They both were anxiously searching as quickly as they could.

Kennedy eventually found one laying on its side under one desk, deeper into the lab. "Found a computer doctor," he said.

"They should back the data up on the CDC database, but I want to find as much physical evidence as possible. I am not confident that we will continue to have access the more out of control the situation becomes." Dr. Costa sounded concerned.

Kennedy pulled the computer out and removed the side. He found the hard drive, ripped it out and stored it in the backpack that Webb had given him. It used to be Myles's, but the mission overrode emotion.

Webb posted at the door and shouted over his shoulder, "Finding anything, Doc? Time is getting tight." She didn't answer, because she was much too focused on the documents she was reviewing. Abarra had a string bag he used to scavenge items while on missions and tossed it to her, "Put them in there and let's go." She just started shoving the documents in the bag, not sure if they were all relevant, but she would take as much as she could.

Webb heard in his earpiece, "Spider, this is Overlord, you copy?"

"Copy Overlord."

"The horde is getting close. We are almost at a critical distance to exfil safely and not get overrun. I believe you guys say the pucker factor is quickly approaching 10."

"Copy that." Webb turned to Dr. Costa, "Doctor, we have to go now!"

"I don't know if I have found what I need yet."

"We have run out of time, so what you have will have to be good enough. You won't be alive to review it anyway, unless we boogie right now."

"Damn," she swore. "Ok, let's go then."

"Moving out," Webb yelled. "Overlord, we are leaving."

"Copy, Spider. We have you covered."

CHAPTER 14

Neville and Shin stayed low, but continued to monitor the horde's movement. Shin radioed the Blackhawk for exfil right after talking to Webb. He keyed Webb, "Exfil in 3 mikes."

"Copy," Webb responded.

Shin turned to Neville, "You think the rest of the world is like this?"

"Don't know, but I sure as hell hope not. Thing is, we don't know where this has hit and how fast it is spreading."

"Yes, you are right." "We need to make it out of here alive, first."

With Webb leading, the team made its way up to the first-floor landing, not stopping for anything. As Dr. Costa reached the second-floor stairs, the door burst open into the stairwell and a bloody woman jumped on top of her. She screamed and fell back on the stairs. Kennedy reached out to help Dr. Costa up while Abarra grabbed the woman and pulled her off.

Abarra slammed the infected woman into the wall and held her there, "Go get to the roof. I'll catch up."

Webb was coming back down the stairs to where they were when Abarra stopped him, "Go, I got this. I'll be right behind you." Webb paused for a second, looked into Abarra's eyes, then nodded, leading the Dr. Costa and Kennedy up the stairs.

The woman struggled against Abarra as he struggled to hold her against the wall. "Damn she is strong for a skinny girl", he thought as he held her against the wall with both hands. He kept wanting to remove one hand, to grab his Glock and put a round in her head. Every time he attempted to, she would struggle in his grip and he had to bring his other hand back up.

Starting to get desperate, Abarra began pounding the back of her head against the wall, hoping to crush her skull. She was a skinny paltry thing with dark hair and wearing a sundress with a red sweater, but her innocence was marred by the screaming and biting. He searched for any ounce of humanity in her, but was saw nothing but a feral growl, gnashing teeth and rage filled eyes. Those eyes told him she wanted to not just infect him, but kill him.

His heart sank knowing that this was what things were coming to and that the result may even worse. He didn't know how things would turn around, but what he knew was that he needed to end this and get the hell out of there. He increased his effort and really started going to town on busting her head against the wall.

"Die already, you fucking bitch! Damn head is like a bowling ball." With a few more slams with her head, the first-floor door opened again as another infected was wedging its way in. Abarra had his foot against the door, but it was difficult dealing with the crazy octopus in his hands and keep the door closed at the same time. "Shit!" he yelled.

The rest of the team was on the third-floor landing when they heard Abarra yelling. Webb stopped, "Kennedy, you take the doctor up to the roof and we will join you there. I need to check on Abarra."

"Got it Cap." Kennedy led Dr. Costa on up to the fourth floor while Webb raced down the stairs trying to get to Abarra as quick as he could.

Abarra could feel the woman go limp as he swung her head against the wall one more time. He dropped her to the floor and turned his concentration to the infected trying to make its way through the door. By this time, the man had his arm through trying to use it as leverage to open the door.

Abarra could see the man's face through the little 12X12 window in the top middle of the door. The infected was an older man with a filthy security guard uniform and big jowls that were shaking around while he kept pushing to get in the door.

Abarra's eyes grew wide as he saw other infected running down the hallway behind the security guard. His attention was so focused on the guard and the infected coming down the hallway, he didn't react to the scream behind him before it was too late.

The skinny woman jumped on his back and took a huge bite out of the left side of his face. He screamed as she came away with most of his cheek and the side of his mouth. Flashes of black spots appeared in front of his eyes as he looked down and noticed the woman was gone from the floor.

"That fucking bitch didn't die," he thought to himself. She leaned in for another bite and tore away one of his eyes this time. He bellowed curses at her and then lost his strength to hold the door closed.

Webb appeared on the upper stairs of the first-floor stairwell, looking down at Abarra as the infected girl bit and tore away his eye. He yelled with rage, brought up his M4 and took out the woman on Abarra's back. Then plugged the security guard in the face as a couple more infected busted through.

Webb started down the remaining stairs, but Abarra yelled, "Get the fuck out of here! Now! Webb looked up at him and caught Abarra's eye. Webb knew there was nothing he could do now.

"Fuck!", Webb yelled. He raised his rifle to end Abarra's suffering when more infected poured into the stairwell and dog piled on top of him, blocking Webb's shot. It didn't feel right, but Webb knew he needed to get out of there and there was nothing he could do now, anyway. He fired a couple three-round bursts and took off up the stairs. He made it to the fourth floor and burst out of the maintenance door on the roof.

In all the carnage happening to Abarra, Webb didn't hear the Blackhawk hovering just off the roof with Dr. Costa on board. Kennedy was entering the helicopter as Webb sprinted and jumped in through the side door.

"Go, go, go!" Webb yelled and the pilot lifted off of the CDC building's roof. The pilot hovered over the insurance building to pick up the sniper element. As Neville and Shin loaded into the Blackhawk, the door on the roof of the CDC building burst open and dozens of infected came streaming out. The infected saw the helicopter, the prey on board, and charged toward them like a crazy mob.

The distance was too great between the buildings and the infected started dropping off over the side with their arms still outreached for Webb and his team.

Shin made his way in and the bird ascended. Webb glanced back to the CDC building just in time to see Abarra standing on the roof staring at him. Staring, just staring, head moving side to side, click, click, click, click, click, click....

CHAPTER 15

Doug looked at Priest while he talked to Webb, having previously asked where they were going or what they were doing now. Priest contacted Overlord for a set rep and to relay info to Webb. Shaw was in the back with Allison and Doc. Doc kept talking to Allison about all the stuff they had done and didn't shut up log enough to take a breath. Shaw was getting annoyed because Doc was taking up time, he wanted to get to know Allison better.

"Doc, come up for air. You chatter on more than a damn chipmunk on speed. Give the woman a break, already." Doc looked over at Shaw with a confused look, because Shaw rarely said a lot. Doc clammed up and turned to look out the window, and Allison discretely reached over and gave Shaw's hand a squeeze in thankfulness.

Shaw didn't know how Allison felt about him since they just met and the world was crumbling around them, but he told himself he would find out. "I mean hell, she had blonde hair, blue eyes and a pin up figure," he thought to himself.

Shaw liked that fact that she seemed to possess a strength and intelligence that exuded a certain confidence which attracted him. He used to deal with bimbos, but had changed and would not deal with a woman if she was in that category. He definitely wanted to find out more about Allison, he just didn't know if they would have the time to do that. Unsure about what would happen, Shaw wondered if Allison and Doug would go their separate way soon.

Shaw was kind of quiet, usually saying things when they needed said. He and Priest had become best friends, even though Priest was older than Shaw by about 10 years. They would go fishing, hunting, attend football games and just hang around each other. Neither of them had been married yet. Shaw was close a few years ago, but his fiancé decided she couldn't deal with his military life and his constant deployment. Shaw and Priest had talked about it, and Shaw confided in him he may have been willing to leave the military if she would have been agreeable to discuss it. Shaw had related it pissed him off, because she just made her mind up and closed the door on their relationship. Priest told him it was a blessing in disguise and if she wasn't willing to talk about something as important as that, then it spelled doom for any other struggle in life they would come across.

Thinking about Allison and maybe re-entering the world of dating brought up the past and his last relationship. Shaw sighed, closed his eyes and decided he would let it go for now and he drifted off to sleep in a matter of minutes. One lesson about being a Special Operations Rapid Deployment Unit was that you ate when you could, drank water when you could, and got sleep when you could. Try to wait for that perfect scheduled down time never came during a mission. "Get it, while you got it," the saying was.

The chopper hit some turbulence and swayed in the air, but that wasn't what stirred Shaw in his sleep. The touch on his hand caused him to part his eyes slightly to see Allison had grabbed his hand and was holding it. Her hand was soft and small in his, but they were freezing cold. He didn't know if she reached over for comfort, safety, warmth or just human contact. He didn't know, nor did he care, because he enjoyed it, accepted it and would not put any more meaning into it than it was.

Allison glanced over and saw a smile just at the corners of Shaw's mouth. She let a smile form on her mouth.

After a while, Priest briefed everyone on the info from Webb's group and let them know that they were to find a stage area and wait for further instructions.

"Doug, are you familiar with the Dearborn area?"

"No, Sir. Indiana is my base of operations."

"Ok, then we need to be on the lookout for a safe place to set down and remain on standby."

"Ok, gotcha Sarge."

Doc speaks up, "Make sure it's somewhere safe." Doug and Priest look at each other and roll their eyes.

They entered the outskirts of Dearborn 20 minutes later and immediately began looking for a suitable spot to land.

"How about a parking garage," Doc uttered.

Priest shook his head, "Negative, too many points of entry to cover. We need a roof top with only one access point to secure." They flew around for two minutes when Shaw noticed something.

"Hey, I think that might be a hospital right there. I see a helicopter pad on that roof at our two o'clock." Doug rotated around to see it.

"What do you think Sarge?"

"Hmm, what scares me is that the hospital would be the first place they would take the infected. I bet that whole hospital is full of infected."

"Yep, probably so," Shaw answered.

Abruptly, Webb came over Priest's comms. "Father, this is Spider. Do you copy?"

"Copy. Go ahead, Spider."

"We are bugging out; the site is hot."

"Copy that."

"Father, one more thing?" Webb's voice took a serious tone.

"Yeah, Spider?"

"I don't know how to say this, but we lost two of our boys."

"Shit!!!" Priest was silent for a moment, "Who?"

"We lost Bolin…" Webb paused "and we lost Bacardi."

Priest's face went flush. He was suddenly out of his mind, out of his body and trying to hold on to reality. "Bacardi?" he repeated.

"Yeah, brother, Bacardi," Webb replied solemnly.

"Can't be," Priest thought. Suddenly he came rushing back to himself like falling off a cliff to a dead stop. Once he was back in the present, anger engulfed him. "Fuck, fuck, fuck!" he screamed while slamming his fists into the door pillar, denting it. This caused everyone to jump, and the helicopter swerved as it startled Doug.

"Holy shit, what the hell, Sarge?" Doc yelled.

"Shut the fuck up, Doc," Shaw spat. He reached up with a gentle hand on Priest's shoulder. "What's up Sarge?" Shaw said in a peaceful tone.

Priest looked down. He had tears in his eyes. "We.... We lost Abarra." Doc took in a deep breath but held it.

Shaw just muttered, "Mother fucker."

"They lost Bolin too."

"I'm so sorry," came a small voice from the back. Priest reached back and gave Allison a reassuring pat on the knee.

"Thank you, but it's not your fault."

"But it is. If you guys wouldn't have had to stay back and rescue us, then you would have been there to save him." She broke down sobbing.

"She's right, I am so sorry. I feel horrible," Doug added.

"Look, we are Special Ops and everything we do is dangerous. We know we may not come back from any mission. It's the way it is. We don't deal with what if's and maybes? We'll deal with what is, so don't think you had anything to do with it," Shaw chided.

Priest nodded, "He's right. We don't deal with what ifs in our business. What ifs drive you crazy and leave nothing but an empty shell? We accept it and will get over it," Priest added. He turned back around to the front. "Spider, this is Father. Do you copy?"

"Copy."

"What's our next move?"

"I believe we need to take what we have back to HQ, assess where we are and what we can do with the data we have. Regrouping to plan next steps is the best alternative right now."

"Copy that. Hold on." Priest turns and addresses Doug and Allison, "What do you guys want to do? Marshall Law wasn't declared so I can't make you come with us and we have no jurisdiction over you so, so we can't tell you what to do. If you want my honest opinion, I believe you are much safer with us, but where you go from here is your decision."

After a few minutes of silence tick by, Doug speaks up, "Hmm, I haven't really thought that far ahead. I was accepting my fate because I thought I would die. Allison, what are your thoughts?"

"Well, from what I have been hearing, all communications are out because I even tried my cellphone and nothing. I guess our news station is no longer broadcasting, so there goes my job and career. It looks to me like going with Sergeant Priest and his men is our best bet."

"What about your boyfriend, Tom?" Doug asked with a slight grin on his face.

"Huh, what? Tom? Fuck Tom! He was an asshole." Everyone in the helicopter turned to Allison with shocked expressions. "Well, he was, and he treated me like shit."

"Do you hear the nastiness coming out of her mouth?" Doc chided.

"I do and it ruins my image of you, Miss Reeves," Priest jokes as a smile came across his face.

"Yep, safest choice... you all will be better off sticking with us... it's safer that way," Shaw added, stuttering. Priest struggled to hold back a snicker.

"What, safer? Are you serious? You two have been getting cozy over there and..." Doc started to say.

Shaw cut Doc off by reaching over, grabbing his plate carrier and pulling him around Allison until their faces were an inch apart. "Let me tell you something, Hoss. You are this close to me snapping you in two and having the halves facing in opposite directions." Allison reached and patted Shaw on his arm and he let Doc go and leaned back in his seat.

Allison took his hand and put it on her lap between her two hands. She gave Doc a look that said, "I just saved your life, so back if off some." Doc raised his eyebrows and then looked out the window.

"Spider, this is Father."

"Copy Father."

"The two civilians are coming with us to HQ."

"Sarge, I will need to get fuel soon, Doug said

Priest nodded at him, "Spider, how are you set for fuel? We are low and will need to make a pit stop."

"Copy that. We are low as well. Stand by for refuel location coordinates."

They planned two fuel stops because the aircraft wouldn't make the 467 miles back to Fort Campbell. Webb chose Toledo, Ohio, and Louisville, Kentucky for the two fuel stops.

The shock of Myles and Abarra's deaths were weighing heavily on the team. Some of them had been together for three or more years. They could measure the life of a soldier in dog years to represent the bond that brothers make in an account of time that others may take ten years or more to achieve. That they had been a team for at least three years, some longer, was a testament to the connection of his brotherhood.

Priest's group turned around based on the orders from Captain Webb. They had made the preparations to change course to Toledo Express Air Guard Station Airport. They would make it there sooner than Webb's team, so he and Webb discussed the mission and tactical protocols as far as providing security while fueling.

After a considerable amount of flight time, Doug glanced down at his GPS and made a face like he smelled something bad. Priest looked over and saw the confusion. "Hey Doug, what's up?"

"Not sure, but I think something is wrong with my navigation controls, specifically my GPS. I've flown this area many times and we should come up on Toledo Airport right about now, but I see nothing resembling an airport. The GPS says it's 5 miles northwest from our target location, but I'm looking at what looks like Marble Lake, which means we are way off course."

Priest asked, "Doug, can we monitor Webb and Eagle One?"

"Negative. We can communicate with them, but not track them. This bird can only monitor aircraft in its general vicinity. They are too far for us to track."

"All right. Spider, this is Father. Do you copy?"

"Go ahead, Father."

"What are your coordinates? We are having trouble with our navigation equipment and our GPS has us off course."

Webb relayed his coordinates and his trajectory flight path. "Shit," Priest said to Doug. "We are approximately eighty miles off course."

"What, that can't be." Doug checked his instruments again and according to them; he was right on course.

"Spider, our GPS has us eighty miles off course. Be advised, we may have to set down in an unfriendly area to refuel."

"Damn, Father. I don't like it, but we don't have enough fuel to come to where you are."

"Understood. We will refuel and meet you in Louisville."

"Copy that. Keep your damn head on a swivel and get to Louisville ASAP, Spider out."

Priest turned to Doug, "Where do you think we are?"

"Well, based on the horizon and the land, I would say close to Coldwater, Indiana somewhere."

"Are you aware of any close airports or refuel points?"

Doug acknowledged and remembered a small airfield he had come across a few times.

Twenty minutes later they sighted the airport. They circled the area looking for any infected, so they buzzed it three or four times with no movement. After the final flyover, Doug located the fuel tanks.

"They're over at the maintenance building right there." Doug was pointing to a tan painted building sitting to the right of three small hangers, which probably housed two or three single engine airplanes. Across from the hangers were two buildings that housed support vehicles for the airport. Most of the pavement on the flight line wasn't in the best of shape, and there were cracks throughout with various weeds growing out of them. Most of the buildings had seen better days suffering from peeling paint, rusted pipes and faded signs.

"Guess we will have to take a chance and see what we find."

Shaw quipped, "Famous last words."

"Ok boys, you know the drill. Doc, Shaw and myself will provide security. Doug stays in the bird and Allison pumps."

"Wait, what?" Shaw stutters. "Why is Allison going out to pump fuel?"

Priest looks at Allison, "Can you fly a helicopter?"

"Ah….no, I can't."

"Ok, there is your answer. Doug is the only way any of us have a way out of here. If it makes you feel any better, Shaw, you can cover that side. Her safety is strictly in your hands. Feel better?" Shaw just looked at him and Priest gave him an enormous ass smile.

Doc started giggling. Shaw leaned over to face Doc, but Allison patted his arm.

"It's ok, I got this. You can cover my ass, but just don't stare at it too long." Shaw blushed, which made Doc laugh even louder. Allison slapped Doc hard on the shoulder.

"Ow" he howled.

"Cut it out or I will let Shaw do whatever he wants." Shaw then leaned forward past Allison, looked at Doc with a shit-eating grin, and cracked his knuckles. Doc stopped laughing and turned to look out his window.

"Ok, heads up," Priest barked. Doc and Shaw immediately went into business mode, which was one thing Priest liked most about the two. Doug navigated the helicopter down and rotated to get the fuel port next to the tanks. Doug kept the engine running as the team jumped out. Shaw took the copilot side with Allison, which was the side with the fuel port. Doc took the pilot side and Priest took the nose and Overwatch. With the noise of the rotors, it was hard to hear, so Priest used his squad comms. "Shaw, report."

"All good here, Sarge. Allison is fueling as we speak, and I see no infected."

Doc reported, "All good here too, Sarge. No infec....". A shot rang out and struck the chopper a couple feet from Doc's head. "I've got contact," Doc came over the comms.

"Who the fuck would shoot at us," Priest thought. He rotated behind the aircraft to see where that shot had come from, and Doc did the same. It didn't take Sherlock Holmes to figure it out as several soldiers came out of one hanger with weapons a hundred yards away.

Priest shouted, "We're with the US Army, 13th/101st. Do not shoot." The soldiers continued to fire but not accurately and as they got closer, Doc could see the blood on their faces and the twitching head movement.

Doc keyed the comms, "We have infected. These soldiers are infected."

"You sure?" Priest asked.

"Positive."

"Then fuck them up," Priest replied. Priest and Doc opened up sending 5.56mm down range and started taking the soldiers out. Shaw stayed guarding Allison and his area of responsibility, which regardless of his feelings for Allison, was what they trained him to do. There were a dozen of the infected, who were easily dispatched. However, behind them another wave of soldiers come pouring out of the hangar.

Shaw keyed, "We are full. Let's get the hell out of here."

"Copy that. Move people and I'll lay down suppressive fire," Priest took out the front runners of the group, jumped in the chopper and they took off heading for Louisville.

CHAPTER 16

Eagle One's pilots had received no communication back from the tower at Louisville International Airport. It was also strange was that they had not picked up any comms from any other aircraft when they entered Louisville's airspace responsibility.

"Can this shit spread this quickly and be this devastating? I mean, no response from the tower, no aircraft identified in the general area. It's just nuts," the pilot proclaimed.

"From what we have seen since this shit started, I can believe it. People don't see the infected as anything less than their friends or family at the start, and then when the shit hits the fan, they realize something is horribly wrong way too late. That's how they get close enough to bite or they just overpower them," Webb stated.

The pilot buzzed over a few times, and the scene was like Fort Wayne Airport, only a hundred times worse. Webb was taking in the scene and the seven levels of Hell from Daunte's Inferno came to mind. This place literally looked like an esoteric scholar would have described as Hell or what Hell should look like.

There were fires all over the airport, they destroyed planes, bodies littered the ground and pools of blood covered multiple areas. Buildings ravaged and fires rolled out the windows. Papers and furniture littered the ground, while husks of bodies hung out of broken windows.

A massive wave of dread froze Webb's heart as he looked upon the "End of Days". The rest of the team were just as dumbfounded by what they were witnessing.

"I spent some time in Somalia, Uganda and the Congo and have seen mass destruction, massacre and complete annihilation of villages. Nothing I saw was even close to this scale," Dr. Costa muttered. She had tears in her eyes as she spoke. She watched as the scenes of Armageddon rushed past her eyes. "My God, what have they done?" she cried.

Webb didn't know who she was talking about, seeing how many people were culpable. Was she talking about the Dutch and German scientists who created the first strain? Was it the faction of Iranian, Palestinian, and Pakistani scientists who distorted and corrupted the strain to their warped sense of satisfaction? Or was it the ISIS fighters who stole the strain and exposed the world to it? It was difficult to nail down who she really held responsible for what she was witnessing right now.

Kennedy put a soft hand on her shoulder, which startled her at first. She quickly calmed down and gave him a smile in appreciation.

"Well, it's your call Capt." the pilot verbalized. "What do you want to do?"

Webb thought for a few seconds, "I have an idea. Take us down to about twenty feet off the deck and hover."

"Sir?"

"Let's see if it will draw out any infected still in the immediate area. We are getting ambushed a lot and I am tiring of it. I think it might be because these things are still thinking and aren't mindless. Even animal predators have the basic instincts of stalking their prey. Ambushing, springing traps and working together to achieve their results. I have a theory that the infected hold a certain amount of that function in their brains, recall it and act on that instinct."

Webb keyed squad comms, "Everyone be ready. We will see if the kids want to come out and play today." They all acknowledged and opened the side doors to provide lanes of fire, just in case things went to shit. The pilot did as instructed and descended to about 10 feet off the deck and hovered. All held their breath as they waited for what might happen next, and for 30 seconds, nothing did. Just then, a throng of infected came out of all directions screaming and shrieking, heading toward the helicopter.

"Oh no, look at them all," Shin said in amazement.

"Yeah, there have to be thousands," Neville replied. As the horde rushed out, they began throwing debris at the chopper.

"Shit," the pilot yelled. Several objects clanged off the sides and bottom of the helicopter. The front windshield was then covered in a brown substance like mud, which made visibility impossible. "Son of a bitch," the pilot exclaimed, as he turned on the wipers, just smearing the substance. It made visibility worse, and then the stench reached everyone's noses.

"What the fuck who shit themselves?" Neville yelled.

Webb answered, "No way, is that what they just threw at us? It's what is on the windshield."

"Can you become infected with bodily fluids?" Shin asked Dr. Costa.

Dr. Costa showed a face like she was thinking for a moment, then answered in an agitated state, "In the original strain, contagion was not an issue. Somehow, in the original strain's defilement, they have altered the primary chemical bonds between the fundamental elements. My educated guess, from what I have witnessed in the last 48-72 hours, is that yes, it is quite possible to contract the virus through other bodily fluids. Just as long as those fluids haven't been absent from the body for a prolonged period."

"Fuck me running," Webb said. "They can now make weapons from their shit and piss, spreading the virus."

The pilot yelled back, "Buckle in, we got to get out of their range." The pilot jerked the chopper to the right to escape a group of infected throwing the bags of body fluids. People had unbuckled to get a look out the window at the devastating carnage, and it threw Kennedy out of his seat and onto the deck. He came down on his knees hard and let out a howl of pain as they threw a bag through the door. The bag burst, dousing everything with the liquid.

"What the hell was that?" Kennedy yelled. He was covered in the fluid. "Fucking got in my mouth."

Shin smelled his sleeve, which had some liquid. "Ah, Captain his is urine. It smells like urine."

"Holy fuck, he's right." Neville adds as he smells his own clothes.

Kennedy's eyes bugged out of his head. "It's in my mouth. That fucking shit is in my mouth!"

There was a loud bang, followed by a repeated scraping sound. Before anyone could react, a deafening crack echoed and then warning wails started sounding, as the Blackhawk started spinning out of control. "Fucking hell, we just lost the tail rotor." The pilot yelled.

Webb yelled, "Hold on!"

Neville and Shin reached out to grab Kennedy, but the Blackhawk tilted to its side while spinning and Kennedy slid out the open door screaming.

"Fuck!" yelled Neville. "I couldn't grab him."

Dr. Costa screamed and covered her face.

"We need to clear out some of this crowd. Get on that Minigun, Corporal!" Webb screamed at the crew chief. The crew chief charged the weapon and started firing. The Minigun began chewing up figures running around as clouds of mist with blood, brain matter, bits of bone and significant amounts of bodily fluids dispersed tens of yards from the epicenter of the mass. Firing of the mini-gun continued as the helicopter approached the ground.

With the tilt of the aircraft, the rotors were now meeting the mass of infected with a blood bath rivaling any slasher film ever made. Bodies separated at the torso and arms, legs and heads detached and launched yards away. The amount of blood spewing from all the bodies caught in the helicopter's rotor wash became an enormous cloud of crimson falling hundreds of yards over the flight line.

Finally, the rotors contacted the ground and churned up more of the already mutilated bodies along with chunks of concrete. The rotors spun for a few seconds before a couple snapped off and flew through the encroaching crowd of infected.

The Blackhawk came to rest on its left side. A smell of blood and gore mixed with jet fuel and burning flesh made the team gag. Smoke hung in the air and made seeing their surroundings near impossible.

"Move, move, move." Webb barked. "We have to get the hell out of here." The team was already unbuckling and climbing up to the open side door facing the sky.

Shin reached the opening first and surveyed the area. "Help us, Buddha." Shin uttered. He was sitting on the side of the Blackhawk, looking around the crash site. There were bodies, piles of viscera and seas of blood spread across the landscape as far as the eye could see. Many of the infected were still alive, but were not in the best shape. Shin put a few down as the rest of the team made their way to the top of the open side.

"Jesus H. Christ," Neville spat. He slid over to set up his sniper rifle to cover the team's exit of the downed aircraft.

Webb exited and looked on the ground. "Unfortunately, we will have to wade through all this shit. My Team will use their balaclavas, all others make a scarf out of your shirts. Keep your mouths covered and don't let any of this stuff enter your body."

Dr. Costa, who was still in tears, made her way out of the helicopter. Her face turned ashen when she viewed the scene in front of her. "Oh my God?"

"Come on Doctor, we have to move," Webb persuaded. She slid down to the ground, and he caught her.

"Aargh," came from inside of the Blackhawk. "Shin help me, he's stuck," the copilot pleaded. Shin went back down inside and made his way to the cockpit. The copilot was trying to help the pilot, but wasn't having much luck. "My leg is pinned. I can't seem to pull it out," the pilot cried. Shin looked down at the pilot's legs and the control panel and center console smashed his shins.

"We must try to apply leverage to free his leg," Shin instructed, motioning to the copilot.

"Ah, Capt., we have company arriving," Neville reported. "A couple dozen infected making their way toward the crash site directly on our six. Estimate 325 yards and closing."

"Copy that. Shin, be quick. We have infected heading this way quickly."

"Working on it, sir,"

Neville adds to his previous report, "Sir, Kennedy is in the group's front leading them right to us."

"Damn it," Webb responded. "Neville, give him some respect, please."

"Yes, Sir." A shot reported as Kennedy's head exploded and his body hit the ground. "Sorry, brother," Neville whispered.

"Shin, how's it going in there? We got to go!" Webb inquired.

"It's not budging Sir; the panel is smashed against his legs."

"What if I come in and help?"

"Negative, Sir. The space is too tight. The two of us can barely fit."

Neville's head was beading sweat. "Sir, they are still coming, you want me to thin the herd?"

"Only the ones that are breaking away in front of the pack. Don't waste ammo on the rest."

Boom… boom. "Got the two front runners, but they are getting closer," Neville reported.

"Get me the fuck out of here. Come on!" Shouted the pilot.

"We're trying," the copilot responded. The pilot started thrashing and bucking, trying to get loose. Shin was trying to calm him down while they tried to free him.

Boom, boom, boom… "We're getting friendly close sir and we will play tonsil hockey with these fucks in the next minute."

"Shin, sit rep," Webb barked.

"No good, Sir. He is wedged in too tight."

"Fuck!" Webb spat. He sighed heavily. "Shin, we must show respect."

"Understood, Sir," Shin quickly pulls his Glock and fires a round in the back of the pilot's head. He says a quick prayer, then turns to exit the helicopter as the copilot just stood there with his mouth open. "Come on, Sir. We have to leave." Shin climbed his way up, but was grabbed by his leg and pulled down. He fell on the deck and was suddenly having to fend off punches.

"You fucking asshole! You murdered him!" Shin was getting ready to retaliate when the punches stopped. He looked up to see the copilot pointing his pistol at him, tears streaming down his face. "You motherfucker! You just fucking killed him in cold bloo...." Bang! The copilot slumped and fell to the ground with a hole in his forehead.

Neville re-holstered his Glock. "Come on brother, we don't have time for this shit." He stuck his hand out to help Shin out of the downed chopper. They joined Webb and Dr. Costa running into the nearest hangar.

"We need to find some transportation, because it's looking like we're driving from here on out," Webb looked at Dr. Costa. "Look for any available vehicles." He stopped her, "With keys. That BS in the movies doesn't work with any vehicles made in the last 20 years." She nodded, and they separated, leaving Webb to look around the hangar and not finding anything. He went out the side door of the hangar to check the parking lot.

The lot was mostly empty except for a few sedans, which he quickly checked two of with no luck. He went to check a third when he heard an engine and then a high rev. Running to the front of the hangar, he saw a 4-wheel drive pickup coming at him at a top rate of speed. It jumped the curb, scraped the corner of the building and stopped about 10 feet from Neville. He was white as a sheet and cussing in some French/Cajun/English mangle.

Dr. Costa opened the door. "Come on. Let's go."

"Shit," Webb exclaimed. They started running for the truck, "Neville you drive, Doctor in the back with Shin and I'll navigate." They all were in and Neville took off quickly, putting distance between them and the horde.

CHAPTER 17

Priest continued to hail Webb on the radio and the lack of contact had him worried about connecting back up with the rest of the Team.

"I can't reach Webb, but our plan stays the same. We make our way to Louisville and regroup there." They had been in the air for about 15 minutes when they felt vibrations in the aircraft.

"Doug, you feel that?" Priest looked over to him.

"Yeah, and I don't like it. Feels like it could be our vertical stabilizer or our tail rotor linkage. Either way, we should set down and check it out."

"Copy that." Priest turns around, "We need to check out some mechanical issues with the bird and we must set down to do it. You boys know the drill."

"What do you think, Sarge?" Doug asked. "Either a huge parking lot or in the middle of a highway so we can see anything coming from a mile or so." They were out in the middle of nowhere, so the places to set down were plentiful.

Doug looked around at the landscape, "If I can guess to our location, I would say somewhere around Auburn, twenty miles from Fort Wayne. I have basically just been following Rt. 69 south since we determined our GPS is tits up."

A spot in the middle of Rt. 69 with excellent 360-degree visibility was identified and Doug descended. The vibrations had gotten worse and were much worse when they landed. The team exited and deployed to provide security.

Priest kept his head up to search for any potential threat but followed Doug. He noticed quite a few more bullet holes in the side than he previously thought were there. Doug stopped three quarters of the way down the tail boom. He stuck his finger in quite a sizable hole in the sheet metal. He opened the tail motor drive shaft cover and started cursing.

Priest walked up behind Doug, "Not good, I take it?"

"No, not good at all. Looks like a couple of those rounds hit us and damaged the tail rotor drive shaft." Doug was inspecting the rest of the tail.

"Is it safe to fly?"

"Normally, no. We would usually ground a bird for something like that, but these aren't normal times. It won't last forever and with the centrifugal force during rotation makes the damage feel a lot worse in flight."

Priest thought for a second. "Ok, we take it back up and fly fairly close to the ground in case this thing goes and we drop from the sky. We should be able to auto-rotate and perform a skid landing. On our way to Louisville, we will scout for other transportation, possibly a vehicle, and drive the rest of the way? It shouldn't be but a few hundred miles."

"Yeah, that's our best bet." Doug said nervously.

Priest whistled loudly, stuck his finger in the air while moving his hand in a circle, the hand sign for mount up. They ascended back in the air and Priest relayed the plan to the team. "Doug, try to get us past Fort Wayne, because we already know what that place is like."

The sky was blue, with no clouds, and was as peaceful as Priest had ever seen it. The peacefulness almost made you forget about everything that had happened. It offered a facade that everything was ok, that everything would be ok, the past long forgotten. It made you think the events of the last 48-72 hours were nothing more than a nightmare and something that no longer existed while you were in the air. He knew that wasn't the case, but pretended for a few moments and enjoy the serenity while it lasted.

The aircraft was a sight, speeding along the highway only 30 feet off the ground. Much of the vibrations had gotten increasingly worse, and Doug was struggling to keep the helicopter flying straight. The tail rotor shaft was vibrating so much it made their teeth rattle in their skull. None of the vehicles that had come across were operational. Just a few multi car crashes, some burned out husks and a few vehicles lying in ditches that would take way too long to pull out even if they had the means to do so.

During the flight, Priest had found a map in the helicopter and was tracking their progress as best he could. By his calculations, they were getting close to Muncie Indiana and had discussed this should be a suitable place to find other transportation. They had agreed to do a flyby of the Delaware County Regional Airport to see about acquiring another helicopter. They flew within sight of the airport and took in the scene. The raging fires were not there, the littering of bodies and debris were absent, and no chaos was clear among the tranquil scene. Doug and Priest just looked at each other in amazement.

"There is no destruction, no anarchy, no infected that we can see. It is calm down there." Priest surmised. "It doesn't give me a warm and fuzzy." They came closer to the airport where the rest of the team could now take in the view. Priest was surveying the area, "Ok, with the lack of obvious trouble visible, but do not let your guard down.... same tactics, same training, HUA?"

They responded, "HUA."

Allison looked confused, "HUA?"

Shaw turned to her, "Yeah, HUA. H-U-A. It stands for hear, understand and acknowledge. In the military, it's a question and a response."

"Oh," she said. "I get it. Hua, Sir," she proclaimed. Priest snickered.

Doc scrunched his face, "He's not an officer, he's not a sir. He is a Sargent. He works for a living."

"Ok, I'm confused. I talked to Captain Webb back at the terminal. So, he doesn't work? Are you saying he is lazy?" Allison questioned. Doc did a face plant into his hand.

Priest spoke, "Yeah, that's correct. He's a lazy piece of shit and doesn't know his ass from a hole in the ground."

"Why do you follow him, if he doesn't know what he is doing?" She said with a serious look on her face.

"Well, we felt sorry for him because no one else wanted him," Priest continued.

"Well, that was nice of you," Allison with actual sympathy in her voice. Everyone giggled, rolled their eyes or shook their head.

Doug performed a few fly byes but no other aircraft was out on the flight line. "There may be something parked in one of the two hangars." The airport was a small local airport, but there were two small hangers, two maintenance and support buildings, along with a small diner attached to the terminal.

"How is she handling?" Priest looked at Doug.

"To be honest, my arms and legs are like jelly trying to hold this pig as straight. I won't be able to hold it much longer."

"Ok, set it down in the middle of the flight line. That is give us enough distance to react to anything threatening."

Doug nodded and brought the aircraft down while spinning it a few times to clear the area before setting it down.

"Ok, team deploy. Doug, keep it running in case the shit hits the fan. Allison, you stay in here, we may be hauling ass back here." She nodded hesitantly.

Priest exited the helicopter, "Ok, on me." Priest took point followed by Doc and then Shaw. They strode quietly to the left of the two hangars. The pedestrian door was to the left of the enormous hangar doors. Both of the hangar doors were closed.

Priest tried the door, and it was unlocked. He nodded to Doc and Shaw. Shaw was ready to breach and with that M48 was ready to inflict some serious damage. They breached the door and found a few small luggage carrying carts. All three exited and stalked over to the office area where a figure stepped out. Immediately they trained their guns on the figure.

The figure spit on the ground, "What ya'll doing here, pointing those damn things in my face?" A man about 65 years old was standing there staring at them. He was wearing old work boots, jeans, a flannel shirt, suspenders, and an old faded Indiana University ball cap that hiked up and toward the back of his head. He sounded like he was from down south as opposed to Indiana.

"Sorry, Sir," Priest spoke up as they lowered their rifles. "What are you doing here?"

"I work here, what the hell are you boys doing here?"

He was a cantankerous old shit, Priest thought. "Sir, are you aware of what is going on out there?"

"Yep, at least what I understand about it. Everybody else skedaddled. That's why all the aircraft are gone."

"Why haven't you left yet?"

"Well," he spit, "I really don't have any other place to go, and besides, I ain't messin' with all that shit with evacuating and whatnot. Being shoved in a shelter with a hundred other people, I can't stand. No, thank you. So, I guess you boys are heading out too?"

"Yes, sir. Trying to make our way back to Fort Campbell," Doc answered.

"Yep, you got a little way to go. So why you here? Need fuel or something?"

"Well, sir, our helicopter has some mechanical problems, and we landed here to see if we could repair it or maybe find another aircraft," Priest answered.

"Well, there is nothing left here, but I could look at what you got out there." The old man said.

"Thank you, Sir." Doc ran out and motioned for Doug to shut it down. They all walked out as Doug and Allison exited.

Priest motioned to the old man, "Doug, this is… Sorry Sir, I didn't catch your name."

"Names Henry Gerald Thompson, but everybody calls me Tug."

"Tug, I'm Priest, this is Doc, Shaw, Doug our pilot and finally Allison."

"Hmm, Miss Allison, you look familiar." He looks at the helicopter and sees News Channel 8 on it. "Ah, that's where I've seen you."

"Oh, you watch our news?" She asked.

"Sometimes, you're all right, but that Steve Atkins fella on there is a complete jackass. Don't know is ass from a hole in the ground. Just saying."

"You're not wrong, Tug. He's an asshole in actual life." Tug's eyebrows went up. He showed something that could pass for a smile and tipped his hat to Allison, "Ma'am." He walked over with Doug to survey the damage.

Priest addressed the Team, "Get some chow and check your gear, one stays on watch." Shaw motions for Doc to eat and that he'll stand watch until he's done. Priest pulls out a protein bar and offers it to Allison. She takes it and then he pulled out one for himself. Doc gives one to Doug and offers one to Tug, but he turned it down.

Priest watches as Doug and Tug talk about the damage and then walk over to him. "So, where are we with this?" he asked the two.

"Well," Tug started, "That shaft is done and I wouldn't get back in the air with that damage."

Doug added, "Yeah, it's much worse than when we inspected it on the highway."

"So, it looks like we will go the vehicle route and drive the rest of the way. Tug, do you have a vehicle we can borrow?" Priest asked.

"You know, I had a nice pickup with 4-wheel drive and a crew cab. Funny thing is, with all the low crime we have here, I always left my keys in it." He takes his hat off and scratches his head. "When people were bugging out, some sum bitch stole it."

"Damn, sorry about that," Priest said.

Tug shook his head, "Shit, my dumb ass fault. You know, there is one vehicle I have here, but it's not the best for traveling. It runs and I guess with what is going on with the world, you all could take it."

"Great, where is it?" Priest said.

"Follow me." Tug walked over to the right-hand hangar and entered the pedestrian door. Seconds later, the hangar doors opened, and a loud sound like something being started reached their ears and the next thing they know, a huge bright lime green truck rolls out.

"What the fuck?" Shaw exclaimed.

Tug steps off of the truck. "Ladies and gentlemen, let me introduce you to the E-One Titan 4X4 Airport Rescue Fire Fighting vehicle. It has a 675 hp Cummins diesel, with 4-wheel drive, self-sealing tires and room for 6 if you squeeze in tight."

The Team looked at the vehicle in awe. The tires alone were five feet tall, and the vehicle looked like something the US Army had, which they called a HEMTT.

Tug was beaming like a father showing off his newborn baby. "They use this for firefighting at the Indianapolis International Airport. They sometimes deliver the vehicles here to get checked out, serviced and graphics applied before they ship them down to Indianapolis." There was just silence as the team just gawked at the truck.

Shaw was half drooling as the beast mesmerized him. "It's the most beautiful thing I've ever seen." His eyes were full of wonder.

Doc was snapping his fingers at Shaw. "Hello, hello? He's gone."

Priest turned to Tug, "Well, it's not a Ferrari, but I believe it will serve our purposes, especially if we run into any infected. Ok, team, mount up, Shaw, you're driving." Shaw let out a giggle like a little schoolgirl and the rest of the team looked at him with confused looks.

Priest motioned to Tug, "Sir, I really would like for you to come with us. You said yourself there is nothing here for you anymore and we don't know how soon the madness will take over this area. We have been through its multiple times and it ain't pretty. There is no way I could have a clear mind if we leave you..." Priest stopped because Tug had walked away. "Tug, where are you going?"

"To get my bag and my guns. You going on long winded like that, we'll be dead by the time you shut up," Tug grunted.

"Son of a bitch," Priest muttered under his breath. He continued to mumble as he got into the passenger front seat, "... bitching old fart... pain in the ass... just say you're going... crusty ass motherfucker."

Minutes later, Tug appears with a couple duffle bags and three guns, two rifles and a shotgun. Allison sat between Shaw and Priest.

Tug and Doc manned the windows in the back because they had rifles with Doug was in the middle. "Ok, Shaw, let's roll out." Shaw rubbed his hands together in excitement, grabbed the steering wheel and pulled out, heading for Louisville, Kentucky. He was whopping like a kid as they started down the road.

CHAPTER 18

The pounding on the door was getting louder, and he was trapped. There just isn't any other way to put it. No ammo, no food and no water made the situation hopeless. The only thing he had left in his possession was his combat knife. He might take out two, three, maybe four. There is no way he could kill as many infected as were on the other side of that door.

Darkness surrounded him and he was in a room he didn't recognize. This seemed to make the situation even more hopeless. He felt lost, and he was totally baffled by how he found himself in this situation, even more hopeless. His mind was muddled, but that wasn't important now because he had bigger issues to address.

The pounding was constantly getting louder. Was it because there were more fists pounding or was it because the rage was increasing in the ones already at the door? He didn't know, but he was sure that the door wouldn't hold much longer. Think, come on, think, there has to be a way out of this.

His eyes were used to the dark now, so he could somewhat see the room. It was empty except for another door on the far wall. That's it, has to be it. There is no other way out. The door the infected were pounding on was rattling and sounded like it was about to be ripped off its hinges. He had no other choice, but to run for the other door which he does puts his ear up to the surface. Listening for any sounds, he hears nothing.

Another knock to see what stirs on the other side of the door and again hears nothing. The infected started breaking through the door he had originally come through, so that decision was easy. Salvation had to be on the other side of that door.

He reached, twisted the handle and jerked the door open. Without warning, a swarm of infected charged through the open door and took Webb down. They started sinking their teeth into his face, neck and arms as Webb screamed, trying to fight off the dog pile on top of him. A faceless man with nothing but an enormous mouth and giant serrated teeth lunged and bit out half his throat. The blood gushed out of his body along with his life.

Neville almost ran off the road, responding to the scream and jerking movement from Webb. "Whoa, whoa, Captain. You all right?" Webb was breathing heavily and was wide eyed. He was trying to gain his bearings as he closed his eyes and slumped back in his seat.

"What a fucking nightmare," he exhaled. "How long was I out?"

"Couple hours, I guess." Neville was looking at him with concern.

"Where are we?"

"We just passed through Bowling Green." Neville answered.

"Seriously? That means we have an hour left."

"Yeah, Captain. You think the rest of the team is ok?"

"I sure hope so, but getting Dr. Costa back to Campbell is the highest priority. As soon as we deliver her, we resupply, grab another chopper and go after them."

"Copy that." Webb turned around to check up on everyone. Dr. Costa and Shin were both asleep. Best to leave them that way, Webb thought.

They got close to Fort Campbell and Neville stopped the truck. "Jesus Christ," he muttered as he stared out the windshield.

Webb saw it as well and tried to process it. They all exited the truck with their eyes wide and disbelief written on their faces.

The sky over Fort Campbell was black with smoke. It reminded Webb of the Saudi Oil Fields that the Taliban had set on fire. Even from this distance, they could see the overwhelming number of fires blazing out of control and the debris floating on the air current the fires generated.

"Did we enter Hell?" Dr. Costa added.

"Sure as hell looks like it," Webb answered. "No pun intended." No giggles, snicker or chuckles followed as everyone was in shock.

Just then, a police siren wailed in the distance. It got louder, as if it was coming in their direction. "Maybe we will get some information from these guys," Webb said. They could see the police car coming up the road about a quarter mile away.

"Hey Captain. Does it look like that cop car is swerving all over the road? Looks like they're drunk." Neville said, his hand shielding his eyes.

"Yeah, but I'm liking it. Neville, get some eyes on that car. Shin take up a defensive position. Doctor, head behind the truck but put about 20 feet between you and it." Webb took a knee and sighted on the car.

Neville was prone and had his scope trained on the car. He attempted to zoom in on the vehicle, but it was difficult because of the constant swerving. His skills as a sniper to track moving targets was what he was best known for. He dialed in and could get enough of a picture to assess the situation. The view of bloodied bodies, wide eyes and laughing faces was all he needed to make a determination.

"Sir, those are not normal cops. Looks like infected to me. I am seeing lots of blood and laughing faces in that patrol car."

"I trust your judgement, so take them out before they reach us."

"Will try, Sir. With that zig zagging going on, it makes it difficult."

Neville took aim and tried to lead the car in its hectic pattern. Bang! Neville puts a round through the windshield, but misses the two in the car. Bang! Another miss. The police car speeds up toward them once the shots begin and they were getting close.

"Neville, how you doing?" Webb asks in a heightened tone.

"Can't seem to get a bead on them, sir?"

"Ok gentlemen, let's get ready to receive some guests."

The Team set up in a defensive position. "Let them get a little closer and then give them shit." The car was driving erratically as it came into range.

The passenger began leaning out the window and firing a rifle in their direction. Shin had to take cover as a couple rounds landed right in front of him. Those rounds kicked up asphalt that peppered Shin's face. Webb riddled the passenger side of the car.

"Ah... Ça c'est bon," Neville grinned as he sighted the infected leaning out the passenger side window. Bang! A round flew from Neville's muzzle and found the chest of the infected. He jerked back and lost his balance off the open window. As he flipped back, he fell and rolled under the rear tires of the police car. The tire caught the side of his face, crushing the side of its skull and ripping the skin off. The face of the passenger was flung to the side of the road like a discarded piece of trash.

The team opened up, trying to eliminate the threat, sending rounds into the car, through the windshield and into the engine block. Neville took one more aim with the sniper rifle at the driver. The car had steadied some as the infected aimed the car right at them and toward the sitting truck. Bang! The driver's head exploded, and he slumped over, although the car didn't slow down much.

"Move!" Webb yelled. Everyone jumped out of the way as the police car slammed into the pickup. The police car wedged underneath the truck and with the momentum caused it to flip over and roll down into the ditch. The truck finally ended up on its roof.

"Mother fucker!" Webb screamed. "I am really tiring of this shit! Everyone okay?" The Team took a few minutes to take stock of their sanity and their equipment and weapons. They stared at the wrecked truck lying in the ditch. With their mode of transportation now inoperable, their inability to get around made things much more dangerous.

Webb stood up and stretched his back. "Well, shit," he said.

Neville looked at him, "You sound like Shaw." Webb smirked.

Shin looked at the wreck. "The journey of 1000 miles begins with one step."

"The trip to an ass whopping begins with one punch," Neville responded.

Shin looked confused, "That is not Confucius, I do not think."

Webb spoke up, "We need to assess what is going on. Is all of Campbell lost or are some of our elements still intact? None of that will happen without transportation, so the first order of business is to find some wheels."

After 20 minutes of walking, the Team came across a golf course. Neville and the Doctor stayed back out of sight while Webb and Shin scoped out the course. There were several vehicles in the parking lot and they tried each one. Shin checked the fourth one in line and it was open with the keys were in it. He motioned Webb over to join him. A couple minutes later, Neville and the doctor came out from hiding as Webb and Shin drove up in the vehicle.

Neville just stared at Webb and Shin sitting in a light blue minivan. "C'est tout? That's all you could find?"

Webb looked offended, "What? You don't like it?" He turned to Shin, "I knew we should have taken that armored Hummer instead. I just thought the minivan would serve us better as a disguise," Webb said sarcastically.

Neville should his head, "Ok, Laissez les bon temps rouler."

They entered the base with caution, driving toward their division HQ. They passed by multiple fires and various scenes of destruction as they made their way toward their unit. Some were because of car wrecks and some because of buildings that were on fire.

It was getting dark, and the fires were casting eerie shadows across the road and on the sides of buildings. It made this trip unnerving as shadows produced an atmosphere of trepidation. In highly stressful situations, your mind can deceive you and trick your eyes into seeing things that aren't really there. Combine that with the shadows created by the flickering glow, and you have a recipe for extreme paranoia.

"Do you guys see things moving around out there?" Shin was shifting his gaze from shadow to shadow.

"Nah, it's just the light from the fires," Neville explained. Immediately a figure slammed against Neville's window, screaming and trying to bite through the glass. "Bordel de merde," he shouted, and the whole car jumped in surprise.

"Go, go," Webb prodded. "Should have shot the fuck, but we don't need the added attention." They turned on the road leading up to their

HQ's and when they got within 200 yards, were forced to stop. They erected a roadblock across their path. "Shin, check it out."

"Copy." Shin got out with Webb and Neville, covering him out their windows. Shin approached the road block cautiously, climbed over the barrier and disappeared from sight. Seconds later, he came running back, hurdled the barrier and then stopped, bent over with his hands on his knees. He puked all over the ground in front of him. Everyone ran up to him as he tried to articulate what he saw, "Must have been large battle.... worst thing I've ever seen."

"Doctor, stay here, please. Neville, with me." Webb and Neville made their way over the barrier and through a mass of military vehicles. As they came out on the other side, their breath caught in their throats.

CHAPTER 19

Shaw was like a kid in a candy store. "Damn, if we had one of these on the farm." He was in love with their newly gained transportation, a brand-new E-One 4X4 AFPP vehicle. A massive tire truck that was built like a tank.

They were rolling down Rt 69 and approaching Indianapolis, as they had planned to say out of downtown and take the beltway around. They had had no communication in the last 24 hours, either with their team or command. Stopping just outside of the city limits to top off with fuel.

"Ok Shaw, take it easy. We have to navigate some of these roads, as we enter populated areas, potential road blocks from abandoned cars are likely." The route around Indianapolis was uneventful. There were a few cars piled-up they had to navigate, multiple sightings of infected who were a little distance away but posed no threat.

They made the decision that Franklin, Indiana, would be a fit place to refuel. The truck wasn't the most fuel efficient, but it made up for that in utility. Two traffic pile-ups they encountered required them to detour off-road, which wasn't a problem. The huge 5-foot tires, the 4-wheel drive and the weight of the vehicle enabled it to run right through the ditches and mud. Priest had to admit he was impressed with the vehicle, and Tug had an enormous grin on his face during the sloppy detours.

As they came down Rt. 65, they could see a roadblock ahead. Shaw spit a glob of tobacco juice out the window, "You see that, Sarge?"

"Yeah, hold on." Priest gets his bino's and looked. "Well, it looks like a bunch of rednecks have blocked the road. I don't know what their intentions are, but be ready in case they get stupid. They could take advantage of the evacuation and trying to rob everyone coming through here, or they could be legitimately trying to steer people away from harm. Seeing how we don't know what is going on further south, these guys might offer us some decent information. Proceed slowly and we'll see how they react, but be on your toes." Doc and Tug checked their weapons, with Shaw and Priest doing the same. They were approximately a half mile away and Priest trained his binoculars back on them.

"They don't appear infected, but they can't seem to stand still. The boys are looking a little fidgety." As the team grew closer, the men at the roadblock leveled all their rifles at them.

Priest looked back, "Allison, get on the floor just in case the shit hits the fan." The vehicle had a loudspeaker, so Priest keyed it, "We are with the US Army Special Operations on our way to Fort Campbell. Please lower your weapons and we will pass through nice and easy."

Priest lifted the binoculars back up to his face and gave the Team a play-by-play. "Ok, they are looking at each other a little confused and seem to argue about what to do. Looking at the surrounding area, I see some stuff thrown around the area like bags, suitcases, clothes and such. I don't think all that shit is theirs, so we could be heading into a shakedown roadblock. They haven't lowered their weapons either."

Priest keyed the loudspeaker again, "Please lower your weapons and allow us to through and we will be out of your hair in no time." One man took a shot, and it ricocheted off the metal frame on the front of the vehicle. "Well, that was rude. Shaw, my good man, would you be so kind as to ram through that mother fucker? We really don't have time for this shit."

With a huge shit-eating grin on his face, Shaw sped up and got the truck up to speed.

Priest turned back, "Get ready for impact and stay down as much as possible." Priest took one more look through the binoculars.

The men took up their positions behind their truck. "Horrible place to stand," Priest thought. Shots peppered the vehicle, but none of the shots seem to be very accurate.

Shaw started giggling like a maniac, which made Priest take a quick look at him just to make sure he wasn't infected.

"Ramming speed!" Shaw yelled. It took the men at the roadblock too long to realize that the vehicle approaching them would not stop. They tried to jump out of the way or run down the ditches on each side of the road, but most were a day late and a dollar short as the old saying goes.

Shaw plowed through the middle of the two pickups they had blocked the road with, causing them to spin out of the way and the one on the right to flip over. Two men got dragged underneath the spinning pickups and the front of the truck struck another man trying to run. The crumpled front launched the man into the air and into the ditch, while another man became wedged underneath as the front tire slid across his body. The tire flayed him open, taking half his skin with it. His entrails spilled out as it pressed him into two separate pieces.

One truck flipped and landed on top of one of the fleeing men. The side of the truck ground his body and face into the ground, decapitating him. Another other man was pinned under the truck when it stopped rolling.

Shaw stopped the truck and Priest walked over to the pinned man, screaming in pain. "Give me a perimeter while I talk to this gentleman, "All right, all right, calm down."

"You almost cut me in half, you fuck!"

"Well, I tried to be nice before and you shitheads got stupid. So, what is going on in this area as far as the infected?" The man just kept screaming and cussing them. Priest stood up, shook his head and pulled his Walther PPQ. "This guy is worthless." Finger, trigger, bam. The screaming finally stopped, and he walked over to verify the rest of the men were dead. The last man on the right side, launched by one of the spinning trucks was still moving, so Priest walked over to him.

"My back is broke and I can't move. Help me." Priest kneeled down to get closer to the man.

"How would you like me to do that?"

"Kill me."

"Well, no problem there, but I will need something from you first."

The man groaned, "What?". Still in excruciating pain.

"What is the infected situation farther south?"

"We-we are from Columbus, that's a-about 20 miles south of here." Distant pounding and muffled voices yelling for help interrupted their conversation.

Priest turned his head to the direction of the noise, "Shaw, Doc, go check that out."

The two listened to see where the noise was coming from and followed it to a batch of trees a hundred yards from the highway. Parked in a clump of trees was a white box truck, and the pounding seemed to come from the back. The truck was strategically placed as to not be viewed from the highway.

"Could be an ambush, so let's go nice and easy," Shaw said. They scanned around for any potential hiding spots, but came up empty. Doc creeped up to the back of the truck and saw there was a combination lock on it.

Doc looked at Shaw, "We will have to blow it off."

Shaw nodded and then banged on the side of the truck. "You inside, back away from the back door, we are blowing the lock off." They met his command with a couple screams from inside. Doc leveled his M4, shot the lock off and lifted the roll-up door. A powerful smell of urine and feces smell came wafting out to accost their noses. They could see movement coming toward the opened end of the truck box.

"Come on out with your hands up," Shaw yelled. They heard some shuffling coming toward them and slowly, three females staggered toward the open door. They had one hand shielding their eyes from the daylight.

The girl in the front spoke in a whispered tone, "P-p-please don't hurt us, we just want to go home. Let us go, please. There were tears streaming down all three of their faces.

Shaw reached out his hand to them, "US Army Ma'am, we will not hurt you. We're here to get you out of there, you are safe now." The girls broke into wailing and repeated thank you's. Doc and Shaw helped them down off the truck and the girls hugged each of them as they continued to cry.

The three girls looked like college students, based on the sweat shirts they were wearing. All three were dirty and looked like they hadn't had a shower in a week. They were trembling with wide eyes, and they huddled together for comfort.

"What happened here?" Doc asked.

One girl who introduced herself as Kim, who was the first one to speak while on the truck. She told the story, "We were heading to Louisville to visit my friend Dana's parents. With all the craziness going on, we figured they were the closest to us and the best place to go. We came up to this roadblock and stopped because the men had guns. They asked for money to allow us through their roadblock, but we didn't have much. They changed their mind and didn't want the money anymore." She stopped and her body started to shake and tears were streaming down her face. "T-T-They took other things instead." She started sobbing and Doc gave her a hug, which she held onto to him for some time.

"Mother fuckers!" Shaw spat.

Kim composed herself and thanked Doc.

"How long have you been in that truck?" Doc asked.

"I don't know, but it has to be three or four days, maybe."

"Ok, let's get you guys out of here." They trudged out of the woods and onto the highway.

Doc led them to their truck, but Kim stopped, "We have some suitcases somewhere around here and would like to get out of these nasty clothes. Could we please change?"

"Sure," Doc said. By this time, Allison and Doug saw the girls and climbed out of the truck. They ran down to offer help.

"We'll take care of them," Allison told Doc.

"Ok, the truck has water in its tanks if they want to wash off. We all have soap in our rucks so just grab anyone's." Allison nodded her head and looked at Shaw. He gave her a sympathetic look, and she went with them to find their clothes.

Doc and Shaw formed up as Shaw whispered in Priest's ear about what they found out.

"Son of a bitch," Priest yelled. He looked at Shaw. "You're not serious?"

"Yeah Sarge, we are." Rage boiled up in Priest and he knew he would blow. He turned back to the man lying on the ground, "You fucking little piece of shit! All this fucking shit going on and you cock suckers are preying on innocent girls? What the hell is wrong with you fucking scum bags."

The man was squirming some, "It wasn't my idea. I swear."

"Well, did you stop it?"

"It was one against four. What was I supposed to do?"

"Yeah, you are such an innocent. How about we go ask the girls how you were involved."

"No-no, they will say anything. They want to get back at all of us."

Priest walked over and kicked him in his teeth, knocking out two them. "Can't feel your legs, but I bet you felt that shit," Priest spat.

Doc walked over to where the women were on the other side of the truck, but Doug stopped him and called for Allison. She came over, "They are taking showers over there and trying to wash away the filth. I'm not talking about dirt either."

Doc looked at her, "Oh, sorry." He stopped, "Washing away filth, all three of them?" Allison nodded. "Shit, could you ask them if it involved a guy with a buzz cut and a neck tattoo of a spider?" Doc asked.

Allison disappeared behind the truck and came back a couple minutes later, "Yes, he was the leader of these assholes and apparently liked it rough. All the girls have bruises all over their bodies." Doc just shook his head. He walked back over to Priest and relayed the information.

Priest was hot, and this was definitely something he didn't like dealing with. He turned to the piece of shit on the ground. "What's your fucking name?"

"Randy."

"Well, Randy. It seems we have a problem; well, you have a problem. You mind explaining to me how those women got all those bruises."

"I don't know, maybe they're clumsy."

Priest waked over and stomped Randy's wrist as a loud crack echoed amongst the team. Randy screamed in pain and started sobbing, "I told you my fucking back is broke and I can't move, just fucking kill me already."

"In due time, Randy, in due time. Now, what does Louisville look like as far as the infected. What have you heard?" Between the sobs and pleading, Randy tells them that Louisville is lost and the infected are all over the city. "If that is the case, then why are you morons out here bullshitting around? What if the infected found their way here?"

"I dunno, we didn't think about that."

"You fuckheads only thought about violating girls!" Priest saw movement out his peripheral vision and turned his head to see the three young women walk around the AVFF truck. They were all still scared and standing there with wet hair. Two of them had a black eye and one with a split lip and cuts on her cheek. "Wow, Randy. You like to soften them up first, don't you?" Randy said nothing, just laid there blubbering.

Priest walked over to join the girls and the rest of the Team. He looked at them, studying the girls' faces. This was when his steely blue eyes showed compassion. "I am sorry this happened to you girls and I wish we would have gotten here sooner." The girl with the shorter brown hair named Dana ran over and hugged him with tears in her eyes.

He didn't know if it was the shock wearing off or if it was because she might need reassurance from a father figure. Whatever the reason, it didn't matter. It was what she needed at the time, and he would not deny her that. She held on for quite a while, sobbing, and then finally let go. She apologized, but Priest waved it off and told her it was perfectly all right.

The girl with the long black hair, named Mia, seemed like just couldn't stand there and the human exchange of comfort and assurance. She ran up to Priest and stood there looking at him with tears in her eye.

Priest was a hard man who had killed countless people, but those people had made their choice to do evil and he was just the one to bring forth the day of reckoning. Yes, that was who he was, but in these moments, he realized he was someone else. Someone who he didn't truly know, but someone he didn't mind sharing with others in these types of situations. He fought to hold back tears as he saw Mia standing there with obvious pain and fear on her face. He reached for her and she grabbed onto him like he was her last breath of oxygen. Almost like her entire existence depended on her ability to hold on to him. It was too much for him, and tears began flowing down his cheeks and into his beard.

Tug was also in tears, knowing what these girls went through. Kim, who was standing next to him, reached out and grabbed Tug's hand with both of hers. He accepted the gesture. Hell, he welcomed it. Dana was holding onto Allison with Shaw close to them. Except for crying and some sniffling, it was dead quiet. Mia pulled back and Priest asked if she was ok. She nodded.

Priest turned to Allison. "Could you please get them settled in the truck?"

"Come on girls, let's get you settled in."

As soon as they left, Priest turned around and now his blue eyes turned stone cold as he walked back to Randy. "You know, it's bad enough people must deal with all this fucked up shit as the world looks like it's ending. Then we have you mother fuckers causing terror and violating any innocence these poor girls have left. Shit, that these young women will have to deal with for the rest of their fucking life."

"I can't take things back and really who gives a shit. They will die; you will die, we're all going to die. Just kill me already."

"Whoa, getting a brief rush of courage suddenly, are we? Ok Randy, you're right. I should give you exactly what you deserve." Priest pulled his combat knife and squatted down to face Randy. He reached out his knife towards Randy's throat as he braced himself for the killing blow. Lightning quick, Priest moved the knife from his throat to his face to cut out one of Randy's eyes. Randy screamed and wailed like a banshee.

Priest let him squirm around for a bit before slapping him in the face, "Focus Randy, focus on me!" Randy lifted his head to look at Priest. He was sobbing with blood running down his cheeks.

"You know Randy, you seem a little scared and in pain. I want you to think about how those girls over there felt when you and your piece of shit buddies raped and terrorized them." Randy just screamed and cursed Priest and the girls.

"Good bye, Randy," Priest said just before he cut out his other eye.

Priest stand up and yelled over the screams, "Guess what, you fuck? I won't kill you and you will exist for a little while lying in your own disgusting filth, not being able to move and not being able to see. Whether it's dehydration, hunger, exposure, being ravaged by animals or shredded apart by the infected, you will die eventually and you won't see it coming. You won't even know what it is. The only thing you will know is that death is coming. We are the Light Reapers, so reap the whirlwind, you fucking piece of shit."

Priest walks away, but stops to turn around back to Randy. Priest smiles and then stomps on Randy's other wrist. He lets out another scream between his sobs as Priest walks back to the truck and gets in. They drive off, leaving Randy screaming and wailing on the ground.

CHAPTER 20

"God help us all," Webb mutters as he feels dizzy and his legs get wobbly. He puts his palms on his knees and doubles over. Neville wasn't faring much better witnessing the scene revealing itself before them. The two were standing on the edge of the parade grounds, which was up as an evacuee shelter.

They erected twenty to thirty large tents on the grounds along with various pallets of MRE's and bottled water. First aid and Red Cross stations were scattered among the tents set up to house evacuees.

The scene looked like a well-organized support facility except for all the dead bodies littering the ground. Hundreds of bodies were lying in various states of death. The white tents were a background of contrast for the ominous red blood splattered throughout the camp.

Actual puddles were forming because of the significant amount of blood spilled during the massacre that seemed to have taken place here. Piles of bowels, intestines and every other internal organ were lying next to the bodies that once contained them. So many people had died with looks of terror on their face, with eyes still open and mouths agape.

The flies had already made themselves at home with the feast laid out across the landscape. Crows, buzzards, and every other scavenger had found their way here to gorge on the bounty. These two men, who had seen the battlefield many times, were now seeing civilians massacred and ravaged.

Women bloodied, children disemboweled, old people with their throats torn out. Brass was laying all over the ground as thousands of spent shell casings cluttered the landscape as far as the eye could see.

They overran soldiers who were here to defend these people. Military vehicles to transport to the civilians and those made to provide security just sat abandoned. Some vehicles had bodies of soldiers still contained in them.

"Jesus Christ," Neville whispered. "Looks like the infected took this place down quick."

"Yeah, probably had people coming in here who were already infected," Webb responded. "Question is… where are all the infected now?"

"I don't know, but I don't want to be standing here when they come back." Neville quipped.

"That makes two of us." Webb replied as the two men spun and sprinted back to the truck. Everyone piled in based on the urgency of Neville and Webb making their way back to the vehicle.

"What's happening up there?" Dr. Costa asked.

"You don't want to know." Neville reversed the truck and spit dirt and gravel as he made their way out of there. "Captain, should we try to see if HQ still exists?"

"Yeah, that's our only move, Sargent. After that, I have no idea."

The atmosphere in the truck was draped in stunned silence. Those that had witnessed the scene couldn't believe what they just saw.

"How could it go so bad in such a brief time? How were the troops overrun so quickly? What does this mean for the rest of the world?" Shin pondered this as he attempted to meditate and bring his blood pressure level down.

Webb just stared out the windshield in disbelief, trying to deal with his dry mouth and scratchy throat. He sat there staring and blinking shell shocked as he was unconsciously shaking his head.

"You okay, Captain?" Neville was glancing over at him.

"Hell, no I'm not… but I will be."

"Copy that. Feeling the same."

After a couple more turns, they started down Range Road, which would take them back home, back to HQ, which was the only home they had known for three years. Once they are home, they could renew their spirit, their strength, their sanity. They can resupply, figure this whole crazy thing out and what is still real in the world and what is fantasy. They have blurred those lines over the past weeks and now Webb didn't know if he could distinguish between the two.

They came up on the main road that led to their unit HQ, and the overwhelming smell assaulted their noses long before they laid eyes on their HQ building. The powerful stench of decay, rot, cordite, sweat and fear all amassed into something living on its own. It all manifested into an environment of despondency and desolation. The demeanor inside the truck completely changed and the tension and anxiety were palpable. They exchanged looks between the team and as they proceeded closer, their breath caught in their throats.

The picture in front of them was one of barbarians assaulting the ramparts as those behind the walls were trying to repel the assailing horde. The two things missing to complete the scene were a drawbridge and a moat.

Surrounding the HQ garrison were convex containers stacked one on top of another, creating a barrier wall. There were rows of concertina wire along the ground about 10 feet in front of the barrier and mounted on top of the barrier at the front facing corner. Infected were strung up in the wire at the foot of the container wall, still wriggling and trying to reach for the uninfected.

They lined soldiers along the top of the barrier shooting into the multitude of infected trying to breech the fortifications. Countless bodies littered the ground for hundreds of yards in every direction. By the looks of the fortifications, this fight for the compound has been taking place for quite a while.

Acrid smoke ascended into the air from countless fires raging all around the HQ. Fires were burning from roasting bodies, destroyed vehicles and scorched earth. All the fires produced a nauseating and toxic haze that seemed to float around looking for lungs to pollute like it had a mind of its own. Countless infected could be seen attempting to gain access to the compound like a frenzied mob. Their deep-rooted instincts driving them into an agitated state of wanting to spread the virus and just kill what was in front of them.

The question that kept gnawing at Webb was how were they going to get through this substantial horde without getting bitten, ripped apart, or shot. They needed to gain access to the compound, and the logistics were not as simple as they should be. Webb looks at his team. "Ok, options?"

Neville and Shin thought for a minute. "Captain, do you think any of the other units are in the same situation?"

"Probably not. It looks like all or at least most of the infected have made their way here. I am not sure if any of the other units are intact, but I doubt it."

Shin looked at him, "Maybe we could acquire an armored Humvee with .50 cal turret, blast through to clear a path, or possibly even lure some away so we can get through their makeshift gate."

Webb looked at the gate and the compound and then to Neville. Neville nodded his head. "Out fucking standing, Shin. Let's move on that."

Neville slowly backed the truck up and then turned it around. They had been stationed at this post for a few years, so they knew quite a few of the other units and possibly where to find the vehicle they were looking for.

The 358th Rakassans were a combat unit a mile or so from their HQ. They drove up slowly, even though the entire area looked abandoned. All the buildings looked desolate, not revealing any signs of life. The team made their way to the motor pool to scout out some vehicles. To their surprise, the motor pool was practically full.

"Should we roll with one or two vehicles?" Neville asked.

"Two would definitely swing the scales in our favor, so Dr. Costa would either have to man a weapon or drive one vehicle," Webb stated. They all turned to Dr. Costa.

"What, I can do either. I have driven the Rubicon and Telluride courses in my Jeep Wrangler so driving wouldn't be a problem. Bring it on." The team's eyes went wide, and they looked at each other.

"Oookay, Dr. Costa, you are with me. Neville and Shin, you are in the other," Webb directed.

Dr. Costa looked at the rest of the guys, "We really need to get rid of this Dr. Costa, shit. My name is Isabelle, but my friends call me Izzy."

"Check the vehicles and make sure you have ammo and are ready to go." The team accessed the armory to gain ammunition and ready the M24's mounted on the Humvees. They then assembled around Webb's Humvee with a map spread out on the hood.

"Here's the OP. Izzy, you and I will take the lead. We will roll right up to the larger mass in front of the gate, fire on the infected, and attempt to draw them away. Neville and Shin, you come in from the west side and flank the horde. Hopefully, we will catch them in a crossfire and thin out a significant amount of that damn herd. Do not let yourself get trapped or bogged down by the mass of numbers. Stay on the fringes of the crowd, keep your distance and pick off as many as you can. We will assess later on into the OP. Questions?"

Dr. Costa had traded in her skirt and blouse for ACV's. She was fit, which Webb had no problem noticing. She had knuckle reinforced gloves and looked like she was ready to kick some serious ass. Webb gave her a thumbs up and she smiled at him as they all loaded up and moved out toward the HQ building.

CHAPTER 21

The infected were constantly jumping against the barrier, trying to grab at the soldiers. Their ammo was running low, so the order had gone out to only fire on any immediate threat. Other than that, the soldiers were to just observe and report any issues. Their morale was lower than the remaining ammo, and desperation was setting in.

In the early morning darkness, the soldiers on top of the barrier heard automatic fire in the distance. The recognizable sound of an M24 was heard coming out of the morning gloom, followed by a Humvee unloading .50 caliber rounds into the mass of horror raging at the gate.

The red tracers looked like flaming arrows as they slammed into the agitated crowd. Appendages were torn off; bodies were shredded and blood spewed everywhere like water out of a garden hose.

Izzy drove straight at the large accumulation of infected while Webb rained .50 cal projectile death on the horde. A barrage of rounds didn't stop and ripped through multiple bodies, removing larger and larger chunks of flesh and tissue as it traveled unmercifully through the throng of infected.

The infected switched their attention and turned and advance toward the approaching Humvee. The horde moved closer, so Izzy turned and drove parallel with the crowd, while Webb sent burst after burst of lead into them. Toward the end of the HQ compound, Izzy turned left and drove at a 90-degree angle from the line of infected. They followed her and Webb just as the Team had planned.

Neville and Shin's Humvee appeared out of the dimness to the west and came toward the barrier wall. Trying to peel off the back of the group, Neville opened up with his M24 and began decimating the crowd of infected.

Shin had to keep moving as not to lose momentum due to the amount of bodies, viscera and blood that had accumulated in front of HQ and mixed with the mud. The ground was so slick the four-wheel drive spun the Humvee's tires and the vehicle was fish tailing. Rooster tails of blood and mud shot out from the tires, which reminded Neville of times back in Louisiana when he and his friends went mud bogging down in the bayou.

The crossfire between the two vehicles was eliminating scores of the infected as Webb and Neville continued firing. As the chaos was mounting to an incredible level, a truck horn blasted in the distance and headlights illuminating came from the east at a top rate of speed.

"Maybe this is another team coming to help eliminate these fucks?" Webb shouted in his squad comms. "Izzy, take us toward that truck so see can see who we are dealing with."

"Copy that," she replied.

As part of her uniform, the team made sure they gave her a squad comm rig so Webb could communicate with her. Izzy steered in the truck's direction, which was still a couple hundred yards away. The truck seemed to notice the Humvee and changed its direction to meet up with them. "Shin, continue with what you're doing and take out as many as you can. We'll meet up with this truck and report back."

"Copy, Captain."

Izzy and Webb continued on their course toward the truck as it continued to blast its horn. As the two vehicles came closer to one another, Webb saw people hanging off the side of the truck. The erratic way the truck was being driven reminded him of the police car they encountered earlier driven by the infected. "Izzy, pull off and head back toward HQ. Something tells me this truck isn't friendly."

"Copy." Izzy pulled a hard "U" and took off back the way they came. The truck still heading toward them was an US Army-5 ton, which was a good size hunk of steel and horsepower bearing down on them.

Webb could see clearly now that the truck filled with infected. A dozen were hanging off the side, screaming and brandishing homemade weapons from table legs to car parts. They had patterns draw on their bodies with blood and displayed multiple wounds. It was a sight of nightmares with the truck screaming towards them and the frenzied infected hanging off of it.

Webb turned the .50 cal toward the truck and squeezed the paddles to fire, but clicked after firing several rounds. "Fuck," he yelled. "Reloading… Izzy, get them off our ass."

"Hold on to your pelotas." Izzy steered the Humvee toward a line of trees off to their left. The pine trees were space apart and used for accenting a property line. She blasted through two of the trees that was such a tight squeeze, she clipped the outside mirrors.

"Jesus Christ, Izzy."

"I got this, I got this." The truck, being too large to fit, swerved to the left so it could go around the line of trees.

Webb was having a hard time get the .50 cal reloaded, but Izzy was doing a fine job creating distance between them and the 5-ton. This came at a price of jerking Webb from left to right, back to front and almost launching Webb right out of the turret. A close explosion to his right jolted thoughts from his mind.

"What the fuck?" Webb could feel the heat and heard shrapnel wiz past his head. He looked up and witnessed one of the infected who was hanging off the side, throw a small ball-type thing at them. Another explosion rocked them, this time to their rear. "Mother fucker! Where did they get fucking grenades?"

Webb was hot and now he was fully loaded. "Get ready for the pain, shitheads!" Webb wrenched back the charging handle and grinned as he depressed the handles. Chunk, chunk, chunk, chunk. The tracers lit a streaking red path across the darkness as the rounds slammed into bodies and machine.

Rounds decimated the 5-ton's grill and hood, sending bits of metal back into the infected hanging off the running boards. A couple dropped off, killed by the initial damage, then Webb raised the barrel up a few inches and plowed round after round into the windshield of the cab. Blood splattered on the back window and sprayed out through the open windows onto the infected still hanging off the running boards.

The 5-ton lost control as the driver slumped over the steering wheel, causing the truck to pivot and flip on its side. Webb adjusted his fire, aiming for the exposed gas tank now sticking up in the air. Baboom! The 5-ton exploded with an a-bomb inspired cloud, reducing any infected left alive to a smoldering piece of charcoal. Webb and Izzy turned their attention to the restseemed scared of the infected horde. A few stragglers remained between them and HQ. Izzy and Webb made a B-Line for the compound.

Shin and Neville were continuing to lead the infected, doing something close to a vast figure eight. They would lead a group of infected in a direction, only to circle around behind them where Neville would unload on them. It was effective, but only pulled small numbers away from the larger group.

The rest of the horde was several hundred yards away from the HQ. The make shift gate was now open and soldiers were frantically motioning for the two Humvees to drive through. Izzy was almost to the gate when Neville noticed them. He turned toward HQ and made a B-Line for it. A moment later, both Humvees had entered the open gate, and it was immediately slammed shut.

The vehicles came to a stop in the make-shift courtyard a couple hundred feet inside the gate. Webb dropped through the turret and stepped out of the vehicle. A couple soldiers ran up to and saluted as they saw that he was a captain. "Who is in charge here?" Webb asked.

"Major Harwell, Sir," a young private who was scared shitless, answered.

"What about Colonel Madison?"

"I am afraid he is no longer with us, Sir."

"No longer on this earth or no longer on this compound?" "No longer alive, Sir."

"Shit. Ok, take me to Major Harwell, ASAP!"

"Right away, sir."

Izzy had come around the front of the Humvee to have the private stop for a second and stare. "Private, this is Dr. Isabelle Costa, and she is a VIP, so let's pick it up and get her to Major Harwell, shall we?"

"Y-y-yes, sir. Follow me." The HQ building was once a showpiece for other units, posts and countries to visit and admire. It had a tall roof held up by four large columns similar to the White House. Large curving staircases were on the left and right, leading up to a central double door in the middle of the building. It had six large arborvitaes standing twenty feet tall with multiple round bushes surrounding them. They distributed flowers amongst all of them.

What was sitting before them was now a shell of that magnificent visage. Debris, dirt and supplies littered the once beautiful white marble stairs. Some bushes and arborvitaes were burned because of the Molotov cocktails thrown over the wall by the infected. They led the team up the stairs and past a make-shift communications center in the main lobby.

Soldiers were scrambling around in a fluster, trying to monitor and assess the situation after the latest infected effort to storm the compound. The Private continued to the back of the large lobby and then down a hall to the right. At the end of the hall was a large wooden door. The Private stopped at and motioned the team in. "He is in there, sir."

The team entered the room and were met by an officer, "Sorry, the Major is busy and is not seeing anyone right now." Captain Webb looked at the female captain across from him. She wore a neatly pressed uniform and shined boots with her brunette hair in a tight bun. He thought it was actually too tight and made her face look like a dog when they poke their head out of a car going down the highway. Webb looked at her name tape, which read "Simmons."

"Captain Simmons, I am quite sure that your astuteness enables you to discern, based on our appearance, that we have been engaged in multiple conflicts, which were considerable and lengthy. Our uniforms are dirty and covered in blood, and I can imagine they have a fragrance that is less than desirable. We are battered, bruised, injured, tired and hungry. This team has waded through three states full of infected trying to kill us and survived a helicopter crash. We have run for lives more times than I care to count, not to mention that we lost some damn fine soldiers and friends during our journey. So, excuse me if I don't give a flying fuck how busy he is or what the hell he is doing right now! He WILL see us now!

She protested, but Webb interrupted her, "With all things being equal in this fine United States Army, if you don't get the hell out of my face, I have no problem fucking you up six ways to Sunday. Questions?"

"Whoa, whoa." Major Harwell came running in. "Let's take it easy. Captain Simmons, I will take it from here."

"Yes, sir." She never took her eyes off of Webb, but neither did he. Harwell led them into the War Room and the team sat down.

"Wow, a little intense out there, huh?" Harwell tried to ease the obvious tension in the room.

"Just a little, but we are not in the mood for her protocol bullshit." Webb answered flatly.

Harwell looked nervously then turned to Izzy, "You must be Dr. Costa, I am Major Harwell, nice to meet you." They shook his hands. "Let me give you a sit rep, then you can do the same. After that, we will determine where we go from there."

Harwell continued, "Unfortunately, Colonel Madison is no longer with us. During one of the earlier waves trying to lay siege to HQ, a wounded soldier who he was trying to help, turned and…" He trailed off, "… ripped out his throat. We did not understand they turned that quickly and had to change protocol to deal with the wounded after that painful realization. Anyway, here is what we know based on what limited intel we have been able to gather."

Harwell continued, "Communications are spotty to non-existent; satellite comms are sporadic and I have a feeling all satellite comms will be out soon. Terra comms work pretty well, but the issue is that we are losing people to communicate with. We were in contact with a few other divisions a couple days ago, but recently some stopped sending, and a couple others we heard the infected attack while they transmitted and then went black. Some infected transmitted while they were killing the soldiers left alive. It was horrible to listen to and I don't think I'll ever get those screams out of my head. I even hear that fucking clicking noise they make in my sleep." He stopped for a moment, looking at the ground, shaking his head.

Harwell regained his composure a second later and cleared his throat, "Based on that, we are virtually blind, and any new intel is scarce. What intel we gathered is this: As far as we can tell, they overran most of the other divisions and if there are pockets of command who are still alive, we have no way to communicate with them. Most of the world's governments are dead or possibly in a coop site somewhere. If it is the latter, we still have no communications with any of them."

Harwell looked toward Dr. Costa, "The CDC in Dearborn is toast, which you saw yourself, however, there is a CDC lab functioning over on the east coast in Maryland. That is the location we need to deliver Dr. Costa to, which we can discuss a little later. The fucking scumbags who started this entire thing fled to Dearborn initially. We intercepted communications between the ISIS faction members with the virus, who call themselves Allah's Vengeful Hand and their sister cell down in Philadelphia.

They are heading down to Philly now to regroup with the rest of their faction and they have about a five-hour jump on us. That location is approximately 600 miles from here and from your Team's experience, it won't be easy going, so that will give us some time. We could hack into their vehicle's GPS nav, so we get random updates on their progress when we can receive satellite intel. As of our latest update, they are just 20 miles east of Cleveland. We need to either intercept them in route or be able to catch all of them together and eliminate the entire group. We would like to keep one or two of them alive for interrogation."

"Understood, Sir. Any word from Priest?" Webb inquired.

"Negative. We are keeping comms open to in hope he communicates with us. Now, as far as we can determine, this virus has made it across the country and to other parts of the world. It's a Goddamn pandemic."

"Do we know what their end game is?" Webb asked.

"Well, from the communications we intercepted, they want to bring their caliphate to fruition as is always their goal. Initially, their intent was to have everyone succumb to their religion and if not, they wanted to reign over us infidels as their slaves. When they discovered how the mutated virus turned people into mindless murdering machines, they unleashed it on the world."

"That's stupid, they would kill themselves in the process," Neville chimed in.

Harwell nodded, "Their thinking is that they would be isolated from the virus in their home countries. Killing anyone who attempts to come into the country who isn't Muslim, they just assumed we infidels would kill each other. I guess that..." Just then, a Private burst into the room. "What the hell?" Harwell yelled.

"Sorry Sir, but we have MSGT Priest on the radio."

CHAPTER 22

Bodies were lying all over the place. On the seats, on the floor and anywhere else there was open space. The E-One was not designed to seat that many people in the cab, but they made due and weren't leaving anyone behind.

They rode in silence for a good while before Dana spoke up, "The one that was still alive, did you kill him?"

Priest turned around to look at her, "Do you really want to know?"

"I do." Dana replied.

"No, he was still alive when we left," Priest said, then added, "technically." Dana seemed upset with this answer.

"You left him alive? What if he sets the roadblock back up and kidnaps some other girls? I would not have allowed him to live to do this to someone else."

"That will not happen." Priest turned back around to stare out the windshield.

"How do you know?"

Priest took a deep breath, "Because his back is broke and he can't walk, I broke both his wrists and cut each of his eyes out. The shithead is blind, helpless and will never know when death is coming for him, but he will die… scared and alone."

"Oh my God," Dana covered her mouth with her hands.

Priest turned around, "I told you, you didn't want…"

She interrupted him, "That was awesome, thank you so much," she said.

"Huh?" Priest said, a little baffled.

"Are you kidding me? After what that piece of shit did to us, I wanted to rip his fucking nuts off myself."

Priest's eyes widened, and he just turned back around in his seat. Shaw glanced over at him, but Priest didn't even look over at him and just shook his head.

After a stretch of silence, Priest asked the girls what their plans may be for the future. It turned out that they still wanted to go to Louisville and check on Dana's parents. Priest didn't have the heart to tell them he thought her parents were probably dead and that their trip would be futile. He explained to the team that they will visit Himsel Air Force Base first and try to gain another helicopter.

After that they would take Dana and her friends to Dana's parent's house and on to Fort Campbell from there. Doug admitted had flown into Himsel a few times, but wasn't completely familiar with the layout or aircraft storage there.

"Ok, Shaw, when we get there, it's all about hauling ass. We blast right through until we get to the airfield. I am really tired of dealing with ambushes, infected hordes, and roadblocks. Just keep the fucking hammer down until we reach our destination. Priest turned to the back seat, "Tug, Doc, you guys load up and be ready to take out anything that moves. Girls, stay down and hold on."

About 20 minutes later, Shaw called out, "Approaching front gate, Sarge."

Priest had his binos out already. "Stop right here and let me get an initial assessment first." He looked down the road to Himsel AFB. "Well, the gate is wide open and I don't see anyone in the guardhouse. I'm scanning farther and it looks like a roadblock on the main road. Don't know if it is just a car pile-up that happened during the mass evacuation or an intended ambush or roadblock point. Either way, we need to get through there. You ready, Shaw?"

"Damn straight!"

Priest took in a deep breath and then exhaled. "Ok, shit and git!"

Shaw whooped and slammed forward, "Here we go people, hold on to your butts!"

The E-One APFF rocketed forward with amazing speed for such an enormous truck. As they blew past the front gates and approached the car pile-up, the Team noticed vehicles on each side which made it impossible to go around the roadblock.

"I see movement around the cars, which definitely are not normal Air Force personnel. Everyone down." As they moved closer, some infected starting shooting at them. Their shots weren't wide and were not very accurate. Just as they came near, bags exploded against the windows and windshield and the smell of urine and feces permeated the cabin.

"What is that smell?" Mia asked. Doc told her that the infected threw their urine and feces on the uninfected to contaminate them.

"They only exist to spread the virus, which seems to be some deep-rooted instinct they develop when the infection takes hold of their brain."

Mia looked confused, "That's crazy."

"Yeah, it's what we have been dealing with since we came across our first infected." Doc answered.

Just then, Shaw burst through the roadblock and sent cars and bodies went flying. The Team didn't stick around to view the devastation as Shaw hit the window washers to clean the filth off. "Damn that's nasty".

"Yeah, but smart. They throw this shit to keep us hunkered down and not able to open the windows to return fire." Priest added.

"Hmm, never thought about it like that," Doc said. They continued on and made their way to the airfield and as they got closer something dark and they could see rippling far in the distance. It looks similar to a wave, was the best way to describe it.

Priest brought up his bino's. "Holy shit." His voice had an element of astonishment. "That is a wave of hundreds of infected coming this way. We do not have even close to the firepower to deal with this mass, no matter how many the truck takes out." There was silence for a moment.

"What about the cannon?" a voice said. Everyone turned to Allison.

"What?" Priest questioned.

"I've been reading the manual for this thing to pass the time and it has two water cannons that produce about 1500 gallons a minute."

Priest thought for a second, "That is some serious pressure. It won't kill them, but it could take a lot more out and give us some time to take down more of these things." "Good work, Allison." She showed him how the controls worked. The water cannons were on the front and on the top of the massive truck, and the operating controls were on the passenger side dash board. "I was wondering what all these buttons in front of me were."

Tug looked out through the windshield. "My God, there is a shitload of them."

The horde was about 50 yards away when Priest opened up with the water cannons. Pressurized water came bursting out at a high rate of speed, and they took completely the initial dozen of the closest infected off their feet. The half dozen behind them caught the high-pressure blast of water in the upper chest or in the face. Those that caught the water stream to the face had their necks snapped by the pressure.

"Holy shit! Do you see that?" Shaw laughed.

Priest aimed the cannons to the front and the sides as dozens more of the infected dropped like bags of wet cement. Those taken down by the first blast were now being crushed under the massive 5-foot tires. It was comical to see the infected screaming as they approached, only to have their mouth fill with water right before their head snapped back and took them off their feet.

"Looks like slaughter time in the chicken coop. All those infected flopping around with their heads barely hanging on their bodies," Tug commented.

The sound of multiple bodies deflecting off the truck was deafening. The crescendo of the noise along with the screaming of the infected was enough to drive you mad. Those who were not used to the shocking sounds of battle had their hands covering their ears as the truck continued on its journey of destruction and mayhem.

Unhindered and unimpeded, the massive truck plowed through the hundreds of bodies littering the ground.

The water cannons were causing considerable damage in taking down massive groups of the infected. Some of those who had been infected longer had sizeable pieces of skin and tissue blasted off their face and bodies. None of them could keep their balance, much less attack the bucking truck. The feelings of dread and despair displayed as they entered the horde were now cheers and shouts as they came out the other side of the throng.

"Holee shit, that was a first," Doc yelled.

"First time for me too," Priest added. "Everyone ok? Doug, are we on the right road?"

"Yeah, should be another mile or so."

A few minutes later, they came across an empty flight line. Without knowing exactly how many infected they just killed, the team knew they needed to work quickly searching for a helicopter. After the rest of the Team bailed out, Shaw turned the truck around to face the way they just come.

Meanwhile, the team frantically spread out to search the hangars for any aircraft. Two hangars produced nothing, but as Tug entered one of the last hangers, he stopped in his tracks.

"Well, my, my." He walked in through the pedestrian door and a moment later the team flinched as the sound of the hangar doors groaning to open reached their ears. They turned around to see Tug standing in the open hangar bay right in front of an UH-60 Pave Hawk. The Air Force's rendition of the Army's Blackhawk.

"Shit," Priest cursed. "Sweet ride, but we cannot use it,"

"Why not?" Tug asked.

"Because this differs significantly from a Bell Ranger, Doug is not familiar with it."

"Says who?" Doug chimed in.

"You know how to fly that?"

"Well, yeah. I flew Blackhawks in Desert Storm, back when I was a warrant officer in the Indiana National Guard."

Priest just stared at him. "Why in the hell didn't you say that before?"

"It never came up whether I was familiar with military aircraft. Plus, you never asked."

"I ought to slap the shit out of you," Priest chuckled. They all pushed the aircraft out of the hangar and Doug entered the pilot's seat. He started his pre-flight checks as they removed the wheel dollies from the skids, removed engine intake covers and all the tie-downs. The girls got in while the team posted to provide security.

There were a couple dozen infected making their way toward them from the killing field they had just driven through. Shaw made a couple more passes, and he took off for the group approaching. Shaw moved through the crowd mowing down people left and right and was having a field day doing it. Priest and Tug looked at each other.

"He ain't all there, is he?" Tug joked dryly.

"No sir, he ain't, but I'll take him that way any day."

Tug shrugged his shoulders and went back to scanning for any other infected.

Doug hit the ignition switch and the twin engines sparked to life. He brought the engines up to operable RPM and the rotors rotated. Priest keyed his squad comms. "Shaw, we're ready to roll. Bring it in."

"Copy." Shaw was on board a minute later. With everyone strapped in, the Pave Hawk lifted off, heading for Louisville, Kentucky. When they were in the air and at cruising speed, Priest plugged into the bird's comm system and hailed HQ.

CHAPTER 23

Everyone jumped up and ran to the communications area in the lobby of the HQ building. Harwell grabbed the handset. "Priest, this is Harwell. Do you copy?"

"Copy, Sir." Everyone let out a loud breath that the entire room was holding.

"I'm here with Webb and his team. Can you give me a sitrep?"

"Affirmative. Glad to hear the rest are safe. We are in route to HQ with an ETA of 45 mics. We have the three of the existing Team, and six civilians are with us."

Webb broke in, "You could fit all those on the news chopper?"

Priest chuckled, "Negative. We traveled to an AFB in Indiana and found a Pave Hawk. When we get to HQ, you must ask Shaw how we got to the base. It's an interesting story he loves to tell. Anyway, the places we came through are royally fucked. We even had a run in with some redneck scumbags who set up a roadblock and were kidnapping women."

"Can't wait to hear. I assume Doug is flying you." Webb inquired.

"Copy that. We had no idea he flew a Blackhawk back in the Army."

"Ok, it will be good to see you guys. Handing you back to Harwell."

Harwell took the handset, "Sergeant Priest? We have infected all over the place. You must land directly on top of the HQ building. We were almost overrun, so we have barriers all around and no devoid space outside the walls."

"Copy. You want us to thin out some infected?"

"Negative. Save your ammo, you might need it later."

"Copy. Priest, out."

A while later, HQ came into view of those on the Pave Hawk. Priest and his team saw the destructive scene that was now the HQ building.

Doc made the sign of the cross, "Holy Mother, Mary and Joseph. It looks like the end of world down there."

Doug maneuvered the chopper to set down on the roof while Webb and his team walked out to meet Priest and his team. There were hugs, tears, introductions and reminiscing. Soldiers from HQ took Dana, Mia, Kim, Allison and Tug to shower, eat and get some rest. They escorted the others to the War Room to meet with Harwell.

Harwell addressed the team, "Priest, Doc, Shaw, it's good to see you. Doug, it's nice to meet you. I'm sorry, but we really need you for this briefing because of that fact you are our only pilot right now."

"Don't worry about it, Sir. I completely understand the weight of the situation. Plus, I am kind of like being back in action."

"Good to hear and we really appreciate it. So, we have two objectives in our immediate purview. One: We need to intercept ISIS from getting to Philly or take the entire group down once they make it there. Two: We have to get Dr. Costa to Site R in Maryland where the CDC has moved operations including the Bio-Warfare group from Fort Detrick, Maryland. Doug is our only pilot, so we have one pilot and two objectives. I am open to options." The team thought for a minute.

Priest spoke up, "Doug, how comfortable are you flying with a sling load?"

He thought for a second, "I have flown with ammo pallets and fuel blivits before. What do you have in mind?"

"I was thinking we could sling load a M1114 Humvee and drop it and a team in Philly to take the ISIS faction and their sister cell out.

The other team takes the bird and continues to deliver Dr. Costa to Site R." The room was silent for a moment while the others processed the plan. A knock on the door broke the silence in the room.

A private poked his head in, "Apologies Sir, you asked for Sargent Dahan. Would you like me to ask her to wait?"

"No, no.... please ask her to come in, she may assist with this. The private moved over and a woman walked in the War Room. She was about 5'10", with olive skin and deep, piercing hazel-green eyes. She had her long black hair in a bun and was wearing an olive drab uniform.

"Team, I would like to introduce Chief Sargent Lia Dahan. She is from the MOSSAD, Unit 217. You may know it as Duvdevan (counter-terrorism) unit within the Israel Defense Forces. She is here to partner with us in developing an integrated tactic process for the US and Israeli forces before this shit hit. They attacked her cadre along with some of our escorts." After they introduced her all Priest heard was blah, blah, blah, blah. He also didn't hear Harwell call on him.

"Priest. Sargent Priest?"

"Huh? What? Sorry, did you say something?" The rest of the team was grinning at him.

"Priest, could you brief Sargent Dahan on your suggestion?"

"Sure." He laid out his plan to address both objectives to her, while she held his gaze. When he finished, he gave the same hands up shoulder shrug.

She looked around the room, "Does everyone approve of this plan?" She had a light accent and her voice was like honey. Everyone acknowledged they agreed this was the best plan. "I agree it is a solid plan, based on present resources and the intel available. We should go over any tactical plans before shipping out."

"Ah, we?" Priest asked.

"We?" Harwell asked.

"I assume that is why you brought me in here, is it not?" She turned to Harwell as she spoke.

"Ah, well, no. I brought you in to assess the plan and give me your opinion."

"Yes, well, I have done so and now we need to execute, yes?"

"Yeah, well, I wasn't expecting to send you out there."

"I believe I could provide some tactical value and having another gun out there doesn't hurt either." The team was watching the back and forth between the two like a tennis match. Harwell looked at Webb and then Priest.

"We're not dealing with normal circumstances here, Sir." Webb said, "We need all hands-on deck. The risk factors have increased, but if we don't get some kind of lid on this shit, we will lose everything."

Priest added, "I am sure, Sgt. Dahan could provide some added value out in the field and if she thinks she can contribute to the mission, then we would be happy to have her along."

Webb responded, "Well, Priest and his team are experts on breach, search and clear. So, Priest, Shaw and Doc will take the M1114 and tackle the ISIS objective. Neville, Shin and I will deliver the doctor to Maryland and come back for Priest's Team on our way back. We can also scout out some other areas for non-infected?"

"That sounds solid. I will accompany the breach team," Sargent Dahan added. Priest raised an eyebrow and nodded his head.

"We could use you. What is your specialty?"

"Weapons expert, tactical assessment and sniper operations."

Priest's smile got wider. He stood up and stuck out his hand, "Glad to have you aboard." Lia looked at his hand and wrinkled up her nose. Priest forgot just how nasty he was. He was filthy from his head to his boots and didn't smell any better than he looked. He chuckled, "Yeah, could use a little freshening up."

"Yes, with a sandblaster, maybe," she replied with a smile on her face.

"How about a hug? I think there are still some bits of intestine and any other body part you can think of stuck to me. Going once. Going twice."

"I think I'll pass." She smiled.

"Ok, suit yourself." He liked her already. He ran off for a quick shower and some food.

Harwell dismissed the rest of the team and they were all left to shower, eat and resupply.

An hour later, the whole Team reassembled, fully geared to move out to their objectives. Sgt. Dahan had her combat load out equipped with plate carrier and helmet. She was toting a 1W1 TAVOR 7 assault rifle, and Priest noticed a Glock 19 on her hip along with a long rifle case she was toting.

"Nice, what do you have in there?" Priest asked.

She acknowledged the case, "Oh, it's an 1W1 DAN .338 Sniper Rifle."

"Sweet."

Just then, Allison ran into the room, wearing a flight suit and sporting a flight helmet.

Harwell spoke up, "Excuse me, may I ask, why are you wearing a flight suit?"

"I am going too." She answered.

Harwell was taken slightly aback, "Wait? What for?"

"I have been flying Doug and I can help him navigate and monitor flight readings."

Harwell looked over at Doug.

Doug nodded, "I could really use the help, and she is a skilled navigator."

Harwell shook his head, "Point taken. Ok, what the hell are you people doing standing around for? Move out!"

As the team walked out to the Pave Hawk and stowed their gear, Dana, Mia, Kim and Tug came up behind them. Allison ran over to hug the girls while Tug moseyed up to Priest.

"You know, you and the boys are a little nuts, but you're honorable people. If I was younger, I would go with you kids. Just think, I would be more of a pain in the ass than a help. I see how you boys operate and it's quite impressive. Good luck to you 'all and we'll be waiting for you to get back." He then turned, shook hands with the rest of the team and walked off.

Priest watched him go until Dana appeared in front of him. She didn't wait for permission, or even an acknowledgement, before she ran over and hugged him. Priest hugged her back and told her it would be all right. She nodded, kissed him on the cheek and thanked him for everything. Kim and Mia followed suit and walked off to join

Tug. Priest hadn't noticed that Tug had stopped and was there waiting for the girls.

Priest yelled over to them, "Once we get back, we'll take you girls and see about Dana's parents and get you to Louisville." The girls smiled and waved at him before turning and walking back in the HQ building.

CHAPTER 24

Priest turned to the Team and spoke up, "Before we load up and go out in the middle of hell again, I just wanted to say something. You are the best team I have ever led and served with. I have deployed more times than I can count and to more places than I care to remember. In all of that time, I have never encountered an enemy who does not show fear, has no regard for self-preservation and who seems not to possess an ounce of humanity.

That being said, everyone here has performed well considering what we have faced. Not to mention, you all have volunteered to go back out there and brave the storm again. Those whose job is not in the military and do not deploy regularly, have stepped up and face this enemy exceptionally well. I wanted to say thank you and I feel blessed to have all of you with me.

Now, the next thing I am about to do, I have never done before and I don't do lightly. The Light Reapers are a strong brotherhood who would die for one another if needed. These are not regular times and the brotherhood needs to accept others into our ranks." He looked at Webb as he spoke. Webb nodded at him as he continued.

Priest reached in his rucksack, pulled out some items and held them out in his hand. "I want to welcome the rest of you to our Team." Doug, Allison and Lia each reached out and took one. "These are patches displaying the Light Reapers Unit insignia. It holds them in high regard among the brothers and sisters in uniform. Being part of the Light Reapers sets you apart from others who wear this uniform. That patch represents skill, courage, loyalty and perseverance. Wear them with pride and pay honor to those wearing it now and those who died wearing it before you. Welcome to the Light Reapers!" All three attached the patch to the Velcro on their shoulder as the rest of the Team shouted, HUA!

Priest looked at the three of them, "Ok, with that sentimental bullshit out of the way, let's mount up."

Doug and Allison entered the cockpit, while Doc, Neville and Shin were stowing everyone's gear and making sure they removed all the helicopter safety equipment. Shaw was loading and servicing the M48 .50 cal mounted on the right side as Webb, Priest and Lia went over the operational plans. Harwell came out to talk to Captain Webb and confirm a few things, leaving Priest alone with Lia.

"You ever been in combat?" Priest asked.

"I am from Israel. Surrounded by some of the most radical terrorists in the world. I'll let you answer your own question." Lia didn't say it in a condescending tone, but more like a matter of fact.

"Excellent point." He continued, "So, what's your story?"

"A little nosey?"

"Negative. When I go into combat with someone, I would like to know who the hell I am dealing with."

"Ok...," she thought for a few seconds, "I am Chief Sargent Lia Dahan. I believe you would me a Sargent First Class. You know my unit already and like Harwell said, we were here on a joint training and tactical planning exercise when my team was ambushed by the infected. I say ambush, because it gave me the impression they planned and executed it with some precision and forethought. Not to mention, since we were on diplomat mission, we weren't geared for combat."

Lia looked straight at Priest, "We had some prior warning, but it came at the price of some soldiers ahead of us and behind us. We ran, but they overtook some of my colleagues. I tried to help them, but they were overtaken so quickly, it was over in seconds." She had her head down and jaw clenched.

Priest laid a hand on her shoulder. She snapped out of her reverie and continued, "I have been with the MOSSAD for the last 10 years. Hand to hand combat and sniper quals are my specialty, if I was to put that down on paper."

"Ah, we need that in Philly." She turned to look at him for a moment,

"What about you, Sergeant Priest?"

"What about me?"

"What's your story?"

"Hmm, not much of a story. Master Sargent Alex Priest, broken home, got into trouble. Court appointed me to join the Army to get straighten out. That was oh 25 years ago. Been with Special Operations for the last 14 years and the Light Reapers for the last six. Me on paper, hand to hand, weapons expert, strategy and leadership. Oh, and don't forget stubbornness and sarcasm. Those are areas of expertise."

Lia laughed, "And what about Mrs. Priest?"

Now it was Priest's turn to laugh, "No, no… got close once. We were engaged, but going out and meeting people was her expertise. She ended up meeting too many people and caught her with one of them when I came home early from a deployment. She and some lieutenant were together in bed, both a little high. I yelled, she screamed, slapped me a couple times for being home early."

"What did you do?"

Priest smirked, "Body slammed her into the closet, locked it, then kicked the shit out of the lieutenant. Kind of fucked his face up pretty bad, broke some ribs. His left arm looked a little wonky too. Oh, yeah… and fractured his collarbone."

"Was she worth fighting over?"

"Ah, hell no. I wasn't fighting over that bitch. I was just pissed that he was in my house, sweating on my sheets, eating my food and worst of all, drinking my good bourbon, mother fucker! Probably would be Sargent Major by now. You? Any eunuch's out there courtesy of Ms. Dahan?"

She smiled, "No, nothing like that. I don't have to deal with assholes like that. I'm a lesbian and my partner respects me better than that."

Priest's eyes went side, "Oh, sorry, I didn't know."

She watched him fumble for a couple of seconds, then burst out laughing, "Hahaha, just kidding."

"Damn, you got my pressure all up," he said with his hand on his chest.

She was still laughing, "Sorry. No, I have had a couple long relationships, and I also was engaged once. We had been together for three years and as soon as he put the engagement ring on my finger, he changed. Became controlling, losing his temper. We got into a pretty heated argument one time in which he put his hands on me."

"Ooh, I bet that worked out well for him."

"Yeah, his arm never really set right after that."

"Damn!"

"Yeah, they had to wheel him out on a gurney."

"Wow." Priest was shaking his head. They both laughed and turned to check on the progress of the team.

Several minutes later, they were in the air, hooked up to the Humvee sling load and were on their way to Philadelphia, Pennsylvania.

CHAPTER 25

Based on the last tracking data Harwell had on the ISIS faction, they should arrive in Philly in approximately four hours. The team had calculated this after infill, three blocks away from the objective location.

Priest had the team assembled around him, "Ok, let's go over the plan one more time. Lia, you're in the building across the street to provide sniper support and overview. I will cover the back door; Shaw and Doc will breech the front door."

Priest's team was in place and sighted in on the target building. It was a dilapidated warehouse which covered half a city block, lengthwise. It was about 100 feet wide and wedged in by other buildings of the same condition. The area was one of older industrial areas in the city with rust covered metal surfaces and windows were near impossible to see through due to the dirt covering them.

The wind was blowing slightly which rattled loose roof tin, chains, wall panels and debris across the pavement. This made it hard to make out sounds they could associate with the targets. Again, here they were; shitty intel that they couldn't completely trust, not enough time to survey the area to come up with an action plan and an incomplete team to execute. This situation pissed Priest off the most, but being what it was, he just needed to overcome and adapt.

Lia was in position on the roof of an adjacent warehouse. She had a 180-degree view on two sides of the building. They chose Shaw and Doc to breech, while Priest was covering the alternate entrance. Shaw, Doc and Priest were off the street and hiding in the shadows, waiting for targets to show. The team had been set for close to an hour.

"Father, this is Overwatch". The Team voted to approve that callsign for Lia. They tossed a few others around, but Overwatch got the most votes.

"Copy Overwatch."

"We have vehicles approaching and I'm not sure if they are coming to the target building, but will call out anyway. Four vehicles in single file, all Suburban's windows are tinted black, so I can't make out several occupants."

"Copy. We will stay out of site in case things go sideways."

"Ok, Father. They are coming to our target building."

"Copy that." "Cotton, give me a sit rep as soon as you make your assessments."

"Copy, roll-up door is opening with three targets inside. All are packing MP5's. Can't see any farther into the building and still can't see into any of the vehicles."

"Ok, let's assume they are full, meaning there is a lot of beef to wade through. We will have Overwatch take out targets before they enter the building. If not, we lose her support. Overwatch, you are cleared to engage as soon as you assess individual targets."

"Shaw, Doc, as soon as she pops the targets, run in and eliminate as many as you can. I will see if I can breech this back door."

The vehicles pulled up near the warehouse and stopped. Pop! The vehicle's driver window shattered, and the driver slumped over the steering wheel with the left side of his face and head missing. The occupants screamed, and there was apparent movement from inside the vehicles.

Shaw answered their shouts with the indistinct repeating sound of his M48 sending .50 cal lead wrapped death into the vehicle. Priest could hear the sounds of destruction as he made his way to enter the backside of the warehouse. The pedestrian door was locked, so lowered his M4 and blew the doorknob off.

Lia witnessed Priest enter the warehouse as she fired on the front vehicle. Her shot went through the driver's window, snapping his head to the side toward the passenger. Blood, brains and skull fragments peppered the passenger. He was in shock and was trying to wipe the gore off his face when a round entered his neck and took the right side of his jaw off. Blood spurted from his neck like an open fire hydrant on a sweltering day in New York City.

The occupants exited the vehicles to return fire. Half were dressed in suits and half were dressed in khaki fatigues with black shirts. They possessed higher end automatic weapons. Most were not the picture of ISIS seen on the news, but were dressed to better mingle around the US. They were exiting the opposite side from where Shaw was laying down fire, which put them in Doc's line of fire.

"Frag out," Doc yelled. The grenade exited his M203 and landed at the feet of the men scrambling out of the second truck in line. BOOM! The explosion drowned out the screams of the ISIS members as Priest entered the door into the darkened back of the warehouse. He could see the opened roll-up door with the light flooding in. Shaw saw the three men position themselves on either side of the door, taking cover. Four other men were coming out of an office from the right side, running to join the other three.

Priest thought this would be an excellent time to make his presence known. He loaded his M203 with a grape shot grenade. "Everyone down. Grape shot down range," Priest yelled into his squad comms. Shaw and Doc took cover. Foomp! Priest launched the grenade then took cover behind an office wall built out of cinder block.

The grenade exploded, sending large metal ball bearings screaming into the combatants standing by the door. They met the several members who were running for cover inside the building with an explosion that took them off their feet. At virtually the same time, multiple projectiles slammed into their chests, face and legs. What splattered to the ground was mangled viscera, unrecognizable limbs and jutting bones. Priest searched the rest of the warehouse for additional ISIS members.

"Holee Shit," Doc yelled. "That really fucked them up." There were a few others who were caught by the blast, rolling on the ground, moaning. The third truck's windows exploded out as the occupants began firing blindly, just trying to lie down enough suppressive fire to allow them to escape into the building.

Priest came over the comms, "Team, we need to snag some prisoners so we can interrogate these fucks!"

Shaw yelled, "Cease fire, cease fire. Ok you fucks, exit the vehicles with your hands up. Now!" Shaw repeated the commands in Farsi and Arabic. Priest made his way to the front of the warehouse as the team had the trucks covered in all directions. There were yells from inside the vehicles in Farsi, "to not shoot".

Shaw continued, "Throw out your weapons and then exit the vehicle (in Farsi.)". A few MP5's and pistols came flying out the window. "Exit the vehicle slowly, with your hands up and lay face down on the ground (Farsi.)" The doors on the last two trucks opened and four middle eastern men slowly got out of the vehicle. Two on the left side, two on the right. "I don't see anyone left in those two vehicles, but I am seeing slight movement in the front one."

"Lia, report." Priest directed.

"I have the front vehicle covered and I see movement."

Priest reloaded a grenade in his M203. "You in the front vehicle, get out now!" Priest yelled in Farsi. There was no movement to exit the vehicle. Priest thought he saw the occupants readying their weapons for an assault. "Times up!" he said.

Priest fired 5.56mm rounds into the windshield and it broke like a spider web with an enormous hole in the middle. He then launched a 40mm grenade into the vehicle through the front windshield. Men were screaming and the sounds of scrambling until.... BOOM! The remaining windows blew out followed by a shower of blood and viscera, ravaged body parts, intestines and the shredded torsos of the men hung out the shattered windows.

This immediately influenced those in the last two vehicles to exit with a renewed vigor. They all exited, threw out weapons and immediately dropped to the ground on their face with their hands behind their heads. Doc, Priest and Shaw closed in while maintaining cover on the men lying on the ground. One man made a quick move to the back of his waistband. He got his hand behind his back before a round entered through his right eye and removed the back of skull.

"You dumb fucks, we have a sniper trained on you. Make a move and die. Check them." Priest covered the men while Shaw and Doc searched them. They found a few blades and a snub nose .357 magnum.

One man was bitching the entire time, so Priest kneeled down and spoke to him. He keyed his comms so the team could hear. "Hey goat fucker," Priest slapped him a couple times to get his attention, "You know your piece of shit friend over there, the one with the back of his skull laying all over the ground? Well, I am sure you would be happy to know that the sniper that killed him is an Israeli. Actually, that sniper is an Israeli woman!"

The man struggled and spit on the ground. Priest knew this would really piss these guys off. The man who spat on the ground began calling Lia all kinds of derogatory names. Priest reached over and bounced the man's face off the pavement, knocking out several teeth and breaking his nose.

Shaw and Doc had just finished cuffing the remaining men with zip ties, when Lia came over the comms. "Priest, we have infected coming our way. They must have heard all the fun. I got approximately two dozen, maybe a few more, about four blocks to the northwest. They are between us and our Humvee, so we lost our transport out of here."

"Do you have a shot if we need you to buy us sometime?"

"I will in a few minutes." Lia answered.

"Okay, we can't wait for exfil. Shaw, check these vehicles and see if one is still operational."

Priest kneeled down to one of the other men, "Who is in charge of your little glee club, here?" The man looked around. He slapped the man, "Who is running the show for you assholes?" The man looked over at the guy whose nose Priest just broke. "Excellent, we are only dealing with two of you." Priest then pulled his Walther PPQ and shot the other five of the remaining men in the head.

"Sarge, we got one vehicle here in great shape," Shaw yelled.

"Ok, great. Lia, come on down and let's roll out."

Priest and Doc loaded the two ISIS members in the truck as Lia came running over to them. "Where is the virus?" Priest barked at the leader. The guy just looked at him. Priest busted the guy in the mouth with the barrel of his pistol, knocking a couple more teeth out. The other squirrelly guy talked nervously and fast and told him it was in the second truck.

Priest ran over and pulled out a medium-sized hard-shell case. He ran back to the running truck just as Lia got there. She loaded her sniper rifle in the back as Priest dropped the case in. He looked at her, "You want to ride shotgun or you want babysitting duty?" She walked over to look in the back seat at the two ISIS members. They noticed her look at them and they glared back in disgust.

"Oh, I'll take babysitting duty."

"I thought you would say that." They both laughed as they got in and the truck. Shaw pulled out of the warehouse area and headed southwest.

The ISIS leader seemed to have calmed down some. The woman sitting next to him with a pistol leveled against his temple seemed to have subdued him. Priest didn't know which was deadlier, the gun pointed at him or the stare Lia had locked on him. He was laughing on the inside but didn't let a smile come to his mouth as he was turned around looking at the leader.

"Where did you guys get the virus from?" The man didn't answer. "Look, I don't have time for your bullshit, so either answer my questions or I will fuck you up six ways to Sunday. It's just that simple, so I will repeat. Where did you get the virus from?" He waited a couple minutes, and the man said nothing. Priest quickly pulled his combat knife and sliced the man's knee deep into the joint cartilage just below the kneecap. The man screamed in pain, his eyes teared up and looked like he was getting dizzy.

Priest slapped him, "Don't pass out on me. That cut I just gave you is extremely painful, but since I went into the joint cartilage there is almost no bleeding. That way, you suffer extreme pain, but you won't bleed out. Cool, huh? Now, we can go at this for as long as you want, but I will get the information I want. Again, where did you get it the fucking virus?" Nothing. Priest drove the pommel of the knife in the middle of the man's chest just enough to crack his sternum in half. The man screamed in agony.

"Whew, now I know that mother fucker seriously hurt...... hell, I can feel it over here. With that broken sternum, it will hurt to move, breathe, talk, sleep, you name it. You care to answer me now?"

The man tried to take a deep breath and winced in pain. "I give you nothing." Priest shot his knife out and took out the man's right eye.

He screamed, "Go ahead and kill me."

Priest chuckled, "Oh no, I wouldn't do that. That would be cruel." He shot out and punched the man in his broken sternum. The man howled in pain, and Priest asked again. No answer.

"Stop the fucking car," Priest commanded. He got out and Lia slid out. He pulled the man out and threw him on the ground. "You tell me where you got the virus and I'll kill you quick and painless. If not, I will blind you right here and leave you for the infected."

The man thought for a second, "Ok, ok. I tell you and you send me to Allah. We stole the virus from the lab in southeast Turkey."

"Ok, what happened with all these people turning into monsters? I thought the virus was just supposed to make people able to control."

"It was, but the collection of scientists that were working on it, changed the formula into effecting the basic impulses of the brain. The virus isolates the violent impulses and brings them to their consciousness. It blocks all other emotional receptors including fear, compassion, pain and others." The man was struggling to talk with the pain he was in.

"How did it get released?"

"One canister was damaged on the journey from Turkey. When we took it on the plane and airports, it leaked out and spread the virus quickly to all parts of the world."

"Was it your plan to decimate the entire planet?"

"No, things went wrong because the release was to be controlled."

"Yeah, no shit." Priest spit as he shot his blade out and took out the man's other eye. The man screamed at the top of his lungs.

Priest kicked him in his face. He then turned and walked back to the truck.

"No, no. Where are you going?" The man screamed, "You are to kill me, you will do it now!"

Priest yelled over his shoulder, "You're blind and there is nothing out here that can kill you, yet. The infected 'll find you and they'll eat you alive or you will slowly die of starvation. One way or another, you will die a slow, painful death. So, have a delightful day and go fuck yourself."

Lia spit in his face as she walked by to the truck. "You fucking whore. How dare you spit on me, you fucking Jewish pig!" The truck drove off with him screaming and cursing. As the engine drowned out the curses, Priest leaned back in his seat, closed his eyes and a smile crept over his face. An equally enormous smile crept on Lia's face as she leaned back in her seat.

CHAPTER 26

Webb spoke into his helmet's microphone to Doug and Allison. "Have you been able to raise anyone at the CDC compound?"

"Negative," Allison responded. "How do we even know this place is still viable?"

"We don't, but we still may be out of range."

Doug added, "We are still 60 miles out."

"Ok, keep trying." "Doctor, what do you think you'll find there?"

"I am hoping they have samples or maybe even an infected cadaver. If we can reverse engineer the virus, then hopefully that will allow us to produce an antidote. If Priest's team can acquire the sample of the original viral strain, that would make it much easier and quicker."

"Got it."

"Captain," Allison's voice reached Webb through his helmet, "We have contacted the CDC compound and they are expecting the doctor and preparing to receive us."

"Copy that." Webb relayed that to the rest of the team as the compound's helipad came into view. The rest of the compound was underground, so they could not see it. Doug circled and set down when Allison started talking to someone.

She came back on internal comms. "Priest just checked in, they have the virus and a prisoner for interrogation. They are in an SUV making their way down Rt. 95 and just passed Wilmington DE. He said if you want the virus quicker, then you must come get it."

"Tell him to keep driving and we will head out as soon as we deliver the doctor."

"Copy." A few minutes later the Pave Hawk had landed as was winding down. There were a couple CDC scientists along with four armed guards from the US Army. The one scientist was a tall, lanky man with light brown hair, graying on the sides. He had squinty eyes and wore rimless glasses. A short Asian woman with shoulder length black hair, round face and rosy cheeks accompanied him. She was a little overweight and walked with a slight waddle. They met Dr. Costa with enthusiasm.

"Hello, hello. I am Dr. Caulfield and this is my colleague, Dr. Choi."

She spoke up excitedly, "We are happy to be working with you, Dr. Costa." She talked as if there wasn't an apocalypse going on.

"I am happy to meet you both and I am excited work with you and see what progress you have made."

Dr. Caulfield responded, "Excellent. We will show you to your quarters and then head to the main lab."

"Sounds great." They walked off, but Izzy turned and looked at Webb.

"We'll be back with the virus samples."

She had a concerned look on her face, but nodded and continued into the underground compound.

Webb ran back to the chopper. "Ok, Doug. Let's go get our boys."
"Copy that, Captain."

Priest had dozed off and woke up with a jostling. He shot up, drawing his pistol.

"Yo, take it easy, Sarge." Shaw's voice said.

Priest looked over at Shaw, "Shit, sorry. What's going on?"

"No problem. We all go 0 to 60 from time to time, it's an issue, though. We're coming up on the bridge to make it across the Susquehanna and from what we can see through the binos, ain't nobody getting through there. They have it blocked."

Priest looks to see the bridge blocked by some jersey barriers and military vehicles. There were a couple police cars parked closer, between them and the barrier. "Shit. These wackos didn't build those barriers, those are regulation. By the looks of the surrounding condition, I would assume this was a checkpoint to stem the flow of infected and keep them from crossing the river."

He lowered the binos. "Damn, trying to plow through there would be stupid. We don't have a map and with GPS down, we are blind. Shaw hand me that radio." Shaw reached in and pulled out the pack they had brought from Campbell with the radio.

"Spider, this is Father. Do you copy?" Priest waited and nothing. He repeated it and waited.

"Father, this is Spider, go ahead."

"What is your ETA to our location? We are just north of the Susquehanna River on Rt. 95. We are near the town of Perryville. Over."

"Wait one… ah, give us 15 mics on that."

"15 mic's, good copy."

Priest stows the radio and then Shaw pipes up, "Sarge, it looks like the police cars are pulling out and coming this way."

"Ok, set up a defensive line and take those two assholes out." Shaw stopped the SUV, and the Team exited to set up a defensive firing line. As soon as the two police cars pulled out an enormous horde of infected rushed through the barrier and followed the cop cars toward the Team.

"Shit, everyone back in the SUV, we don't have enough ammo to fight that entire crowd." They all jumped in and took off north, heading away from the bridge. Up ahead at the next exit they could see movement coming towards them from the east, "Fuck me sideways. There is a large horde coming from the road on the right. He looked over and saw them cross the railroad bridge and then swarming the road and the intersection. "Fuck, fuck, fuck," Priest yelled. "Ok Doc, you come up here and drive. I want Shaw hanging that M48 out the window and trying to buy us some time. They are coming over that railroad bridge. How did they know we were even here, much less key on us that quick? Did they hear us, smell us, see us? What?" They drove north a little way until they saw a country road to the left.

Doc drifted sideways on the road and straightened as Priest was looking at him. "What? I did a little street racing back in the day." Priest returned his eyes forward and shook his head.

"Shaw, throw that ruck up here." Shaw dropped the radio ruck up front.

"Spider, this is Father. Do you copy?"

He received an instant reply, "Go ahead, Father."

"We are on the move with a shitload of infected climbing up our ass. They had the bridge barricaded, and another mass came at us from a parallel railroad bridge. We are heading west on a country road parallel to the river. We are spitting up a cloud of dust, so it should be easy to track our location."

"Copy that. We are flying over the river now."

Shaw yelled from the back seat, "Sarge, the police cars are almost on us. Time to introduce them to Jimi Hendrix." Lia looked over quizzically. Shaw patted his M48. "Jimi Hendrix, cause he rocks like a motherfucker!" She just grinned.

Shaw leaned out the back window and began sending rounds toward the lead police car. Even with the dust and dirt flying around, he could see the wild eyes and erratic movements of the infected inside the car. Their faces were visible until his rounds entered the windshield and tore the two occupants to shreds. The police car careened off the road and went nose first into the ditch, while the second police swerved to avoid the first car and continued the chase.

The ISIS prisoner freaked out and thrash around. "Why are these police trying to kill us? This is not right."

Lia gave him a hammer fist to the nose, breaking it. He screamed a high pitch scream and tears streamed from his eyes. "They aren't cops, there're infected. This is what you fuck heads unleashed on the world." She was visibly disgusted by having to speak to the prisoner. "How does your precious Allah feel about you killing other Muslims, huh? The caliphate is to eradicate the infidels, but you assholes eradicated the entire world population." The man's eyes were wide as he started praying in Arabic.

Shaw looked over at him, "Ain't gonna help you now, jackass." The man had his eyes closed and was continuing to pray. Shaw was about to aim his M48 out the window when rounds rained down from the sky, shredding the police car in seconds. The rounds stopped as the helicopter flew overhead. Shaw looked back to see the police car stopped in the middle of the road with two bodies slumped in the front seat.

"Father, this is Spider. Do you copy?"

"Affirmative."

"Half a mile up the road from your position, there is a field off to your right. Regroup there for exfil."

"Copy that."

Minutes later they all met up in the field. Allison, still in the co-polit's seat, saw Shaw and waved at him excitedly. He returned her wave with a look of admiration. They threw the ISIS prisoner in the chopper and Priest noticed his broken nose. He looked at Lia and she gave him her innocent look and shrugged her shoulders. Priest chuckled and got on the chopper as they lifted off for Maryland.

As they ascended, they got a good look at the coming horde. Thousands had massed around the area; some were crossing the bridge, and some were standing there like they didn't know what to do.

"Damn, look at all of them," Doc uttered. "It's out of control and no way to turn the tide."

"There's a way. There's got to be or we should just give up right now. Just nose dive this son of a bitch right into a bank along the river." Priest looked over at Lia and she was staring out the open door.

Priest turned back to Doc, "I'm not ready to die just yet." Doc raised his eyebrows looking from Priest to Lia. Priest lightly slapped Doc on the side of the head and put his finger to his lips in a shhh sign.

The Team had made their way down the Eastern Bay and were over Baltimore. "Captain," Allison came over the internal comms. They patched Webb and Priest in.

"Go ahead," Webb replied.

"We received a message from the CDC compound, but was cut off. I only got "We are being" and then it cut off. I haven't been able to raise anyone else since."

"Ok, there could be trouble brewing over there. Doug, get us there ASAP."

"Copy that." Doug cranked the RPM's and increased their speed, heading for the CDC compound.

CHAPTER 27

As the chopper approached the CDC compound, they could see plumes of smoke rose over the trees. "Shit, that doesn't look good." Webb was staring at the smoke rising and he had a sinking feeling. He didn't know if the place had been overrun or just one of those issues with someone not divulging that they might be infected.

It was sometimes hard to test people who had the virus before they turned. That, added with the basic need for human survival, often caused people to hide information on whether they were exposed. So many people had been affected felt perfectly fine, but that changed quickly and then they would have a serious problem on their hands.

People wanted to give others the benefit of the doubt, and it was that kind of thinking that had gotten so many people killed over the last few weeks. They flew over the last of the trees, which now gave them an excellent view of the compound area. It was a site they had witnessed too many times recently.

The military and civilian vehicles parked near the compound entrance had suffered incredible damage. Destroyed and on fire, the smoke everyone could see from miles away. There were a few bodies lying around and the door into the underground compound was wide open.

"Ok team, full battle rattle. Watch your lanes and keep your head on a swivel," Priest barked. The chopper touched down, and the team exited and immediately went to one knee to provide 360-degree security.

Webb spoke into his comms, "Doug, keep the bird hot in case we need to exfil quickly. Allison, close all doors and provide a watch for any infected. You see the infected, you let Doug know, and you guys lift off. We will come up with an exfil contingency plan if it comes to that."

Priest surveyed the scene, "Shaw and me first, then Neville, Shin, Lia, Doc and Webb will cover our six. The Team drifted to the entrance. There were definite signs of a battle here. The strange thing was that the signs of battle were from outside - in and inside - out. "Captain, signs point to soldiers outside wanting in and soldiers trying to keep said soldiers out," Priest articulated in slight confusion.

"So, we may deal with infected solders who might still know how to fight?"

Priest nodded his head, "Looks that way, Sir."

"Fuck, now we have to fight our own?" A black cloud descended on the group and an all familiar seriousness hit the team. The seriousness produced a feeling of trepidation and regret. Since this complete shit storm started, the killing of citizens and soldiers of their own hadn't sat well with the Team.

Being a soldier meant always dealing with competing feelings and the best could compartmentalize them. They each had their own box, which you could open or close when you felt you could deal with it. There was almost a collective deep breath before the Team entered the underground compound.

The Team entered through a corridor that had staggered entry doors. One door stayed closed, while the other opened. This way someone didn't have entry all the way into the building, but of these doors were now wide open and blood was smeared all over the walls. Pools of blood lay chaotically throughout.

The smell of cordite from spent rounds along with body waste and offal was nauseating. Everyone pulled their baklavas up over their noses. The sounds of electricity shorting out along with the haze of smoke hanging in the air gave the environment one of anxiety and heaviness.

The Team made their way out of the corridor into a larger hall. Priest broke out to the right of Shaw while the rest of the team filed in behind the two. This hall was like the previous one with revolting signs of battle, massacre and inhumane violence. Human heads with their spines still attached were hanging on the wall like a trophy displayed. Their faces frozen in a state of fear. Forever a reminder of how horrific their last moments had been.

"Jesus Christ," Shaw whispered. "They aren't just killing or infecting, they are mutilating in an almost ritualistic way. When did they turn the corner into this kind of shit?"

Priest turned to him, "Yeah, I'm not getting this. They said the virus increases the rage and violence while subduing compassion and sympathy. So, where the hell is this mutilating ritual type behavior coming from? We have heard nothing involving this kind of stuff."

Suddenly, a scream came from inside the compound. "Ok, swift but smart. Let's find out who is left alive here." Priest turned to the team. They took off at a fast duck walk, covering doorways as they progressed farther into the building. They passed a small lunchroom, two offices, and came to an elevator with stairs to the right going down. Priest made a cut sign and pointed to the elevator and motioned toward the stairs. The screams came again, but much louder this time.

The team then moved to the second landing and noticed the door to this floor was open and damaged. They could see down the long dark hallway with multiple doors on each side. Some doors were open, and some were closed. They broke most of the lights down the hallway, which created eerie shadows that danced and moved, creating a surreal view. At the end of the hallway was an open door.

The room on the other side was also dimly lit, and a figure appeared with his back to them in the doorway. He was naked except for a pair of ACU pants, and his back had multiple deep lacerations going down it. He also had some strange hat on with a tail coming down his back and was dancing around with some items in his hands. As he rotated, he spied the team at the end of the hall, cocked his head to the side and stared at them.

A large unnerving smile spread across his face and he spoke to them in a husky voice, "I see you. I see you, yes. Yes, you could be brothers, but no poison. You need the poison to truly be brothers." He started toward the team. "Brothers, brothers come. I know you wish to be one with us. Yes?" As he came closer, the team finally realized what the hat was. It was the skin stripped off of a young woman's head and face, which he had on his head like some kind of animal pelt. The tail was her hair, braided down his back. There were bones from the spine braided in with it. He also had a severed arm in each hand that he was swinging around.

"That is some fucked up shit," Doc uttered.

The infected man stopped and cocked his head again, but his demeanor changed to one of sadness. "You-you don't want the poison? You don't want to join your brothers? You are not here to join us?" Not waiting for an answer, his face changed from sadness to one of insidious rage. He yelled and launched himself toward the Team. He was foaming at the mouth as he screamed and ran toward the group.

Priest pulled his Walther PPQ and put a .45 round right in the infected forehead. That brought the world down around them as infected started pouring out of the same doorway the man had just came out of.

Webb and Doc rotated to cover their backs in case any came up or down the stairwell. Priest and Shaw took a knee while Lia and Shin stayed standing. Neville joined Webb and Doc, protecting the rear.

Shaw began dropping infected left and right as his M48 was dealing out some serious devastation. Bodies shredded, limbs torn off, and heads exploded. The hall was awash with blood, guts, bone fragments, brain matter and bodily fluids. Everything you need for a nice slaughter soup. Priest added to the bodies stacking up in the hallway.

"Reloading," Shaw yelled. Neville swung around to help with the oncoming infected. The dozens were slowing down to a trickle.

Priest ended this while clearing some bodies. "Grenade," he yelled. Everyone squatted down for cover. Priest pulled the trigger on his M203 and Foomp! The grenade launched into the doorway. Priest got down just in time as the explosion rocked the building and debris rained down all over the Team.

"Let's move," Priest urged. A substance covered the hallway which could only be described as "human paste". Shaw turned the corner through the doorway and came out into a lab space. The lab showed signs of killing and mutilation. Blood smears and handprints which couldn't have come from the grenade explosion, along with human remains littered the lab floor and counters.

Webb pondered as he looked around, "What makes them kill as opposed to just try to spread the virus? How do they decide who gets infected and who is slaughtered? There doesn't seem to be any rhyme or reason to how they select."

"Not sure, but when they choose to kill, it's not a clean, quick death," Priest responded. Looking around, Priest could see Shin visibly shaken.

Shin was a Buddhist, and everything could be explained through enlightenment. Things were evil or divine. Even those things that are evil have a certain amount of humanity in them. Shin was trying to find the sense in what he was seeing, but he couldn't find meaning or purpose for what was going on. His faith was being stretched to the breaking point, so he kept trying to use meditation to center himself. To ground his thinking in order to wade through all the pain and destruction. To find a place of peace and renewal. He didn't know how much longer he could go on without bringing his being to focus.

"Shin, Shin…" Priest was talking to him, "Shin, you okay?"

"Yes-yes I am well." Shin looked at Priest and tried to show a calm appearance.

"You sure?"

"Yes, I am fine."

CHAPTER 28

The lab didn't look used much and definitely not used recently. A door on the far side of the lab was in poor condition. An exit sign dangled from the ceiling in front of the door.

"There must be another stairwell somewhere. This lab is definitely not the only one they have been conducting their research in," Webb pointed out.

"Agreed," Priest said as they moved forward toward the door.

Shaw penetrated the door. "It's another stairwell going down," Shaw observed. They started down the stairwell and heard a scream, but they couldn't determine whether it was the same scream they heard earlier.

The rest of the Team trotted down to the next landing as Shaw looked through the small window. "Short hallway with three doors, Two on the right, one at the end of the hallway. No sign of infected. The door at the end has some significant damage to it. Looks like the infected were trying to gain access to it."

"Maybe the scientists are holed up there?" Priest said. They entered the hallway and Priest and Shaw checked the first door. Supply closet. They moved to the second door on the left and it turned out to be a compact locker room for the scientists.

The door at the end was a sturdy steel door that had severe damage from what looks like an axe. Shaw knocks on the door. "US

Army, is there anyone in there?" They waited a couple minutes. Shaw knocked again, this time a little harder. "US Army. Are there any survivors in there?" After a couple minutes they could hear a muffled voice.

"Who is it?"

"US Army, Ma'am."

"I need to know who," the voice replied.

Shaw turned to Priest, he nodded. "It's Shaw, Priest, and Webb."

The team heard running toward the door and moving of items. The lock unlatched, the door slowly opened, and a disheveled Dr. Costa's face peered out. She looked around at the team until she locked on Captain Webb. She rushed out the door and into Webb's arms and broke down, weeping uncontrollably.

Neville and Doc performed security while Shaw, Priest, Lia and Shin continued into the room. Webb and Dr. Costa entered the room, and he spoke to the two scientists. "Dr. Caulfield, Dr. Choi, it's good to see you again." They both greeted him.

Priest called all three scientists and Webb over to him. "Ok, I don't know how much they compromise this compound, but it's pretty obvious this place is toast. How much of your samples and data are still viable? Remember, we have the samples of the original strain."

Dr. Caulfield's face lit up, "You have the originals?"

"Yes, and a prisoner. One of the ISIS members. Where do we go? Are there other facilities like this? Maybe one that is not compromised?"

Dr. Caulfield nodded his head. "Absolutely. I have access to two other facilities like this one."

"Ok, which one is the closest?"

The doctor tapped his finger on his chin, "Hmm, I would say that would have to be our facility in Boone, North Carolina, located up on Snake Mountain. The other one is out west, in Colorado Springs, Colorado."

"Ok, gather anything you absolutely need and let's get the hell out of here. Like I said, I do not know how many more infected are in this compound and I don't want to find out. You must tell me what the hell happened here."

Dr. Choi began talking about what had happened and Webb cut her off.

"Sorry, Doc, maybe later. We need to go." She nodded and then went to gather her items.

Abruptly, the team heard distant gunfire, followed by static on their comms. Webb and Priest exchanged looks. "The chopper might be engaged and the comms won't work down here."

Priest motioned to Shaw, "You, Neville and Lia on me. Shin, Webb and Doc, you guys get these scientists gathered up and follow some distance behind. We will let you know when it is clear. Ok, let's move!" They were down the hallway and up the stairwell in a shot. They appeared in the outside doorway and stopped to assess the situation.

Five infected were clawing and biting, trying to get in the chopper. Two bodies were lying on the ground, apparently taken out by Allison on the M24. Doug looked over and caught Priest's gaze. He motioned for Doug to lift off. Doug saluted, said something to Allison through his helmet and lifted off. Two of the infected were hanging onto the landing gear as the helicopter rose. The Team opened up on the ones still on the ground.

Priest sighted on one of the infected, but his head would put Priest's round trajectory right into the fuselage. He lowered his aim and put a round right in the spine of the infected, which caused it to lose its grip and plummet to the pavement. The fall finished it as its head hit and exploded like a ripe tomato. The sound of the crunch and then the sick wet splat was enough to make you cringe. Maybe he was preoccupied with clearing the facility, or just didn't notice before, but all the infected they had fought here had been soldiers. None of them were the surviving scientists. All were dead or infected. He wasn't sure if this was note or just the way things panned out. Priest made a note to talk to Webb about it later.

A call from Allison snapped him to. "Father, we have a problem."

"Go ahead."

"We have a herd of infected coming this way up the access road."

"Estimate and ETA?"

"Couple dozen and I would say about 10 minutes." Priest turned to Neville and had him get the scientists out now.

"We will set up a defensive perimeter toward the access road. Shaw, get me a couple claymores with a trip wire about 100 yards down the access road."

Neville appeared in the compound doorway. "Sarge, they said 5 mics."

"Shit, tell them we lift off in 5, so they better be here. We've got company."

"Copy that." Neville ran back into the facility. Doug brought the chopper back to land, but kept the rotors spinning.

A few minutes later, Shaw regroups with Priest. "I heard them coming when I was setting the claymores. Ten minutes was more like seven."

Neville joined them. "They are on their way up."

"Copy. Let's set up a perimeter here in case we need to give them more time." They just saw the head of the pack cresting a hill on the access road. Priest keyed, "You people gotta fuckin move. We got company and we should be in the air by now!"

"Copy," Webb responded. They were exiting the facility and loading them and their equipment. That is when the infected locked eyes with Priest.

"Ah shit." The infected man dressed in ACU's let out a shriek and started running for them. The rest, coming behind him, did the same and quickened their pace. Priest, Shaw, and Neville stared to unload on the approaching horde. "Just take out the sprinters. Leave the rest to hit those claymores as a mass." The other two acknowledged.

Allison's voice came over the comms, "We're good. All are on board and Webb is on the fitty." Allison had learned from the guys you don't call it a fifty caliber or even a fifty. They called it a fitty. She was getting the hang of it, which made Priest smile. Shaw smiled too, but for a completely different reason.

As they turned to load up, the horde hit the claymore trip wire. The sounds of all those ball bearings ripping through flesh, bone, trees and brush proceeded a deafening boom. The concussion of the blast knocked a few of the infected off their feet.

The devastation of the ball bearings ripping through the mass was jaw dropping. Various appendages were shredded while it eradicated faces and heads. It lay torsos to waste and rendered them incapable of holding any organs or intestines within the body. Although there wasn't much body left on any of the infected, they still tripped on their entrails and fell face first like a little kid's hockey team out on the ice.

The guys laughed as they got on board and gave Allison the thumbs up. She motioned to Doug to take off and within seconds; they were airborne and surveying the damage the claymores just delivered.

Doug's voice came over the comms, "We will need to set down to refuel soon. I'd say in another 50 miles."

"Copy that," Webb responded. He and Priest brought out a map to scout out some regional air parks to refuel. It was much safer than the major airports or anywhere close to a city. After consulting, they made a plan to refuel at Frederick Municipal Airport in Frederick, Maryland. That would get them close enough to Boone, North Carolina. They would probably stop one more time, because they didn't enjoy flying around with little to no fuel.

CHAPTER 29

Major Harwell barked out orders as soldiers scurried around the Command Center.

"Get some ammunition over to the east wall. The infected are amassing there and are trying to breach the wall!" Harwell commanded.

The sergeant in front of him saluted and ran off to execute the order he was just given.

Harwell walked up behind a corporal who was manning a bank of monitors.

"How we looking on the west wall?"

"Not much better, Sir. I don't know where the new mass of infected came from, but a large group is assaulting the west wall." The corporal responded.

"Well, with the gunfire, explosions and the massive smoke signals we are sending from the various fires burning, I'm surprised we don't have infected from half the damn country at our doorstep." Harwell said absently.

Captain Simmons ran up to Harwell, breaking him from his funk.

"Sir, we are getting low on ammunition and the soldiers on the wall are reporting vehicle headlights coming this way from the west." She said.

"Corporal, rotate that camera to get me a wider view of the west side." Harwell ordered.

"Copy, Sir." The corporal said as he rotated the camera to get a better view.

The three watched as headlights came into view and were approaching quickly. As they continued to watch, they could make out the infected hanging off the side of a 5-Ton truck.

"Tell the west wall to take the fucking truck out! Now! They are going to ram the wall!" Harwell yelled.

Tug continued to fire at the turned up infected faces. He had been on the west wall for a couple hours now and things were not looking better. He felt this was where he was needed most and where he could do the most good.

A scream broke his gaze from the scene in front of him. He looked to his left to see a soldier being pulled off the wall by the infected. As he landed into the waiting mob, they started tearing off arms and shredding his torso to grab at his insides. Tug took aim and put one in the young man's temple to end his suffering…and his screams.

Another infected used the young soldier's body as a bloody ladder and scrambled up to the wall before the body was pulled completely into the churning mass.

Tug leveled his rifle and fired, taking off the right side of its skull. The impact snapped the rest of its head back and sent it falling back into the horde.

"Sum bitch. This whole thing is getting ready to go tits up." Tug mumbled to himself.

That's when he looked up and noticed the truck barreling toward his section of the wall.

He yelled, "They're going to breach the wall, everyone down!"

He turned and started down the ladder when a thought crossed his mind…the girls. He climbed down as fast as he could and hauled ass for the HQ building. His breathing became labored as he reached the stairs.

"Should have laid off of all that beer, you old fuck." He said to himself.

His legs felt like Jello as he ascended the stairs, but he didn't stop. He had to reach the girls. He felt like they were his responsibility. It was his job to protect them.

Tug was wheezing by the time he reached the front door, and he stopped for a couple seconds to keep from passing out. He heard a loud crash followed by a massive explosion. He turned to see the west wall was on fire and the spot where he was previously standing was no longer there. Instead, the mangled husk of a large truck engulfed in flames now stood in its place.

He shook his head, sucked in another deep breath and ran into the building. The Command center was complete chaos. No one was manning the monitors, and soldiers were running in every direction. As Tug passed the monitors, he stole a quick glance. He could see the infected scrambling over the destroyed wall and a pile of bloody ammo cans sitting on the ground unopened.

Tug continued his mission; he has to get to the girls. He focused on reaching them even though his old body was screaming at him.

He finally reached the third floor and ran down the hall. His body was ready to give out, and he had lost feeling in his extremities. His lungs were burning. He tried to suck in another breath, but it was like his chest was filled with concrete. It was heavy and vibrating as his heart pounded away.

A minute later, Tug was at the girl's door knocking excitedly. Dana opened the door and looked out.

"Tug, are you okay? You look terrible. Come on in." She said.

Dana opened the door wider to reveal Kim and Mia, who were inspecting Tug with wide eyes. They rushed over to Tug and led him to a chair to sit down. Kim ran over and brought him a bottle of water.

Mia looked at Tug with concern, "What's going on, what's happening?"

Tug took a large gulp of water before speaking, "The infected have breached the west wall and are flooding into the compound."

Dana looked at Tug with fear in her eyes, "The military will take care of them, won't they?"

Mia and Kim leaned in to hear the answer. Tug dropped his head and shook it.

"They don't have the ammo or the soldiers. The horde has grown again. There are as many now as there was before." Tug went silent for a moment.

The girls went silent, but continued to stare at Tug intently, hopefully waiting for him to finish with a "but we will be okay".

Tug felt the stares on him. He looked up and forced a smile.

"Hey, I believe if we hide and let this mob run through, we should be okay. We will just wait them out."

The three girls exchanged glances, and then Kim broke the silence.

"We don't have any other options." She said to the other two.

Dana and Mia slowly nodded, but did not look too convinced.

Tug stood up. "Come in girls; it will be alright," he said with a reassuring smile.

All four of them stood up and gathered food and some water. They entered a decent size storage closet and settled down with Tug at the very back.

"We might want to shut this light off in here," Tug suggested.

Dana reached up and switched it off. The four of them sat in the dark, straining to hear what was going on around them. They could hear distant weapon fire along with yells and shrieks. The girls stifled their sobs as they held on to each other. Tug's breathing was rapid, and he tried to be as quiet as possible.

The weapons fire died down, but the screams and screeches continued.

The noises became louder and louder the longer the four of them sat in the dark. Running footfalls came closer and the girls inched closer together.

A brief silence fell on the group huddled in the closet. Quiet sniffles and whimpers came from the three girls as the silence made them nervous. They waited for any sound to clue them in to what was going on.

Suddenly a screech split the silence and a pounding against the wall in the hallway startled the group. One girl involuntarily let out a slight scream. More footsteps found their way toward the group's location. Another scream, followed by two more, came from the hallway, closer to where Tug and the girls were hiding.

With the screeching getting louder as the infected keyed on their location, the girls were panicked and cried loudly.

The infected knew where the group was now, and they came pounding on the door. The girls were screaming and sobbing, trying to hold on to each other.

Tug whispered, "I love you girls, just as if you were my own." BANG! BANG! BANG!

Tug fired three shots from the Glock he already had pointed at the back of the girl's heads.

"I told you I wouldn't let them these fuckers take you. You girls will be just fine now. No more fear, no more sorrow, no more of this fucking hell!" Tug was yelling now.

A tear rolled down Tug's face as he closed his eyes and the door finally gave way. The pistol was already in his mouth, and he only needed to provide a few pounds of pressure on the trigger.

Tug's eyes shot open and in a last act of defiance, he swung the pistol out in front of him and shot the two closest infected right in the forehead. He smiled and quickly turned the gun on himself and pulled the trigger before the rest of the infected reached him.

"I need a fucking sit rep! Captain Simmons, give me a mother fucking sit rep!" Major Harwell spat out.

Captain Simmons stared at the monitors as she tried to raise any of their squad leads on the radio.

"Sir, both the east and west walls are compromised and the infected are inside the compound," Her voice and her hands were shaking.

"Fuck me to hell!" Harwell raged.

He grabbed the handset, "Pave One this is HQ, do you copy?"

The Reapers were a few miles out of Frederick when Harwell came over the radio. "Pave One, this is HQ. Do you copy?" He sounded out of breath and stressed.

"Pave One, go ahead."

"We are being overrun. The infected have breached the outer walls." Harwell's voice raised an octave or two, and the fear could be heard in his voice.

At this point HQ's front doors were being assaulted, and Simmons was trying to search the monitors for the cameras that were facing the doors.

"Are you in a position to support?" It sounded more like a prayer than a question.

Webb answered, "Sorry, Sir. We are over the east coast. The CDC facility was overrun, and we're heading to North Carolina." There was a lengthy silence, then some mumbling from Harwell.

The front doors gave way, and Simmons pulled her pistol. She leveled her Glock and took the right side of the closest infected's face off. Harwell ran towards her and fired at the next two closest.

"Simmons, come on! Come the fuck on!" Harwell screamed at her.

She back peddled as she continued to fire, but the infected were much too fast. They ran and pounced on her even as Harwell was firing into the mass.

The closest infected jumped on top of Simmons and drove her down. Before they even hit the floor, a gangly woman took an enormous bite out of the front of Simmons's face, coming away with strips of flesh and most of her nose.

Simmons let out a gargled scream as blood spurted from the front of her face. The infected woman didn't waste a moment and dove in for another bite. This time she tore out most of Simmon's throat as blood bathed the both of them.

Harwell turned and took off running for the war room. He made it there a couple of seconds before the horde of infected, slamming and locking the door. He turned around frantically, trying to come up with what to do next.

He heard a voice come over the radio.

"HQ this is Pave One, do you copy? HQ, do you copy?"

Major Harwell stared at the radio for a few moments while the infected scratched and pounded on the door, trying to get in. After a pause, his shoulders slumped, and he trudged to the radio.

"Captain Webb, this is HQ. You are not in the vicinity to provide support? Is that correct?" Harwell said solemnly.

"Correct, Sir. What are your orders? Continue to the CDC Facility?" Webb asked.

Harwell then started rambling, "Then it's over. It's fucking over. I guess I knew it would all come to this."

Webb tried to talk to him but Harwell had the transmit button pushed, keeping the line occupied.

"I knew when I had to kill Madison that it was all over. Just too stupid to let it all go, but it's time."

There was another long silence, then a click. Webb shouted in the mic, "Major Harwell! Sir, can you hear me? We can redirect and head your direction...." BANG! Then there was dead silence.

CHAPTER 30

"Harwell, Harwell, are you still there? Major Harwell, do you copy? Speak to me, Sir." Webb looked stunned. He then yelled, "Fuck, fuck, fuck! HQ is gone; it's fucking gone!"

Priest and the rest of the team looked down, their faces not revealing the emotion inside them.

Dr. Choi looked worried, "What does that mean?

Shin turned to her, "It means we have a home no longer."

Priest sighed, "It also means that Command is gone, and we have no idea whether any other command still exists. In a nutshell, we are on our own."

They set down at Frederick Airport and Priest old Doug to shut down. Priest directed everyone to continue to provide security, but to be in earshot to hear. "Ok, unfortunately, we have to bring everyone up to speed, and I'm sorry but we can't pull any punches on this. Our HQ is gone, overrun. We have tried to hail other command structures along the way with no luck. Basically, we are on our own with no command infrastructure that we know of, no orders beyond what we have already executed, and no idea what's going on in the rest of the country. Hell, we have no idea what's going in the world."

Dr. Caulfield spoke up, "Does that mean you no longer have any responsibility to us anymore?"

"Technically, yes. We can take off and leave all this shit behind," Priest exclaimed. Worried looks shot all around.

"Don't worry, we will not do that." Webb nodded, "We took an oath that transcends any command structure or world event. You guys are stuck with us until we find a place that you will be safe."

Izzy moved closer to Webb while he spoke, and it was quite obvious that she had gotten close to him during the craziness they recently experienced.

Webb continued, "So, the plans are to get you guys to Boone, North Carolina. Hopefully, it is still intact. Speaking of which, what the hell happened back there?" Dr. Caulfield and Dr. Choi exchanged worried looks, and you could see the fear behind their eyes.

Izzy spoke up. She was shaking, but grabbed Webb's arm to steady herself. He didn't seem to mind and even put his hand over hers. "We were performing analysis on the samples we had, but they were quickly becoming non-viable. Fresh samples were needed and the only way to acquire those was to pull them from actual infected people. We met with the head of facility security… Sargent Collins, I think his name was. He had agreed to send a couple of his men to retrieve what we needed. From what we could determine, his men became infected, somehow trying to obtain the samples. Then they faked their way in. Nobody knew who was infected or not, so the actual infected gained their way in and started infecting everyone in the facility."

Izzy continued, "When the chaos broke out, we locked ourselves in here. They tried to gain access into the lab by telling us they were security and were here to help us. We almost opened the door as they sounded somewhat normal, but then we heard the clicking noise they kept making. I could see them through the camera outside the door before they destroyed it. Their wild eyes and the way they kept tilting their head back and forth was disturbing. It was one of the creepiest things I have ever seen. Gave me shivers," she finished.

"Wow, we're just glad you guys are ok," Webb patted her hand which appeared to give her some courage. She wiped away the tears and stood up straighter.

Izzy looked at the Team, "I want my combat gear back." She went to a duffle she had brought and removed the gear she had worn previously. She stripped right there and got dressed.

Webb noticed with a quick glance that she didn't have the stereotypical scientist body and hers was fit and quite nice. Being from

Puerto Rico, she had caramel skin and black hair. Webb turned around and glared at those who were still looking. They immediately spun to put their backs to her.

Priest turned to Lia, "You have a second?" She nodded, and they walked off. He led her away and finally stopped and turned towards her, "Look, things have changed quickly and not for the better. We are in an "end of the world scenario" here, and we have no idea what could happen next. I guess what I'm saying is."

He stopped and took her hands in his. "Normally I would wait awhile to say anything about my feelings. Hell, to be honest, I might have said nothing at all, but these aren't normal times. I have not felt this way about a woman in a long time. I'm not sure what I'm asking, but whatever we do, or wherever we go, I would like to do it together."

She just stared at him for a long moment. Priest was on the verge of turning around and walking away, sure that he had made a mistake, when Lia spoke, "I thought you would never ask."

Priest stood there dumbfounded. She hugged him, pulled back and kissed him full on the lips.

"Damn," Doc yelled. "Didn't see that coming!"

Priest turned toward the chopper, his face a little flush. He floated back to the aircraft, and Lia followed with a grin on her face.

Webb walked over to Priest, "We good with the plan?"

"Huh, what?"

Webb laughed, "The plan. Are we good with the plan?"

"Ah, yeah, yeah. We're good." Webb slapped him on the shoulder, shaking his head.

They refueled without incident and were in the air headed to Boone, NC. Priest had the Team check and clean their gear. Lia and Izzy followed suit because they were now part of the Team. Webb had given Izzy a pistol and an M4 and taught her how to fire and clean it.

Dr. Caulfield and Dr. Choi wanted nothing to do with any weapon, which was cool with Webb and Priest. They didn't want to spend the time trying to teach them, anyway. Training people to shoot, who have never dealt with a weapon before, was a serious pain in the ass.

CHAPTER 31

After an hour in the air, Allison's voice came over the comms. "Webb, Priest. We are approaching Roanoke Blacksburg Airport. We need to stop and refuel here to make it to Boone, North Carolina."

"Ok, give us the flyby so we can assess the scene," Webb replied. "You guys land after we assess Me, Shin and Neville will roll out and provide cover on the east side. Priest, Shaw, and Doc will take the west. Lia and Izzy will provide support from the chopper. You guys take off and hover after we unload, that way we don't' risk losing our transportation."

Doug buzzed the airport a couple times to lure out the infected. A few people appeared out of the buildings and were easily dispatched. Lia was manning the .50 cal and Izzy had an M4 providing support.

Priest's and Webb's team exited and knelt down in an outward facing semi-circle on each side. Doug ascended to about 20-30 feet and hovered. Each team spread out to 100 yards, then made their way to the fuel tanks by one of the maintenance buildings.

Priest, Shaw and Doc checked the building for any infected while Webb, Neville and Shin posted guard out front. Priest reported all clear, and they brought the chopper in.

Doug set down near the tanks and spun down to refuel, kept the engine running just at lower torque. Allison exited and refueled. A couple minutes went by, then they heard a siren, and all looked around.

Webb spat, "2 o'clock, emergency vehicle." They saw a bright lime green emergency fire truck coming their way.

"They have active emergency services working here?" Shaw asked. Nobody really knew the answer to that one, but saw the truck came around one of the main buildings and headed towards them. As the fire truck came closer, they could see the people hanging off of it and the way it was erratically being driven.

"Aw shit," Shaw spat. "Fucking infected." The team opened up on the truck.

Priest yelled into his comms, "Allison, stop fueling and get this bird the fuck out of here!" Allison stopped the pump and threw the handle. She jumped back in the chopper and Doug cranked the RPM's getting the rotors up to takeoff speed.

The team was throwing as much lead down range as they could and rounds were slamming again the truck's front, shattering the windshield. Two of the infected fell off the sides of the fire truck after being shredded by all the bullets, but the truck was eating up the distance by the second.

"This shit is getting hairy," Webb shouted. "Get that chopper out of here, Doug!"

"I'm trying, but I have to get enough lift first. It doesn't just jump in the sky in a second!" Doug yelled. Just then one of the front tires blew out, which caused the truck to flip and slide on its side. The speed and the momentum drove the sliding truck toward the chopper.

"Move! Get out of the chopper!" Priest screamed. Doug lifted off, but it was too late. The truck slid and crashed into the chopper, plucking it out of the sky. As the truck hit the bottom of the helicopter, it tilted on its side. Rotors bounced off the concrete, which broke apart, sending pieces of rotor and chunks of concrete in all directions.

Each of the team dove for cover while attempting to dodge all the fragments being hurdled everywhere. The truck slid into fuel tanks and slammed into the side of the building. BOOM! The leaking fuel exploded, and the explosion pushed the truck back into the helicopter, which was on its side now. This sent the helicopter flipping across the pavement.

The shock wave leveled the team to the ground and sent pieces of debris and bodies flying all over the area along with blood and fuel residue. The landscape took on a toxic feel and fire was everywhere. It was difficult to breathe, and the disorientation made it nearly impossible to gauge their surroundings.

There was screaming and moaning, which faded in and out because of the explosion affecting their hearing. Fear and panic gripped Webb, and he bled from multiple cuts and the mist caused by the fuel in the air bit at every open wound on his body. He was disoriented and was trying to regain his feet under him, as he yelled out, "Reapers, sit rep. Reapers, I need a sitrep."

The call out was to see who was still with him. Priest tried stumbling to his feet, but the earth was shifting back and forth under his feet and he found it difficult to find his equilibrium. "I'm here, but don't know shit beyond that." He looked around at the total devastation surrounding him, which was difficult to see with the fuel mist floating in the air. He also tried to locate the rest of his team. "Shaw, Neville, Doc, Shin, call out!"

"Mother fucker!" Well, there was Shaw. A couple seconds later he came stumbling over to Priest. He was dirty and bloody, but none the worse for wear.

"You see anyone else?" Priest asked.

"Negative Sarge, but we better find them quick. This situation is deteriorating fast." There were fires all around that were creating columns of smoke. The two were navigating the debris and the fires as best they could.

Shin opened his eyes and was immediately beset by excruciating pain, and he moaned at the stabs of agony. He looked down to see an enormous piece of the tail rotor embedded in his abdomen.

Blood was seeping around the wound, and he couldn't seem to move his legs. He could hear faint voices calling out, which he tried to clear his throat and answer. His voice was horse, and he was having trouble catching his breath to call out. He managed a yell with no audible words, hoping it was enough to be heard.

A minute later, he saw a figure through the smoke. He couldn't tell who it was but could determine they were hurt. His voice was low and raspy, "N-Neville, is that you? Doc?" The figure wasn't big enough to be Priest, Shaw, or Webb. "Hey, I need help here. I am quite injured." The figure seemed to hear him and made its way toward Shin. "Thank you, I am in some trouble. Your assistance is greatly appreciated. Doc, is that you, I hope?" The figure came out from the smoke and the nearby flames illuminated their face.

It was not any of the team, but one of the infected from the fire truck. Half its face had melted off its skull showing a bone jowl and exploded cheek bone. The eye on that side was a bloody mess and looked like slime dropping out of the eye socket. On that same side, its arm and leg were at weird angles and barely functional. "Shit!" Shin uttered. He tried calling out, but his voice just wasn't loud enough. The infected figure had locked on him with its single eye, which spurred its shambling toward him with a renewed vigor.

Shin reached around him, searching for some kind of weapon to repel the creature. He could see his backup knife sticking out of his boot, but being paralyzed prevented him from reaching down to grab it.

Shin panicked and tears streamed down his face. There was nothing in his reach to use, so he tried to move, using any function his body was allowing him to use. The panic was grabbing him and squeezing his breath out of him. The creature was only a couple feet away when he heard Shaw's voice calling out for him.

Shin gathered all his strength and called out to Shaw.

"Coming buddy, you hold on." He saw Shaw stumbling over and witnessed his eyes lock on the creature almost on top of him. Shaw was off balance, but fired on the creature, causing it to fall. Shin closed his eyes in relief until he felt the hand grab his arm, followed by intense pain. He opened his eyes to see the infected had taken a mouth sized chunk from his forearm.

Shaw had shot him, but being off balance only managed a couple rounds into its torso. It wasn't a head shot, and it wasn't dead. Shin screamed with all the strength he had left and the infected creature's head blew apart. He looked up to see Shaw holding a pistol at the creature's head.

"Holy shit. Buddy, are you ok?" Shaw had worry in his eyes and you could hear it in his voice.

"No, no big man, I am not," Shin responded.

Shaw yelled, "Sarge!" And a second later Shin saw Priest running toward him.

"Fuck Shin, this is no time to take a nap." He turned to Shaw, "See if you can find Doc." Shaw got up and started off, "Or Dr. Costa," Priest called after him.

"Got it," Shaw called back.

Priest looked back at Shin, "Sargent, I am not well. I will not survive here."

"What are you talking about? We going to get you out of here and you'll be all right." Shin showed Priest his arm. A bite mark was evidently clear.

"No, I will not. I am bitten and you need to send me away before I turn. Do not let my tranquility be tainted by that. Please, Sargent."

Priest pulled his pistol with such speed; it was almost a blur. He fired a round into Shin's forehead before he knew what was happening. Priest shot up to his feet. "Fuck, fuck, fuck," he was yelling when Shaw and Doc ran up. "He's gone," Priest said. Shaw turned to Doc, "He was bitten and wasn't long before he turned."

"Shit." Doc's eyes dropped to the ground.

"We gotta find everyone else and reassess," Priest said. All three left to find the rest of the team.

Webb came to himself and stumbled toward the downed Pave Hawk. The aircraft was a mangled mess and Webb called out but did not receive any replies. The bird was still laying on its side, so he had to scramble up and on top to gain access to the cabin. He peered in the open side, searching for whoever was still in the aircraft. He could see a pair of legs underneath the helicopter with a massive pool of blood on the pavement.

Webb jumped down into the aircraft to see who it was, but once he got nearer, he saw the BDU pants and black boots. The tension went out of his body for the time being. The clothes identified the last ISIS prisoner they had taken, but Webb wasn't shedding any tears for that piece of shit. It upset Webb that they didn't get the chance to torment the fucker and then have the joy of killing him themselves.

Webb looked toward the cockpit and saw the side of Doug slumped over in his seat, so he made his way over to him. With his initial assessment, Doug looked okay, but as he got closer, he saw Doug had a huge wound on the left side of his head.

Webb put his fingers on Doug's neck to check for a pulse. He pulled his hand back as there was no pulse. "Fuck," he mumbled under his breath. He closed Doug's eyes, which were still open, and said a small prayer over him. He called out to see if anyone was left in the aircraft, when he heard a muffled voice coming from the back of the helicopter. "Call out," he yelled, trying to locate where the voice was coming from.

"Here," came a voice. Webb followed the sound and under some supply boxes and gear bags and found Lia. She looked a little frazzled, but otherwise okay. Webb keyed his comms, "I got Lia. She is okay."

"Shaw and myself found Shin, but he didn't make it," Priest's voice turned a noticeable down turn.

Webb responded, "Shit. Okay. Doug didn't make it either. We need to find Allison, Neville, Izzy and the doctors.

Lia and Webb heard a voice, "Get this shit off of me!" It was coming farther back toward the tail section. He and Lia moved MRE cases, load out bags and other items. As they removed things, a pretty tanned face in a scowl appeared. Izzy's features softened when her eyes saw Webb's face.

"We got you. We got you," Webb reassured her. "Anything broken? Are you hurt?"

"I don't think so," she answered him. They extracted her from the wreckage and she immediately grabbed Webb and hugged him. She held on for dear life and he stroked her hair as he hugged her back and reassured her.

Lia saw Priest come through some smoke and flames. She ran to him and embraced him just as Izzy did Webb. Priest had no problem reciprocating the squeeze. He really cared for her and he was at a place in his life where he couldn't care less what anyone thought. Lia pulled back with tears in her eyes and kissed him urgently. He felt the passion, fear and reassurance in her kiss. She pulled back again and looked at him.

"Well, hello," he stuttered. They both laughed at one another.

"Let's go find Allison," she said. They called out for her. Shaw had already begun frantically looking for her and was yelling her name when he heard a noise in front of him. He couldn't see but made out a figure moving on the ground. As he approached slowly, he noticed Allison's long hair.

Making his way toward her, another figure jumped on him from his right. Trying to get to Allison to see if she was all right, Shaw raged on this fuck. He used the infected man's momentum to grab him underneath the armpit and slammed him to the ground, head first. The man's head hit the pavement with a sickening crack, followed by a wet splat sound. The rest of the infected body followed his head in, slamming to the pavement. He no longer had any resemblance of a head after Shaw was done. He ran to Allison and saw that she had a sizeable piece of debris laying on top of her. She was conscious and was in pain.

"Hey babe. I knew you would find me," she said as she looked up at him.

He had concern in his eyes, "Don't worry babe, I will get you out of here." He yelled for help with Webb and Izzy showing up a second later.

"Pull her out when I lift this up," he said.

"You can't lift that by yourself," Webb said.

"I need your strength to pull her out. Now just do it." Webb and Izzy both nodded. That big son of a bitch lifted that piece of debris with a grunt. Webb and Izzy grabbed Allison under her armpits and pulled her out from underneath. She let out a small scream when they pulled on her. Shaw slammed the piece of debris on the ground and ran over to where Allison was. "How is she?" he asked. Izzy had her shirt pulled up, checking her abdomen and ribs.

"I'm checking her over now." Webb turned to Shaw, "Let her work. We still need to find Neville."

"Okay, captain." The two took off looking through the wreckage, looking for their missing brother.

Priest and Lia had met up with Doc. "How you doing, Doc?" he asked.

"A little banged up, but I'll be all right." "Any sign of Neville, Caulfield or Choi?"

"Negative." The heat from the fires was getting intense, and the team was running out of time to find the others. As they continued to wander through wreckage, they spotted Dr. Choi. Her stature gave her away, but as they came closer, something didn't look right. Upon further inspection, they noticed her left arm was missing and just a stump and the shredded remains of her lab coat sleeve. She locked eyes on them and a recognition flashed in her eyes. She let out a scream and ran straight toward them.

"Aw shit," Priest raised his Walther PPQ and put a .45 caliber round in her forehead. She immediately dropped to the ground. They walked over to her and immediately saw the bite and chew marks on the stump of her missing arm.

Priest keyed his comms, "Team, keep your head on a swivel. Infected are still milling around. I just had to put Dr. Choi down after she tried to attack us. We are down to Neville and Dr. Caulfield, so we need to find them ASAP."

The Team called out for Neville and Dr. Caulfield. After a couple of minutes of searching, they heard gunshots. Some seconds later, a couple more shots rang out. They all ran toward the noise with their weapons at the ready. They cleared a few enormous pieces of debris and saw Neville standing over Dr. Caulfield with a crowd of infected advancing toward them.

Shaw yelled to pull their attention away from Neville and Caulfield. The rest of the Team opened up on the infected as Neville kneeled over Caulfield. They dispatched the infected in several seconds and in hearing the gunfire, Webb showed up a second later.

"Shaw, Neville, go perform security for Izzy while she works on Allison." They took off and Doc ran over to Caulfield to assess his injuries.

"My leg hurts terrible," Caulfield said as Doc reached him. Doc pulled up his pant leg and triage the injury.

"Well, your leg is fractured and we need to splint it. Let me run back to the chopper and get my med kit. I have a splint in there." He ran off to locate his med kit.

"We need to get Caulfield and Allison stabilized and get the hell out of the middle of the wreckage. It's nothing but a beacon for those infected, and we're sitting ducks here."

Doc quickly returned and could splint Caulfield's leg. They made their way to where they found Allison. She was sitting up with a grimace on her face.

Izzy looked at Priest, "Some bruising and sore ribs, but otherwise okay." He nodded in acknowledgement. The Team quickly scavenged anything they could from the downed bird. Webb had scouted a small air traffic control tower while searching for the rest of the Team. It would give them a 360-degree observation and contained only one point of entry to defend.

While Izzy, Doc, Lia and Neville stayed with the injured, Webb, Priest and Shaw cleared the small air traffic control tower to set up for the night since it was getting dark. They only encountered a few infected they dispatched and threw off the catwalk at the top of the tower.

After getting Caulfield and Allison settled in, the Reapers met to go over objectives. Webb laid out where they were, "Ok, our mission, as I see it, stays the same. We have to get Izzy, Caulfield and the samples to North Carolina and the CDC lab. HQ is gone and we haven't been able to contact any other command. Hell, we haven't made contact with any people, period. Opinions?" Priest continued to mull over their options to make sure he wasn't missing anything.

Shaw spoke up, "Way I see it, I think it is our only option right now. If the facility is still intact, not only will the scientists have the lab and equipment we need, we will have a base of operations which will be easy to defend and limit our exposure."

Priest nodded, "That was exactly what I was thinking. We could scavenge for equipment, vehicles, supplies and try to plan out our next move or moves. I say regardless of how we find it; we clear it and use it. Well, within reason, that is."

Webb agreed, "Any objections?" There was silence. "Ok, it's settled then. Now in the morning we will have to find our next mode of transportation, load up and make our way to Boone, which isn't but about 120 miles from where we are now. We'll split the teams up and occupy two vehicles. Priest, you, Shaw and Lia will be one team. Me, Neville and Doc will be the other. We'll put Allison and Caulfield in with you, and we'll have Izzy. Izzy can shoot so that gives us a little more firepower to measure up to Shaw over there. Plus, if we separate the scientists, it will increase our chances that at least one of them makes it to the research facility. We'll post two on watch and rotate four hours."

Priest spoke up, "I'll take first watch with Neville. Shaw, you and Doc release us after four."

Webb looked at them, "Whoa, that leaves me out."

"Yeah, your brain needs to be functioning to get us through this shit. Enough said," Priest finished. Webb didn't argue, and they left the circle.

CHAPTER 32

Priest was sitting outside of the tower on a catwalk that wrapped around the circumference of the tower. He focused on the ground; as the moon's glow illuminated the area. The NVG's took that light and made the view light up enough to see just about anything. A faint sound to his left, Priest had his pistol out and pointed as fast as a rattlesnake strike.

Lia standing there.

"Holy shit, not a good idea," he said as he re-holstered his pistol. He looked back up to see her face was stoic, eyes were wet and glistening. Tears were forming but not falling. "Hey, what's wrong?" His voice took on a gentle tone. She said nothing, but sat down next to him with her head into his shoulder and chest. He put his arms around her. He could feel her shivering, but knew it wasn't because of cold. "Hey, talk to me." he whispered.

The tears were coming now, and she was fighting to speak, "W-we lost so many today. Kind people. People who didn't deserve to die. I didn't know them half as well as you, but I still feel the loss."

"I know. I have lost so many people in my life, I almost lost count. I can remember every one of them though."

"I too have lost people in my life, but it doesn't get any easier. Actually, the more people I lose, the harder it gets. Sometimes I wish I could just shut people out, close myself off. That's just not me though, and I don't think I could if I tried."

Priest pondered this for a minute. "They say God will never give you more than you can handle, so it seems you have a huge heart for a reason. Few can love like you do, and that is a rare trait. One that is definitely missing in this world. It was missing before all this shit started. I am undeserving to know you like I do now, although I'll take it and thank God for it. I would have loved to know you before all this, without the death and chaos. Regardless of what you are going through now, you're still a light to me!"

"You sure spread it on thick."

"Yeah, just like Shaw, I'm from Alabama. We know nothing else but thick.... syrup, gravy, bullshit." She kissed him and pulled back for a few beats. He looked at her and couldn't believe how beautiful she was, and what was more unbelievable was that she loved his dumb ass. He watched her walk back inside and thought, "Just say thank you and move on, dumbass".

The next morning came without incident. Priest and Webb were kneeling down on the catwalk with their bino's searching for viable transportation options. There were some infected lumbering around off in the distance, but nothing that was an immediate threat. "You seeing anything?" Priest asked.

"Negative. All these snowflakes with their Prius' and these other little shit cars. We need at least two SUV's or pickup trucks."

"Agreed. With all the abandoned cars along the road, I don't want to get stuck because this little car can't drive through a fucking puddle, much less a couple of infected," Priest mused out loud. They continued to look for several more minutes. "Oh, wait a minute. Hold up," Priest sounded excited. "Look at our two o'clock. Right past the base of the water tower." Webb turned toward the direction Priest described. Priest continued, "Is that a Chevy and Jeep dealership over there?"

"You know, I think it is."

"Hot damn. We get our pick of some brand-new shit!" Priest was even more excited.

"I believe you are right, my friend. So, we need to check out a couple of these pieces of shit and see if they are operational. As long as they can get a team over there, that's all we need out of them."

Priest nodded, and they both went back into the tower.

Priest started directing the team, "Neville and Lia, you stay on the catwalk and provide oversight, sniper style. Webb, Doc, Shaw and myself will take two of these puddle jumpers to get us to the Chevy dealership a few miles northeast of our location. We get in, find the keys for two Tahoe's, Suburban's, Jeeps or whatever, and we bail the fuck out. Questions?" Everyone shook their head. "Ok, gear up. Check your equipment, weapons and ammo. After we gain transportation, we will have to locate a facility to resupply. A base or National Guard Unit." Everyone nodded.

Everyone was in place and the deployment team made their way down to the cars in the parking lot. They had checked the office in the tower for keys as they progressed down to the ground level with no luck.

At full battle rattle, the team systematically waded through all the cars. They found one with an extra set of keys in a magnetic box under the car. The other was an older model, which Shaw busted the steering column and used his Leatherman to crank over.

From their previous recon, they could see that the highway was extremely congested with abandoned vehicles and a quick glance down the streets of the town revealed a much less hindered route. They made their way through a quarter of the route when the Old Grand Marquis Shaw was driving shuddered. It was gasping and wheezing and sputtered to a stop. "Damn piece of shit Ford," Shaw spat. They all got out to pull security, while Shaw checked out the car. Doc pulled up behind them and they all got out. Webb came running up.

"What's the problem?"

"Looks like a vacuum leak issue," Shaw responded. As Shaw continued to work, a distant wailing started. They all were on their toes were looking for the source. It was early morning, and the sun hadn't burned off the morning mist and fog yet. This made it difficult to see very far.

"Dude, what the fuck is that?" Doc asked wearily. He was becoming frazzled as the sound got louder and more voices joined in. "Seriously, what the hell is that?" In front of them, barely seen through the fog, figures appeared. They appeared as small shadow figures and were aggressively tilting their heads from side to side. Instead of the clicking noise, they were making those screeching/crying noises. They were slowly coming toward the team as the fog dissipated.

"Mother fucker!" Webb said as he looked closer. "They're fucking kids. Little infected kids!"

Doc turned to Shaw, "Come on big man, get his thing started. I don't want to shoot no kids." His voice was trembling.

"I'm trying, I don't want to shoot any either," Shaw barked back. They could now see the building up the street was a daycare facility.

"Aw, shit. This ain't right," Priest added when he saw the daycare playground. The scene was something out of a Clive Barker Novel, think Hell Raiser, but with children.

The tiny figures were infected kids from toddler to maybe six or seven. They slowly shambled towards the Team as they emitted the crying/screeching sound. It was high pitched and creepy as hell.

The breath caught in Priest's throat when he saw the playground. The kids had killed, no mutilated, some adults. Possibly those that worked there. One woman was sitting on the merry-go-round with her abdomen ripped open. Her intestines were splayed all over the merry-go-round and draped over the bars. Some were using them like ropes to hang on while other kids spun the merry-go-round.

Another woman was swinging back and forth on the swing set, looking like one of the swings. She was hung by her own entrails from the top bar of the swing set by her neck. Two kids pushed her legs and watched her swinging back and forth while they giggled. All the while, their heads were tilting left and right.

"Fuck me," Doc uttered. "Holy Mary Mother and Joseph." He made the sign of the cross. Just as the first kids were now 25 yards from them, they heard the car's engine start up. They all turned and ran back to the car. The kids let out a horrifying shriek and came after them.

Everyone was back in their cars and Shaw was ready to speed off. The kids were running straight for them, so Shaw gunned the engine and his face was white with fear and guilt.

"I hate to do this, I really do." He closed his eyes and stomped the accelerator. The car lunged forward and the sickening sounds of the kid's heads bouncing off the hood was sickening. Everyone in the car winced with the noise as the sounds of thuds and crunches as the car ran over the little bodies being thrown under the wheels reached their ears.

Shaw was looking straight ahead when they cleared the last of the kids. He was ashen and sweat was rolling down his forehead and it was weird for Priest to see Shaw like this.

With the amount of combatants Shaw had killed over the years while never batting an eye, to see him this shaken, let Priest know how much Shaw loved kids and this had really gotten to him. Hell, it had gotten to them all.

As the brothers they were, the rest knew to leave Shaw alone and let him work this out. Priest just put a reassuring hand on Shaw's shoulder and that's all that needed to be said.

They encountered a few more groups of the infected. Those they could go around and those they had to dispatch. They arrived at the dealership, took a few laps around, but with no infected present, they got out.

Shaw and Priest looked for a straightforward way in, while the rest of the team pulled security. None of the doors were open, so Shaw used his expertise as an expert in the fine art of breaching to gain access. Most doors couldn't resist the Jeremiah Shaw charm and they all opened, eventually. Shaw and Priest cleared the dealership building and went to look for the keys.

Doc's voice came over the squad comms, "I used to be a car detailer back in the day. The keys are usually in some safe that has a screen on it. You have to put in a car code and a salesman's code to access the keys. I bet Shin could have those keys in no time..." he trailed off. There was a pause before Doc came back on, "Shit, sorry, guys. I -I,"

Priest cut him off, "It's ok Doc. We can't act like Shin never existed. Shit like that is how we keep his memory alive. And yeah, he would have those bastards in a minute." Priest chuckled. "Big Daddy Shaw will have to go old school on it."

"Shit yeah," he replied. A couple minutes later they located something that fit Doc's description. Shaw backed up and put one .50 cal round in the vault lock and the safe opened. In the safe were multiple rows of keys, which were labeled by make, model and style. Sedans, trucks and SUV's were all laid out in their respective rows.

There was also a row of keys near the bottom that caught Priest's eye. The label read "Special Orders" and Priest cocked his head with curiosity. He kneeled down and picked up the key fobs one at a time to read them aloud. "2020 Jeep Wrangler Rubicon, Rock Ridge Special Custom."

Shaw's eyes got gigantic, "Aw fuck yeah!"

Priest laughed, "I guess that is one specially outfitted vehicle."

"You bet your ass it is. Four-wheel drive beast!" Shaw said excitedly.

Priest continued to look, and he found another one similar to the first.

"Grab it. Grab it!" Shaw was like a kid in a candy store. He hadn't seen Shaw this excited in a while. They ran out of the dealership and into the parking lot and walked over to where the Jeeps were parked. Priest pushed a button on the first key fob. A vehicle chirped over to their left and the Team turned as Shaw let out a gasp.

There sat a royal blue 4 door Jeep Wrangler. It had a four-inch lift kit, oversized off-road tires and LED light bars. Huge steel reinforced front and rear bumpers with brush guards were mounted on the front and rear of the Jeep. Steel side steps and armor reinforcement on the rear quarter panels graced each side. A snorkel system was mounted, coming out of the side of the hood. "Fuck yeah!" Shaw shouted. He snatched the key fob from Priest's hand and took off running for the vehicle.

Webb sauntered up beside Priest. "Shit, what is he, sixteen again?"

Priest laughed, "Looks like it." He handed the other fob to Webb. "Here you go."

Webb took the fob and hit the button. A similarly outfitted Jeep chirped, which was a few vehicles down from the first one. Webb tossed the fob to Doc and walked over to the black Jeep that had just chirped. They all piled in to the Jeeps by team and drove around to the parts door.

"Let's see if there are extra fuel tanks, sky jacks, or anything else helpful to keep these bad boys maintained," Priest said. They found a few items that would be helpful and took off back to the tower at the airport. They took another route as to not pass the daycare center again. It was too much for the team to take the first time, much less revisit.

As the team made their way back, they turned left onto Braden Street and saw a few infected in the street. They stopped and saw the team instantly, screamed and came running for them. Shaw looked over at Priest with a shit-eating grin.

"Go ahead," he chided. Shaw punched it and took off toward the infected. They kept right on coming.

Within 25 yards, Shaw yelled, "Ramming speed," and then hit all three infected. Their heads bounced off the top bar of the brush guard, smashing into what looked like broken eggshells. Brains, skull fragments and blood littered the hood as the three disappeared from view. Only a couple dings and crunch sounds were heard from underneath the Jeep as the infected bounced off the skid plate.

Shaw laughed, but Priest just shook his head, grinning. They arrived back at the tower, and everyone was impressed with the new modes of transportation.

The welcoming back was a strange one, because of the team usually being composed of a group of guys. Lia came out and gave Priest a hug and kiss.

Priest looked at her, "I guess you don't give a shit what anyone thinks anymore."

"Never did, just had to scope you out." Inspired by Lia's lack of giving a shit, Allison came out to Shaw with the same welcome, followed by Izzy.

Izzy hesitated in front of Webb for a second, then decided "Aw fuck it" and laid one on him. He didn't seem to be put off by it, and his arms wrapping around her was all that needed to be said. Doc and

Neville bitched about their situation and Caulfield was in the tower, so he had no idea if he needed to bitch.

Neville straightened up and looked at Doc, "Hey don't worry. We will get to this CDC facility and there will be some hot scientists."

That got a reaction from Izzy, "Hey what do you mean?" Neville tried to recover, "I-I-I didn't mean you. I mean, you are hot too. Not that I'm looking or anything. Cap, I wasn't looking, I mean she is special." Izzy released Neville from his self-manufactured foot in mouth syndrome.

"Aw, you are so nice." Izzy planted a kiss on Neville's cheek. Even though he was mixed, he blushed just as hard as anyone and it showed. Izzy walked back over to Webb.

"I think you are special too," Doc whined. She gave him a kiss on the cheek. He blushed, even though he was supposed to be a lady's man from the Bronx. That just encouraged Allison and Lia to do the same. Both Doc and Neville blushed after each kiss.

"It was kind of pathetic, but let them have a little fun," Webb thought.

They decided not to waste any more time and immediately loaded up. In Royal Blue (as Shaw called it) was Shaw, Priest, Lia and Allison, along with gear and supplies. Black Plague (as Doc called it) had Doc, Webb, Neville, Izzy along with Dr. Caulfield all cozy and laid out in the back.

The team took off down Route 81 heading to Wytheville before they would get on Route 27 heading south to get on Route 421. During the journey, the teams practiced contingency tactics if they became overwhelmed or the shit hit the fan in some other way. This comprised stopping and a shift in personnel.

Shaw and Doc were both excellent drivers, so keeping them behind the wheel was the best plan. Trying to keep them out of a fight was the principal objective. If the fight went south, then Allison switched with Shaw and Izzy switched with Doc. This freed up their guns to join the assault. It felt like when you were teenagers and you stopped in the middle of the street, yelled "fire drill" and everyone changed seats.

CHAPTER 33

The team made it to Boone, NC at about 1:00 in the afternoon. Boone was a quiet town in the foothills of the Appalachian Mountains. It was also the home of Appalachian State College, which was almost as big as the entire town.

They weren't here to sightsee, so "Black Plague" took the lead since Dr. Caulfield was the only one who knew how to get to the CDC facility on Snake Mountain. They traveled up the access road leading to the CDC facility and as they approached, they noticed the outer security fence had the gate blown off its hinges.

"Shit," Webb breathed out. "Is this fucking place overrun as well?"

"It definitely looks like a battle has happened here," Doc added. They moved in closer, but at a more cautious pace.

Webb keyed Priest, "What do you think?"

"Hmm, there has been a battle here, but the way it looks and the damage I am seeing, I don't feel the infected attacked here."

"Are you sure?"

"I'm not sure about anything anymore, but it's a gut feeling I have." They stopped their vehicles and got out slowly, with weapons at the ready. They could see the bullet impact marks on the front metal door.

As they advanced closer to the door, a voice came over a speaker, "What do you want? You need to vacate the premises or I will release our security force if needed."

"Hello, Sir. I am Captain Marcus Webb and this is Master Sargent Alec Priest from the United States Army. We have Dr. Caulfield and another scientist, Dr. Costa. We fled from a CDC facility in Dearborn, Michigan, and were ordered to bring them here."

"Oh, really. Please wait for one moment and we will open up." Seconds later, the front steer door opened, and a short, disheveled scientist type poked his head out. He had crazy red hair, tons of freckles, and a brown house robe on. He was quite the picture and reminded Webb of Hawkeye Pierce from MASH. The scientist looked around nervously.

Webb walked up to him, "Hello Sir. Is everything okay here?"

"Huh, what? No-no, things are terrible."

"Have you been attacked by the infected?"

"What, infected? No, this is from some crazy mountain people trying to take this facility over."

"Really? A bunch of rednecks trying to play warlords?" Priest asked. He had made his way up to Webb's side.

"No-No, they are much more than that. They are organized and have sufficient numbers."

Webb tried to give the man a reassuring look, "Ok, we will deal with them. Don't worry." "How many of you are left?"

"Just four of us are left. That's it."

"Ok, we can get everyone up to speed later. Let's get everyone inside and set up a perimeter in case the rednecks show back up," Webb directed. They hurried to get all their gear stowed and got Caulfield settled in one of the dorm rooms. He wanted to go straight to the lab, but they convinced him to get some rest. Once he was taken care of, the team gathered in the front section of the facility.

Webb had the Team form up on him, "Ok, we need to set up a perimeter and install some deterrents. Priest, get that taken care of."

"Got it. Let's move people. I don't want to get caught outside by these guys and lose our element of surprise. We should be able to take a bunch of the guys out before they know what hit them. That's IF they still don't know we are here" The team acknowledged and went to work.

Neville moved the Jeeps to the backside of the facility. Shaw rigged up Claymores just like at the other facility, but set up three stages. He came back and he and Priest welded hinges back on the perimeter gate and reinforced it with some rebar that was lying around from a maintenance building. They set up a couple more Claymores at the fence, constructed some surveillance points, and a couple sniper supported positions on top of the facility entrance. Neville and Lia will start there. If things got too hot, they have a way on the backside to get down, and the team would provide suppressive fire to allow them to get into the facility. Priest and Shaw will start on the opposite sides of the facility entrance, with the same contingency.

As they finished their preparations, Doc spoke up, "You know, it's bad enough out here having to fight all the infected, but to have to deal with regular people acting this way is bullshit."

Priest nodded, "Yeah, but remember that in most places we have been overseas, it's the same thing. Over in Somalia, Congo, Botswana, they all have civil war, ethnic cleansing and border skirmishes. You had these warlords trying to take advantage of the situation by hording food, natural resources, etc. Just so the people will bow down to them."

"Yeah, their own fucking people!" Shaw got fired up whenever he talked about what they saw over there.

Priest continued, "Why should this be any different? Just a bunch of fucking assholes taking advantage of a seriously bad situation." They all shook their heads. They had all seen the injustice and the corruption of people selling out their own.

The killings were brutal, and it didn't matter if you were a man, woman or child. They all were killed, tortured and or raped. It was amazing that soldiers or warlords were there for ethnic cleansing, but would still rape people they were there to kill because they hated them. The Team finished up preparations and went in the facility for chow and a little rest. They had cameras set up at the bottom of the access road that would give them an early warning.

Inside the facility was basically the same layout as the other one, and they were probably all cookie cutter construction. However, the team was in full battle rattle up in Dearborn and didn't have time to take a breath and enjoy the scenery.

The facility had a lunchroom, workout room, dorms, shower facilities, storage and a massive laboratory with all the latest technology. This facility was much better outfitted than the Dearborn one. Dr. Caulfield was extremely excited to get to work since he had gotten a few hours' rest.

The Team took one of the storage rooms as their tactical load out and armory. It was the room right next to the Command Center (CC) of the facility. The CC had all the camera feeds inside and outside that monitored all lab environments and had access controls for the facility. It also had controls for the massive generators housed in the underground facility. Along with generators, there were underground fuel and water tanks making the facility self-sufficient.

There was an infirmary, which Doc and Izzy checked out together. It was nicely outfitted and could handle just about any emergency except for major surgery. If worse came to worse, it even might give it a go. There was enough emergency food to sustain 45 people for 6 months.

Webb had called an all-hands meeting in the large conference room. This was to meet everyone, establish rules and procedures and to update everyone on what was going on. "Hello everyone, I am Captain Marcus Webb of the U.S. Army. I would like to go around the room and have everyone introduce themselves. Please state your name, what you do, and any special traits or abilities. I want to take an inventory of all capabilities at our disposal."

"Master Sargent Alex Priest, second in command."

The rest of them went after Priest. "Dr. Isabelle Costa, microbiologist… I was also a medical doctor and was trained in minor surgery."

"Allison Reeves, news reporter. I can navigate and monitor flight controls, but never got enough flight time to fly a chopper. Don't think that will benefit us much."

"You have no idea," Webb smiled.

"Chief Sargent Lia Dahan with IDF, now a Light Reaper." That got some "damn rights" and a couple claps. "I have training in light weapons, sniper operations, hand to hand combat and I was a communications officer, so I am trained in various radios, computers, GPS, sat phones, etc.".

"I am Dr. Caulfield, virologist with research in Hematology. I can make wine and beer." A few faces lit up in the room.

"I am Dr. Diane Santiago, Pathologist dealing with body tissue and disease. I have a green thumb and can grow things in dirt and using hydroponics."

"I am Dr. Bethany Rand, Immunologist. I also sew as a hobby. Dresses outfits, couch covers, etc."

"I am Dr. Arnold Holtz (the scientist with the crazy red hair), Biotechnologist, disease and medicine research. I am involved in husbandry to some extent."

"Ok, we are not here to take over or to bully you guys around. We are here, at least for the foreseeable future, to provide security and to keep all of you safe. Now, to do that efficiently and properly, there will need to be some procedures to abide by. First, let me tell you what you are dealing with." Webb continues to explain the state of the world as he knows it. He explains what they have encountered and fought through. He talked about the reactions and mannerisms of the infected and the way they have been evolving.

When Webb finished, a general silence evaded the room along with shock, tears, and obvious disbelief. The scientists sat there for a few minutes, saying nothing.

Priest broke the silence. "We have some samples of the original virus strain to test with. Dr. Costa resealed the containers, but they dragged this virus through all those airports that spread this shit like wildfire. Hopefully with these samples, you may find a cure or antidote. I sure as hell hope so, at least!" As Priest finished, their faces lit up.

"Untainted sample," Dr. Santiago said. "Yes, Ma'am." Priest slapped Doc on the shoulder because he had been staring at her since he laid eyes on her. "You're staring. You look like a mental patient."

"Sorry, I can't help it." Dr. Diane Santiago was something to look at. A Hispanic woman who has black hair, big brown eyes, and she carried a few extra pounds, but they were all the right places. She was attractive and had a full figure, and it mesmerized Doc.

Dr. Santiago noticed him looking a couple times, but never really said anything to him. Dr. Bethany Rand was slightly older and closer to Priest's age, but didn't show it. She wasn't a "hot" woman but was the pretty girl next door type. Being shy, she didn't look at people much and seemed to have a low self-esteem, but was a damn talented scientist.

CHAPTER 34

Webb created a schedule of watch personnel, which included everyone since it didn't take military training to monitor the cameras for issues. The plan was that if someone saw something suspicious or an obvious threat, they would wake up the Sargent at arms for that night, which floated back and forth between Webb and Priest.

There was an alert sound and intercom in each of the rooms. Instead of going for her own room, Lia stayed with Priest with no protest. Izzy followed suite with Webb, but Allison was still a little nervous about it. Shaw told her not to worry about it and it was ok. Everyone else was in their rooms.

Neville started off as the first watch when everyone went to bed. Priest showered and was in bed when Lia came out of the bathroom naked.

Priest was a little wide-eyed at first, then composed himself. He could see various scars on Lia, one on her stomach, on her thigh and across her collarbone. She saw him looking and self-consciousness spread across her face.

She turned to get a robe, "No, no. It's okay, come here," Priest whispered. She walked over to him and sat on the bed. He softly and slowly ran his hand across her scars. He looked up at her, "Combat?" She teetered her head back and forth, "Kind of.... abusive husband."

Priest's face went from concern to rage. She put her hand on the side of this face and kissed him. His rage dissipated.

"Don't worry, I had enough one day and kicked the living shit out of him." Priest grinned. She pointed to her collarbone, "It's how I got this. He threw me down the stairs in our home. I was dazed, but it knocked something loose and I had enough from that moment on. I was wearing heels that night and one had fallen off as I tumbled down the stairs. One was still on and as he came down after me and I kicked him with my heel into the side of his knee. It buckled, and he fell, so I kicked out again, this time at his groin. The heel entered."

"Did you say entered?"

"I did."

"Holy shit." Priest made a squeamish face. "I bet that hurt."

"It was enough for him to pass out!"

"Sweet."

"We were both in the IDF and so I went to his Command and told them the entire story. They put him in the "brig" as you call it. I filed for divorce two days later."

"Damn." Priest looked at her for a long moment, "You are beautiful to me, scars and all, seriously." Lia bent down and kissed him, her wet hair tickling his face. As she straightened back up, she ran her fingers over the multitude of scars that covered his body. She asked him to roll over, and she saw even more on his back. He turned back over and a look of concern swept across her face, "Battle? She asked.

"No, crazy ex-wife," he snickered. She jumped on him and they wrestled around with her squealing and him laughing. They stopped after a while and were laying side by side facing each other.

She looked into his eyes, "Where did you get all those?"

He took in a lengthy breath, exhaled it, "Some from combat but almost all on my back from being a prisoner in Yemen. They like to use the whip over there."

"Oh my gosh," she gasped.

"Don't worry, my boys busted me out, and we made them pay. Took their whole fucking compound to the ground. A few survived and we...", he paused, "Well, let's just say we sent them to find their

72 virgins with missing limbs, missing teeth, mmm… missing eyes, etc.". She just laid there grinning at him. He lay there looking in her eyes. "Can I ask you a question?"

"Sure," she said.

"Why are you here?" She was taken aback slightly.

"What do you mean?"

"Why are you here with me? Why did you choose me?"

"Why not you?"

His eyes held a deep sadness and she could see hurt there. He didn't believe it to be true, like he was waiting for the punchline. She ran her fingers through his beard softly.

"My God, has life given you nothing but hurt and sorrow? No one that has loved you for who you are?"

Lia had tears in her eyes, "You want to know why I am here?" She paused for a second and made sure he was looking into her eyes.

"I see strength in you and not just in your body, but in the way you lead, in the way you care for your men and others, in the way you feel the need to do what's right. I also see the way you look at me, with what I can only describe as pride. I don't know why, but I can see it in your eyes when you look at me. You are hard and rugged, soft and caring, loyal and humble, all rolled into one. So, yes. I am here with you because there is no other place I feel as safe and happy."

That brought tears to his eyes, and he dropped his head. She pulled his head back up, wiped the tears away with her thumbs and kissed him again.

After a few moments, he touched her face, "Just to clear one thing up. When you came out of the bathroom, that look I gave you, was lust." She let out a chuckle and slapped him on the shoulder. They turned off the light, embraced each other, and that was all the talking they did that night.

The next morning, Priest woke up to an empty bed. He got up, washed his face, put on a t-shirt and sweatpants and made his way down the dorm hall. Half way down, something reached his nose. It was an aroma of meat and spices. It reached up, grabbed his nose and carried him toward the dining hall like in one of those Bugs Bunny cartoons.

Before he reached the dining hall, he heard voices and laughter. It was almost foreign to him since it had been so long since he had experienced that genuinely. Sitting at the table was Lia, Allison and Dr. Caulfield, all drinking coffee and it smelled heavenly. There was giggling coming from the kitchen and he could hear Neville going on about something.

The dining hall had a fully equipped and stocked kitchen. As he reached the dining hall, he saw Neville and Dr. Rand standing at the stove cooking together, joking and laughing. That brought a smile to his face, then he was startled by a pair of lips on his cheek. He was focusing on Neville & Dr. Rand and didn't see Lia walk up to him.

"Whoa, you okay?" she asked.

"Yeah, sorry. Probably still torqued up from the past few days."

She stroked his arm, "Sit down and I'll get you some coffee." He gently tapped her on the butt when she walked by. She looked over her shoulder with a giggle on her way to the coffee station. He sat down at the table where Shaw was now sitting next to Allison. He was staring at Priest with a sheepish grin.

"What?"

Shaw elbowed Allison, "You're kind of glowing," she said with a smirk.

"I do not glow."

"Well, you are glowing today," Shaw chimed in. "Honestly Sarge, I've never seen this side of you before."

"The only side of me you're gonna see is the front of my fist if you don't shut up," Priest joked.

"You got it, Sarge."

Lia returned with his coffee and sat down. She looked around the table, "What's going on?"

"They say I am glowing," Priest said over his coffee mug. This caused Lia to blush a little. He looked over at her. She had her thick black hair in a ponytail, barely a few grays throughout. Her hazel eyes sparkled next to her olive skin. She caught him looking at her and knew what he was thinking.

She patted his forearm, "Why not you?" she said. He nodded, closed his eyes for a second to say a quick "thank you" prayer. All the women he had ever been with never affected him the way Lia had. It was strange territory for him, but he definitely didn't mind. "All right, snap out of it and get your shit together, jackass," he thought to himself. He was ready to turn his attention to figuring out what they do next. "Where is Doc?" Priest asked.

"He had last night's shift for watch," Shaw answered

Webb woke up with Izzy still laying there asleep. He got up and used the bathroom and came back into the bedroom with Izzy sitting up in bed. "Shiiit." He said. She started laughing. "You scared the shit out of me."

"I can see that." They bantered back and forth and got ready. She looked at him, "Are you okay?"

"Yeah, sure. Why do you ask?" "You were having a rough time last night. You were thrashing around, having nightmares and calling out."

"Damn, yeah I have issues."

"Marcus, look, I don't have any experience with this, but if there is anything I can do to help, I will."

He leaned over and kissed her, "Just you being here with me calms my spirit. You make me feel more secure in my own mind. You ground me to where things don't feel so out of control and give me a sense that things are okay. Does that make sense?" He looked up at her and saw she had tears in her eyes.

"It makes more sense than you can ever know." She wiped her tears away and gave Webb a hug. She pulled back, and they smiled at each other, and then her eyes got big.

"What?" Webb asked.

"I am starving!"

"Me too," Webb added.

They made their way down to the dining hall, laughing and joking. Webb seemed to have a glow about him as well that Priest noticed. He now understood what everyone was talking about.

Webb sat down across from him and looked up. "What?"

Priest snickered at Lia, Allison, and Shaw. He looked back at Webb, "You're glowing." The entire table burst out in laughter.

Izzy came back with coffee, "What is so funny?"

Webb still with a look of confusion on his face, "They said I was glowing. What the hell is that?" Izzy giggled, bent down and whispered something in Webb's ear. She straightened back up, kissed him on this head and went to the kitchen. If you have never seen a black man blush, Webb's face looked like a red stoplight. "Aw piss off," he said.

Bethany Rand called for everyone's attention and started an introduction, "Straight from the bayou of Louisiana, I give you Chef Renaldo Neville and his Cajun chef-d'oeuvre petite dejeuner!" She turned to Neville, "Did I say that right?"

"That was just fine, Chere," Neville responded.

"Damn, that smells good. What is it?" Shaw asked.

"It's a little something I whipped up. Eggs, onions, sausage, cheese and some spices."

"Where did you get the sausage?" Shaw asked.

"Okay, it's hotdogs, but with the Cajun spices I always have with me, BAM! andouille sausage."

Priest leaned over to smell it, "Whatever it is, it looks and smells delicious." Neville dipped some out for everyone. He was smiling a smile that hadn't been on his face in quite some time. It was good to see.

Just then, the doors from the opposite hallway burst open and Dr. Holtz came power walking through. In his hand was a huge insulated coffee mug the size of a full-size coffee can. He walked up to the coffee station, emptied both pots into his enormous mug and zipped off back towards the labs. Everyone turned and looked at Dr. Caulfield.

"Yeah, well, get used to it. That is an everyday occurrence. Actually, it occurs multiple times a day. He is a brilliant scientist, but a tad bit quirky." Caulfield said with a look on his face that signaled acquiescence.

"Ya, think?" Neville said.

Priest shrugged and grabbed his plate, "I got to watch so I'll take it with me." He got up and turned when he heard a throat clearing. He turned back around to see Lia looking at him with a smile on her face. "What? Oh shit, sorry. Just not used to it." He bent down and kissed her and then turned to walk away.

"That's ok," she said and then slapped his ass. Priest jumped and let out a girlish scream and then walked away shaking his ass way too much.

"Damn, didn't need to see that," Webb laughed.

"You and me both," Shaw added.

Priest just started singing "Jealousy" by Queen as he went down the hall to relieve Doc.

A few hours later Webb showed up in the CC while Priest was scanning the perimeter with the cameras.

"What's up Cap?"

"Nothing much, just seeing what was going on."

"I've been thinking. I think we need to scout the town down there and see if there is anything we can use. Plus, I wouldn't mind finding out if the "Redneck Mafia" that attacked this place before, has a base of operations in that town."

Webb looked pensive for a moment, "I had the same thought myself. A little recon would do us good for some local intel."

"Agreed. Another thought I had was possibly looking for a chase vehicle. You know, something small, quick and maneuverable. Something we could scout out the infected with or possible even use as a bait vehicle to lure the infected away if needed."

"Hmm… I like it."

"Okay. I'll take Big Man with me and we will see what is what tonight." Webb nodded and left the CC.

CHAPTER 35

The town of Boone was a small to medium size country town, anchored by Appalachian State University. The college was a major source of employment and commerce. It supplied consumers for the town's goods and services and was the lifeblood of Boone's existence.

The town was as dead at night time. The streets held an even more eerie feel since power to the town had shut off. With no one manning the nations' power plants, it was a crap shoot which towns had power and which ones didn't. The CDC facility has its own generators, along with a solar farm and battery banks.

Deep into the night, a vehicle made its way down the gloomy streets. No lights illuminated from the vehicle interior or exterior while the two figures rode silently.

The figures had their NVG's activated, which allowed them to move undetected and still being able to see everything as if it were daylight. The vehicle traveled through the town at a slow creep, looking for other signs of life.

Priest wondered how many kids made it home or succumbed to the virus, never to go home again. He couldn't imagine being a parent and worrying whether your child, not knowing where they were, if they were safe, if they were dead or not. The anxiety in trying to get to them through all this shit.

Shaw noticed Priest was more quiet than usual, "Hey Sarge, you okay?"

"Yeah, just thinking about this place when it was in full swing. Wondering how many kids made it home or got infected before they ever made it there." He couldn't imagine being a parent and worrying whether your child, not knowing where they were, if they were safe, if they were dead or not. The anxiety in trying to get to them through all this shit.

"I know what you mean. I think about that myself." They both fell silent as they navigated through the empty streets.

Shaw broke the silence again, "You think any of those rednecks are out here somewhere. Maybe occupying a couple of these buildings out here?" Shaw asked.

"They got to be somewhere, but I imagine they're out in the sticks. They are probably better prepared for this situation in their own homes than in the town." Priest replied.

The two continued on, passing grim building after grim building. None showed signs of life. They turned back onto the major road, heading through town.

"Whoa, stop the truck." Priest called to Shaw.

"What? Why? What's wrong?" Shaw was looking around for something he might have missed.

"No, no. Take it easy. Look over your right shoulder. What is that?"

Shaw turned to look, "It's a motorcycle shop. And?"

"So, what are we missing with other mission needs?"

Shaw thought for a while, "Ah. Maybe something quick and more maneuverable. Maybe to scout or lead the infected somewhere. I like it, but you feel up to riding?"

Priest looked at him with an enormous grin, "Hell yeah! I'm ready to ride."

"Well then, let's go look and see what they have for sale."

Shaw turned off the engine, and the two sat there for a couple minutes listening for any movement from the infected. After hearing nothing, they exited the Jeep and walked over to the door of the bike warehouse. Priest walked up and grabbed the padlock on the door.

"Shit. How are we going to remove that quietly?"

"Let the doctor operate," Shaw said as we moved past him with a pair of bolt cutters.

"Where the hell did you find those?" Priest looked at him in disbelief.

"One never reveals their secrets. Ok, I picked them up at the 4x4 dealership." Shaw grinned as he made quick work of the padlock. "After you, fine sir."

They entered the warehouse and found themselves in the maintenance shop. There were a few bikes in pieces and a couple other waiting for repairs. Those repairs were probably never coming. They continued through a doorway on the right and came out into the showroom.

There were a few used bikes sitting there, but in pristine condition. With it being dark and Priest's vision being filtered through the NVG's, it made it hard to see the immaculate condition of the bikes in the showroom.

As he continued to scan, his eyes stopped on a particular bike sitting by itself. We walked over to it and ran his hands over it. Shaw joined him after noticing that he had stopped.

"Brand new Kawasaki Ninja 1000," Priest said, somewhat in a daze.

"Yep, you think it fits the bill?"

"Shit, yeah!" Priest said, trying to contain himself. After a quick search, they found the keys and some riding gear in the pro shop. Priest turned the bike on to walk it out of the shop. They were back out at the Jeep and with Priest straddling the bike.

"Okay, when I crank this thing it will be loud as shit, you ready to roll out?" Shaw gave Priest the thumbs up. Priest cranked the Ninja, and it growled to life. He put it in gear and took off like a shot.

"Shit," Shaw had to stomp on the Jeep to keep up with Priest. "Crazy son of a bitch!"

Priest had a feeling come over him he hadn't experienced in a long time. The freedom of riding a bike on the open road. He thought about Lia holding on to him while they cruised all day and experiencing the freedom together. Probably why he had grabbed an extra set of gear from the shop.

The two reached the compound and settled in for the night.

The next morning everyone was in the dining hall, eating breakfast and listening to Shaw and Priest tell the story of obtaining the motorcycle. They all joked about riding it and how cool it was to have it as part of their transportation options.

Webb looked at Priest as he was pouring hot sauce on his eggs, "I think we need to check in with the scientists and see where we are with things.". The eggs were powdered, but with the hot sauce, they weren't too bad.

"I was thinking the same thing, but I kind of thought you were already in the know," Priest said with a sly smile on his face.

"Dude, shut up," Webb said shyly.

Priest just laughed, "Yeah, we can go down there and check it out." Minutes later, the two entered the lab. Everyone was busy looking through microscopes, mixing samples and other research type actions. That's what it looked like to Webb and Priest, anyway.

They saw Dr. Holtz zipping around to all the different stations with his bucket o'coffee. As Webb and Priest walked in, he noticed them with a look of annoyance on his face. He didn't stop to address, but kept on doing what he was doing. Webb and Priest looked at each other with a smirk.

"I think we ought to get our update from Caulfield," Webb said.

"Agreed." They walked over to Dr. Caulfield, who was now out of his splint.

"Hello gentlemen. What can I do for you?" Caulfield greeted them.

"Just came down to see how things are going," Webb said.

"Well, we are making some progress in reverse engineering this virus but we keep hitting a brick wall."

"How so?"

"We can reverse engineer the virus, find all the chemical components, the composition strings and compound links. The issue is we still need to know how all this works with the human body. We have a theory that the virus interacts and alters the chemicals in the brain to elicit specific behaviors and reactions. We don't know that for sure, but we are speculating. What we don't know is the complete affects the virus has on the body. How it affects specific organs, what does it do to the cells in the blood? Does it mutate a person's DNA? Based on the things we have seen with the infected, this is much more than just a chemical imbalance in the brain. Where does the strength come from? What about the indestructibility and the extreme rage, while maintaining the coordination and instincts to work together? Bottom line, there is still so much we do not know."

"Ok Doc, so hearing everything you are saying, it sounds to me you don't have everything you need. So, let's hear it," Webb prodded.

"You will not like it."

"Probably not, but spit it out," Priest interjected.

"We need a viable infected specimen." Both Webb and Priest did a face plant.

Priest spoke up, "When you say viable, am I to assume you mean "live" specimen?"

"You assume correctly, Sargent. If you were to acquire a dead specimen, then we would have no way to measure any electrical impulses from the brain, which is one of the big mysteries we need to solve."

"Shit, I knew he was going to say that," Webb groaned. He looked at Dr. Caulfield, "You are sure that it is that important or are you just satisfying your curiosity?"

Dr. Caulfield looked at him for a minute and said, "Yes."

"Damn, that will be a cluster fuck," Priest said.

The two left the lab and were walking back toward the CC when they ran into Izzy.

"Hey babe, what kind of trouble are you doing getting into today?"

"We just had a conversation with Dr. Caulfield and he said you have no more viable samples."

"Well, that is true."

"We are discussing getting a specimen for you today."

She looked at him, "You guys are really going to trap an infected?"

"Well, Caulfield says you guys have to have one. Is that not true?"

Izzy let out a breath, "I don't know if we exactly have to have one, but it would probably cut our time significantly, if we did."

"So, when you say cut time, what do you mean?"

She looked up at the ceiling and then back to Webb, "I'd say weeks, maybe a couple months versus 6-8 months."

Webb's eyes got bit, "That much impact?"

"Afraid so."

"Well, I guess that confirms it. We go out today and capture a specimen."

"Ok, but be careful, please."

"I will."

"We might need you for our objective planning. Can you be in the Load Out room in about an hour?"

"If you need me there, yes." She then gave Webb a kiss and walked off towards the lab.

Webb turned to Priest, "Let's round up the team and see about planning this OP," Webb instructed. Half an hour later, the entire team including Izzy was in the Load Out Room. Webb was addressing the group, "We have an important mission to execute ASAP. The scientists working here have hit a brick wall as far as progress. Bottom line, they need a "live" infected specimen to test."

There was an audible groan from across the room. "Believe me, I don't like it any better than you do, and I'm not comfortable putting the team in unnecessary danger trying to catch one of these infected. I am less comfortable having a live infected INSIDE the facility, much less the compound, but there you go. So, we need a plan to capture one of these things as safely as possible." Webb looked around, then nodded to Priest. "You're up, Sarge."

"Ok, here is how it will go. I will run as the chicken on the bike to flush out any infected. Hopefully, the bike's speed and maneuverability will allow me to stay a few steps ahead of any infected. To maintain as much safety as possible, we will take this out on the highway and out of the town. The town has way too many ambush opportunities, but out on the highway, we can see them coming. Shaw, Doc and Neville will be in the Jeep and they will be in the chase car."

Webb looked confused at Priest, "Whoa, whoa, whoa, I didn't hear my name in there."

"No Sir, you didn't, and it was on purpose. If this thing goes sideways, and I mean worst-case scenario, then we need someone here who can maintain command. We both can't be out there and risk both of us being killed. Things are way too important here for both of us to be out of the picture."

Webb protested, but stopped. He knew Priest was right, no matter how much he hated it. "Fuck!"

"You must stay home with me," Izzy joked. Webb sighed.

Priest smiled at him and continued, "Once you guys narrow down a target, Neville will take out its legs. This will decrease its mobility and make it somewhat easier to capture. Shaw will have on thick protective gloves and arm and head protection. We will manhandle the infected and get it secure enough for us to slap on cuffs and bind its legs. Also, to make sure we slap that belt on its mouth."

Shaw added, "I got a sack we can throw over its head so none of the nasty spit and saliva gets on anyone during the melee."

"Excellent idea!" Priest nodded his head. "Questions?"

Doc spoke up, "What if you run into the guys who shot this place up?"

"Good question. I'll run and let Shaw light them up with the M48. If the shit hits the fan like that, then we bail on the infected and regroup back here at the compound. We face them together on our turf. Ok, gear up. We leave in thirty."

CHAPTER 36

Priest had on the riding gear on that he swiped from the bike shop. He looked at the jacket and pants and they made sense. Both were thick leather to protect the rider from road rash, and there was no way the infected could bite through it either. Not to mention, the helmet was protection and a weapon all rolled into one.

Priest checked his M4 and slung it on his back, then secured his thigh holster for his PPQ. He walked out to see everyone out in the compound lot waiting on him. "Ok, we got everything?"

"Yep, all loaded up and ready to go," Shaw answered.

Priest thought to himself, "Your men are top-notch, do you really need to ask?" He cleared his head and focused on the mission. He turned towards the bike, and Lia walked up to him.

She gave him a longing kiss. "Please be careful and come back soon."

Priest cracked a smile, "Of course, you think I want to leave a beautiful creature like you alone with these trolls?"

"Hey, I resemble that remark," Shaw yelled. Priest shook his head as he put on his helmet. He started up the Ninja and looked over at Shaw and he gave him a thumbs up.

They had modified his squad comms to plug into the speakers and microphone inside the motorcycle helmet. "This is Father, testing out the helmet comm. Do you copy?"

"Read you, Father," Shaw responded.

"Ok then, lets rock-and-roll." Priest took off on the Ninja with Shaw following close behind. They made their way east until they reached Rt. 421 and then Priest opened up on the throttle and took off down the highway. "Woo-hoo," He yelled.

"Damn, Sarge. Where did you go?" "Around the earth a couple times," he laughed. Priest backed off and looked around for any infected. There were several car pile-ups that could have been likely ambush locations and Priest gave those a wide berth.

As he proceeded down the highway, some movement caught his eye farther up the road. The high grass on his left moved until suddenly a figure on all fours came rushing out.

Priest saw it and what he thought was all fours turned out to be both legs ripped off right at the knee. This thing was running on its hands and the stumps, but was still incredibly fast and moved out to throw itself in front of Priest's bike. "What the fuck?" he yelled in surprise. As he leaned to the right to maneuver around it, another figure shot out of the tall grass on the right side.

Priest had just enough time to jerk the throttle back and narrowly shoot by the figure reaching for him. He then braked and whipped the bike around in a 180-degree slide. He dropped the throttle and rode back toward the infected now running his way, reaching for him.

Priest shot by him again and then slowed down. As he had hoped, the infected came after him. Priest stayed just ahead of the infected, leading it back toward Shaw.

The infected following Priest was actually quite fast, but not fast enough for the Ninja. Priest kept looking back to make sure it was following and noticed it was a young man who looked college age. He had on an Appalachian State hoodie, and Priest wondered if maybe he had been a track star in the college. It brought on feelings of sadness thinking about who this young man was. Who were his friends and family? Did he have a girlfriend? What were his plans after college?

It made Priest think about how much would have been possible in this young man's life if not for the virus. He thought of the young man getting a job, settling down and raising a family, but all of that was gone now.

Priest felt for the man, and it made him sad to think about everything this young man lost. Now he was about to become a guinea pig and dissected like a class room biology experiment.

Priest saw Shaw heading for him and slowed so the infected could catch up. Priest rode to the opposite side of the Jeep as Neville hung out the rear window and took aim, POP! His first shot blew out the infected right femur and it fell and Shaw slowed a bit as they approached.

The infected struggled to stand for a brief second. POP, Neville's second shot shattered its left femur, and it went down. Shaw stopped just short as the infected was crawling for them. Priest circled back and came up behind the infected.

Shaw ran over and mounted the thing's back grabbing both arms allowing Neville to slap on the handcuffs. Shaw then grabbed its legs and brought them up toward its handcuffed arms, and Neville looped one of the zip cuffs around the handcuffs and secured its legs.

Priest was there putting a belt on the thing's face, but it kept moving its head trying to bite him. He finally attached the belt and cinched it tight. There was a crack sound before he finished securing it.

Priest went to put the mask on when they heard a distant sound. It was faint but getting louder and definitely the sound of vehicle engines.

"Shit, we got company," Shaw yelled.

"Stow that fucker in the back and let's prepare for our guests," Priest ordered. He got on the radio, "HQ, this is Father, do you copy?"

"Go ahead, Father."

"We are about 5 miles east on 421 and we have company driving up our way. Don't know if they are friend or foe, but could use some backup in case things go sideways."

"Copy that Father, we're mobilizing."

Shaw set up his M48 in the open window of the open Jeep door and Neville set up on the other door.

Priest looked over at Neville as he set up his sniper rifle, "What do you got, Neville?"

"Two pickups with 5 occupants a piece and they look to be armed. Small weapons, a couple M4's, an A-K and some shotguns. They are not infected, so they could be the ones who have been hitting the CDC facility?"

"Probably so," Priest replied.

"I don't see anyone in the truck's bed, sitting up at least. They could be hunkered down, ready to spring an ambush."

"Okay, we'll let them get about 75 yards and see how determined they are," Priest ordered. The trucks kept coming at a decent speed, "Ok Shaw, put a couple rounds across their bow." Priest said as they were within 100 yards.

Shaw let off a three-round burst right in front of the lead truck, but both stopped and sat there. Priest raised his hand to stop and walked out into the road where he could be seen. He glanced over to Neville.

"Don't worry Sarge, I got the bead on them. If they so much as scratch their ass, I'll push their off button." Priest nodded. The driver and passenger got out of the truck and walked to stand in front of it. They both had M4 rifles, but were pointed down.

The driver was an older man with a potbelly, salt and pepper beard and had on a baseball cap which had a logo that Priest couldn't make out. His passenger was a young, skinny man with slicked back hair gathered into a ponytail. Both sides of his head were shaved, and he sported a sleeveless t-shirt.

The older man addressed Priest, "You boys ain't from around here. I know that because I know everyone around these parts."

"No sir, we're not," Priest answered.

"You the ones that have moved into that underground bunker on the hill?"

"Yes, sir, we are."

"What are all you people doing up there?" Priest could feel things would go south, eventually.

"Well, that would be our business, but is there something we can do for you?"

"You can start by not givin' me no sass and answer my fucking questions." Yep, this was escalating, Priest thought. Although the thought didn't really bother him in the slightest.

"Neville, what do you got?" Priest said softly.

"Same as before, and I have seen no one reaching for a weapon. They are just sitting there right now."

"If shit jumps off, you take out the passenger. He's young and looks like he may have an itchy trigger finger."

"Got it Sarge."

Priest turned his attention back to the driver. "We'll answer questions, as long as it has nothing to do with what we are doing at the facility."

"All righty then. Who are you fellas?"

"I'm Master Sargent Alex Priest from the US Army and with me is SSG Jeremiah Shaw and Sargent Renaldo Neville."

"Well now, you boys sound mighty important. Where is your military vehicles and all that? That Jeep there don't look like no military vehicle."

"We were flying on a Black Hawk, but when we stopped for fuel, a bunch of infected in a fire truck destroyed it. Then we were on foot until we repurposed two Jeeps."

"Hmm, that sounds like the truth, but there is only one problem. You boys "repurposed" trucks out of my town. That's what we call stealing."

"Ok, let's cut to the chase here because we have things to do. What exactly is it you want?"

"I am fixin' to hurt you 20 ways to Sunday if I don't get my trucks back."

"Sorry Sir, but that will not happen." The driver and passenger raised their rifles.

Priest said quietly, "Neville, passenger." No more did Priest say it. Then you heard the report of the rifle, see the passenger's head snap back and fall to the ground. The driver looked over at his buddy and was in total shock. He ran over to him, knelt down and cradled what was left of the young man's head.

"You shot my boy, mother fuckers. You shot my boy!" Sorrow and anger racked the driver as he held his boy in his lap. By now, the two in the back of the crew cab and the four in the truck behind it got out to see what was going on. The guys from the second truck looked down at the father and son on the ground and showed confusion about what had just happened.

"Get your people together and go on home." Priest said in a calm tone.

The father looked up with rage in his eyes, "You fuckers will pay for this. Pay in blood!" The driver looked at his guys and nodded. They brought their weapons up.

"Shaw!" Priest yelled and then dove behind the Jeep. Shaw let loose and sent round after round of .50 cal into the group standing out in the open. Just then three trucks came from the opposite direction with the beds full of men with rifles.

"Damn, and there they are. They are attempting a Pincher Movement." Shaw and Neville pivoted to engage the 3 trucks coming from the east. Priest rushed around to the front of the Jeep while Shaw and Neville took on the additional threat.

Neville sniped the first driver as he was coming over the median. With the driver out of commission, the truck couldn't navigate the ditch in the middle of the median and the passenger side front tire dug deep into the ditch. With the forward momentum suddenly stopped, the truck dug in and tipped over.

The men in the bed were yelling as the truck tilted over. They tried to jump out far enough to avoid being rolled over on and most didn't make it. As the men jumped, the side of the bed rolled over pinning them to the ground. One guy who was slower than the rest was pinned down by his neck.

The passenger in the front didn't have his seatbelt on and the upper half of his body was ejected out the window as his body became trapped under the truck. The other trucks swerved around the lead truck to continue the assault.

As Priest had made it around the front of the Jeep, he thought to himself, "if I were planning this then I would expect someone else to… he trailed off. "And there they are." Priest saw another two trucks coming from the direction they had originally come. "Hmm, these guys are smarter than I gave them credit for," Priest thought to himself.

Shaw was firing on the second truck that had swerved out to the left of the lead truck to prevent from crashing into it. He raked the front windshield and could see at that the driver and passenger were now dead. Their brains and blood covered the back window and the men's faces sitting behind them.

There was so much blood that Shaw couldn't tell if the blood on their faces was from the heads in the front seat or their own. It didn't much matter, because Shaw kept firing on those in the back seat and through to the men in the truck bed.

This truck was coming in much faster than the lead truck had, and when it hit the ditch, it rolled over multiple times. The men in the bed were thrown out, and the truck rolled over them. Their bodies were more like meat bags than recognizable humans.

The truck came to stop with what looked like rag dolls flopping around inside. Those who were flung out of the bed and lived were shocked and confused, trying to sit up and gain their bearings.

"Neville, swap targets," Shaw yelled. Neville instantly pivoted to target the men who were sitting up from being launched out of the truck bed. One man who was holding his arm, which was bent at an unnatural angle, received a round in the left cheekbone that exited the right side of his head. Half his face exited with the round. Another man lost his throat and half of his neck. Blood spurted out of his ravaged neck as he fell to the ground.

Meanwhile, Shaw had focused his fire on the last remaining truck. The men in the window seats were trying to pull out their rifles to get shots off and were failing miserably. Their shots were wildly off target, but their truck navigated through the ditch in the median.

As they can up on the highway, Shaw shifted his aim to the rear of the truck to take out the back tire. He concentrated fire toward the rear, punctured the gas tank. After a couple seconds and a few rounds, BABOOM! The entire truck went up like a fireball and it launched bodies into the air, looking like Molotov cocktails.

Fire flashed through the truck cab like a back draft and it engulfed all the men inside instantly as they struggled to exit the vehicle. The bodies finally started pouring out as their faces were melting because of the intense heat. They escaped the truck only to have their liberation short lived as Shaw cut them down one by one.

Priest could feel the heat on the back of his neck from the truck exploding, but he didn't take his eyes off of the approaching threat. The two other trucks were about a ¼ mile away when he saw movement behind them. A smile crept on his face, "Right on time," he said to himself. "Shaw, Neville, are you girls done playing around back there, we have company of a unique sort."

"Damn Sarge, I'm getting seasick from all this pivoting around," Neville joked. He scoped down the highway. "Is that the Captain coming?"

"It sure is," Priest responded.

"So, you knew they would send multiple troops from multiple directions during different times?"

"I didn't know, but I assume and planned for it just in case. I gave these guys the benefit of the doubt and expected them to send their people in waves. That's why I radioed the Captain at the time I did. Hopefully giving it enough time for the last wave of these guys to start and our guys come in behind them.

"Father to Spider, do you copy?"

"Go ahead, Father."

"Spider, eliminate those two trucks just ahead of you. They are unfriendlies."

"Copy that." Around Priest, Shaw and Neville all was silent except for the crackling of the car-b-que that Shaw had lit off. The gun fire from the approaching Jeep was heard. Webb and Lia were firing upon the two trucks coming toward Priest's team.

"Shaw, hold your fire but Neville, you can engage if you can put rounds on the target and not into Webb's Jeep."

"Understood, Sarge," Neville acknowledged. Neville sighted on one of the two trucks. He saw the driver looking back to see where Webb was and that's when he put a round in the side of his temple. As with all the others, his blood and brain matter splattered onto the face of the passenger. He freaked out and didn't grab the wheel as the driver slumped over toward him.

The truck careened out of control and bounced off the guardrail, then launched into the median and nosedived in a washout ditch. The abrupt stop catapulted most of the occupants out through the front windshield. Some of them hit the grass and bounced twice, while others hit the pavement and left parts behind on the blacktop.

Scraps of flesh and smears of blood were seen for 50 yards. Captain Webb's team finished any others who survived the guardrail crash. After seeing the destruction of their friends, brothers, sons and fathers, the remaining truck turned tail and ran, heading west. Webb's Jeep arrived at Priest's location.

"You know to throw a party!" Webb said.

"Don't I know it!" Priest responded. "Thanks for showing up, I had a feeling these knuckleheads would try something."

"Yeah, we arrived just in time." Priest was getting ready to answer when Neville spoke up,

"Sarge, that truck is coming back this way."

"What? Are they stupid? We'll shred them to bits."

Still sighting through his scope, Neville answered, "Ahh, I know why."

"You plan on letting us in on it?"

"There is a large horde chasing right after them."

"What is large?" Priest asked.

"Quick guess, I'd say a couple thousand."

"Fuck, are you serious?" Webb got out of his Jeep and he and Priest pulled out their binos for a look.

"Holee shit! There are tons of them." Priest looked at Webb.

"Where the fuck did they all come from?"

"Don't know, but we better get back," Webb said. That's when Webb heard banging on the back of Priest's Jeep. "What the hell?"

"Oh, we have a guest coming over for dinner."

"Bagged one, did you?"

"Sure did." They all loaded up and took off before the truck made its way back to their position. The team hauled ass back to the compound and reactivated the perimeter defenses.

CHAPTER 37

Dr. Caulfield's voice came over the speaker, "Ah, Captain Webb and Sargent Priest, please come to the CC, we have a problem."

"Shit, what now?" Webb said, exasperated. Both men got to the CC and Dr. Caulfield pointed to a monitor whose camera covered the front fence. There were figures banging on the gate and fence.

"How did the infected get here so quick?" Priest asked.

"Those aren't infected," Webb answered. "Looks like people from the town."

"You got to be fucking kidding me!" Priest yelled with annoyance.

"I guess they figure this is the best place to be." Webb turned on the speaker next to the camera and grabbed the mic. They could hear the people yelling and banging on the fence.

"Let us in. The infected are coming. Open up now!" Webb stopped before addressing them.

He clicked over to the internal speakers, "Everyone report to the CC, ASAP." He looked at Priest, "We are not a dictatorship and we need to put this to a vote."

Priest signed, "Yeah, you're right."

A few moments later everyone was present at the CC and Webb spoke to the group, "Ok everyone, we have a situation. There are a couple thousand infected coming this way. Now, we are safe and can maintain for quite a long time while we wait for this horde to pass. The issue is that the people from the town are at our gate wanting access to the compound." The scientists looked at each other in bewilderment.

Dr. Rand spoke up, "Are these the people that attacked us before trying to get in?"

"The same people who attacked us a couple hours ago, and these are the same. I told you we were not here to take over, so everyone has a say. So, we either let those people in or we leave them outside. Those are your two choices and I'll give you a couple minutes to decide." All the scientists got together to discuss.

Dr. Caulfield looked over at the team, "Aren't you going to deliberate?"

Priest looked at him, "We already did and know where we stand." Dr Caulfield still looked somewhat confused, but turned back around to his huddle. Some long minutes later, the huddle broke.

Webb acknowledged them, "Ok, by a show of hands, all those in favor of bringing these people inside, raise your hand." Three hands shot up, Dr. Holtz, Caulfield and Santiago. All those in favor of leaving them outside our gate, raise your hand. Seven hands went up. "Okay, that is 7 against 3, which means they stay outside?"

Dr. Caulfield spoke up, "Are you really going to leave them there? It sounds barbaric."

"Well, these people tried to break in before and they just tried to kill us a few hours ago. So, yeah, I am." Webb went back to the microphone and keyed it. "We took a vote and the majority consider your group too dangerous and untrustworthy."

Screams of anger and pleading were heard through the speakers. "You can thank the group of you that just tried to kill us for that. You have five minutes to clear that fence and get back down that access road. If not, then we will remove with force. Your five minutes have already started."

The team continued to watch the screens. Most of the crowd turned and ran back down the road. Seven or eight stayed staring at the facility entrance. They stood there with their faces pressed against the chain link.

One man spoke up, "You don't let us in, we will die."

Webb responded, "Hey, jackass, you guys tried to kill us with no provocation. Now you want us to just open our doors and invite you in? You can't be serious."

"I didn't have nothin to do with that. That was another group and isn't the ones standing here."

"And we're just supposed to take your word for it?" Webb could understand their plight, but was he supposed to put everyone in the facility in danger, based on the word of a man he didn't know?

"I'm telling you; those people weren't us. You let us in or you will have innocent blood on your hands." The man was staring a hole right into the camera and something about him was off.

Webb couldn't nail it down, but there was something definitely off. He looked to be in his early forties with black hair, a thick black beard, and had on tactical pants, boots and a t-shirt with a tactical vest.

"Sir, we are sorry, but the answer is no. We will not open our gate to you. There are too many unknowns for us to do so."

The man nodded his head. "Ok, ok, that's how it's going to be? That is your last answer?"

"It is," Webb replied.

"Ok then. Have it your way, but remember it was you who put us in this position. The blood is on your hands." He looked around and then a smile crept across his face, "I wonder if this fence could hold back thousands? It would be interesting to watch."

The man turned around without saying a word and walked away. He went about 10 yards, stopped and stared dead in the camera, "The name is Brody. Remember it, because you will hear it again." And he walked off.

Webb looked at Priest. "He will lead all those fuckers here."

"Well, it makes sense. Lead them here, let the infected take us out, then they come in to clean up and take over the facility when the infected move on," Priest surmised. "Fuck, they could screw this entire thing up," he said it low under his breath.

"What?" Webb tried to hear.

"We need to lure them away. We need to make sure they never reach this compound. They need to be led in the opposite direction."

Webb stood there and pondered for a minute, taking in all that Priest was saying. The more Webb thought about it, the more dangerous it sounded. The problem was, Webb couldn't think of anything else that would accomplish what they needed to do.

Webb took in a deep breath and exhaled, "Who are we going to get to do it, and how are we going to execute the plan?"

Priest looked and him with that resolved look, "Me."

"What? You? Why you?"

"Marcus, think about it. It needs to be someone fast, maneuverable, quick thinking and who has experience solving issues in case things go south. Who is better equipped than yours truly on the bike?" Webb hated when Priest made so much sense. It didn't suppress the feelings of worry and dread that one of his team, his brother, his friend was going out there with basically no support.

"I don't like it," Webb finally said.

"I'm not exactly thrilled about it, but do you have a better idea?" He didn't and Priest knew it.

Webb was one to lead from the front, not hiding underground while your people are out doing the job he should do. He hated things to be this way. Priest could see the internal turmoil written on Webb's face and he put his hand on his shoulder.

"Dude, it's fine. It's the only way and we both know it."

"I know, but it doesn't make me feel any better about it."

"It will be fine." They spent the next hour planning the route and coming up with a few contingencies. Half way through, Lia had joined them and asked to go. She was denied, but she stayed to spend time with Priest before he left.

Priest packed a ruck with Lia's help and loaded up with ammunition. He added a second holster with a Glock and outfitted the front of the bike to hold two combat knives.

After a couple minutes to double check everything and make sure it was secure, he kissed Lia goodbye and made his way down the access road, being cautious about whether any of the town's group was lingering around.

All the streets looked deserted as Priest made his way east to intercept the coming herd. As he rode, Priest tried to focus on the feeling of riding, trying to compartmentalize everything he had going on. He exited the town going east on Rt. 421. He went a couple miles, fully expecting to come across the horde by now. What the hell was going on? He thought.

As he continued on, he saw dust clouds in the distance. Priest didn't know if this was because of the horde or something else. He proceeded another ¼ mile, stopped and pulled his binos to get a better view.

He saw a dozen trucks driving in a large circle attempting to corral the infected, like they were on some damn cattle drive. It wasn't working all that well, but it was obvious they were trying to round them up.

"Shit," Priest thought to himself. This makes the mission ten times harder. His team could help, but it was way too dangerous to take on a dozen trucks and the infected. He sat there for what seemed like hours, even though it was five or so minutes. An idea came to him, so he raced back to the compound as fast as the bike could take him.

He keyed his comms, coming up the road. "Hey, get me 10 grenades." Most of the team came out to meet him. When they came out and handed him the grenades, Priest explained what he had seen.

They all wanted to go with him and no one more than Shaw, who was champing at the bit. He assured them it would be like a snatch and grab. Quick and easy. They still didn't like it, but they would follow his orders to stay. He told them to be on standby in case he needed them, then said his goodbye's and rode back down the access road toward the horde.

CHAPTER 38

As Priest rode back toward the shit storm, he thought about how the odds of achieving the desired result was very slim. He thought to himself, "I will have to hit this thing hard and fast. Creating even more confusion than the infected are creating will give me my best chance.

The infected are unpredictable, which is more of a problem for the local yokels than it would be for me." He saw the chaos in front of him and decided the best way to go about it was head first.

He dropped the throttle and the Ninja 1000 launched forward like a rocket. A bright red pickup, with two men in the back, was driving in the circle they had created trying to get the infected bunched up together.

Priest plucked a grenade from his vest, pulled the pin with his teeth. He released the spoon, held it for a second, and then threw the grenade into the truck bed.

The men in the truck were still focused on the infected, so Priest put some distance between him and the truck by letting off the throttle. In front of him, the grenade exploded in the truck bed and instantly killed the two men in the bed.

The explosion sent glass and shrapnel into the cab of the truck, killing both the driver and passenger. The truck went careening into the middle of the circle, slamming through throngs of the infected.

Priest looked ahead and was selecting his next target when a bullet whizzed by his head. He looked back to see a black truck with a guy pointing a rifle at him hanging out the back of the bed.

Priest punched the bike and caught up with the next truck in line in the circle. He had a grenade out and was closing in on his next target as bullets continued to fly by him. He glanced back again, and the truck was trying to gain ground, but with the uneven terrain, it was having a hard time increasing speed. This also kept the man in the back from getting a good bead on him.

The Ninja wasn't the best at handling this terrain, but he was managing. He increased speed, popped the spoon and tossed the grenade into the bed of the truck to his right. This time he sped by the truck before the grenade went off. He heard the explosion and watched out of the corner of his right eye, but saw nothing.

He looked back to his left and saw the truck coming to a stop on the outside of the circle. "Damn," Priest thought to himself. It would be better if they wrecked to the right and killed a bunch of these damn infected. As Priest looked around at the state of things and noticed the circle's formation was deteriorating.

"I need to break this thing apart quicker," Priest said to himself. "Time to get stupid." Priest slowed down and dropped his left foot, lowered the bike and let the momentum bring it around in a 180-degree turn and propelled himself in the opposite direction. Facing the oncoming trucks, he shot right by the truck that was shooting at him earlier.

Priest rode by the next truck, which was brown, and Priest pulled out the Glock and started firing into the windshield. The driver turned the wheel to their right, which angled the truck into the infected in the middle. This also gave Priest an accurate sight picture of the driver's temple, which he did not waste the opportunity of, and put two rounds into the side of the driver's head. He has time to see what happened afterward.

Priest was garnering some attention now and more people were taking shots at him. He knew he couldn't keep this up, but he just wanted to disrupt this operation enough to make sure the infected weren't led to the compound.

He spied a smaller truck, which was a little slower than the rest and took off for that truck. It was light blue and rusted out all to hell. He pulled out a grenade and extracted the pin, but he lost his grip on it and it dropped from his hand.

The grenade went off near the front of another truck and blew the tires and part of the engine. The truck came to a halt immediately.

With the reduced speed and visibility, along with the focus on the infected, another truck came from behind and didn't see the truck stopped right in its path before it was too late. The rear truck, which had six men in the bed, slammed into the disabled truck, launching the men onto the ground. Infected swarmed the men, ripping and devouring flesh.

Priest took this time to call it quits and let the rest play out. He performed another 180-degree power slide turn and headed off to this right.

While riding west toward the compound, multiple things happened at once. The repeat of a loud high caliber machine gun reached his ears as the back wheel of his bike and sprocket disintegrated.

The bike shot out from underneath him and because of high rate of speed; it hurled him 50 feet onto the pavement. It forced all the air out of his lungs and he felt a few cracks form throughout his rib cage. He slid and then rolled a few times before coming to a stop on the shoulder of the eastbound lanes. He was dazed and in some pretty decent pain, and he had trouble getting up. His body just wasn't working like it was supposed to.

He heard a vehicle approach quickly, and he continued to get up. He got to his knees before a blow to the back of his helmet brought complete darkness and he fell back to the ground unconscious.

CHAPTER 39

Priest woke up still lying on the ground. He felt like shit, but at least he was feeling something. He looked around and noticed that his helmet, riding jacket and riding pants were all gone. He glanced over to his left and saw the Ninja 1000 laying on its side. Not expecting the bike to be in any working order, Priest got up painfully and walked over to it. Everything still looked intact, but he thought back to before and was sure the rear of the bike was toast. Maybe it was just asphalt broken up from the rounds that got caught in the rear tire. He inspected it, and surprisingly everything seemed fine. Regardless of the condition of the bike, he needed to get the hell out of there and make it back to the compound.

Apprehensively, Priest started the bike, and it roared to life. He took off, expecting the worst, but it seemed to roll fine. Priest raced back to his new home on the compound. He quickly sped up, but it would not move any faster than 40 mph.

"Must have taken some damage on the throttle when I laid it down," Priest thought to himself. "Just keep it moving and get back to everyone. We'll check it later," was the only thing on his mind.

There was a faint sound of engines in the distance. He craned his neck to see if he could pinpoint where they were coming from and realized the sound was coming from behind him. He looked over his shoulder to see three trucks approaching from his rear and heading straight for him.

Priest dropped the throttle to race out of there, but the bike wouldn't respond. It stayed right around 40 mph. He didn't have to look back this time to know the trucks were getting closer. The revving engines were getting much closer. He was on the highway so there were no alleys, no buildings where he could hide. Nowhere he could hope to lose them. They were bearing down on him and he could sense it, he could hear it, he could feel it.

"Why don't they just shoot me? Why not just kill me and be done with it already?" he thought to himself.

Yelling and screaming along with the roar of the truck engines now reached his ears? Screaming and hooting like wild animals. The anticipation of them reaching him was overwhelming, and the tension was physically debilitating. Every muscle in his body was tight, like steel cables being twisted and stretched. His head was pounding, and he could feel the blood surging in his ears.

Suddenly, he felt hands on his arm, grabbing, clawing, and ripping. He looked to his right to see a pickup right next to him. His eyes went wide when he saw the infected in the back of the truck, heads tilting back and forth, screaming and yelling. A few of the infected in the truck's bed had a hold of his arm and were trying to pull him off the bike. He attempted to wrench his arm out of their grip, but they were incredibly strong. A couple other infected in the back reached out and grabbed his shirt and pulled him off the bike. Although he was fighting them with everything he had, it seemed futile. Feeling the situation was reaching a desperate point, he stretched down to his left thigh and grabbed his Walther PPQ. He cursed loudly as his hand came away empty. His pistol was gone, both of his pistols were gone.

"Fuck," he yelled, as they pulled him off the bike and slammed him into the bed of the truck. They jumped on him, screaming like banshees as he fought to keep them off. He was swinging, kicking and thrashing about, trying to gain some freedom from their grip. Trying to create some space between them, so he could wriggle out from underneath them and maybe jump out the back. There had to be something....something to give him a fighting chance.

Priest screamed as the excruciating pain overtook him as he felt them taking bites out of his arms and legs. Then they ripped at his skin. They pulled his entrails out, laughing and screaming as they held them up as trophies. One leaned in and took a bite out of his throat as he attempted to scream. The scream wouldn't come, only gasping and gurgling. He rocked his head, trying to remove the gnashing teeth from his throat. He gathered all the strength he could muster and screamed out.

He jolted awake, gasping and panting.

"Well, look who's awake," a voice called out that he didn't recognize. Priest struggled to open his eyes and look around, but they would barely open. His eyes were pulsating and throbbing and something crusted them halfway shut.

Priest tried to wipe them, but his hands wouldn't move, wouldn't budge. They felt like they weighed 50 lbs, and he had lost feeling in them. He rotated his head to the left and right and saw he had handcuffs on each raw and bleeding wrist. Priest was on his knees with his arms stretched out, cuffed to a railing on each side. Stripped down to a t-shirt and jeans, they were both covered both in blood. He felt his lips with his tongue, and they were split and bleeding in various places. His throat was parched, like he had gargled with barbwire. As Priest regained his wits about him, every inch of his body screamed out in pain. Every inch protested movement and cried out, trying to gain his attention all at the same time. A slight grin came over his face as he embraced the pain as a welcomed friend. The pain allowed him to focus, allowed him to keep his mind in the present.

"Take it in. Take it all in. You aren't home anymore," that same voice said to him. He opened his eyes as much as they would allow to look around the room.

Priest analyzed his environment and thought, "A maintenance building of some sort? No, it looked more like a horse barn and tack shop. There was a man sitting in a chair facing him with three more men standing behind him. The man in the chair was leaning on a sledgehammer with the head against his cheek.

"Ah, there he is, it's about time too. I worried I hit you too hard." The man said as he held the hammer up to his face and examined it.

"It split that helmet, though. Just like cracking an egg. Oh, and the boys here worked you over quite a bit as well. I mean, with you killing so many of their friends, I'm sure you can understand how they might be a little upset. Truth is, we had to pull them off you before they beat you to death."

In a low raspy voice, Priest finally spoke, "Yeah, they did a pretty good job on the dog pile seeing how I was already down. If they would like to try me now, I would be more than happy to return the favor."

The man in the chair looked at him quizzically. A smile broke on Priest's face as he snickered, then spat out a wad of blood and phlegm. The man stared at him for another brief second and then broke out in laughter like that was the funniest thing he had ever heard. He went on for a while, tears rolling down his cheeks.

"My God, you are funny." The man was wiping the tears off his face. It took a few minutes for him to compose himself. "Whew. That was good. You know what makes this even funnier?"

Priest shrugged, as much as he could with the shackles on his wrists. "Because my associates here, probably don't realize just how true that is." He laughed again, but nowhere close to the spectacle as before. The men behind him started shifting nervously.

Priest didn't know if they enjoyed being called out, but he didn't give much of a shit either.

"My, my, my, where are my manners? Let me introduce myself. My name is Thomas, Thomas Baker. I am the mayor of our little paradise here, called Boone."

When Priest pictured mayors he thought of fat, balding men with floppy jowls and a handkerchief to mop up the sweat constantly rolling off their head. This Thomas guy had a southern accent that sounded like an old southern gentleman of high society. His appearance, however, differed from the image his voice projected. This "Thomas", was fairly tall from what Priest can determine with him sitting in the chair. He was lanky, a little on the thinner side, and wore khakis with a button-up shirt. Except for the fact that he tried to cave his head in, Priest thought he might have sat down for a beer with him under different circumstances. He had sandy blonde hair that was cut short and a close-cropped beard. Thomas Baker noticed Priest analyzing him and answered the unasked questions.

"No, I am not really the mayor, well one that was voted upon, anyway. This group, however, has made me the mayor."

"No shit," Priest uttered.

Thomas looked at him for a moment.

"My boys really messed you up, didn't they? Perhaps seeing the picture I have in front of me, might clue you in to the seriousness of the situation at hand. Thomas got up from his chair and walked out of the room.

He was getting a kick out of this, Priest thought. Thomas came back into the room with a small mirror and held it out in front of Priest.

"Holy shit, they did a good job. My compliments to the artist," Priest said. He could see that his eyes were practically swollen shut, crusted together with dried blood, and were black and blue. He had cuts all over his face and his lips were busted and split. He had blood crusted in this beard and cuts all over his face and head.

As Priest looked at the broken face in the mirror, he said in a raspy voice, "I've been tortured by the best and you fuckers are going to have to do better than this."

That seemed to amuse Thomas. "I really like you; you know. I'm afraid you have me at a disadvantage. You know my name and I'm curious to know what yours is?"

"Priest."

"What?"

"They call me Priest."

"Is that your first name, last name or a nickname?"

"Just Priest."

"Well, Mr. Priest. Let's you and I have a little heart to heart talk, shall we?"

"Please, let's," Priest replied.

Thomas laughed again. "Ah, I love this guy. Okay, Mr. Priest, here's the deal. Our little family here is all about survival. It's been a major part of our life to prepare for this event, for this series of events leading to the end of the world as society knows it. If I may be so blunt, you and your people have encroached on our property and have interrupted our plans. We have included that facility in our plans ever since they started building it. They hired many people from this town to build it and so, have intimate knowledge of its amenities and how those fall so perfectly into our plans. They have been in that facility, seen how self-sufficient it is. Oh, yes. It is everything we have been planning and living for. So, we will not just let you and your people come and take it away from us."

"Are you bitching about your ass hurting?" Priest replied.

Thomas was taken aback for a second, but a sly smile comes across his face. "Lawrence, please teach Mr. Priest some manners?" The man to Thomas's left stepped forward and punched Priest in the jaw with a gloved hand.

Priest spit out some blood.

"Lawrence, I'll remember that shit," Priest growled.

"Now, before I was so rudely interrupted. Mr. Priest, what I need from you is a key, so to speak. A way to unlock that facility. Actually, it is better defined as a way in. I would appreciate it if your people just left and gave us that facility with no trouble, but I feel that will not happen. Mr. Priest, you are my key to get in there, and I don't much care how it happens. Whether you talk them into it, whether we use you as a hostage, or whether you walk right up and let us in. One way or another, you will be the way to our salvation, which includes that entire compound on the hill."

"You don't sound like the rest of these country fuck Cro-Magnons. How is that?" Priest answered.

Thomas again looked at Priest with amazement, "Well, that was a compliment and a slight in the same sentence. Even though it was quite rude, I will answer it anyway. I am the orator for our grand movement. The voice for public meetings, assemblies, etc. They have appointed me the "mayor" of this town, and my job is to talk to other groups, communities or other entities in power and negotiate treaties, alliances or any other means necessary for our survival."

Thomas leaned forward on his chair, narrowed his eyes at Priest and spoke carefully," That also includes articles of war if we deem it necessary."

Thomas leaned back in his seat and his face took on a more casual demeanor, "People take you seriously when you can speak to the level of the room or above it, such as in my case. Mr. Priest, knowing the answer to this question before I ask, I still feel compelled to ask, anyway. How would you like to join our little family? You and your fellow soldiers, that is. You could help with ensuring our existence, providing much needed security and tactics advise, while you help to spread our authority across the region to re-establish humanity?"

Priest looked at him and the smile left his face, "I assume we would just be the silent minority? The spearhead to further your cause? Just doing what we're told and keeping our mouth shut? Does that sum it up accurately?"

Thomas thought pensively, and Priest could see the diplomatic wheels turning in Thomas's mind.

Priest knew a lot of shit was getting ready to spew from Thomas's mouth and he didn't wait for an answer, "With the prior attempts to kill us earlier, the nice job your associates did on my face and body, I am afraid I will have to decline. You understand that with my pride, it's hard to let that just fly. I have killed people for much, much less than this. I will miss our little talks, though," Priest spoke in a raspy voice.

He continued, "The fact that I considered your offer for a split second, might earn me some water?"

"Ah, Mr. Priest. I would love to accommodate you, but I feel that would confuse our relationship. It might be seen as a betrayal to the rest of our group."

"Well, I expected as much. Thought I'd ask, though," Priest said and then spit on the floor. Blood and phlegm mixed in a small pool by Thomas's boots.

"You might want to keep that in your mouth, Mr. Priest. No telling when the next time you'll have something to drink may be." Thomas said as he looked down at his boot.

"I'll be fine, but thank you for your concern. To reciprocate your kindness, sans the beating you levied on me. Let me extend an offer to you. Our group could use an educated man who knows the area and could assist us in acquiring needed resources. How about you join our group instead? You let me go, I take out these fuckheads, and we mosey on up to the compound together. What do you say?"

Priest knew Thomas wouldn't accept his offer, but for a moment, he swore he saw consideration flash across Thomas's face.

Thomas laughed and stood up. "Mr. Priest, you paint a rosy picture. Had we met a little while ago, I might have taken you up on that tempting offer. Just the opportunity to listen to your various quips is reason enough to join."

The men behind him bristled about and mumble to themselves, but Thomas raised his hand to silence them.

"I am afraid I will have to decline. You see, Mr. Priest, here I am the one in charge; the one making decisions, the one with the last word. I have no illusions to the fact that with your group, I would be regulated down to just a participant. One who may offer an opinion, but who would be ignored and looked upon as a lesser contributor."

Priest shook his head, "Honestly, as soon as my hand was free, I would have ripped out your fucking windpipe, then waded through these fucking skirts you use as soldiers."

Priest grinned as he spat another wad of blood and phlegm on the floor. It was quickly becoming more blood than phlegm.

"Ah, again with that humor of yours. I would love to stick around and entertain you further, but I am afraid I have to leave you now. Don't worry though, I have a special "skirt" coming to spend time with you and he will provide his complete and undivided attention. Mr. Priest, let me introduce you to my right-hand man, Mr. Brody."

Priest thought he recognized the man as the one from the gate at the compound. As Mr. Brody walked a little closer, Priest recognized him. It was definitely the same man, and he didn't look all too pleased.

"Ahh, Mr. Brody. I think I remember him from the yacht club," Priest chuckled. Brody walked up to him and kicked Priest in the gut, causing his chains to bounce back and forth.

"Shit!" Priest yelled. "That was fucking uncalled for. Your dingy never measured up to my cabin cruiser."

Brody started towards Priest again, but Thomas stopped him.

"I apologize, Mr. Priest. My friend, Mr. Brody here, is not as cordial as myself. He is a little more direct, and I must admit, I don't have the stomach for this kind of stuff. You know, we can skip all of this if you would just agree to allow us access to the facility."

"Well, I would love to have you over for tea, but our neighbors are extremely judgmental and I just don't have the patience to get into it with them again." Priest showed a bloody smile.

Thomas was laughing and shaking his head, "Mr. Priest, I really enjoy your company. Unfortunately, I don't think you will be in the same frame of mind after your "quality" time with Mr. Brody."

"That is a shame," Priest retorted.

Brody walked up and pulled a large hunting knife from its sheath. He put it on a nearby table and walked over to Priest. Grabbing the collar of Priest's t-shirt, he ripped it in two. He scanned Priest's body and looked back at Thomas. With Priest's heightened adrenaline level, the multiple scars all over his body were radiating a sickly redness. Thomas showed an instance of shock but quickly tried to hide it.

"Well, Mr. Priest. You have had some troubles in your lifetime, I see. Had a rough go of it?"

"Yeah, rough childhood. Fell off a few jungle gyms back when I was a kid," Priest responded.

"Oh goodness, Mr. Priest. Such a character, even though you're facing undue torment. I must go now, because like I said before, I can't stomach this kind of thing. We'll talk later."

Thomas walked away, stopped and turned back towards Priest, "Maybe." He turned back around and left the room.

Priest shifted his eyes to Brody, who had picked up the knife again and stood there looking at him.

Priest looked down at his scars, then raised his head with an evil, bloody grin. "Bring it bitch!"

CHAPTER 40

"Where the fuck is he?" Shaw yelled as he went berserk.

"We don't know, Shaw, calm down." Webb was trying to reason with him. In the last few hours, they had lost communications with Priest, and the infected were making their way toward the facility. Doc had just come back from a surveillance run, and he couldn't find any sign of Priest or his bike. They cut his search short because of the progress the horde had already made.

"We got to go out and find him! Are you sure you looked? Probably didn't know what the fuck you were doing out there," Shaw spat. Doc's mouth stuck open as he looked down and then walked away.

Webb looked over at Doc with empathy, but needed to address Shaw first.

Webb reached out, "Stay with me, brother. We'll find him, I promise. You know I wouldn't leave anyone out there, least of which, Priest. I need you to stay focused."

Shaw huffed, but Webb could see him visibly come down a few notches. Shaw was showing the most emotion Webb had ever seen from him, except for the rage he unleashed in battle. Webb knew Shaw and Priest were tight, like brothers, and that Shaw would take the fact Priest was missing the hardest. Webb saw the rage in Shaw's eyes dissipate, but not the determination.

"Sorry, Cap. I'm good. I'm good to go." Shaw said with a slight bit of embarrassment showing on his face. He looked over and saw Doc walking away down the hall.

Shaw called after him, and Doc stopped and turned around. Shaw thought about how he lashed out at Doc for no reason, and tears formed in his eyes. He reached out and grabbed Doc in a bear hug.

"I'm sorry, brother. I didn't mean it. I know you did all you could out there. I have been too hard on you lately, and I am sorry."

Doc said nothing.

"Are we cool?" There was silence. "It would mean a lot if I had your forgiveness, so I can move on and concentrate on the mission ahead."

Silence.

"Come on, Doc, I said I was sorry. I...."

A small voice interrupted Shaw.

"I - I would answer... if... if....I....could....breathe." Doc squeaked out.

"Oh, shit! Sorry." Shaw let Doc go and watched the color came back into his face.

Doc looked up at him, wheezing. "How the hell can you hug Allison and not kill the poor woman?"

Shaw laughed and slapped him on his back.

"We're good, brother. I know where your head is. It's cool, Shaw."

Webb walked over. "We'll find him, big man, you have my word on that."

Webb then walked back over to the console in the CC and announced on the facility comms, "I need all hands on me ASAP."

Within minutes, all were present. "Ok, here is our situation: We have lost communications with Priest and after a preliminary search, we can't find him or his bike." Lia's eyes went wide.

Webb put his palms up, "Believe me; we will find him. I promise. Unfortunately, we have a bigger problem at the moment. These local fucks are leading a massive horde this way. Their plans are to have the infected storm this place, kill all of us, lead the infected away and then take the place for themselves. This is all speculation at this point, but we strongly believe that is their intentions from the get-go. So, our immediate effort is to address this large group of infected. Whether we kill them, redirect them or something in between, they are the immediate threat. I don't like leaving Priest out there any more than you do, but we have to prioritize our risks and plan accordingly. We have a few ideas, but I want to hear from the scientist staff. Dr. Caulfield, any opinions?"

Dr. Caulfield looked at him quizzically, "You gentlemen are the problem solvers, why are you asking me?"

Webb walked closer to him, "Based on what little you know about the behavior and trends of the infected, we wanted to know your opinion on the matter."

"Hmm, well, I believe once they focus in on this place, it will become a beacon for them. Once they realize they are uninfected in here, they will do everything they can, to get in. So they will need to be put down."

Webb turned to Bethany. "Dr. Rand?"

"I would have to agree with Dr. Caulfield. They will key on this place. So, I believe you will have to deal with them again if not eliminated."

"Duly noted. Dr. Holtz?" He wasn't really paying attention. Once they brought the live specimen in, Dr. Holtz had been totally focused on it.

"Yeah, whatever. I agree with them," he said with a wave of his hand.

"Okaaay, Dr. Santiago. Any opinion?"

"I really have little to offer. Once I spend more time with the specimen, then I will figure out where I stand on things."

"Last but not least, Dr. Costa?"

"From interaction with these things, I believe they will have to be eliminated. Once, they have become focused on a potential killing field, they will focus and will continue to return. Especially if they have nothing else in the region to focus on."

Webb nodded. "Ok, then eradication is our agreed upon solution?" All nodded in agreement "Then let's plan for Armageddon."

CHAPTER 41

Brody walked into Thomas's makeshift office with a dejected air about him.

"Well?" Thomas asked, as he eyed the man.

"He ain't going to tell us shit, and I don't think he will help us get into the compound. Between you and me, that is one hard ass mother fucker. I've seen no one take that kind of punishment."

"Hmm, well, if all those scars were any indicator…" Thomas made a face like the image repulsed him.

"You didn't see all the ones on his back. It was like they whipped him like a dog." Brody added.

"Ok, we haven't dealt with anyone like him before, but no worries. We will see if his friends are as hard as he is. Bring his gear here, and we'll see if we can contact his friends over at the facility. We will use him as a bargaining chip. If that doesn't work, then I guess we will just let the infected do the dirty work. It's much more cumbersome, but we have waited this long to take over. A few more weeks won't kill us." Thomas had a satisfied grin on his face.

A little while later, Brody returned with all of Priest's gear and his communication equipment. Thomas patched it in to their equipment.

He looked at Brody, "Hopefully, it is still on the correct frequency." Thomas keyed the mic. "Hello? Hello, I am trying to reach those in the CDC facility in Boone, North Carolina. Can you hear me?"

The Light Reaper Team had been planning their defense against the infected when a voice came over their comm system. The team looked at each other and then all turned to Webb. He cautiously walked over to the microphone like it was a rattlesnake ready to strike.

"This is the CDC facility, go ahead."

"Ah, excellent. My name is Thomas Baker, and I'm the replacement mayor of our little community here. I would like to welcome you to our little town."

"Well, we appreciate the hospitality." Webb asked.

"Just a miscommunication, I assure you. With whom am I speaking with?"

"This is Captain Marcus Webb. Commander of the Light Reapers/101st Airborne, U.S. Army."

"Oh, my goodness, that is a mouthful."

"Just giving you all of it. I believe in transparency."

"I couldn't agree with you more, Captain Webb. Let me cut to the chase, if I may. You are in possession of a facility that we truly believe is ours. We have planned for years for this exact situation. Those plans specifically included the facility you now occupy. Hopefully, you can see the situation for what it is."

"Ok, so let me understand this. You want this facility because it is part of your "plans", and you want us to just hand it over to you?"

"It seems that my oratory skills have not diminished. You understand completely."

"Mr. Baker, I am afraid we cannot do that. We have important work going on here that could benefit us, your community, and the entire country."

"Now, that sounds quite important, and I'm sure you believe that you are doing what's right. Here is the reality of it; you are trespassing on our property and holding on to that site when you have no right to do so. You and your associates can walk out right now, and we will allow you safe passage to go wherever you wish."

"That sure is kind of you, Mr. Baker, and it is a generous offer. I am afraid we will have to respectfully, decline."

Thomas let out a heavy sigh, "Captain Webb, I was hoping you would see things with more clarity, so let me see if I make things clearer for you." Webb could hear his voice change tone.

Thomas continued, "You were engaged because you have trespassed on OUR facility, on OUR town, and on OUR carefully laid out plans. You will vacate that facility and set up in another area."

"We are not leaving and will take our chances with the infected with which you are leading right to our doorstep!"

"Captain Webb, you are in no position to refuse or to dictate how things will go. I hold all the cards here."

"Frankly, you hold shit, Mr. Baker."

"Is that so? How about we ask our new distinguished guest, Mr. Priest."

Webb let go of the mic.

Shaw was enraged again, "That cock sucking mother fucker! I'm going to rip out his fucking heart!" Allison was trying to calm him down.

"Quiet it down, Shaw. We can't let him know he has us," Webb pleaded.

"Captain Webb? Cat got your tongue? I'll take it by your silence that you were not expecting that." Thomas's voice came over the radio with a sly and condescending tone.

"It doesn't change things, Mr. Baker."

"Oh, it doesn't? Hmm, well, I can tell you Mr. Priest has been a lovely guest."

"How do I know that you have even have him? You could have picked up a name by hearing our communications."

"Come now, Captain Webb, do you think I would play those types of games? Mr. Priest here is a big man, with a shaved head, longer type salt and pepper beard, although his beard is quite red at this moment. Come to think of it, his entire body is significantly red. My associate, Mr. Brody, has spent some quality time with Mr. Priest. He is extremely stubborn and a tough and rugged man. There is no doubt about that. Don't worry though, we will break him. That is, unless you give us what we want. What is rightfully ours."

Shaw was seething at this point and was nearly at berserker mode. Webb knew he had to think of something.

"Mr. Baker, it appears you hold more in your hand than we initially thought. We will need time to mull over your offer, especially if we are to plan where we go from here. Our survival is as important to us as yours is to you."

"Of course, Captain Webb, we completely understand. A decision of this magnitude takes some consideration. However, what you will not do is stall for time and make this a difficult transition. Do you understand me, Captain Webb?"

"Yes, I understand, Mr. Baker."

"Good, good. You have 30 minutes, and that is all I'm giving you. I would offer you the same opportunity as I gave Mr. Priest, which was to join us. I say "would", because I understand your answer would probably be the same as Mr. Priest's, so there isn't any reason to delve into futility. 30 minutes, Captain Webb. 30 minutes!"

Webb turned to the team. "We have two issues to address. Stopping the infected and rescuing Priest."

"I'm going after Priest!" Shaw growled.

"Hold on, Shaw. If we lose this facility, then we are all screwed. We have to be smart about this. Neville, what are the odds that when we roll out, these assholes will be watching?"

"I would say pretty high."

"Ok, I believe we didn't send everyone out last time we dealt with these locals, so they don't know how many we have here."

Shaw looked at Webb, "What are you thinking, Cap?"

"I tell this guy that the infected are too close, and we have to fight them, just to make it out alive. While we send out a team to engage the infected, we send another small team out the backside of the facility to find Priest. Shaw, I am going to need you on the assault team against the infected. Your firepower and ordinance expertise." Shaw let out a big troubling sigh, but nodded in agreement. Ok, here are the teams: Shaw, Izzy, Lia and Allison are with me. Doc and Neville will make their way through the town and try to locate Priest. Make the assessment on whether or not you can extract him. Do not engage without talking to me first. Since they have one of our comm rigs, take one of these, and we will be able to communicate without being monitored." Webb handed Doc and Neville a couple of two-way radios they had found at the dealership.

"Questions?"

While the team were making their last-minute checks, Thomas Baker's voice came over the comms.

"Times up, Captain Webb! What say you?"

"Look, Mr. Baker, that throng of infected you so graciously lead to our doorstep is practically here. If we don't engage this threat now, not only are we are not even making it out of here alive, you will not have any facility left to move into. That, Sir, is completely unacceptable. We also have scientists in here who cannot exit the facility until we deal with the infected. Once we deal with the infected, we will vacate the facility and head to the next closest CDC facility."

"That will not work, Captain Webb."

"It's going to have to work. You led those fuckers right to us, and the only way out is that access road. We do not have enough time to pack up and evacuate this facility without running headfirst into the infected. If that is the case, then we stay where we are and we blow the facility with us in it. That is a much better outcome than being eaten alive. We have enough C4 here to do it. At that point, we both lose."

"Come now, Captain Webb. I believe I can recognize a bluff when I hear one."

"Hmm, ok. If you think we won't do it, then tell me where Priest's head is right now? I bet you he has reserved himself to die. He is willing to drift off into darkness, right? So, will we do it if you try to remove our only chance for survival. As soldiers, we have reserved ourselves to die. As far as the scientists here? Well, they don't have a choice. We will deal with them mercifully and then blow the fuck out of this place."

"Well, my goodness, Captain Webb. You paint a dismal picture, don't you? You are really tugging on my heartstrings."

Brody motioned toward Thomas and let go of the comms button.

"What?!," he said, annoyed.

"Thomas, I think they mean it. That Priest fella in there is tough, but I think he is ready to die and doesn't seem to mind doing so."

"So, what do you suggest, Mr. Brody?"

"Let them go out and fight the infected. We will wait for them to leave and be ready for anyone that makes it back. If anyone does makes it back, then we will kill them easily. The scientists won't blow that place and will be ready to give it up."

"Mr. Brody, where have you been for the last few weeks? We have tried to get into that facility and "those scientists" who you seem to think are so meek have denied us every time. What makes you think they won't continue to repel us?"

"Thomas, they knew people were coming to help them. They knew these soldiers were going to be arriving and helping them defend this place. No one else is coming, and they will have no help. They had the initial soldiers who were assigned here and then knew about these guys. It's over for them."

"Mr. Brody, you have given this some thought, I see. I do like the picture you paint. They go out and fight the infected. Their health, ammo, supplies and spirit are depleted. We will wait like vultures and pick clean what is left of their little group. Which means, they eliminate the horde for us, we remove whoever is left and get the facility. I'd say that is a win-win for us. This may well be the only option we have to come out on the other side of this with everything we need."

"Captain Webb?"

"Go ahead."

"I have thought over what you said and there is some truth in what you say. We will allow you to exit the facility to engage the crazies coming your way. Once that is complete, we will resume our discussion to negotiate how you will vacate our facility. Oh, we'll hang on to Mr. Priest if you don't mind. He is in no condition to go out there and fight. He can barely stand." Webb didn't respond to that.

"Go ahead, Captain Webb. Do your best against your adversaries, and we will be there to mop up the mess. We will be watching you, Captain Webb. Have a nice day and good luck."

"Mr. Baker, make no mistake about it. We want Priest back alive. If anything happens to him, every ounce of our knowledge, every round of ammunition we possess and every breath in our body will be used to remove you and the shitheads that follow you off the face of this planet. That is the only outcome I can personally guarantee," Webb said stoically.

There was no response.

CHAPTER 42

They geared both Teams up in no time. Webb and his team took both Jeeps and drove down the access road. They activated the perimeter traps behind them as they went.

A figure in the woods watched as both Jeeps exited the facility. The figure-maintained surveillance on the Jeeps from a distance.

"Yes, both Jeeps exited the facility. We are staying with them to make sure they eliminate those infected. Good thing too, because I am tired of losing men trying to filter out this infected mob."

"I know you are Mr. Brody. You have my word; we will not lose one more brother to this."

"Thank you, Mr. Baker."

"You are welcome. We will keep Mr. Priest company; however, I am moving him to Site B. The town could easily become a war zone depending on how the infected mass travels. Once you have completed your surveillance, meet us there."

"Understood, Mr. Baker."

Doc and Neville made their way through the fence at the back of the facility, which was surrounded by a thick forest. They re-wired the fence and took off through the woods. Traversing the outskirts of town, they kept to the tree line. Doc and Neville recon'ed houses from the tree line, only coming out if they spied a potential mode of transportation. They came across a few cars, but passed them up.

After a half-dozen houses, they came across a house with tan brick and brown trim which had its garage door open. Parked inside was exactly what they were looking for. A black Toyota Prius sat there waiting for them. Neville went into the empty house and found a set of keys, probably the backup set. They got in and Doc turned the key and the engine came on.

"Sweet," Doc whispered. The hybrid car was just what they needed. As long as they stayed under 45 mph, the electric motor powered the car quietly which would allow Doc and Neville to approach their potential target unnoticed. They continued to stay on the outskirts of town, taking all less traveled roads. Seeing exactly what they were looking for, the two soldiers pulled off the road and behind the building they had scoped out.

The building was one of the tallest in the town and would give them an adequate view of the town. As they traveled up to the top floor, they set booby traps to warn them of any enemies making their way up the stairs. They set up an observation point and looked for any signs of Priest.

Meanwhile, a mile out from the facility, Shaw started to set up claymores, white phosphorus grenades with trip wires and remote C4 mounds with jars of shrapnel. They equipped each mound with ten jars full of nails, screws and any other scraps of metal the team could find. If the infected got through that, then the team planned to mow down the rest with small arms fire.

Thomas and four of his men opened the door to a dark room. The room had once been a small office, but now all the furniture and carpet had been removed. Laying in one of the far corners was a figure that resembled a man lying in a bloody heap. He was dressed in only pants, no shoes, no shirt. There were fresh cuts all over his body that were crusting up. Priest was lying on his side; his eyes closed, his beard was soaked with blood and his nose didn't sit straight on his face. Bruising along each side of his ribs had showed. The blood pooling right underneath the skin was turning a sickly shade of purple. The men with Thomas looked uneasy at the sight, and it was apparent that Thomas was not comfortable with the view either.

"Damn, Brody may have gone a little overboard on this," Thomas said almost at a whisper. "Well, we need to move him, so ahead."

The men moved into the room and two of them grabbed him underneath his arms to lift him up. He was so slick with blood that the men couldn't get a good enough grip to lift him. The men slung their rifles over their backs and each grabbed an arm or leg. They lifted him off the ground with his head dangling down. He didn't stir; he didn't cry out in pain; he didn't react at all.

"Wait," Thomas commanded. He reached over and placed his fingers on Priest's neck. "Ok, take him away. He is still alive.....barely." They exited the building and headed for one pickup.

From an observation point on the top floor of a building across the road.

"Shit, we got movement," Neville said to Doc.

Neville zoomed in, "Holy fuck! They are carrying Priest out to one truck. They really fucked him up and you can barely make out its him. He looks dead."

Doc came over with his binos and his mouth hung open. "Jesus, Mother Mary and Joseph. Look at all that blood. We stay with him no matter what."

"Fuckin-a-right we will!" Neville said in a loud whisper.

"Those fuckers are going to pay for this one way or another! Come on!" Doc exclaimed.

Thomas's men loaded Priest into the back of one pickup and drove off, heading north. Doc and Neville were already in their Prius and following at a safe distance.

The Team had fallen back from the field of death they just constructed. Never the patient one, Shaw was getting agitated. With Priest out there in whatever state, Shaw was chomping at the bit. He liked to take the fight to the enemy, not the other way around.

Webb had his binos out and could see the infected coming their way, but not making good time. They were milling around, seeming to locate their have lost prey.

"Looks like they don't know which way to go. Allison, Lia, hit those horns. Let them know we are here."

Allison and Lia started laying on the Jeep horns. The infected's heads looked up, snarled, and then came running towards the team. Webb observed all this in his binos.

"Oh shit, that caught their attention. They're coming now. They are thinned out, but it still looks like several hundred and they are coming this way in a hurry."

They positioned Lia in a wood line to the north of the highway. They had found the deer stand in the woods and thought it would be a perfect sniper point.

Shaw, being the first line of defense, was positioned behind a berm they built along with his M48 on the southern side of the highway. He had all the claymore triggers, C4 detonators, and a planned out contingency if the LZ got too hot.

Webb was on command point and Izzy and Allison were ready to drive the Jeeps out of there so they were not lost. Webb, Izzy and Allison were equipped with M4's and grenades.

Webb trained his bino's on the advancing host of infected and was the one who would call out the firing and shock positions. Shock positions (the locations they had placed the explosives) were staggered in a way to provide maximum damage. Since the infected didn't react the same as regular human troops, it was slightly easier to set up the fields of impact to take out as many infected as they could before the team ever fired a round. The fast runners of the infected were a about 25 yards ahead of the main pack.

Webb keyed his comms, "Ok, Shaw. Get ready to engage."

"Ready to rock, Cap."

Webb keyed Lia. "Take out those runners. I'm waiting for the bulk of the crowd to enter the blast zone."

"Got it, Cap," Lia replied.

"Shock A, hit it!" Webb shouted.

Click, click, click, Shaw activated the claymore trigger. Baboom! The first string exploded, sending thousands of ball bearings into the pack of infected. Bodies shredded, bones shattered and viscera scattered. With some infected already suffering decay, the devastation was indescribable. Those who were freshly turned the landscape crimson. There were a few of the runners who were already ahead of the blast zone.

Webb saw them coming out of the smoke, "Lia, you have…"

Bang! Bang! Bang! "Yeah, I got them," she said with a giggle.

"Nice," he said. "Ok, ready, Shock B, go!"

Shaw activates the next set of triggers with the same effect. Things were looking manageable, Webb thought. As soon as that thought entered his head, he saw something coming over the horizon that he couldn't make out. There were flashes of bright orange.

"Lia, can you make out what those flashes of orange are that I keep seeing? Way behind the mass of infected." A moment of silence went by.

"Shit! It looks like three county maintenance trucks. Judging from how they are being driven, I would guess it's infected behind the steering wheels."

"Damn, they are fucking unpredictable," Webb expressed. "Ok, guess we have another factor to plan for."

Lia continued, "Ah, Captain. That's not all. Those maintenance vehicles are dump trucks and are filled with infected. I'd say another 30 per truck."

"Fuckin A. Shaw, heads up. We got 3 dump trucks filled with more infected coming behind the mass on foot!"

"Shit Captain, they are getting smarter." Shaw barked.

Izzy spoke up, "They appear to be evolving. Advancing their thought patterns, being able to think and process. At least elementary cognitive functions. Possibly a basic memory recall of muscle memory behaviors."

"Well ain't that a fuckin peach!" Shaw spat.

Webb was still monitoring the battlefield, "The first two blast zones worked fairly well. Not only did the blasts take out quite a few of the infected, it also slowed the mass down considerably with all the bodies on the ground they now have to negotiate. Tripping over bodies, slipping and sliding on blood and internal organs, they can't keep their footing."

Shaw took a minute to pull his binos and survey the field. "Yeah, we took out about a third, but those trucks coming are going to be a pain to deal with. Hopefully, those C4 mounds will give us the edge."

"Copy that," Webb replied. The next wave of infected had made their way toward the half-way point of the field. The first of the trucks was coming up behind them at a high rate of speed. It wasn't even trying to maneuver around the infected who were on foot. The crazy bastards were driving right over them, trying to get to Webb and company.

Lia was attempting to dial in a shot on the driver, but with the uneven terrain and the irrational head tilting back and forth, it was nearly impossible.

"I can't dial in the driver, Captain. They are bouncing around in there like a couple of kangaroos," Lia communicated.

"Ok, Shaw. It's up to you. See if you can take them out."

"I'll give it a go," Shaw replied. He had one hand holding up his binos to his eyes and the other hand on the detonator. He watched as the truck got near the first C4 mound and he depressed the trigger. BABOOM!!! The C4 detonated with a huge spray of dirt and cloud of smoke. The projectiles could be seen penetrating bodies and embedding into the truck. A couple of tires popped from the nails, but didn't slow the truck too much. Dozens of infected on either side of the truck went down, but the truck kept coming.

The last explosion caused the following two trucks to steer wide on the left and right to avoid the explosions. Shaw saw the course correction and cursed. "Yeah, these infected aren't acting like the others."

The front truck was already committed to its course and couldn't change. The other two changed their paths to go around the explosive mounds.

Shaw called on Webb, "Switching to the M48 to take these trucks out. I need you to man these detonators."

"On my way," Webb replied. He ran over just as Shaw opened up with the M48. He concentrated on the lead truck, trying to put it out of commission. The .50 cal rounds rained all over the truck, taking out chunks of metal and infected. The driver and passenger were eliminated, and the truck lost direction. It drove directly over one of the C4 mounds and Webb pulled the trigger on the detonator. Whoom! The force of the explosion lifted the driver's side of the truck off the ground and it tipped over on its side. The fuel tank was also hit with shrapnel and was punctured. Fuel was leaking out all over the ground.

Lia witnessed the whole thing and now targeted the fuel tank. Meanwhile, the infected were crawling out of the bed of the truck. A bunch made it to the ground and stood up to run and attack when, WHOOM! The truck went up from a shot Lia put in the fuel tank. It blew the infected around the truck off their feet. The next second, dozens of figures were stumbling around and on fire. It looked like a bunch of match sticks dancing around. It also blew a dozen that had come upon the truck as it wrecked off their feet, but escaped the flames. The other two trucks were coming up the east and westbound lanes of Rt 421.

Webb surveyed the scene as it unfolded in front of him. The rest of the ordnance could take out the rest of the infected who were on foot, but it would do nothing to the two trucks coming up each side of the highway.

Webb turned to Shaw, "Guess we will have to take these things out, old school."

Shaw chuckles, "That's fine by me." He rotated his M48 to send rounds toward the truck coming east. He immediately took out the driver and passenger, which sent the truck careening off the road and into the woods on the south side of the highway. The truck plowed into a couple large trees and stopped. You could hear the infected in the truck bed bouncing off the sides of the metal walls.

Shaw and Webb laughed as they looked at one another. The infected scrambled out of the truck and running for the two. Shaw opened up and Webb shouldered his M4, putting three-round bursts together. They dispatched the couple dozen infected in a couple minutes.

The truck coming west on the highway was coming in hot. Lia was taking shots at the windshield, trying to take out the driver, while Izzy and Allison were aiming at its tires to slow the truck down. The truck was getting close to Lia's strategic firing point.

A couple well-placed shots exploded the front tires of the truck, sending it lurching to one side. The truck flipped, and it crashed into the north side of the woods. Izzy and Allison started celebrating until they realized the truck crashed right into the wood line where Lia and her tree stand were. Allison pushed on her comms, "Shaw, Captain Webb, that truck wrecked right where Lia is."

"Shit!" voiced Webb.

"You finish the rest of these fuckers, I'm going to help Lia."

Shaw nodded and went back to work. Webb jumped over the berm and ran toward the wrecked truck. Allison and Izzy were right behind him. The infected that were in the dump bed came pouring out from around the back end of the truck.

"Take them out!" Webb yelled.

Lia saw the truck flip over and head right for the tree she was in. She scrambled to jump out of the stand, but it was too late. The truck hit the tree and propelled her a distance into the woods. She hit a few branches with the back of her head as she tumbled in the air before it knocked out her.

Moments later Lia stirred and heard sounds in her darkness. They weren't cheerful sounds either and developed clarity. There were screams, shouts and gunfire. She thought she heard her name but wasn't sure with all the noise and her cloudy state. As she opened her eyes, she was looking up at the sky and lying on her back. She sat up, then felt the wave of dizziness wash over her. She eased back down for a second and tried to make out the sounds she was hearing. She shook the cobwebs from her mind and starting to get up. A searing pain radiated from her leg and she let out a cry.

Lia looked down to see a seedling tree, about an inch in diameter, protruding out of her thigh. Blood was pooling all around it and it had her impaled to the forest floor. She grabbed the small seeding tree to snap it off, but the pain was excruciating and it was too thick. The pain made her see little starbursts. She then looked around to make sense of where she was. In front of her to the right, she could see the wrecked truck wedged against some trees, lying on its side. The top of the truck was facing her and she could see that the dump bed was empty except for two infected that had gotten caught between the side of the truck bed and a couple of trees. One was wedged hanging in the air and was almost cut completely in half. Its upper body was smashed into the trees and just hanging there. Its bottom half was hanging close to the ground with a trail of intestines connecting the two halves. Blood and other fluid, Lia couldn't make out, was trickling down onto the ground. The sight was disgusting, but the accompanying smell was even worse. The second infected had its hips and legs wedged in a "V" from a splitting tree trunk. The top half must have fallen to the ground after the crash.

Lia knew things would not get better unless she called out for help. She called for anyone of the team and then was quiet to hear a reply. She thought she heard someone repeat her name. Was that Webb?

"I'm here. I'm hurt and cannot move," she yelled. She heard voices telling her they were coming for her. She allowed herself a slight release of anxiety, but couldn't let everything go because of the pain she was in. She heard rustling to her right and looked over to see no one coming. She called out for Webb, for Allison and for Izzy, with no response. She heard rustling again, but still saw no one coming. She cocked her head to locate where the sounds were coming from. She heard it once again, and this time saw some ground brush move to her front left. She called out to whoever it was once again. The rustling was still 10 yards away.

A figure slid out from the brush. It was one of the infected, well half of one of the infected. It was crawling on the ground, using its arms at the elbows. The entire lower half of its body was gone. Only scraps of flesh were dragging behind it like some kind of macabre cape. Its intestines and spine were also trailing behind the creature. It locked eyes on Lia and then hurried its effort to reach her.

Lia screamed and panicked. She heard voices calling for her, but they still seemed too far away. She reached down to her other thigh to pull her pistol, but felt that her holster was empty. She looked down and could not locate it.

Fear gripped her, and she thrashed around in panic, which brought waves of pain and threatened to cause her to pass out. As the thing continued to crawl closer, Lia thrashed around harder which brought more pain. As pain racked her body, it took over her headspace, pushing the fear away. She embraced the pain, which manifested into anger.

The anger consumed her, and she felt extreme hate for this thing. Her mind cleared the panic and the need to fight took over. With her mind somewhat clear, she reached down to her boot and withdrew her back up knife. She was now egging the thing on to come closer.

She was screaming at the top of her lungs, "Come on fucker, come on!" The infected crawler had now come close enough for Lia to strike. She shot out her blade, which raked across the side of its head, skipping off the skull and toward the thing's face. She didn't just wait there to see what damage she caused. She continued to strike out again and again, growling like an animal. She eventually caught it in the side of the head by the ear and felt her blade sink in. She heard more rustling, but kept plunging the blade into its skull. With her last stab, she looked up to see Webb coming through the shrubs toward her. He looked surprised when he saw her plunge the blade into the infected's skull for the last time.

"Holy shit, girl. You got it. Are you okay, Lia?" Webb asked and then looked down to see the stick protruding through her thigh.

"Shit! Izzy, we need you over here! Bring the med bag!" He bent down to assess the damage.

She looked at him, "I can move my toes and bend at the knee, so I'm good to go there."

"We'll get you out of here and back to the facility. Shaw, how are we looking out there?"

"We're good, Cap. Cleaning up a few stragglers. We will need to regroup quickly and go get my boy!"

"Understood." They extracted Lia and with Shaw's help got her back to the facility. Izzy worked on her while Shaw and Webb resupplied and prepared to find Priest. They received a call on the two-way radio.

"Go ahead, Doc."

"Captain, they moved Priest to another location 4 cliques away from the original target."

"Did you put eyes on him?" There was a long pause.

"Doc, did you put eyes on him?" A little more forcefully this time.

"Copy, we saw him."

"Good, we will work with him to extract him out."

"Sir, w-we saw him but it wasn't good."

"Explain. Cut to the chase, damnit!" Webb wasn't mad at Doc, it was his anxiety surging from thinking Priest may be in serious trouble or worse.

"Captain, they carried him out. He was not under his own power and was unconscious. At least I think he was. He looked bad, covered in so much blood. I couldn't even tell if he was breathing or not."

"Fuck!!!," Shaw had come up behind Webb. "I am going to kill every one of these motherfuckers! I swear to God, I am killing every fuckin one of them! No, not just kill them, I'm going to make them pay!" Shaw was shouting and completely full of rage.

Webb didn't even try to deal with him. "Tell us where you are. We are on our way."

"Copy that."

An hour later, the four team members regrouped just outside the new location of where they held Priest. Webb asked for a sitrep and Neville looked solemn as he briefed Shaw and Webb.

"They brought him in a couple hours ago. Six contacts were with him and we've seen four additional plus that fuck stick was at our fence."

"That Brody guy?" Webb articulated.

"Yeah," Neville responded. Neville filled them in on the layout of the building based on what he could see. They had Priest in a room at the mid north-west side.

"What's the call, Captain?" Shaw inquired.

Webb thought for a moment, "Neville, you and Doc take the front but stay out of sight and find a strategic firing point. You guys will keep them busy and cause a distraction. Shaw and I will breach the rear door and search for Priest. We need to hit quick, so they don't have a chance to execute him. Questions?"

"What if you have issues breaching the rear door?" Doc asked. "If so, have Neville shoot that lock out and you guys breach the front."

"Copy that, Cap."

"Ok Reapers, move out."

CHAPTER 43

Priest's entire body was screaming. He was lying on the floor of a space he didn't recognize. He slowly looked around and knew this wasn't the room they had him imprisoned in before. He was fighting to stay conscious so he could attempt to assess his surroundings and situation. The room was an empty bedroom from what he could determine. No furniture or carpet, just a hardwood floor covered in his blood. The blood was drying and was sticky now. His ribs hurt and were making it hard to breathe. He attempted to sit up, but the pain was agonizing. He worked through it and sat up against a wall. His breath was coming in rapid gasps. His mind was a muddled mess, and he was reaching out for a memory or a thought to grab hold of. Anything he could remember to center himself on.

Just at that moment, Lia flashed in his mind. He squeezed his eyes shut and visions of her came rushing in. The first time they met, the first time they made love, the first time they fought side-by-side. He opened his eyes and tears were running down his cheeks. His mind was in overdrive now, with memories and visions flashing like an old movie projector. Lia flashed in his mind, Webb, Shaw, Doc and Neville flashed, Izzy, Allison and the scientists flashed, Myles, Doug and Abarra flashed.

He was still taking stock of himself as the door opened and Brody, along with Thomas, came inside. They both had metal chairs that they unfolded and sat down looking at Priest. Priest was doing everything possible to not look as broken as he felt. It was hard for him to do when his body was betraying him. He was going into shock and his body was shaking. His lips were so swollen and split, he wasn't able to keep his saliva in his mouth so he had drool running down his chin. His drool was dark crimson from all the cuts inside his mouth. All the adrenaline his body had been pumping out was stiffening his joints and making it painful to move. Thomas looked at him for a long moment.

"It didn't have to be like this, Mr. Priest. We gave you many chances to make this right, and you refused. Now, all your friends must fight that massive horde and I guarantee you they will not survive. But just like you, they were stubborn, and they refused. So, that brings me to where we are now or will be soon. The horde will be whittled down some thanks to your friends. Unfortunately, the horde will ultimately kill all of your remaining team. We come in, mop everything up, and ultimately get what we started out to obtain. With your group and those infected crazies taking each other out, you have eventually eliminated both threats we would have had to deal with. So, I guess I should say thank you. So, thank you." Thomas said in a condescending tone.

Priest said nothing. "What, nothing funny to say? No little quips or bouts of jocularity?" Thomas asked in a patronizing tone.

"I – I would, but I'm trying to hold everything in so I don't shit all over myself. Leave me a little dignity, would you?" Priest whispered out.

Thomas let out a huge belly laugh. "Mr. Priest, you never disappoint. I sure wish you had joined our group. I know you would keep us in stitches"

"I was thinking about it, but then you guys kicked the shit out of me. That hurt my feelings."

"I guess that's true. Well, Mr. Brody enjoys his work. He may get overzealous sometimes."

"Speaking of stitches, give me five minutes with Brody and I'll think about joining you." Priest said while trying to smile through his destroyed lips. Thomas looked over at Brody and smiled.

"Ok, forget about it. The shape I'm in, I doubt I could whoop a paper bag," Priest joked.

"Well put, Mr. Priest. I guess...."

BABOOM! The building shook and debris rained down on them from the ceiling. Weapon's fire followed immediately the explosion. The firing was repeating after each other, so it was definitely a fire fight. Priest's ears knew exactly what that sound was.

Thomas's eyes got wide, "What the fuck!" That was the first time Priest had heard Thomas curse. He and Brody exchanged looks before Thomas ran to the door and opened it. Men were running back and forth.

"What the hell is going on?" Thomas asked one man.

"We're being attacked from the front, Brother Thomas," the man said. Thomas let him go and looked back at Brody.

He caught Brody's eyes, "Kill him and then meet me up at the mountain post." Then Thomas took off running.

"I hope this works," Doc said as he fired an 40mm high explosive grenade from his M203 into the front door. The blast took out the door and part of the frame and wall on the right side. Neville scoped out the remaining windows for faces. He saw two appear in the left window. Pop, the one man went down. Neville put the round through the wall about mid-ways down on the left. Doc sent another grenade through the door, BOOM!

Shaw heard the second explosion and kicked in the back-door. He rotated out and Webb entered the doorway. Two men were running for the back door before Shaw kicked it in. They stopped in surprise, but Webb didn't give them any time to think. He fired at them on full auto and cut them down in seconds. They heard a couple of yells from farther down the hallway, then running footsteps approaching.

Shaw entered through the door, squatted and trained his rifle down the hallway. A man poked his head around the corner of the long hallway in front of them. Webb squeezed off a few rounds at the man, but he ducked back just in time. Shaw trailed some rounds through the wall and they heard a scream. A body fell out from the corner and hit the ground. More yelling could be heard from down the hallway.

Webb pulled a grenade from his vest, pulled the pin and let the spoon fly. He waited a second, then threw it. It hit the left wall just before the corner and bounced to the right into whatever room or space was there. Yells and shuffling were heard, and then nothing but the explosion. The dust settled, but they heard no more voices.

Brody stood up from his chair and reached for his pistol. He took a couple steps toward the open door and raised his pistol. Voices yelled "grenade" and then there was an explosion. Brody was stunned and was stumbling around. The hand holding the gun dropped to his side and Priest decided it was now or never. With every ounce of strength he had left, Priest lunged for Brody, putting one of his hands on the wrist of the hand which held the pistol. With his other hand, he snatched the blade Brody stored in a sheath on his side. Priest let out a yell, swung the blade around and plunged it into Brody's neck. He gave it a quick twist and then fell away in exhaustion.

Brody's jugular vein spurted blood out like water from a garden hose. He dropped the gun and wrapped both hands around his neck. Priest watched Brody's life literally drain from his face as the blood rushed out onto the floor. Priest was staggering from the effort of swinging the blade, but could lean close to Brody, who was trying to keep as much of his blood in his body as he could.

"Next time you take a prisoner, make sure they're tied up or dead, before getting close to them, you fucking piece of shit!"

Brody was stumbling and slammed against the wall.

"Where is Thomas?" Priest yelled into Brody's face. Brody tried to articulate something, but all he could manage was a gurgling sound. Brody then collapsed to the floor and Priest soon followed.

Priest was exhausted, in pain and couldn't hold himself up. He heard more voices outside the door, so he crawled over to Brody's lifeless body and took his pistol. He used the wall to prop himself against and stood up with great difficulty. He stumbled to the door and cracked it, looking out into the hallway. His sight wasn't the best, but his ears were as sharp as ever. Minus the slight ringing from the earlier grenade blast. He could hear footsteps coming toward him from down the hallway. Three men ran by the door. Priest leaned against the doorjamb with his should and unloaded on each of them.

All three dropped to floor, dead. Immediately, Priest heard footsteps echoing from the opposite end of the hallway, coming toward him.

As the footsteps came closer, Priest threw open the door and stumbled out as fast as he could, holding the pistol up as high as his broken body would allow him. A large figure raised its rifle, but then stopped. Priest and Shaw were facing each other standing within 20 feet. Priest recognized him instantly, but it took Shaw a couple of seconds for things to register.

"Jesus fucking Christ!" Shaw thundered. Priest, recognizing his friend, had all the strength rush out of him and his legs gave way. He dropped to his knees, and the pistol fell out of his hand and clattered against the wall. Shaw ran over and caught Priest before his face bounced off the floor.

Webb appeared behind Shaw. "Oh my God," is all he could say.

Shaw was in tears, "Mother fuckers, what did they do to you?" Shaw was holding Priest up looking at him.

Priest raised his head and spoke in a raspy voice, just barely above a whisper, "H-H-Hey, big man. It's-It's that really you?" Priest had tears in his eyes, which were basically shut now from the swelling.

"Yeah, it's me, Alec. I'm here, man, I'm here. Shaw was holding Priest's broken body.

Shaw heard Priest whisper something else, "I-I almost g-g-gave up back there. C-C-Couldn't t-take anymore."

Shaw hugged Priest and was sobbing now. "Don't worry, brother, we are going to take care of you. We got you, we got you. These fuckers are gonna pay.... as God is my witness, they are gonna fucking pay!"

Priest weakly tapped Shaw on his shoulder and lifted his head higher with great effort and croaked out, "T- T- That you Cap?"

"Yeah, it's me, Alec."

"G-good to see you too, Mar... Marcusss," Priest passed out and went limp.

Webb was trying to stem the flow of tears as well. "Love you too, brother. We're getting you out of here, right fucking now!" Webb hit the radio, "We found Priest and we are exfiling out the rear. Give me a sitrep."

"The rest of the locals in the facility are dead. I can't be sure, but I think a few escaped out the side window. We were engaged already, but Neville could take one out. We were going around there to confirm. We'll meet you at the Jeep," Doc responded.

"Copy that." Webb nodded at Shaw, who was carrying Priest. They just arrived at the Jeep when Neville and Doc came around the corner. Shaw was putting Priest in the passenger seat.

"Jesus, Mother Mary and Joseph," Doc said as he made the sign of the cross.

Priest moaned something inaudible.

Webb motioned to them to get in. "We're going, Alec. Just hold on."

Shaw drove like a madman, getting the team back to the facility. Shaw and Webb along with Doc rushed Priest to the infirmary and left Neville to get the gear and clean up all the blood.

They burst into the infirmary, which startled Lia, who was resting her leg a couple of beds away. They rushed in and laid Priest down on one bed.

Lia looked at them in horror, "That can't be!" She trailed off. Webb looked back at her and nodded his head. She let out a cry and was struggling to get out of bed. Izzy came rushing in from another door.

"Lia, be still and rest that leg."

Lia was yelling, "Get me over there. Get me to Alec!" Izzy looked over and saw a bloody mess.

"Oh dear God," she gasped. "What did they do to him?" She was still staring when Lia's yelling snapped her out of her shock.

"Get me over there, damnit!" Izzy grabbed a wheelchair and lifted one of the leg braces. She helped Lia in and wheeled her over.

Lia grabbed Priest's bloody hand, "Alec, it's Lia and I'm right here, I'm right here, baby." She was in tears, but was trying not to lose it. That isn't what Alec needed right now.

Izzy wedged herself in, and she and Doc worked on him. She told Webb and Shaw to leave because they were getting in the way. She knew better than to tell Lia to move.

Shaw and Webb moved out into the hallway. Shaw was still in tears and was looking up at the ceiling with his hands folded on the back of his head. He was taking deep breaths. Webb was bent over at the waist with his hands on his knees. They heard footsteps running toward them and looked up to see Allison running toward them.

She ran to Shaw and was about to hug him, but stopped. She looked at him up and down with shock on her face. Shaw cocked his head and looked at her strangely, then realized why she stopped. He looked down, and he was covered in blood.

He looked at Allison with tears streaming down his face, "It's Alec's," was all he said. Allison put her hand to her mouth. She rushed in and hugged him, anyway. Shaw paused for a second and then hugged her back.

Izzy came out. "It's going to be awhile. You guys should go clean up. You're not going back in there with all the germs and dirt, anyway. Go, go. We will take care of him and we will let you know how he is doing." The three paused for a couple of seconds and then left to go to their dorm rooms.

CHAPTER 44

Shaw stripped off his clothes and sat back on the bed in his underwear. He felt a wave of emotion sweep over him. Thinking back to Yemen and when they pulled Priest out of that terrorist compound. He wasn't in as awful shape as he was now. Priest had sacrificed himself back then. He always took the hit for his men, but this shit needed to stop. He shook his head, got up and went to the bathroom. He looked at himself in the mirror. He thought to himself, this is all he had left. This was his family, and he was going to hold on to it no matter what.

Once Priest was better, if he gets better. He raged and smashed his fist against the wall. He WILL get better and we're going to cut this shit out right now. He walked over and started the shower. He adjusted as hot as he could stand it, stripped off his underwear and got in.

The scalding water felt like magic running over his body. He was a machine, but machines break down once in a while. His sore muscles needed this. As he let the water flow over his back, he heard a noise. The steam from hot water covered the glass and he couldn't see out. He thought he saw the outline of a figure, so he opened the shower door. Allison was standing there, still wearing the bloody clothes, tears streaming down her face. He looked at her, but said nothing. He reached out his hand to her, which she grabbed with both of hers and gave it a squeeze. She let go of it and then undressed. Shaw watched her, but his expression was one of understanding but also of need. She finished removing her clothes and joined him in the shower. The steam surrounded them as they embraced.

Webb had gotten out of the shower when Izzy walked in. She looked disheveled and completely exhausted. She looked up at him and tears started flowing when she saw him. He went to hug her, knowing what she had just seen. She held on to him tightly and he could feel her body shake as she sobbed.

"I have seen nothing like that before. I can't imagine how much pain he must have been in." Webb said nothing, but just held her until she stopped crying. She pulled back from him and wiped her eyes.

"Marcus, it was horrible. Once we got him cleaned up and saw the extent of damage," she shook her head, "it was like nothing I have ever seen. The amount of damage Alec took was astonishing. We also took x-rays and looked at his bone structure too." She shook her head again. "I can't even fathom the amount of pain he was in. I know I keep repeating that, but my God."

Webb looked at her, "Do I really want to know?"

"Probably not, but I'll tell you."

"Yeah, I need to know."

"Okay, he was severely dehydrated and had multiple deep lacerations all over his body. It took 128 staples, 38 stitches, and three tubes of surgical glue to close. He has a concussion, along with a fractured skull and a broken left orbital bone. Luckily, he didn't lose an eye with the damage and swelling involved. Most of his ribs were broken, he had a punctured left lung, lacerated spleen, bruised kidneys, and fractured left collar bone. His knee joints were swollen and bruised like someone was stomping on them." Izzy stopped and shivered like a frigid breeze just blew across her. Webb just stood there in silence. He knew she was severely affected, and that it was hard seeing someone you cared about in that state.

Webb's face had a wave of concern flow across it, "We need to quit taking risks like that. We are all we have left. This is our family and we need to protect what we have." She looked and him with what seemed like relief in her face. Izzy got up and kissed him and went to take a shower.

She stopped and turned around, "We put him in a medically induced coma while he heals. He is not in pain right now. That's all we can do for him. The rest is up to Alec."

Webb nodded and put on his clothes. He was making his way toward the infirmary and almost ran into Shaw coming around the corner.

"Whoa, sorry, Captain."

"No problem, Shaw. Heading to the infirmary?"

"Yeah, I need to see him."

"Me too."

They both walked together in silence and entered the infirmary. Priest was lying in bed with multiple wires and tubes. A ventilator machine pumped to help keep his lung inflated. Tons of tubes and wires, monitoring this, measuring that. Lia was there next to his bed, sitting in her wheelchair. She had Priest's hand clasped between both of hers.

Both Shaw and Webb walked over and kissed her on the top of her head. They glanced up to look at Priest, and he was completely unrecognizable. With all the swelling and bruising, it was tough to make out who it was.

Lia spoke up, "They hurt him, hurt him bad. Fucking human beings.....not even those infected psychos out there, but fucking human beings." She had tears in her eyes, but there was rage shining in them as well. Lia looked up at Shaw, "They all need to die! Every fucking one of them!"

Shaw just nodded his head with his jaw clinched and this seemed to be all the answer Lia needed. She rotated her head back to look at Priest.

Webb didn't protest either. The rules had changed, and this was a new reality. The law of reason and negotiation were out the window. They were following their own rules now. Like everyone had been saying, including him. This group, this unit, this family were all that mattered now. Anyone trying to break this family apart or trying to destroy it will pay the price. This was something Webb swore to.

He reached down and put a hand on Lia's shoulder, "Do you need a break? I can watch over him." She shook her head no, and he left it at that. Just then the door opened and Doc, along with Neville, walked in. They had cleaned up and came to check on Priest. They all hugged each other.

Shaw looked at Doc with big, wet eyes, "Thanks for patching him up, Doc."

He smiled, "I did what I could, but I am afraid most of the credit should go to Izzy. Some of this stuff was beyond my expertise. Izzy is a little more advanced than she lets on."

Shaw took a deep breath, "How long, Doc?"

"Well, he stays in the coma for another three days, then he will be left to wake on his own. He will be the gauge to measure progress based on his pain and what he can tolerate. He will have to work out and do physical therapy, but if I was to take a guess, I would say at least three months. That also was based on his work out level, so he can't overdo it either."

"Don't worry. We will put Lia on his ass and she will straighten him up," Neville replied.

After some time to joke and talk with each other, the team went to their load out room. They all assembled and looked at each other solemnly.

Webb addressed them, "Great job getting Priest out of there. What we need to discuss is where do we go from here? I want to hear about where your heads are." He turned to the Big Man, "Shaw."

Shaw thought for a second, "I want these fuckers dead. I don't know how many got away, but I want these fuckers dead!" He took a breath, "I know we have no idea where they are but I can't get past it. As far as us here, this is my family and I will protect what we have here with my life."

Webb nodded, "Doc?"

"Cap, I have seen nothing like the shape I just saw Priest in. I'm with Shaw, based on that. We need to hunt these scumbags down and eliminate them. I also feel the same way about us. This is our brotherhood and all that matters right now."

"Ok, Doc. What about you, Neville?"

"Seeing Sarge like that has started a rage in me I have never felt before. I want these sum bitches dead. As far as all those here, Bethany and I are getting along great and I want to protect that." Webb nodded again.

"What about you, Cap? Where are you at?" Shaw asked.

Webb looked around the room at his team, "I'm not going to lie. Izzy and I have a good thing going, and I don't want to jeopardize that. I will protect that and everyone here with everything in me. I'm also with you guys in hunting these pieces of shit down. What we need to consider is whether we have a larger obligation to reconnect with the rest of the world. If there is a world left, that is. Do we have a more important obligation to find out if any more of these CDC facilities are functional? Are there any remnants of government left? Are there any remaining military bases still operating? That is something we need to take into consideration." The room fell silent as they pondered Webb's words.

Neville spoke up, "I think we eventually need to investigate the possibility of other entities existing in the country. I think we need to get our house in order and take care of our backyard, as my momma used to say."

Webb took a deep breath, "Okay, so it looks like we are all in agreement. This is my proposal; 1I) We fortify this facility with more deterrent measures. Maybe get some cameras strategically installed. Give us some eyes around the town and on the highway entrances into the town. We could use the cable tv grid to transport the signal over long distances. We'll just have to remove the additional splitters so no one can just turn on their TV and see the camera feeds. 2) We need to conduct surveillance a couple times a week during the day to make sure we don't get surprised by any infected. We will also run a few night recons to see if we can locate those fucks who jacked up Priest. 3) Once Priest recovers and is back in commission, we will see about mapping out locations to evaluate viable locations of survivors. This will also include locating facilities for gear, food, medicine, etc. 4) We will build or expand our ability to communicate. See if we can connect with others at great distances. Oh, one other thing we need to address. I don't know how long the electrical grid is going to stay up. I know we have the solar farm and generators. We need to do some calculations on power consumption versus power generated."

"Wow, that was a mouthful," Doc joked.

CHAPTER 45

Priest was in an induced coma for a few more days, before Izzy removed the medication from his IV. Lia asked her when he would wake up, but Izzy said it was unpredictable.

"It could be hours. It could be days." She patted Lia on the shoulder and started to leave the room.

Izzy turned back and looked at Lia, "We need to get you up on those crutches and work that leg. You could really use a break right now. Come on and we'll get some coffee. Get you started on those crutches."

Lia nodded and looked down at Priest. The swelling in his face had gone down, and she could see that his eyes were closed. It had been days since she could actually see he had eyes. The swelling had been so bad, she knew it would have been extremely uncomfortable if he was awake. She had been talking to him for the past couple of days, hoping he could hear her. She would talk some, read to him and had the guys come in to have conversations around him.

She sighed and grabbed the crutches off of the wall. She followed Izzy out the door.

Sometime later, Lia came back into Priest's room. It had felt good to move around some after sitting by his bedside for so long. Hobbling over to the side of his bed, she turned to set the crutches back against the wall.

"Damn, your ass looks good even on crutches," Priest croaked out in a dry, raspy whisper. She snapped her head around to look at Priest. His eyes were open, and he had a slight smile on his face.

"Alec! You're awake, you're awake!" She spun around and grabbed him in a hug.

"Ow," he said.

"Oh, shit, sorry. Sorry." Her eyes welled up with tears. "It's so good to hear your voice."

"Waking up and seeing your face was what I hoped for," he breathed.

She stood over him and put her hands on the sides of his face, "We thought we were going to lose you. I love you, Alec Priest. I sat here thinking about how I don't know if I could go on without you."

"You won't have to. They could take the grizzly down, but they couldn't take him out." She kissed him on his forehead. "For the record, I love you too, Lia."

He took a deep breath and winced in pain. "Could use some water."

"Yes… yes, babe. I have some right here." She grabbed a cup with a straw and put it to his mouth. She cringed as he pursed his lips to drink. His lips were crusted over and still swollen.

"Do they hurt?" Lia asked.

Priest let out a slight chuckle, "Everything hurts."

She leaned down and kissed him gently on the lips.

He smiled, "How long was I out?"

"Well, Izzy, put you in a coma to recover. It's been about four days."

"Four days! Holy shit. What about the infected? Is everyone ok? Why are you on crutches?" He croaked.

"Slow down, slow down. Yes, we killed all the infected, destroyed the compound of the men who took you, and a stick impaled my leg. When you are better, we can fill you in on more of the details."

"Shit, I need to know what happened. What is our status? I need a sitrep," Priest barked as he shot up in bed.

"What you need, is some rest. Everything is fine." Lia said as she delicately pushed Priest back down to the bed.

"Rest! I've been resting for four days." He went to sit up again this time wincing in pain. He gently laid back down. "Damn, those boys did a number on me."

"Those assholes damn near killed you," Lia replied.

"I'll recover, and then it will be time for payback. That, I fucking guarantee!" Priest spat with hate in his blue eyes.

The doors to the infirmary slowly opened, and Shaw poked his head in.

Lia motioned him over. "He's awake."

Shaw's eyes went wide, and he rushed over to see Priest's eyes staring back at him. Shaw grabbed his hand and tears welled up in his eyes. Priest could feel some moisture forming in the corners of his eyes, also.

"Thanks for coming to get me, brother. I wouldn't have lasted much longer. That's two I owe you." Tears were streaming down Priest's face now.

"You don't owe me shit. You have saved my ass more times than I can count. Alec, we got to stop doing this shit like this, taking chances. We have everything here, and we need to protect it."

Priest looked over at Lia and then back to Shaw, "You're right. No more unnecessary chances. We take everything on together."

"Thanks, bro. It's just I have had nothing to fight for, except my country. Allison and this compound, are as much of a family and a home as I ever had."

"I understand, Jeremiah and I agree. This place is somewhere we can put down roots again. Protecting what we have here is important. We do things smarter from here on out."

"That's all I wanted to hear."

Webb, Doc, and Neville came bursting in the room.

"Hey guys!" Priest said excitedly.

"We thought we heard a bunch of noise in here. Damn Sarge, you look like shit." Doc joked.

"Shut up, Dude!" Shaw barked. "The man's been through hell."

"Pipe down, kids," Webb scolded. "How you doing, Alec?"

"I would be doing better if I knew what the hell went on out there. Plus it's killing me not being with you guys." Priest pouted.

Shaw laid a hand on Priest's shoulder, "You'll be out there soon enough. Don't try to rush it, everything is cool. Besides, if you get too froggy, Cap will sick Lia on you."

Webb crossed his arms and gave Priest his best stern father face.

Izzy checked Priest's vitals and then looked at the Team.

"He will pull out of this and be the old Priest in time. It is just going to take him a little while with the injuries he suffered," Izzy said solemnly.

Priest gave a thumbs up in agreement.

"Yeah, those fucks have no idea the nightmare coming for them and the price they are getting ready to pay." Shaw spat as he slammed his fist into his open hand.

"Take it easy, Big Man. We are going to them back for this. The Reapers are not into the revenge business, but we'll make an exception in this case." Webb said grimly.

Priest nodded his head with purpose.

Izzy quickly changed the subject back to Priest's health, "He needs some more rest."

"With Lia taking care of things, I'm sure he'll be just fine." Webb added.

"Whether he likes it or not." Shaw chimed in.

Priest widened his eyes and looked over at Lia. She pointed her two fingers at her eyes and then pointed them at Priest, like she had him under constant surveillance.

The group laughed and then settled down around Priest's bed. They shared their stories about all that had gone on. The fight with the infected and the plan to get him out of the hands of Thomas and his followers. They laughed some, cried some, it was a good day.

A familiar feeling washed over them. It felt like a brotherhood…no, it felt like family and it felt like home.

ABOUT THE AUTHOR

Born into a violent childhood, Gary Hickman was led to join the military and was assigned to the 101st Airborne, serving in Desert Storm. He was then recruited by a security contract company and performed clandestine missions overseas for a number of years. Now the Director of Operations for an IT company, Gary has also been a martial arts instructor for twelve years.

He spends time with his wife, their two kids and their boxer. Gary lives with his family in central Maryland.

NOTE FROM THE AUTHOR

Word-of-mouth is crucial for any author to succeed. If you enjoyed *The Light Reapers,* please leave a review online—anywhere you are able. Even if it's just a sentence or two. It would make all the difference and would be very much appreciated.

Thanks!
Gary Hickman

Thank you so much for reading one of our **Sci-Fi** novels.

If you enjoyed our book, please check out our recommendation for your next great read!

People of Metal by Robert Snyder

The well-intentioned leaders of China and the U.S. form a grand partnership to create human robots for every human vocation in every country in the world. The human robots proliferate, economic output soars, and the entire world prospers. It's a new Golden Age. But there are unintended consequences—consequences that will place biological humanity on a road to extinction. Ultimately, it will fall to the human robots themselves to rescue biological humanity and restore its civilization.

CPSIA information can be obtained
at www.ICGtesting.com
Printed in the USA
BVHW031657040821
613532BV00023B/155

9 781684 337347